THE SHAPE OF THE WIND

DRAGON SHIFTER ROMANCE

(MOSAURAN BOOK 2)

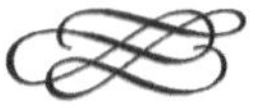

JESSICA GRAYSON

Published in the United States by Purple Fall Publishing. Purple Fall Publishing and the Purple Fall Publishing Logos are trademarks and/or registered trademarks of Purple Fall Publishing LLC.- purplefallpublishing.com

Publisher's Cataloging-in-Publication Data

Names: Grayson, Jessica, author.

Title: The Shape of the Wind / Jessica Grayson.

Series: Mosauran

Description: Purple Fall Publishing, 2020.

Identifiers:

ISBN: 978-1-64253-552-5 (paperback)

ISBN: 978-1-64253-534-1_(Ebook)

ISBN 978-1-64253-561-7 (Audiobook)

Subjects: LCSH Vampires--Fiction. | Dragons--Fiction. | Shapeshifting--Fiction. | Fairies--Fiction. | Human-alien encounters--Fiction. | Science fiction. | Romance. | Love stories. | Paranormal romance stories. | BISAC FICTION / Romance / Science Fiction | FICTION / Science Fiction / Space Opera

Classification: LCC PS3607 .R3978 S53 2020 | DDC 813.6--dc23

Edits by Holly Ingraham and Tera Cuskaden

Cover Design by Maria Spada

PRINTED IN THE UNITED STATES OF AMERICA

Rev 02 07 2024

To my husband: Thank you for being so supportive of my writing and joining me on this amazing journey. You are my rock and I love you more than words can say.

CHAPTER 1

TR'LANI

Flashing red lights and blaring sirens strike terror in my heart as the deafening sound of weapons firing echoes from outside the medical complex. My fellow Aerilons scatter in every direction. Some search for places to hide while others grab blasters to arm themselves against the invaders trying to break in.

Panic coils tight in my chest, my wings fluttering in agitation behind me as I scan the crowd, searching for On'aro. I call out for him but can hear nothing over the terror-filled cries of my people in all of the chaos.

"Tr'lani!" I whip my head in the direction of his deep, booming voice.

He races toward me, and I push through the mass of people to reach him. His golden eyes are wide as they meet mine. "Take this." He holds out a blaster. "You need to go. Zovian slavers are raiding the colony. It's only a matter of time before they breach the building. Take the access tunnels to the transports. Get off this rock, and don't look back!"

I can hardly believe what I'm hearing. Where is our military? "The Defense Force. Why aren't they—?"

"They're on their way, but they won't be here for at least another hour." Another explosion rocks the complex, and his gaze darts nervously to the front entrance before sweeping back to mine. "You have to go! Now!"

Still in shock, I search his eyes. "What about you? I can't just leave you here."

He reaches out and tucks a stray tendril of long silver-white hair behind my ear before giving me a quick kiss. "I love you, Tr'lani," he whispers against my lips. "I should have told you sooner."

I'm stunned by his admission. I open my mouth to speak but the words won't come.

He takes my hand. "There isn't time. You must hurry. We'll try to hold them off as long as we can. Go! Now!"

His gaze holds mine a moment more before he turns and runs toward the entrance with several more of our people. On'aro trained with my brother Al'aneo in the Aerilon Defense Force before he became a Healer, and now I desperately wish that I'd done the same as I awkwardly palm the blaster in my hand.

I race down the hallway toward the back of the complex. The main access tunnel isn't very far, but I pause long enough to scan every room, not wanting to leave anyone behind. As I pass the nursery, several golden eyes stare back at me through the darkness, and I skid to a halt. It's the medical staff, each of them holding a fledgling, trying to hide.

"We have to get out of here!" I motion to the hallway. "The Zovians are coming! We have to get to the access tunnel and the transports!"

Frozen in fear, none of them move. An explosion splits the air. Shouting and blaster fire echo from the lobby, followed by the clicking of dozens of clawed feet along the tiled floor.

Panic stops my heart. The Zovians have breached the complex.

"You can't hide in here!" I yell at the staff. "They'll find you. Follow me!"

We file out into the hallway, racing as fast as we can toward the access tunnel. The harsh cadence and click of Zovian speech follows us, seeming to grow louder as they close in on our position.

My pulse pounds in my ears as I glance over my shoulder and notice at least a dozen Zovians coming this way. Their large mandibles click in a frantic tempo as they pursue us. The excitement is easily read in their compound eyes as they chase after their quarry. Aerilons are worth thousands of credits in the slave trade.

When we reach the access tunnel, I motion everyone inside. As soon as the last person is through, I turn to the control panel to seal the entrance. Out of the corner of my eye, I notice the deep maroon chitinous shells of our enemies as they rush toward us, but I don't bother to look up. They're almost here, and we don't have much time.

My hands shake as I punch in my code to close it from inside. As the doors begin to slide shut, bright light arcs and explodes on the keypad, frying the panel. A low, buzzing hum comes from the doors, halfway open and frozen in place.

Ice fills my veins as I look to the Healers and fledglings in the tunnel, their eyes wide in terror as they stare gaping at the still-open doors. The slavers will be on us in moments. We're not all going to make it to the transports. "Go!" I yell, startling everyone into action.

I turn back to the hallway. The Zovians rush toward us with their weapons out but not firing. No. They want us alive and unharmed so they can sell us later. One of the fledglings cries out, the scared and pitiful sound echoing from the access tunnel behind me as the adults rush to get them to safety. A warm hand claps my shoulder, and I look back to see one of the elderly females, the badge on her uniform identifying her as the Healer in charge of the nursery.

"Run, my child. There isn't much time." She holds out her hand for the blaster. "I'll try to slow them down as best I can."

As brave as she is, it won't be enough. I realize this, and so does she, but there aren't any options. Unless…

"No." I meet her gaze evenly. "Go. I know how to stop them."

She gives me a confused look as I adjust the weapon to the highest setting and then step out of the tunnel and into the hallway.

Her eyes go wide. "What are you doing?"

"Move away from the entrance. Get to the transports; evacuate as many as you can. I'll buy you the time."

"Healer Tr'lani, what about you?"

A tear slips down my cheek. "Tell my family I love them."

Before she can reply, I aim the blaster at one of the overhead support beams and fire. The tunnel entrance collapses in an explosion of dust and debris, sealing my fate.

My hands shake and my body trembles as I spin to face the Zovians. I raise my weapon and begin firing rapidly. Two of them stumble and fall dead as I continue to shoot blindly into their ranks.

There are dozens more behind them, and as they get closer, I bring the blaster to my left temple. As a Healer, I've treated many, and I know exactly what happens to Aerilon slaves. I'd rather die than be taken.

The barrel is warm against my skin. I close my eyes and draw in a shaking breath as I picture my family. "Forgive me," I whisper, and then begin a silent countdown in my head. *One, two, three.*

I start to depress the trigger, but the blaster is ripped from my grasp. The shot hits the wall beside me and the weapon clatters to the floor.

I open my eyes as a clawed hand swings toward my face. I duck, but too late. Pain explodes across my cheek, and I go flying backward. The air is forced from my lungs as I slam against the wall.

My head spins as I collapse to the ground in a crumpled heap. Huge compound eyes rake over my form as one of the Zovians looms overhead. Paralyzing fear snakes down my spine as my own terrified golden eyes reflect back at me from the multiple lenses. Light reflects off the chitinous, deep-maroon shell that covers its entire body like armor. Two of its four arms reach down and grab me roughly, dragging me to my feet. A thumb and three fingers tipped with lethal black claws on each hand trace over my cheek as it studies me intently.

Using the last of my strength, I kick out wildly. A sharp crack slices the air as I make contact, creating a fine hairline fissure across the torso of its shell.

A high-pitched screech blasts my ears, and the Zovian jerks on my arm, throwing me to the floor. Blinding pain ripples along my skull, and my world goes dark.

* * *

IT'S BEEN at least two cycles since the day I was taken. I haven't felt the sun on my skin in all that time. I'm so cold, and everything hurts. I pull my knees up to my chest and curl into a ball as the last client exits the pleasure simulator.

Tears stream freely down my cheeks as my Zovian master removes the restraints from around my arms and legs. Five clients paid handsomely to take their pleasure from my body in the simulated environment. Patrons like it because it feels real for both partners, and slavers like it because it keeps their merchandise intact.

Although none of these males physically touched me, my body aches as if they actually did.

My master jerks on my collar, dragging me out into the hallway to return to the ship and the cage that awaits me in the dark cargo hold. As we exit the pleasure house and onto the station promenade, two enormous yellow eyes with vertically slit pupils stare at me with a hungry gaze.

It's the Anguis who took his disgusting pleasure from me in the sim. He snarls, baring two large fangs. His red, forked tongue comes out as he scents the air. With two arms, two legs, and a long, tapered tail, his body is all sinewy muscle beneath shiny interlocking scales.

What little clothing he wears only covers the lower half of his body, and as my gaze travels down his sinuous form, it's easy to see that he's still aroused. He fists his hand into my silver-white hair and jerks my head back to look up at him. Despite my fear at his close proximity, rage twists deep in my gut, and I meet his dark glare with my own.

He looks to my master. "I'll give you 40,000 credits for this one. I want to have her in the flesh, not the simulator."

My lips curl back in a feral snarl, and I lift my hands to rake my claws across his face before I remember that I no longer have them.

The masters broke my wings, filed down my fangs, and removed my claws and the venom sacs in my mouth. My ruined wings rattle with fury behind me a moment before sharp pain arcs along one of the damaged tendons. The slavers took every defense I had and left me completely vulnerable.

My master draws his blaster, pointing it at the Anguis. "You've already had your fun. Now, move on."

The Anguis relinquishes his grip on my hair, baring his fangs with a loud hiss.

When we get back to the ship, the master throws me back in my cage.

My body still aches terribly. Liana embraces me, and I wince slightly in pain, biting back the worst of it because I don't want her to feel bad.

"Thank god you're back," she whispers into my hair. "You were gone so long this time, I was worried. Are you all right?"

Her sea-green eyes stare at me in concern. I may be alive, but just barely, and I'll certainly never be all right. Even if we're somehow rescued, I'm broken beyond saving. My damaged wings flutter softly behind me of their own volition as if emphasizing my point. Liana is as close to me as a sister. She hasn't been a slave as long as me, and I'm desperate to shelter her from the worst of all of this. I reach out and take her hand in my own. "I will be fine."

The cargo bay doors whoosh open. One of the Anguis masters runs a sonic wand over our cage to cleanse us, removing the dull grime from my violet skin and my wings, restoring the membranes to clear, sparkling clarity. His obsidian eyes rake over our forms. "You made us quite a bit of money today," he hisses. His eyes shift to Liana. "Perhaps if I offer the two of you, we'll make even more tomorrow."

I pull her behind me as if to shield her. He means to put her in one of the pleasure simulators too. I meet his gaze evenly. "Not her. She is V'loryn. It would break her mind, and then she would be useless to you."

His yellow vertically slit pupils contract and then expand as he tips his head to the side, considering. "Perhaps you are right." He stares at her a moment more and then leaves the cargo bay. The doors close behind him, plunging us into total darkness.

Liana turns to me, and I automatically reach for her, taking her hand in my own. Her shoulders sag forward in relief. She's essentially blind right now. Her species is unable to see anything in the dark, unlike mine. Aerilon night vision is not as sharp as many of the other races, but it is better than nothing. She's Terran, but everyone assumes she is V'loryn since she looks very similar to their race.

But if they were to study her closely, they'd realize she's something entirely different. She has curved ears instead of pointed, like the V'loryns have, and her green eyes do not glow like theirs would either. There is also the matter of her golden skin covered with a fine dusting of slightly darker spots across the bridge of her nose and cheeks. Not to mention that her long brown hair has a hint of red in the coloring. With all these differences, anyone should realize she is not a V'loryn.

But the master doesn't notice, and we need to keep it that way. V'loryns bring thousands of credits in the slave trade, just as my people do. This makes her valuable enough that they won't sell her to the gladiator rings as a prize to the winners or sell her body for a few hours at a time to potential customers. They still might put her in the pleasure simulators like they do to me if they become desperate enough for credits. But it's risky to place V'loryn slaves in the sims because they are naturally strong telepaths and it often breaks their minds.

I've never seen Liana's species before. I do not think anyone has in this quadrant. And I can see how she'd be mistaken for a V'loryn. She says she went to sleep on her ship, on the way back to her home world —Terra—and woke up in a cage. Her people have never even traveled beyond their planetary system and did not realize that other life outside of their own existed in the universe.

Her soft voice calls me back from my thoughts. "Tr'lani, I know you're trying to shield me, but you can't keep taking all of the punishment. I'll go to the simulators tomorrow. Not you." She gently squeezes my hand. "I don't want you to be hurt anymore."

Holding her hand, I know she speaks truth. She *would* sacrifice herself for me. My people are able to take someone's measure—to discern their intentions through the touch of our palms. Liana may be small, but she is brave. She has not been a slave as long as me, and she has yet to be broken. I don't want that for her.

It's too late for me, but she might still be saved. We have been through much together. She has taken several beatings from the masters that were meant for my small acts of defiance. I would already be dead if not for her. I love her as if she were my own flesh and blood—as if she were my sister.

I hug her back tightly. "I don't want you to be hurt either. I would never recover if something happened to you, Liana."

We lay down in our cage, huddled together. I'm so exhausted I can barely feel the pain anymore. Closing my eyes, I allow myself to drift away.

CHAPTER 2

ROWAN

I hate these outer stations. As the airlock door opens, putrid air wafts in from the Vylax docking ring, burning my lungs with each inhalation. The smell of blood, filth, and fear is so strong my entire body instinctively reacts. Every station and port that allows the sale of slaves reeks of it.

My silver-gray scales darken to match my already dark-gray wings folded tightly against my back. My obsidian claws extend, and the muscles ripple beneath my scales as I struggle to suppress the urge to shift into my draken form. Much larger than my current form, I know I'd probably damage much of the station if I were to change right now. Although it is difficult, I force myself to calm.

I am no stranger to places like this. I spent a little over two cycles searching for my brother, Soran, when he was a slave. Our enemies had told us he was dead, that he'd been killed alongside our father at the start of the civil war. But I felt in my heart this was not truth. I knew he was still alive and—against my mother's wishes—I set out to find him, vowing that I would not return until I'd done so.

I can only imagine the dark memories Soran carries from his time in slavery, forced to fight in the bloody arenas. I place a hand on his shoulder. "I am sorry we had to stop here, but it was the closest place to refuel."

His silver reflective eyes, so like my own, look to me intently as we walk down the platform. "I understand. But the sooner we leave this place and reach V'lora, the better."

I smirk. "I never thought you would be in such a rush to see the V'loryns." I detest their race, but now that the civil war is over, my mother, the Mosauran Empress, needs to formalize a new trade agreement with them. We need their L'sair crystals to power our ships. There is still much dissension among the Great Houses of Mosaura, and we cannot afford to let our guard down. My mother's fleet must be prepared if any should challenge her right to rule. And if that means dealing with the V'loryns, so be it.

Soran turns to me. "The V'loryns may be a deceitful, duplicitous people, but on one thing, our two races can agree: We both detest slavery. If we can convince them to engage in shared patrols of the neutral zone between our two territories, it will make it harder for slavers to practice their despicable trade."

"I agree. As much as I dislike the V'loryns, at least they enforce antislavery laws in their region of space as we do in ours."

When we reach the bottom of the ramp, a dockworker rushes to meet us. Trembling slightly, he lifts a cautious gaze to me. "Refuel?"

Part of me hates that so many other species are afraid of us. Our race—the Mosaurans—are known as fierce warriors; we are feared throughout every sector of space. There aren't many who would dare cross us. But another part of me realizes that this reputation works in our favor. Like now, as I snap at the dockworker. Because he is fearful, he will do his job that much faster so we can leave this wretched station. "Yes. Work quickly and contact us as soon as the glider is ready."

Soran is tense beside me. This place is affecting him. I do not know the extent of what my brother went through as a slave in the gladiator rings. He will not speak of it, but I can only imagine how terrible it must have been. The arenas are known for their brutality.

Trying to distract him, I clap a hand on his shoulder. "It will be at least a few hours until the ship is ready. Let us go find a meal. And perhaps," I grin, "I can win a few hands of kartu."

Soran smirks. "I have a better idea. Why don't you watch *me* play kartu? We'll lose far fewer credits that way."

I narrow my eyes. "The only reason I lost so much at the last station was because that corsair must have been hiding extra zari up his sleeves. I'm certain of it."

He arches a condescending brow. "Is that the story you're going with, for when I tell Caryn about our trip?"

I lift my chin. "Yes, because it is truth."

"*Sure*, it is," he grins. "You forget that even when we were children, you were unable to hide your expressions during a game of kartu. Caryn and I could tell just by one look on your face if you'd drawn a winning hand or not."

Annoyance flares through me. As a child, I was always trying to win the approval of my two older siblings and to no avail. "The two of you always used to team up against me. Why was that? Is it because *I* was the youngest?"

Soran laughs. "Don't start this again. I've told you many times before: you're my favorite brother, and Caryn is my favorite sister. Therefore, you are both equal in my eyes."

"That doesn't mean anything," I huff. "We are your *only* siblings."

"Then…what is the problem?" he teases.

I purse my lips. "I wish our parents had decided to have more children. Then, maybe I'd have had someone on *my* side for a change when we were growing up."

Sensing my foul mood, he elbows my ribs teasingly.

I shove him away, slamming him against the side wall.

He grimaces and then rubs at his shoulder. My heart stops. I didn't mean to push him so hard. Quickly, I move to his side, studying him in concern.

A slow grin curves his mouth, and I narrow my eyes. My worry instantly replaced with anger. I hit his shoulder. "You, maltak. I thought you were really hurt."

He laughs.

Shaking my head in mock frustration, I struggle but fail to suppress the smile that tugs at my lips.

We banter back and forth as we make our way further into the station, but our mood quickly becomes more somber as we take in the filthy, decaying state of the interior. Rusted metal panels line the dozens of shops along the promenade. Bright flashing signs promise customers all kinds of illegal indulgences.

We pass by a pleasure house, and bile burns its way up my throat at the slaves displayed in the windows, waiting to be picked by a customer and forced to service them.

Soran shakes beside me with anger. His scales darken, and his claws lengthen into lethal tips. The muscles of his arms ripple beneath his scales as if readying to shift. I grab his forearm, drawing his attention back to me. "We cannot. The station is too small to shift into your draken form."

He bristles slightly but then reluctantly nods. He knows I'm right. At best, he'd injure several bystanders if he changed forms now. At worst, he could tear a hole in the station's hull. I meet his eyes evenly. "When the V'loryns and the Aerilon agree to enforce the laws in these unpatrolled regions, we will be able to free the slaves that are held here."

What I don't voice, however, is my worry that they will not accept our proposal. They would be fools not to though. It would benefit all of our people if we worked together to end slavery.

It is rare for slavers to dare take any from our three races because the punishment inflicted by our laws for such crimes is death. But many still risk it for the high price our species fetch in the illegal markets.

Off to the side, a Patiko female nestles her three small fledglings under her wings. My heart clenches when I notice the stack of crates they've turned into a makeshift shelter. They are all so thin the outlines of their bones are easily visible beneath their tattered clothing. Their crimson and green feathers are dull instead of the usual vibrant shade typical of their species. During the two cycles I spent searching for Soran, I saw things like this many times. And it always broke me.

I motion to my brother to wait for me, and then I walk toward them.

I kneel before the female, and she cowers slightly, spreading her feathered arms even wider to shelter her children. I hate that she fears me when I want only to help. I reach out to her.

"Please," I implore. "Give me your arm."

Reluctantly, she nods and extends a trembling arm out to me. I touch her wristband to my own, transferring enough credits to her account that she will be able to feed and shelter her children, or if she so desires, to even book passage and leave this terrible place.

Her eyes light up as she realizes what I've done, and she bows low. "Thank you, Mosauran warrior." She swallows thickly and then fans her back tail feathers, spreading them wide in a mating display. "I—I can repay you." Her voice quavers softly. "If that is what you—"

"That is not necessary," I reassure her. I would never take advantage of another in this way. When I mate, it will be for life, as is the way of my people. I give her a subtle nod of parting and then start back to my brother.

As we walk away, she calls out. "Mosauran warrior, wait!"

I turn back to face her with a questioning look.

She rushes toward me, her three fledglings in tow and tears gathering in the corners of her eyes. "May the Creator bless and keep you, warrior of Mosaura."

I dip my chin. "And you as well." In my quest to find Soran when he was a slave, I learned that although it is not possible to save everyone, you can still save some.

We make our way to one of the relatively nicer eating establishments, and the host greets us with a nervous grin. He trembles slightly as he motions us to the nearest table.

I stare down at the menu, my appetite nonexistent after all the suffering we just saw. Perhaps I will simply order a drink. Anything to dull the emotions that course through me as I think on all those I cannot help.

Soran tenses beside me. "What is—" I start to ask, but then stop as I follow his gaze across the room.

Two females, an Aerilon and a V'loryn, are collared and chained. Rage fills me as their Anguis master drags them behind him, parading them in front of the customers.

The Aerilon trembles with fear. Her long silver-white hair falls down her shoulders and back, drawing my attention to her wings. I gasp when I notice they are broken and deformed, fluttering pitifully at her side. Her slave dress barely covers her body, and as the over-sized neck slips off her left shoulder, I clench my jaw at the deep purple scars on her back that mar her otherwise light violet skin. Her golden eyes sweep over the room as if pleading for anyone to save them, but no one moves. Not even us. The V'loryn embraces her, trying to soothe her fear, and I've never felt so ashamed as I do now.

I am a warrior. How can I just sit by and watch this happen? It goes against everything inside me, and I move to stand but stop abruptly as an A'kai approaches the Anguis.

I go still as I realize who he is. Remarkably similar to the V'loryns, all A'kai have glowing green eyes, cranial ridges, and pointed ears, but their green skin and white hair are unique only to their species. As he turns in the light, my eyes go wide when I notice the long, jagged scar that spans the entire length of the left side of his face.

This is Talel—brother of the First Prime of A'kaina. A dangerous and lethal male indeed. He is the one who gave my brother the deep scar that runs from the top of his right brow down to his cheek.

Quickly, I scan the room for any other A'kai soldiers. I'm almost certain he has an entire regiment with him.

The Anguis master motions for the females to step forward, but the Aerilon remains still, frozen in fear. He jabs the shock stick into the Aerilon's side, and she cries out, collapsing to the floor in agony.

Talel watches with a tight smirk on his face as the V'loryn tries to defend her and then gets shocked as well. Sick delight dances behind his eyes. He enjoys watching them suffer.

The Aerilon gathers the V'loryn in her arms as tears stream down her face. Curling my hands into fists at my side, I cannot bear it.

Everything inside me wants to charge at the Anguis and Talel for daring to harm them. Fire licks at the back of my throat as the muscles flex beneath my scales with want to change into draken form and burn them to ash.

But this space is too small to shift without injuring others, and if I'm right about the A'kai having more soldiers nearby, we'd be rushing into our deaths if we attacked them now.

"We must help them," Soran says in a low voice.

His thoughts echo mine, but it is too dangerous. "Do you not recognize who is purchasing them? We wouldn't make it out of this sector before A'kai Centurions descended upon us, shredding us and our glider to pieces. We would be fortunate to even make it off this station alive. We must contact their people first. If they have a ship nearby, they will come for them."

Although it goes against every instinct inside me, it is the only logical choice. The only way we don't both end up dead.

Soran starts to protest, but I interrupt him and add. "And—more importantly—they will bring reinforcements. We do not know how many A'kai he travels with. He is the First Prime's brother. I'm certain he must have an entire contingent of soldiers somewhere nearby. We will both surely fall in battle if we attack him now, Soran."

He clenches his jaw. "There is no time to contact their people. Do what you will, but I cannot leave them with him a moment longer. You *know* what he does to his slaves."

Dark memories surface of the Aerilon female I tried to save long ago. Talel violated her mind in the R'ugol—a forced mind link. It is the most terrible of crimes—the equivalent of force-mating, except it involves the mind instead of the body. He passed her around to the rest of his men, and they did the same. I close my eyes against the pain. Even though it was many cycles ago, I still carry the guilt of not being able to save her.

Clenching my jaw, I look to my brother. "I cannot bear the thought of leaving them in his hands either. We will have to free them diplomatically. We will be killed if we openly challenge him here."

Soran gives me a reluctant nod, his anger brimming just beneath the surface.

I am just as enraged as him, but we have to think this through. "We do this my way. We cannot rush into this without careful preparation. Understood?"

"Fine," he grumbles.

A sharp cry draws my attention back to the females. The V'loryn charges at Talel, and he wraps his hand around her throat, lifting her into the air as if she weighs nothing. My heart stops when she stills beneath his hand.

Soran stands to move toward them, but I catch his shoulder to stop him. "R'ugol," I whisper as I stare in shock.

Anger burns through my veins as a single tear slips down her cheek as he violates her mind. After a moment, he slings her over his shoulders.

He jerks on the Aerilon's chain, dragging her behind him as he steps onto the promenade. Her terrified whimpers tear at my heart as she desperately struggles to free herself.

My claws extend into sharpened points, and I want nothing more than to rip out his throat as we follow discreetly behind them.

CHAPTER 3

TR'LANI

Liana's limp form hangs over Talel's shoulder as he drags me behind him. Her eyes are open but empty as he violates her mind, forcing her to remain still.

Fear wraps tight around my chest. He will kill us both. I'm certain of it. I struggle against my collar, desperate to escape, but it's no use. The A'kai are strong, and aside from the V'loryns, they are the fastest of any species. Almost all other races fear them.

As we continue through the station, everyone moves out of the way for Talel to pass. This is the first time during my enslavement that I haven't been groped by strangers as I'm pulled behind my master. No one dares touch what belongs to an A'kai.

We make our way to the docking bay and toward an A'kai cruiser. The large ship is menacing; its obsidian hull seeming to absorb all the light around it. We walk up a ramp where two more A'kai stand sentry at the door. As we pass through the entrance, the nearest one licks his lips as he meets my gaze. I shudder inwardly.

The A'kai are blood drinkers. Aerilon blood is considered a delicacy among their people. When the airlock seals behind us, we're plunged into almost complete darkness. Only a dim green glow lights our path down the hallway.

Their home world—A'kaina—is known as the "dark planet." Bright light does not seem to affect them, but it is well-known they prefer the darkness.

From what little I can make out, the walls, floor, and ceiling are seamless black metal panels. We pass several doors, but none of them are marked to signify what they are or where they lead to. I wonder how the A'kai navigate their way throughout the ship. With their superior night vision, perhaps I am only unable to read the markings. I count each step in my head, praying that it will help us if we can somehow escape later.

Liana has taught me to never give up hope, and despite how desperate our situation is now, I must hold onto it or else I'm as good as dead already.

Talel jerks on my chain again as he pulls me into a room full of decadent furnishings. A stark contrast to the utilitarian décor of the rest of the ship. He drops Liana onto a large bed and then spins back to me. He grabs my arm in a bruising grip and then drags me to a small cage along the wall, throwing me inside. Pain explodes across the back of my skull as I slam into the bars, and my world goes black.

ROWAN

When Soran and I approach the A'kai vessel, the Centurions guarding the door eye us warily. One of them steps forward. "What business do you have here, Mosaurans?"

I tilt my chin up and look down my nose at him. "Inform your Lord Talel that Prince Rowan and Soran of House Mosaura request an audience."

He relays our message into his communicator. A few moments later, the airlock hisses open, and we're met by another soldier. His fangs extend into sharpened points in a not so subtle show of aggression before he motions us forward. "Follow me."

When we step inside, we're greeted by almost total darkness. My nostrils flare as I try to identify the scent of the two females. The smell of their fear is thick like a cloying blanket, and my muscles tense with want to shift. Rage twists deep in my gut, but I push it back down as we move through the ship.

The A'kai leads us through another doorway, and I blink several times as my eyes adjust to the sudden and unexpected brightness of the room. Large gray sofas sit across from each other, separated by a small table.

"Make yourselves comfortable." He gestures to the couches. "My Lord Talel will be in to meet you shortly."

Soran and I take a seat on the sofa facing the doorway as we wait for Talel. He turns to me. "Do you really believe this will work?"

I clench my jaw. "It has to. There is no other way to safely free them."

Soran huffs. "We should just kill him and take the females."

While I agree in my heart, I also know how foolish it would be to try something so bold while we're so heavily outnumbered. "If we fall in the attempt to free them, then we are dead, and they are still slaves. It would solve nothing. We must be patient, brother."

He holds my gaze but says nothing. He knows I am right.

Myriad scenarios play out in my mind of how this could turn out. Of the two of us, I am the more level-headed. I have always prided myself in my ability to weigh risk before making a rash decision. But the overpowering scent of blood and death on this ship claws at my mind. Many slaves must have met their end on this vessel, and I can barely concentrate enough to think beyond my rage. I want Talel and every soldier on this cruiser dead by my blade.

As if my thoughts have summoned him, the doors whoosh open to reveal Talel, dragging the collared V'loryn female behind him. With her eyes downcast, he jerks on her chain. My heart sinks when I realize the Aerilon is not with them. Has he already killed her?

Anger boils inside me. Females are sacred. How dare he treat life-givers this way.

Clamping a firm hand on her shoulder, he forces her to sit at his feet as he takes a seat on the sofa across from us. His lips twist up in a tight smirk. "What brings you two here today?"

Soran glares at him. "Slavery is illegal, Talel."

His grin widens. "So it is, Prince Soran. But we are in the neutral zone, and the laws are a bit vague here, so you'll have to forgive me if I indulge in a few guilty pleasures."

My brother growls low in his throat. "Give us the females. I vow if you give them to us, we will return them to their home worlds and not mention your name, for you know it is death if their people find out you kept them as slaves."

Talel narrows his eyes. "I will not give up my pets. I haven't finished playing with them. Perhaps you can have the scraps when I'm done."

I'm about to demand to see the Aerilon when Soran shoots up from his chair. "Brother!" I wrap a firm hand around his forearm. "You must calm yourself and sit down."

His eyes dart to mine briefly before he turns a dark gaze to Talel. "What do you want for the females? Name your price, and we'll pay it."

A wicked grin spreads across Talel's face. "I never thought *you'd* be so interested in something outside of your own species." With a casual air, he relaxes back in his seat. Now that he knows how much we want them, I suspect he will draw this out. "Let us have tea and discuss our terms."

He taps on a panel, and a few moments later, a male enters the room with a teapot and three small cups. He arranges them on the table and then leaves.

My eyes travel over the V'loryn as Talel pours our tea. I grit my teeth when I notice the two puncture wounds on her neck. He's already fed from her, and my thoughts turn again to the Aerilon. The A'kai consider their blood a delicacy. Did he drink from her first?

I study Talel. It is very likely he will refuse to sell us the females simply to spite my brother. Soran and I may die here today after all, for I will not leave here without them.

"I don't want tea," Soran snaps. "Just tell me your terms. How much for the females?"

Talel gives him a sly grin. "Tea is a part of every A'kai negotiation. It is part of our custom, and we will honor it."

My every muscle is tense, but I try not to appear impatient. Talel already knows he has the upper hand, and he will not give up his slaves easily. Whatever he wants, though, we will pay it. I cannot bear to leave them in his grasp.

Soran reaches for his cup, and I do the same. Without warning, the V'loryn female jumps up and swipes the cup from my brother's hand, throwing it back at Talel.

The liquid splashes across his face. He cries out like a wild kraven as his skin sizzles and expands into bubbled welts.

He meant to poison us!

The world shifts into slow motion as he jerks the V'loryn female's chain, sending her flying across the room. She hits the wall with a sickening thud, crumpling to the floor.

Enraged, I leap from my chair and rush forward, slamming him to the ground. I wrap my hands around his throat, squeezing the life from his body as he claws at my arms and chest. But his talons are no match for Mosauran armor. I tighten my grip on his neck as I grit through my teeth, "Where is the Aerilon?"

He gasps, only a choked sound escaping him. I relinquish my grasp just enough to allow him to speak. "She is mine!" he wheezes. "You cannot have her!"

The V'loryn cries out, drawing my attention away from him.

Taking advantage of my distraction, he twists in my grip and then pushes me away. Pain explodes across my body as I fall back, crushing the wood table beneath me. Soran rushes forward, slamming him back to the ground. I pull out my blaster, but Soran beats me to it.

A shot rings out as he fires a direct hit at Talel's chest. Obsidian blood blooms from the site as Talel writhes in agony on the floor. The fact that he's moving means the weapon was not on the highest setting, but it is easy to see it is a mortal wound.

We must leave before his men discover what we've done.

Soran rushes to the V'loryn, gathering her in his arms while I stand by the door, bracing myself, ready to defend us if anyone enters.

I motion for my brother to hurry as he carries the wounded female. "We have to go before someone comes. We cannot fight an entire regiment of A'kai by ourselves."

He gives me a firm look. "We cannot leave without the Aerilon."

It was never my intent to abandon her, but I'm worried how we're going to locate her now that Talel is dying. I'm certain he won't tell us where she is. My only hope is that the V'loryn knows. I lean down to meet her eyes evenly, stunned when I notice their green coloring is dull instead of the glowing brightness that is standard for her people. I can only imagine what the slavers must have done to her to cause this. "Where is your friend? We have to hurry."

"Left down the hallway. Third door on the right," she barely manages. My gaze drifts to her left leg, swollen and bleeding. If we do not get her back to the ship soon, she could die from this injury. But we cannot leave the Aerilon here. We must rescue her first.

Cautiously, I open the door and peer out into the hallway. "It's empty," I whisper over my shoulder, motioning for my brother to follow me.

Since he is carrying the V'loryn, I go first. It is not her fault she is unable to walk, but there's no way he could use his blaster and keep hold of her at the same time. Sweat trickles down my back as we move quickly and quietly down the corridor. Laughter echoes from somewhere nearby, and while I do not know exactly how many A'kai are on this ship, I'm certain it's more than my brother and I could take down on our own. "Are we almost there?" I whisper over my shoulder.

"Almost," she replies weakly.

I send a silent prayer to the Creator that we're not too late to rescue the Aerilon.

CHAPTER 4

TR'LANI

My head is still throbbing, but I force myself to focus and push down the pain. Talel and Liana are gone. Before they left, I overheard him speaking with a female that I assume is his mate. Although I could not see her face on the viewscreen, she must be a different species from him. They talked of creating an empire through an alliance with their people to conquer the rest of the quadrant, including the Mosaurans.

But I cannot worry about that now. I have to figure a way out of here. I have to save Liana. The A'kai are known for their cruelty. They'll rape us and drink of our blood until we're dead.

I reach my hands through the bars of my prison, fumbling with the lock and hoping it will somehow open. The subtle whoosh of the doors draws my attention, and my eyes snap up to see an A'kai guard stalking toward me.

"Going somewhere?" he asks with a sinister grin as he kneels before the cage.

I scramble backward, slamming into the bars behind me, desperate to get as far away from him as possible.

Closing his eyes, his nostrils flare and he licks his lips. "It's been a long time since I had Aerilon blood. You smell delicious. I think I'll have a taste."

A terrified whimper escapes me as he opens the cage and reaches inside.

In desperation, I lunge forward, trying to push past him. He catches my leg. Pain rips up my spine as I twist onto my back, and the hulking mass of his form moves over me, pinning me beneath him.

He grins, and his canines extend into sharpened points as his eyes turn into feral, obsidian orbs. A broken sob escapes my lips as he lowers his head to the curve of my neck and shoulder, running his tongue along the flesh, directly over my artery.

Trembling, I draw in a shaking breath. "Please. Don't."

He takes my jaw in a bruising grip, turning my head to bare the long column of my neck. I struggle a moment before the sharp lash of his thoughts whips through my mind, forcing me to still. The heavy press of his mind as it invades mine is an unbearable weight. Long tendrils snake and wrap around my consciousness as he tears through my thoughts, asserting his dominance and forcing me into submission.

A tear slips down my cheek as he forces my legs apart and settles between my thighs. His hardened length presses against my center, and I bite my lip to stifle a whimper of fear. Dark memories rush forward of all the abuse I endured in the simulators.

Perverse delight ripples through his thoughts as he replays the terrible images, deriving sick pleasure from my remembered pain when he discovers that I've never physically joined with anyone before and he will be my first.

His dark desire floods my mind as he scents along my neck. I choke on a scream as he sinks his teeth deep into my flesh. The horrible pull as he drinks of my blood is agony, and I cry out a moment before his consciousness wraps thickly around mine, forcing me to go silent and still.

He reaches between us, fumbling with the clasp of his pants. My pulse pounds in my ears as my body begins to weaken. Powerless to stop him, tears stream down my face as he struggles to free himself.

The doors whoosh open, and he rips his fangs from my neck and spins toward the entrance.

My eyes go wide as two Mosaurans enter. One of them holds Liana in his arms, a long, jagged scar on the right side of his face. The other rushes to attack.

A burst of light races toward the A'kai, hitting him square in the chest. He stumbles back and falls dead to the floor. The shot came from a blaster in Liana's hand.

Weakened from my blood loss, my head swims as I try to stand. One of the Mosaurans steps forward and grabs my arm to keep me from falling. His species are natural enemies to mine, and I instinctively recoil from his grasp. "Don't touch me, Mosauran!"

They are a race of warriors—lethal and dangerous. The history between our people is long and bloodied. They are not to be trusted.

I bare my teeth, and my wings rattle behind me in warning. Aerilon venom can incapacitate an enemy for several hours. That's why the masters removed my fangs and the venom sacs attached to them. But this male does not know I no longer have this defense, and he studies me warily.

"They're here to help us, Tr'lani," Liana says. "These are the good guys."

Despite her words, my gaze remains locked on him. I don't know what they've told her, but I'm still not convinced. Large, silver, reflective eyes stare down at me. He's covered in smooth, silver-gray scales that shimmer with iridescent color beneath the light. Accents of red highlight the sharp ridges of his cheeks and brow. A small, bony ridge starts at the top of his forehead and spreads out across his skull in a V, disappearing into short-cropped, black hair.

Dressed in the form-fitting obsidian armor that is common for his people, it does nothing to hide the thick layers of corded muscle that line his entire body. The aristocratic features of his nose and cheekbones lend an almost regal air to his countenance, but it is the kindness reflected behind his eyes that gives me pause. Mosaurans only respect strength. They are not capable of empathy. Are they?

Determined to move on my own, I take a small step. The world spins around me, and I start to fall forward, but the Mosauran catches me in his arms, lifting me to his chest. "Allow me to carry you."

I narrow my eyes. "I can walk."

A faint smile curves his lips. "As you said, I am Mosauran. Your weight is slight; it is no burden to carry you. We need to be able to run if we are going to escape. I beg you not to be stubborn about this."

Reluctantly, I agree. He is right. I'm still weak from blood loss. I'm going to have to trust him and the other one to help us get out of here. We don't have any other choice.

Sweat beads on my forehead as we make our way to the airlock. As soon as we reach it, one of the guards moves into our path. His gaze travels over me, and I shudder inwardly, terrified he's going to capture us again. "Where are you going with these two?" he asks in a booming voice.

The other Mosauran steps forward, and the one holding me leans down to whisper in my ear, "Do not worry. I will die before I let him take you."

His words stun me as his eyes meet mine with fierce determination.

The other Mosauran replies to the guard. "We bought them from Talel."

"Where is my Lord Talel?" he asks darkly.

Before he can answer, Liana fires a blaster at his chest, and he falls dead at their feet.

No doubt alerted by the sound of weapon's fire, several voices begin shouting in the hallway behind us. We escape through the airlock and race across the docking bay.

"Our glider is just up ahead," the Mosauran reassures me. "We're going to make it."

A dockworker moves in our path, and my rescuer stops so abruptly I worry I'll pitch forward, but he holds me firmly against his chest.

The male cowers before him. "Your—your ship is ready, my lords."

Releasing an irritated huff, my rescuer somehow manages to keep me secure in his arms as he hurriedly pays the dockworker for refueling their vessel.

As soon as he's done, we race toward the glider and up the ramp, sealing the doors behind us after Liana and the other Mosauran are through.

Quickly yet carefully, he places me in a chair on the bridge, strapping me securely to the seat. I lift my eyes to thank him and am surprised at the tenderness of his gaze. "Hold on," he whispers. "I'm going to get us out of here."

I nod weakly, and he slams into the station beside me. His hands fly across the control panel as he spins up the FTL (faster than light) engines.

A harsh A'kai face fills the viewscreen, and an involuntary whimper escapes me when I realize it's Talel.

I eye the blaster still in Liana's hand. I won't be taken again.

"You should be dead," the scarred Mosauran says darkly.

"That one." He points to Liana, unconscious in the seat beside me. "Her blood. It healed my wound faster than anything I've ever partaken before." He drags his tongue across his lips. "And I've had the blood of many creatures. Give her back to me at once, or else I will order the entire A'kai fleet to hunt you down."

The Mosauran growls low in his chest. "You *will not* touch her ever again. And when her people find out what you've done, *you* will be the one who's hunted like an animal. You will die for what you've done to her."

Talel narrows his eyes. "I might be worried *if* she were V'loryn. But I've been in her mind, and I've tasted her blood. I do not know exactly *what* she is, but I know, for a fact, that she *isn't* V'loryn."

My heart stops. If the A'kai figure out what she is, they will hunt for her planet and enslave her world. I wait with bated breath for the Mosauran to answer, wondering if he'll decide to help us or turn us over. With the threat of being hunted by the entire A'kai fleet looming over their heads, they may decide we're not worth it. After all, they do not even know us, and I don't understand why they would risk so much to save us. Especially me. Our people are enemies.

The Mosauran leans forward. "I give you my vow as a prince and warrior of the Mosauran Empire. If you come after her, I will end you."

Without waiting for a reply, he slams his fist down on the control panel, activating the engines. Stars begin to blur in the viewscreen as we enter FTL travel.

The male who carried me darts a quick glance over his shoulder. "Do not worry. Our glider has cloaking technology."

I release the breath I hadn't realized I was holding as I fall back in my seat. My relief is short-lived, however, when I turn to Liana and find her slumped forward in her chair. Panic fills me. "Liana needs medical attention."

The other Mosauran quickly gathers her in his arms. He calls out to the other, "I'm taking her to the med bay."

Despite my weakened state, I somehow manage to follow behind him, my newfound freedom granting me strength enough in spirit to at least do this.

He places her in the medical repair unit (MRU). As the scanner passes over her form, I study the readings while the two Mosaurans stare down at her in confusion. No doubt they realize now from Talel's words, the curved shell of her ears, the strange spots on her skin that she calls "freckles," and the slight reddish tint to her hair that she is not V'loryn.

"She's Terran," I offer, answering the unspoken question that lingers behind their eyes. "I've never heard of her race before. She is the first one I have ever seen."

"Where is her home world?" the scarred one asks.

This was the first thing I asked her as well when we met. I remember the sadness in her eyes when she explained that she was lost. At the time, I'd hoped that maybe one of the other races knew of her people and her planet. The Mosauran Empire is vast. If they have not even heard of her kind, her world must be very far away from this region of space. "I do not know, and...I do not think she does either.

Her species has not yet left their planetary system, much less made any contact with other races."

As the med scanner continues to move over her form, I study the readouts a moment before turning my attention back to our rescuers. "It will take a few moments." I gesture to the machine. "I am Tr'lani of the High Clan Al'ani. I," my voice quavers slightly. "I was a Healer back on Aerilon."

That life feels so far away now. Like that version of me was a distant dream instead of reality. Lowering my gaze, something whispers from a dark corner in my mind. *I am no longer that person. Now... I'm only a broken thing.*

The Mosauran steps closer, pulling me back from my despairing thoughts. He places a closed fist over his chest and bows slightly. "I am Prince Soran of House Mosaura, and this"—he motions to the male beside him, the one who carried me—"is Prince Rowan."

Rowan's piercing silver gaze meets mine as he inclines his head and then bows as well.

"Thank you for saving us." I meet Rowan's eyes evenly. "I am sorry for my reaction when you found me. Our two races have fought for many cycles over the neutral zone, and we've been enemies for so long. I—"

"There is no need to apologize," he interrupts. "I would probably have reacted the same if our roles were reversed." He cocks his head to the side. "You are of one of the High Clans on Aerilon. How were you taken?"

Lowering my gaze, I close my eyes against the painful memories and regrets. My family warned me. My brother Al'aneo even begged me not to go anywhere near the outer planets. He insisted it wasn't safe. That those places were raided by slavers regularly.

But I didn't listen. I never thought we would be attacked. What a fool I was. "Zovians invaded the colony I was on, near the border. Those they didn't kill, they sold into slavery. The neutral zone between our two Empires is supposed to be protected." Frustration burns through me. I clench my jaw, fighting back tears for all that I suffered these past two cycles. I don't want to cry anymore. "If your people and mine could stop fighting with each other, perhaps the slavers would not be able to operate so close to the edge of our shared borders."

Something akin to guilt flashes briefly behind Rowan's eyes, but it's gone too quickly for me to be certain.

The scanner beeps, interrupting our conversation. I turn to the readout, and my eyes go wide as my suspicions are confirmed. "The closest match to her anatomy is that of a V'loryn but...there are still so many differences. She is weak from blood loss and has several minor fractures and a broken leg, but I believe she is stable." I take Liana's hand in my own. A low, trilling hum rises in the back of my throat as I seek to comfort her and whisper, "In'ari."

This word is sacred among my people. A sign of deep affection, it is reserved only for Clan and family members. Liana is a sister to me in all ways but blood. And I will ask my family to accept her into our Clan when I find them again. She is all by herself out here, separated from her people and her world. With the protection of my Clan she will never be alone again. I swear it to the Creator.

Out of the corner of my eye, I notice the Mosaurans gaping at me. Acceptance of an Outsider into one's Clan is almost unheard of. Gently, I brush the hair back from her face, staring down at her unconscious form. "She is like a sister to me. We have been through much. She has protected me ever since we met. I would be dead now if not for her. I have never known one so brave or so—" My voice hitches. "So kind."

Rowan inhales sharply as the 3D scanner displays the thick pattern of jagged red scars that mar the full length of Liana's back—a branding from one of her owners. They are difficult to look upon. I have yet to study mine, but I know they are many and they are deep. Zovian slave markings can never be removed. They cut us with Hawkan steel and pour silic acid into the wounds to ensure they are permanent. No MRU can heal these.

My gaze drifts to Soran's face and the deep scar that runs from the top of his right brow down to the hard ridge of his cheek. It must have been made with a silic-acid-tipped bladed or else it would have been fully healed. It is fortunate he did not lose an eye to this injury. If not for this marking, he and his brother would be harder to tell apart. They could almost pass as twins, except for the slight scruff of beard that covers Rowan's square and chiseled jaw.

"Will she be all right?" Soran asks.

"Yes. The MRU is already working to heal her. She's similar enough to a V'loryn that it should be able to repair the damage she has suffered."

Something akin to relief crosses his expression as he stares down at her through the MRU casing. His brother moves to his side and clamps a firm hand on his shoulder. "We must speak."

Soran hesitates a moment, and it is easy to read his concern for Liana, but I do not understand it. Just as I do not know why they risked themselves to save us. Is it merely kindness, or is it something else?

My entire life, I've been told that Mosaurans are volatile, aggressive, and untrustworthy. They are known for their speciest views. They believe all other races inferior to their own, and unlike mine, they do not tolerate any mixed-species pairings. And yet, all they've done so far is to help us, but why?

Only when I tell Soran that I will stay to monitor Liana does he leave the room with his brother.

Everything inside me tells me we can trust them, but my mind demands proof of their intent.

CHAPTER 5

ROWAN

Soran and I have always been close. So much so that I knew in my heart he was alive despite the claim from our enemies in House Caladan that he'd been killed along with our father. When our forces captured Lord Caladan, I tortured him until he gave up the truth that they'd sold Soran into slavery.

My mother and sister did not believe him. They thought he'd say anything I wanted to hear just to end his torment. Despite their protests, I set out to search for Soran, vowing I wouldn't return until I brought him home.

And now, this deep connection that I share with my brother tells me that something troubles him, but I do not know what it is. I meet his gaze evenly. "Something is wrong with you, brother. What is it?"

He looks down at his hands. "Liana is my Ashaya."

This cannot be truth. "You are certain?"

"Yes."

I stare at him in stunned silence. If she is truly his Ashaya—his fated bondmate—I will lose him forever. "But, she's…she is not Mosauran. How could she be your Ashaya?"

He lifts his eyes to mine, resignation easily read in his features. "I do not know, and I cannot change what is."

His words hit me like a physical blow. Despair fills me so great I feel as if I'm drowning in it. Pacing back and forth, I run my hand roughly through my hair and then turn to face him, praying to the Creator that he listens to reason. "It is forbidden to take a mate outside of our race. You would be Outcast. You are a Prince of Mosaura. You cannot bind yourself to her."

"I cannot deny this calling. I already feel her here, brother." He thumps his fist to his chest, directly over his heart. "You do not understand."

"You're right," I snap. "I don't understand. How can you throw away your life for this strange female? A species we've never heard of before? You don't even know her."

He gives me a pleading look. "My soul is tied to hers. It is not something I can just ignore or pretend does not exist."

How can he say this? If he takes her as his mate, he will lose everything. He will become Outcast from our people, and I will never see him again. I give him an incredulous look. "Do you even love her?"

"How could I?" He shakes his head. "I do not know her."

"Then that decides it. You cannot give up everything for a complete stranger."

"She is *not* a stranger," he growls. "She is my Ashaya."

Panic stabs at my chest. After all I went through to bring him home… "I…I do not want to lose you again."

He gives me a pained look and places a hand on my shoulder. "I do not want to lose you either. Perhaps there is another way. If I can convince Mother to accept her, maybe she can convince the Council to change the laws and—"

"There is no other way. You know the laws as well as I. You will be Outcast, and I will never see you again." I gesture angrily toward the door and begin pacing again as my body rebels with fits of nervous energy at his words. "She may not even want you as her mate. Have you even considered that?"

Without meaning to, my eyes drift to his facial scar, remembering how his betrothed turned him away because of it. This female could be the same as her. Shallow and uninterested in a male she considers damaged. The day Maina turned her back on him, she chose me instead. I refused her, but I'll never forget the pain in Soran's eyes, and I'll be damned if I allow him to go through that again. I cannot bear the thought of him giving up everything for someone who might not even want him.

He meets my gaze evenly. "Perhaps you are right. She may not desire me as hers." With a heavy sigh, he turns back to the med bay doors.

"Where are you going?"

Without bothering to turn around, he speaks over his shoulder. "She has been through much. I will sit with her until she wakes. Even if she does not want me, I wish to help her…to help them both in any way I can."

When he goes back into the room, I follow behind him. Tr'lani spins to face us, a wary look in her eyes even now that suggests she still does not entirely trust us. And I suppose I do not blame her. Our people have been enemies for such a long time.

My brother steps forward. "I will sit with Liana if you wish to use the other unit on yourself."

Her broken wings flutter softly behind her, and my heart clenches at her pained expression.

Instead of answering him, she reaches out her hand in the Aerilon gesture of greeting and touches her palm to his.

The Aerilon female I tried to save…she did this to me as well. This is how they read someone—judging if their intentions are good or bad. It's not as sensitive as the touch telepathy possessed of the V'lo-ryns and A'kai, but it is close.

Her eyes are closed in concentration. A small frown creases her brow, and I wonder if she can sense the bond my brother claims exists between him and the Terran.

When she releases his hand, her expression is solemn. "I have taken your measure. You are an honorable male, willing to protect us with your life if necessary. I thank you for your protection. I did not expect to find such kindness from a Mosauran. The A'kai did not intend to let us live."

After all they have been through, I'm sure she must be exhausted. Now that she knows we do not mean them harm, I address her. "Are you hungry?"

She nods but then looks down at Liana's still form in the MRU. "I want to be here when she wakes."

Her concern is touching. "How long does she still have?"

"A few hours yet."

"Then, would you like me to show you to the crew mess?"

I do not understand why, but I feel a strange pull to this female. Something inside me wants only to protect her. At first, I think she'll refuse. But after a moment, she nods. "Thank you."

CHAPTER 6

ROWAN

She follows me out into the hallway, and I make sure to walk beside her. She has not used the MRU on herself, and from her slower gait, I wonder if she is still feeling weak.

I shudder inwardly as I remember how we found her in the clutches of the A'kai soldier, his fangs dripping with her blood. My hands curl into fists at my side. I am glad he is dead.

Her eyes are wide as she takes in everything. The glider is rather small and built for a standard crew of no more than four to six people, but it is my pride and joy. "I personally designed this vessel for stealth and speed. While not as comfortable as our cruisers, it has everything we need," I assure her. "I made certain to spare no expense for its defense capabilities."

She nods but says nothing.

Trl'ani's people are known for their love of aesthetics: gems, ornate furnishings, and such. It is rumored that their ships are built as much for comfort as they are for defense and maneuverability. As a Princess of Aerilon, I'm almost certain she finds my glider to be lacking.

As I give her a general tour of each area, I note the haunted expression in her face. St'lara had this same look after I saved her from the A'kai. We were on our way back to Aerilon when she took her life. Clenching my jaw, I close my eyes against the painful memory. It's my fault she died, and I will never forgive myself for not recognizing the signs.

As I turn to Tr'lani, I vow that she will not suffer the same fate.

When we enter the crew mess, I gesture for her to sit at the table as I retrieve two protein pouches. I offer her one, and she extends a trembling hand out to accept it. I watch in confusion as she sets it on the table before her and then reaches up to take my still outstretched hand in her own.

Ah. She wants to make certain I am safe as well.

Warmth travels across my palm from the touch of her bare skin as she takes my measure. Her hand is so small compared to my own, but I know she is far from delicate. Unlike my species, Aerilon females are smaller than the males. But they are as beautiful as they are deadly.

As her eyes are closed, I take a moment to study her features. Her skin is a lovely shade of violet and petal-soft to the touch. Her silver-white hair spills down her back and shoulders in long, silken waves. The tips of her ears are pointed, her cheekbones are high, and her brows are slightly rounded, unlike the sharp ridges that define mine.

My heart clenches when I notice she is missing her claws. Her broken wings flutter softly behind her, and I suspect her venom sacs have been removed as well. The masters have stripped her of all her natural defenses. Her reflective golden eyes are bright with tears as they open to meet mine. "Thank you," she whispers.

I nod. She looks so thin, it's worrisome, and I gesture to the protein pouch before her. "You should eat."

I watch as she drinks only a half portion and then closes it again to save the rest. I tip my head to the side, wondering if the taste bothers her because surely she must be starving. Slavers are not known for keeping their captives well fed. "Would you like something else?"

She blinks several times and then shakes her head. Her gaze drops to the protein drink, and a small puff of air escapes her. Her shoulders sag forward, and she opens it again. "I suppose it's habit by now," she says softly. "Whenever we were fed, I always tried to save half of it for later. The masters didn't always remember to feed us every day."

I move to reassure her. "We have plenty of food here. Anything you want…it is yours. You need not ask."

She gives me a warm smile. "You are kind. Something I did not expect from a Mosauran."

A slow grin curves my lips as I tease her. "Don't be spreading that information around freely. My people have a reputation to uphold, you know. We don't need others believing we've gone soft."

A stunning smile spreads across her face, and she laughs. It's such a light and beautiful sound, I'm enchanted. "Don't worry. Your secret is safe with me."

She takes another sip of her protein drink, and when she's finished, she asks what else we have. I wish I'd stocked better food besides ordinary travel rations. "Unfortunately, all we have are the protein pouches and nutrient bars."

Her eyes light up. "Nutrient bars?"

I nod.

"I'll take one of those." She grins. "Or two."

I smile and then give her three, glad to see her eating more. Her frame is very slight, almost delicate-looking, as is normal for Aerilon females. I hope with enough time she will regain the weight she lost during her captivity.

I study her discreetly as she eats. She takes a bite of her food, and I notice that even the two prominent fangs that should be on either side of her mouth have been removed.

I ball my hands into fists at my side. I wish I could kill the ones who did this to her.

As if sensing my anger on her behalf, she lifts a pained gaze to me. "The masters removed all my natural defenses. My claws, my venom sacs, my fangs, and…they broke my wings." She pauses. "Paying customers do not want a female that can fight them when they—"

Her voice breaks, and a tear escapes her lashes, but she quickly brushes it away.

Cautiously, I reach across the table and gently take her hand. "I give you my most solemn vow as a warrior of Mosaura that I will do everything in my power to protect you or die trying. I will end any who dare try to touch you against your will. And I swear that I will return you to your people, Tr'lani of High Clan Al'ani."

She draws in a shaking breath and swallows back a sob. "Thank you," she whispers.

In this moment, she looks so vulnerable. Anger fills me. I wish I could kill every male who ever hurt her. I do not push her for any details of what she went through. Even Soran has never told me much about his slavery. In my two cycles of searching for him, I saw so many horrors, I can only guess at the terrible things they must have endured.

I know I cannot change what has happened to her, but I can help her remember the things that are important. The reasons for her to cling to life and not end up like St'lara. "Tell me about your family."

A wistful smile curves her lips. "My mother and grandmother are politicians—the leaders of our Clan. But my grandfather and my father are both Healers like myself. And my brother…he decided to do something entirely different and joined the Defense Force." She shakes her head. "My parents and grandparents were furious at this, of course. They were so afraid he would be—" She stops abruptly. A deep-purple bloom spreads across her cheeks as she nervously tucks a stray tendril of hair behind her ear.

"What were they afraid of?" I ask, curious to know.

She hesitates a moment before answering. "That he'd be killed in a pointless border skirmish with your people."

Ashamed, I avert my gaze from hers. In truth, I know it is my people who are the aggressors in these skirmishes. We are very territorial, and I suspect it is something to do with our naturally possessive instincts.

Clearing her throat, she continues. "My father studied under my grandfather, and that's how he met my mother. My grandparents said they knew it would be a good match from the start." She pauses. "What about your parents? How did they meet?"

"It was the same with my parents. My father was in training with my grandfather to become a warrior. That is how he was introduced to my mother." A smile tugs at my lips. "It was quite a scandal because Father was not of noble blood, but my mother did not care."

"You have a sister, do you not?" she asks.

I nod. "Caryn. She is as fierce as our mother and yet is slow to anger, like our father was. She was the only one who did not try to discourage me from searching for Soran even though our enemies claimed he was dead."

Tr'lani leans forward. "I remember hearing rumors of him. The Mosauran Prince who was rescued from slavery by his brother. I did not realize they were true." Her golden eyes search mine. "He is truly fortunate that you did not give up on him. How did you know he was still alive?"

I place my closed fist to my chest, directly over my heart. "I felt it in here."

"You had no proof?"

"No. But I could not ignore what I knew in my heart. And I vowed to the Creator that I would search for however long it took to find him and bring him home."

She stares at me, a hint of wonder reflected in her eyes before sadness fills them once again, and she looks down at her hands. "Al'aneo—my brother," she says softly. "He begged me not to go to the outer colonies...warned me that slavers operated too closely to those planets. But they were experiencing an outbreak. When I saw how they were suffering on the vidfeeds, how could I not go when I knew that I could help? Al'aneo is my twin and we have always been close. In my heart, I know he is out there still searching for me too."

She is selfless, this Aerilon. Risking her life to aid others. I hate that she paid so dearly for it. "We will find him, Tr'lani. I swear it to the Creator."

She gives me a pained smile. "Thank you, Rowan."

When she is finished with her meal, I ask if she'd like to see her quarters and to bathe and change.

Her eyes light up. I'm captivated as I stare into their reflective golden depths. Her people are known for their beauty. It is rumored that they possess the ability to charm anyone, and as I study her, I realize this rumor is truth. Even in her disheveled state, she is the most beautiful female I have ever beheld.

Pushing down my errant thoughts, I lead her to the room that will be hers. It is directly across from mine. I instruct her to place her hand over the access panel to code it for her entry. As soon as the doors whoosh open, she steps inside.

The quarters on my glider are nothing special, and I worry she will be displeased. There is a small bed in one corner, a desk and chair in another, with a sofa in the middle of the room. At least everything is immaculately neat and tidy. I make sure every surface of this ship is cleaned and polished at all times.

I gesture to the door along the far wall. "That leads into the cleansing room."

She gives me a smile that rivals the brightness of the Mosauran sun. "It's perfect. Thank you, Rowan."

My entire body flushes with warmth. I'm almost certain the red markings on my cheeks and brow are now a deep-crimson hue.

"Is there anything I can change into?" she asks.

Silently, I curse myself. In my obsession with cleanliness, I have recently placed all the spare clothing in the refresher, and it has not finished its cycle yet. "I—I am sorry. Everything is currently being washed."

She looks down at herself, gently tugging at the paper-thin slave dress that barely covers her body.

"I—I have a spare tunic. I wore it for only an hour yesterday before changing. I am sorry it is not entirely clean." I wince as I think of the small grease stain on the chest from when I was in the engine room. I glance down at the shirt I have on. It is spotless. "Here, you can use this one." Eager to please her, I quickly remove it to offer it to her.

She skitters back to the wall.

I freeze at the terrified look on her face. "Forgive me. I only meant to give this to you to wear. Nothing else. I swear it to the Creator."

She gives me a shaky nod. "I—I'm sorry for my reaction. It's just…I was used in the simulators so many times that I—" Her voice catches, and she lowers her gaze to the floor as she fights back tears.

I move to reassure her. "Not many know this about us, but my people do not have casual matings. We mate for life. I would never touch you in that way."

She looks back up at me and extends her arm to take the shirt from my hands. "Thank you. Even a used shirt would definitely be better than this." She tugs at her dress as if in emphasis.

I nod. "I will return shortly to check on you if that is all right. I believe I do have some pants and a belt you may use as well."

She gives me a faint smile. "I'd like some pants."

It doesn't take me long to retrieve the extra clothing, and when I do, I find Tr'lani waiting in her quarters wrapped in a towel. Her long, silken hair hangs like a curtain down her back and shoulders in silver-white waves. A beautiful contrast to her soft violet skin, flushed after her warm shower. Her reflective golden eyes stare up at me, and I've suddenly forgotten how to speak. Unable to form words, much less a coherent thought, I somehow manage to hold the pants and belt out to her.

She smiles, and my heart stutters and stops. "Could you turn around, please?" she asks softly.

I blink several times as I come back to myself and then fumble over my words. "I—I will leave you and—"

She shakes her head. "You don't have to go. Just turn around."

I do as she says. My pulse pounds in my ears when I hear the towel drop to the ground and realize she is standing completely bare behind me. A soft rustle of clothing follows shortly after. "You can turn back now," she says.

When I do, my mouth drifts open slightly. The hem of my shirt goes down to her mid-thighs, and the sleeves are so long, she has rolled them up her forearms. The neck is so large it hangs off to one side, revealing the bare skin of her left shoulder. My pants are so loose on her slender waist they are cinched tight with a belt, and I note she has folded up the ends because of their length. Her bare feet peek out from beneath the material, and I marvel at how small they appear.

Everything about her is both beautiful and delicate. But I know her appearance belies a strength deep inside. As she stands there in my used shirt, my nostrils flare as I inhale discreetly of our combined scent.

Mine. The word flashes through my mind as my possessive instincts flare.

She smiles up at me, and I quickly push down my errant thoughts and force myself to focus. I'm surprised by my reaction. She is not my mate. She is Aerilon, and I am Mosauran. Why am I responding to her in this way?

She turns to me. "I'd like to try sending a signal to my family now."

"Of course. Follow me."

I lead her to the bridge, and she takes the station beside mine. The one Soran normally sits in. I hand her the comm. "Before we send anything out, I must know. Is there a special frequency we may use to contact your people?" I ask this because almost every species has a secret way to communicate with one another. Whether by code or use of a certain channel.

She hesitates a moment, and I realize it must go against everything inside her to share this information with me. I meet her eyes evenly. "I know it may not mean much to you, but my vows as a warrior are sacred to me. And I offer it to you now when I give you my vow as a warrior of the Mosauran Empire, I will not share the secrets you divulge to me of how your people communicate with one another."

She studies me a moment and then nods. "I will record the message first and then show you how to encode and send it."

It is no small thing for her to trust me like this, and I vow that I will never betray it. She presses a button on the console to begin recording but says nothing. When I look over at her, her head is bent and her eyes are closed as her shoulders shake with silent sobs.

Uncertain of what to do, I reach over and gently place my hand over hers, wanting desperately to offer her some sort of comfort. I'm surprised when she does not pull away but instead turns her palm up to mine and squeezes my hand in return.

She sniffs and then wipes at the tears on her cheeks. Clearing her throat, she begins again. Her voice quavers softly as she speaks. "I am Tr'lani of High Clan Al'ani. This message is for my family."

I listen as she records her communication. She was a slave for over two cycles, and I marvel at how she survived for so long. She is much stronger than I realize.

When she's finished, she turns to me. "Here is the code and the wavelength to broadcast it on," she says, pointing to the display. Once it is sent, she looks to the door. "Can you show me the way back to the med bay? I'd like to check on Liana."

"Of course."

As we walk down the hallway, I am surprised when she gently places her hand on my forearm, stopping me abruptly.

Just that simple touch and my entire body fills with warmth.

She stares up at me with her golden gaze. "I sensed something when I took your brother's measure."

I go still, uncertain if I should reveal to her what he's told me.

She continues. "What he feels for her is more than concern, isn't it?" Her eyes search mine. "You know what I'm speaking of, don't you?"

With a heavy sigh, I nod. I cannot be untruthful with her. "He is pulled to her, instinctively drawn to protect her above all else. He believes she is his fated one."

It is truth as best I can describe it. She lowers her gaze, a contemplative look on her face. "Our people have something similar," she offers. "Our wings glow when we find our fated mate."

I'm shocked and yet disappointed in equal measure as I look to her wings, part of me hoping they will begin glowing in my presence. But they do not. If they did, that would at least explain why I am so drawn to her.

She continues. "He is a good male, your brother. As are you. I sensed this was so before I took your measure, but now…I am certain."

Unsure how to respond, I nod. "Thank you."

She dips her chin in acknowledgment of my words, and then we continue on. It is good she has Liana to focus on, but I will monitor her closely. I will watch for all the signs I missed with St'lara. I will not allow what happened to her to happen to Tr'lani. Perhaps this is why my protective instincts are so strong in regard to her. And yet, I never felt this pull to St'lara as I do to Tr'lani.

When we reach the med bay, my brother is seated beside the MRU with his hand resting atop the casing. I've never seen him look as lost as he does now. I move to his side and place a hand on his shoulder.

He opens his mouth to speak, but the MRU panel chirps and glows brightly, indicating it is finished repairing Liana's injuries.

Her eyelids flutter and open, and when she looks up at my brother, I am pleased at least that there is no fear in her eyes. She sits up. As her gaze travels over his face, I detect no hint of disgust or revulsion at his scar, either, and I am glad. I do not think he ever fully recovered from the pain of his betrothed's rejection because of it.

She blinks several times. "Where am I? What happened?"

Tr'lani steps forward and takes her hand. "We're safe. You had many injuries, and you lost consciousness. I treated you and—"

Her eyes dart nervously around the med bay. "You're sure we're safe?"

Soran moves to reassure her. "I am Prince Soran of House Mosaura, and this"—he gestures to me—"is my brother, Prince Rowan. You are both safe. We are going to find your people and return you to your home."

My shoulders sag forward in relief at his words. He's decided to take my advice and not pursue her as a mate.

"Thank you for rescuing us," she says softly. Without warning, she recoils as if struck, her expression fearful as she looks to Soran. "Are you—are you in my mind?"

My heart stops. Only those blessed with the fated bond have a telepathic connection like this. He is right. She *is* his Ashaya. There is no doubt about it now.

He replies. "Forgive me. I did not mean to project my thoughts to you."

I don't want it to be true. It can't be. "You heard my brother in your mind?" I ask, hoping and praying she will deny it.

Instead, she nods, and worry floods my system. "But that is—"

I start to say impossible but stop when Soran gives me a warning look. Despair fills me. In this moment, I already know I will lose my brother.

CHAPTER 7

ROWAN

Tr'lani embraces Liana warmly, thanking her for healing her injuries. I hope now that her friend is well Tr'lani will take advantage of the MRU for herself. It is easy to see that she is still weakened from blood loss, and I know her wings must pain her terribly.

I start to suggest this when Soran looks to Liana. "Tr'lani said you do not know where your home world is. Would you like to study our star charts to see if anything is familiar?"

"Talel's beloved," she says quickly, and we stare at her in confusion. She continues. "I heard Talel speaking to a woman. He called her his 'beloved.' She mentioned the name of a city on my home world. Her people have made contact with mine."

Soran steps forward. "Are you certain?"

"Yes."

"I remember him speaking to a female," Tr'lani adds. "From the way she talked to him…they must be mates. But she was not A'kai."

"How do you know?" I ask. "Did you see her?"

Tr'lani shakes her head. "No. But she is a Princess. Talel spoke of their bonding uniting their two races to forge an Empire that would rival that of your people."

Soran and I listen intently as Tr'lani and Liana relay everything they heard. The A'kai have always been our enemy as far back as the most ancient history of our people. That he would ally himself with another race to conquer mine is unsettling, to say the least. Our mother—the Empress—must be warned.

When they are finished talking, Soran looks to Liana. "She did not say anything that could help us figure out who she was? What species?"

"No," she replies. "And—because Talel doesn't know what I am, he didn't realize she was speaking of my planet…my people. I have to find my home world before it's too late."

I give Liana a pitying look. It may already be too late. "I've already set a course for Mosaura. It is the safest place for us to go now. I am sorry, I wish we could help you, but we cannot just wander aimlessly in search of your planet. It will take us four weeks to reach home as it is, and at least two before we are able to communicate with our home world to request assistance from our Empire."

She frowns. "Why will it take so long?"

"In order for the glider to remain cloaked, the engines must sacrifice efficiency and speed. And I believe it wise that we remain cloaked for the entire journey. On the bridge, I overheard several transmissions. Talel has already placed a bounty on all our heads."

My brother's eyes are full of concern as he meets mine. He understands the gravity of this information. The A'kai are hunting us. And we will not be truly safe until we reach Mosauran space."

* * *

It has been a long day. Everyone else has gone to rest in their quarters. I, however, cannot sleep. I have not left Mosauran space ever since I rescued Soran ten cycles ago. I saw enough of the quadrant in those two cycles that I spent searching for him; I had no desire to ever see anything more. Soran still has occasional nightmares from his time as a slave, but me…I have dark memories and guilt enough to fill a lifetime as I think on all those I could not save. When I close my eyes, I can still see their faces. In my sleep, I hear their sorrowful cries. Yes, I saved many. But I could have saved more. Many times, it came down to the risk of knowing I may not survive. And I knew that I had to, to save my brother. No one else was even looking for him but me.

As I sit at my station, my gaze goes to the communication panel. I am eagerly waiting for a signal that I hope will appear soon. Tr'lani sent out a message searching for her family earlier, and I know she is anxious for any word from them.

Soran joins me on the bridge, and we run a system's check on the ship's computer. "We will have to do this more often now to ensure proper functioning of the cloaking device," I tell him.

He grunts in affirmation. "I am sorry that my actions have placed us in such danger."

I still. He misunderstands. "Do not apologize, brother. Saving the females was the right thing to do. And I am ashamed that I tried to dissuade you."

He frowns. "But I could have gotten us both killed."

"Then we would have died for a noble cause," I reply without hesitation.

He opens his mouth to speak, but the doors whoosh open to reveal Tr'lani. She gives me a warm smile as she approaches my station. "Any messages?" she asks.

Her expression is so hopeful, I hate to give her the news. "Nothing yet," I answer, and her face falls. "But it is probably much too early to expect a reply. After all, we are far from Aerilon space."

She nods, but her disappointment is easily read in her features.

Running my hand across the console, I bring up the nav charts. "Here"—I point to the screen—"is where we are now. And here"—I expand it a bit—"is Aerilon space."

She steps closer to me to view it. Her golden eyes scan the screen a moment before she points at the floating display. "Is that Malorn Station?"

I study the image and then nod.

She hugs her arms to her chest. "Can we avoid that one?"

I don't miss the small shudder that moves through her. "Yes. It will be a while before we must refuel."

Her shoulders sag forward in relief. "Thank you."

That place must hold many dark memories for her. I wonder if there are any others we should bypass. I turn to her. "Is there any place else that you would prefer not to go?"

She lowers her gaze, and her voice quavers slightly. "I wish we didn't have to stop anywhere."

I want nothing more than to grant her this request, but it cannot be done. We will have to refuel at some point. I will just have to make sure to choose locations that are less likely to have slavers. It may add a bit of time to our journey, but not much. And if it gives her even a small measure of comfort, it will be worth it.

A haunted look steals over her face, and I am desperate to chase it away, but I do not know how.

"We could stop at Le'ro," Soran offers.

My brother is smart. Le'ro is one of the nicer planets on our route. Less likely to allow the trafficking of slaves.

I look to Tr'lani, trying to gauge if this suggestion pleases her. I'm so distracted as I study her face that I startle at the loud rumble along the hull.

Spinning back in my seat, I growl low in my throat when I notice the rather large chunk of debris now spiraling away from the glider. Devastating images flood my mind of the damage that may have been done to the outer panels. I give Soran an accusatory glare. "How did you not see that?" I gesture angrily to the viewscreen.

He arches a condescending brow, his eyes darting briefly to Tr'lani with a knowing look. "How did *you* not see it?"

With an exasperated huff, I turn back to the console. My hands fly across the controls as I run a system's check to determine how serious the damage is.

Soran leans back in his chair, his arms crossed over his chest as he sighs heavily. "Here you go again."

My head snaps toward him. "What do you mean?"

"It was a mere scrape. Nothing more." He shakes his head in mock frustration. "You act as though something catastrophic just happened. We're fine."

"Easy for you to say," I grumble as I study the system readouts.

Tr'lani's voice cuts in. "Are we?" She clears her throat. "I mean...we are all right, aren't we?"

I don't like the fear and uncertainty in her voice, so I move to reassure her. "There is some minor damage to the outer hull, but nothing that will compromise the integrity of this glider." I narrow my eyes at Soran. "It's not like the time he piloted us through a large debris field. I woke from a deep sleep to the sound of the engines grinding so loudly I thought the ship was being ripped apart."

Soran waves a dismissive hand at me. "It was not that bad."

"Not that bad?" I give him an incredulous look. "The engines were so overheated by the time I was able to shut everything down, we're lucky we didn't explode. In fact, the entire time it took to make it back to the docking bay, I prayed to the Creator to please spare our lives because I was certain the ship was going to break apart at any moment."

I open my mouth to continue but stop short at the sound of Tr'lani's laughter. She's practically doubled over in her seat. She catches her breath and then looks up at me with a wide grin. "You're just like my brother. So protective of your ship."

Soran laughs with her.

I cross my arms over my chest. It seems that Aerilons find stories of near-death amusing. But after a moment of Tr'lani's infectious laughter, I find myself struggling to suppress the smile that tugs at my lips. I suppose the incident can be considered funny now...especially since we managed to live through it.

"Of course, I'm protective of my glider." I tilt my chin up. "I designed it myself. It is a state of the art, fully equipped masterpiece. Any good captain knows that you must take great care with your vessel."

Tr'lani curiously rolls her eyes—a Terran gesture of mock frustration that she seems to have picked up from Liana. "Just like my brother." She laughs softly. "One time, I accidentally spilled my tea on a control panel, and he nearly had a fit."

My heart stops and my eyes widen at just the mere thought of such a thing happening. I run a gentle hand across the console. A tiny smudge on the glass draws my attention, but I quickly buff it back to a flawless shine, pleased when it sparkles once again like new.

"You see." Soran gestures to me. "He treats this glider as if it were his own fledgling instead of a chunk of flying metal."

I narrow my eyes at him, and Tr'lani begins laughing again. The sound is so light and beautiful, I decide to make it my mission to coax laughter from her as often as possible.

After a moment, she straightens and then looks to me. "I'm going to try to rest. Please wake me if you receive anything from my family."

"Of course."

When she leaves the bridge, Soran leans back in his chair. Crossing his arms, he gives me a pointed look. "You seemed rather distracted by our Aerilon guest."

I turn back to my station, studying the console so as to feign ignorance. "I do not know what you're talking about."

"Hmph," is all he replies before turning his attention back to the viewscreen.

We sit in comfortable silence for a while before the conversation turns once more to Liana. My brother insisting that she is, in fact, his Ashaya. The truth is, I believe him. Especially given that she can hear him in her mind. But it doesn't mean I accept it. To do so would be the same as giving up on him; knowing that he will become Outcast and I will never see him again.

The thought settles in my chest like a heavy stone. And when she comes to the bridge and asks us to teach her how to pilot the glider, I watch as he stares at her with a longing so intense it is a wonder she does not seem to notice it.

She was a pilot on her world, and her entire focus is on learning to survive now in ours. It is an admirable goal, but my ship is not a training vessel. While I understand her reasoning, we cannot afford to risk the glider by allowing her to "train" on it. I cross my arms over my chest. On this, I will not budge.

She meets my eyes evenly. "Look, I can tell this ship means a lot to you. Pilot to pilot, I promise to be really careful with her." She smiles. "What do you say?"

What do I say? "No." That is what I will say. I will not risk my precious glider. She can train on another vessel when she gets to Aerilon if she really wants to learn. My ship is not a training vessel. I open my mouth to break it to her gently, but Soran elbows my ribs so hard I nearly fall out of my chair.

Recovering quickly, I shoot an angry glare at him and then sigh heavily. I can tell this is an argument I will not win. "Fine. But be careful with her." I provide yet another example of how Soran almost destroyed this vessel, asking her to take great care to not do the same.

I run my hand reverently across the control panel, shuddering inwardly as the memory of him nearly destroying my glider replays in my mind. I'm certain I'll regret this later.

Liana gives me a beaming smile, and I return it with one of my own, glad to have given her some measure of happiness after all she's been through.

My thoughts immediately turn to Tr'lani, and I wonder if something like this might make her happy too. My cheeks heat as I think on the way she smiled at me earlier. For all that I'd heard of the Aerilon, I never believe the tales of how captivating their charm could be. But now that I've experienced it for myself, I know it is truth. It seems Mosaurans are not immune to this effect. But I also know that it is probably my concern for her well-being that makes me more susceptible to it.

Soran narrows his eyes at me, obviously mistaking the flush on my face and believing it is directed at Liana. If he only knew what I was really thinking…

* * *

When I decide to return to my quarters to rest, I stop in the hallway outside Tr'lani's door, wondering if she is still awake. I want to check on her, but I hear no sounds inside her cabin. She must be asleep, and I will not wake her.

As I lay back on my bed, I stare up at the ceiling and picture her face. A smile tugs at my lips as I recall her laughter earlier. That she can still experience joy is a good sign. I resolve to make sure she laughs often.

I must be vigilant, however, and observe her closely for any indication she wishes to harm herself. I will not lose her like I lost St'lara.

A loud cry startles me, and I jerk up from the bed. I still, uncertain if I actually heard something or if it was just a dark memory making its way to the surface of my mind.

"No!" Tr'lani cries out.

Panic fills me, and I race out the door to her room. When I enter, my eyes adjust quickly to the darkness, and I find her under the bed, wrapped up in the comforter and thrashing around.

I rush toward her, dropping to the floor. Her eyes are closed. She must be having a bad dream. Carefully, I reach under the bed and place a hand on her shoulder. "Tr'lani?"

Her eyes snap open, wide with fear.

"It's me, Rowan."

"Rowan?" She blinks several times.

"You were having a nightmare."

"Why is it dark in here?"

"Lights!" I command. Brightness floods the room a moment later.

She pulls the comforter even tighter around her like a cocoon. "I made sure the lights were on when I fell asleep." Her voice quavers. "I hate the dark."

Inwardly, I curse myself for not realizing this. Of course, she would hate the darkness. Most slaves are kept in cages and dark cargo bays. "Forgive me. It is a feature of the glider. If there is little movement, the lights automatically turn off to save energy. I will disable this so it will not happen again."

Ready to do just that, I move to stand, but her small hand on my forearm stops me abruptly, her golden eyes staring up into mine. "Thank you, Rowan."

"You are welcome, Tr'lani."

After I adjust the program to merely dim instead of shutting off the lights completely, I turn back to find her still cocooned in the blanket, beneath the bed. I cannot just leave her like this. "Would you like some tea?"

She nods. "Yes. That would be lovely."

I turn to the door, but she calls out. "On second thought. Maybe you could just stay here instead, and we could…talk." She crawls out from under the bed and sits on the edge.

She doesn't want me to leave because she does not wish to be alone. Afraid of falling back into her nightmares, I suspect. Soran was like this in the beginning after I found him. I spent many nights talking to him until he fell asleep and many uncomfortable hours sleeping in whatever chair was near him as he slept. I did this because it comforted him to awaken to a familiar presence.

Crossing the room, I pull the chair away from the table and move it close to her. She is silent, so I try to think of something to speak of. After a moment, I decide to ask more about her family and home, hoping that the reminder of all she has waiting for her will help chase away some of her dark memories. At least for a little while. "Tell me about your twin brother." I lean forward with my elbows on my knees. "I imagine your father must have had a difficult time guarding two eggs. My cousin and his bondmate were blessed with two as well." I chuckle as I recall the memory. "By the time both his fledglings hatched, I'd never seen a male look so ragged."

Tr'lani gives me a puzzled look. "Hatched?"

I nod, and then realize my mistake. "I forget. Your people carry your young to term, like the V'loryns, is that correct?"

She nods. A faint smile curves her lips. "Al'aneo was born five minutes before me, so he's always teased me that he's technically my older brother."

With a heavy sigh, I lean back in my chair. "I was the youngest one among the three of us as well. I swear, if I hadn't come along, I do not know what Soran and Caryn would have done for entertainment. They were always teasing me when we were children." A grin tugs at the corner of my mouth. "When I first learned how to shift into draken form, they convinced me that if I flew during a full moon, I would remain stuck that way permanently."

She leans forward, a small smile on her face. "So, what did you do?"

"I refused to shift during a full moon for several months before my father found out."

She laughs even as she gives me a semi-pitying look. "That's terrible. I can't believe they did that to you. Did your father punish them?"

Sadness creeps in around the edges of the memory as I think of my father and the smile slips from my face. "He was angry, at first, but he never really punished us. Many times, I've lamented that my parents did not have another child after me. At least then, if they had, it might have been even." I grin. "I could have had someone on my side for a change. So that's why I've decided that when I am bonded, I would like to have an even number of fledglings."

"So you are not bonded then?" she asks, curiously.

I shake my head. "Females have challenged me in the shav-rhokan, but I have never accepted. Most of them want me only for my title. But I want a mate that desires me for myself, not for my status among our people."

She frowns. "The 'shav-rhokan?' What is that?"

"The mating battle," I explain. "Do your people not have this?"

She shakes her head.

I give her a puzzled look. "Then how do Aerilon females determine if their mate will be strong enough to defend them and their young? And to provide them with fit offspring?"

"We usually court one another first," she explains. "If a male is interested in a female, he makes his intentions known by presenting himself to her on one knee, asking her to accept him. If she does, then they perform the mating flight."

"Mating flight?"

Her cheeks turn dark in embarrassment as she looks away. "It's about trust." She nervously tucks a stray tendril of hair behind her ear before shifting her gaze back to me. "The female trusts the male to carry her in flight the first time they consummate their bond."

Now my face feels as if it's on fire, and I'm certain the red-orange marking of my brow and cheeks are probably several shades darker.

"Tell me about this mating battle," she says. "It doesn't sound very...romantic."

I cock my head to the side. "It is not supposed to be romantic. It is glorious. The female challenges a male she believes worthy to best her in battle. If he agrees to her challenge and defeats her, he gives her his mark, she accepts him into her body, and they become a mated pair from that moment on."

She gives me a hesitant look. "Does anyone ever get killed in this... mating battle?"

My head jerks back in surprise, and I blink several times. "Killed? What do you think we are? Savages?"

"No!" she replies quickly. "It just...it's different I guess than what I'm used to."

Mating during flight does not sound very normal either, but who am I to judge? I try once more to explain. "Mosauran females are taller and stronger than the males. They would never kill a suitor. They would merely call an end to the battle and move on to the choosing of another male they deem worthy to challenge."

"Oh," is all she says, though her expression tells me she has many more questions.

I'm silent as I wait for her to ask, but she does not. So, I take this opportunity to ask her something else instead. "Do you have a mate?"

"No."

For some odd reason, my heart flutters at her reply, but I quickly push this feeling aside and decide to change the subject. "Do you play kartu by any chance?"

Her eyes light up. "Yes, I do."

I smile. "How about a game?"

"That would be great."

Happy to have found something to take her mind off her nightmares, I rush back to my quarters and retrieve my playing deck.

When I return, I place the table between us and lean forward, arching a teasing brow. “I must warn you that I am an excellent player. But I will try to go easy on you.” Attempting to impress her with my skills, I begin shuffling the deck only to lose my grip and send several of the kartu flying through the air and fluttering softly around us as they land.

She bursts out laughing, and it’s such an enchanting sound, I “accidentally” do this again when I begin to reshuffle.

As we play, I find it difficult to concentrate on the game because I cannot keep my eyes off her. Her face is very expressive; it is rather easy to read her mood each time she draws a card or plays a hand. And every time she wins, a stunning smile curves her lips. I find myself mesmerized. I am a lost male indeed.

When she gets a full span, she slaps the kartu down on the table in triumph. She is practically beaming with joy.

I am thankful that my playing skills are obviously not as great as I believed they were, because I love seeing the happiness that lights her face each time she wins.

After a few hours, she blinks several times as if struggling to keep her eyes open. So, I offer to leave so she may rest. I move to the door and reach up to tap the panel to exit into the hallway, but her soft voice stops me abruptly. “Rowan?”

I turn back to face her. “Yes?”

“Could you—” She looks down at her hands, fidgeting nervously with the comforter a moment before she takes a deep breath. “Would you mind staying in here until I fall asleep?”

I’m both surprised that she would already trust me this much and honored in the same measure. But I must take too long to answer because she lifts a worried gaze to mine.

“Not in the bed,” she adds quickly. “But on the sofa?”

“Of course,” I reply. And before she can change her mind, I cross the room to the couch and sit down. Fluffing one of the pillows, I lean back in the chair.

She lays down, pulling the comforter securely around herself as she curls up into a ball on the mattress. This is progress that she chooses to lay on the bed instead of beneath it, and I'm pleased that she feels more secure. Golden reflective eyes meet mine. "Goodnight, Rowan," she says softly.

"Goodnight," I reply in kind.

I close my eyes even though I am not tired, so that she doesn't know how uncomfortable I am on this cushion. But I've slept in far worse places, and this is nothing new for me. I did this for Soran, and I do not mind in the slightest doing this for her as well.

After all she has been through, I want to do everything I can to comfort her and make her feel safe.

CHAPTER 8

ROWAN

When I wake in the morning, Tr'lani is still asleep. My heart clenches as she shivers slightly.

Quietly, I move to her bedside and carefully pull the comforter up over her shoulders.

She opens her eyes, and they widen in a look I recognize as fear, so I gently reassure her. "You are safe, Tr'lani."

Her entire body relaxes once more. "What time is it?" she whispers.

"It is early morning. Shall I bring you something to eat?"

She gives me a warm smile. "Thank you, but I can get it myself. I—"

"Stay here and rest," I insist. "I will get something for us both and return shortly."

She nods before closing her eyes again and snuggling beneath the covers. It pleases me immensely to see her so relaxed. I imagine this must be the first time she has slept soundly in a very long time.

As soon as I turn to enter the crew mess, I nearly collide with Soran.

"Good morning," he says and then tips his head to the side in a questioning look. "I tried to comm your quarters last night, but you did not answer. Are you well?"

"Yes."

His brow furrows in confusion. "Then why did you not answer?"

I struggle to come up with a plausible lie. Here I am encouraging him to distance himself from Liana because she is an outsider, while I'm spending the night with an Aerilon. But I realize that I cannot withhold the truth from Soran. He knows me well enough that he would see through any false statement. With a heavy sigh, I brace myself to be accused of being a hypocrite. "I stayed with Tr'lani in her quarters."

His eyes go wide. "All night?"

"I slept on the sofa. She...didn't want me to leave until she fell asleep, but I ended up falling asleep as well and only woke up less than half an hour ago."

Instead of accusing me of not taking my own advice, he gives me a look of understanding. "It is still too new for them. I fear they will have many sleepless nights before they finally feel truly safe." He places a hand on my shoulder. "That was kind of you, brother."

Guilt fills me at his words. He believes I do this for purely selfless reasons, when in truth it is because I am inexplicably drawn to her. I cannot admit this to him though. Not when I've been so hard on him about Liana. Unable to lie or tell him my truth, I simply nod and then move to the supply cabinet. "I told her I'd return shortly with something to eat."

A smile tugs at his lips as he holds up a nutrient bar and a protein pouch. "I promised the same to Liana."

I bite back a groan of frustration. It seems we're both enthralled with our new passengers. Him with a Terran, me with an Aerilon. I'm not sure which will displease Mother more: The fact that Liana looks so much like a V'loryn—a species despised by our people, or that Tr'lani is an Aerilon—a race that we have been in various states of conflict with for thousands of cycles.

When I return to her quarters, she greets me with a bright smile as

I present her nutrient bar and a warm cup of tea. She takes the mug in both hands and lifts it to her face, inhaling deeply of the rich aroma before taking a small sip. She closes her eyes, and a low, trilling hum that can only be construed as a soft sound of contentment escapes her.

My body flushes with warmth as I stare across at her, completely mesmerized. My alarm chirps, snapping me back into awareness, and I realize it is time for me to do my routine system checks on the glider. I'm reluctant to leave her company, but our safety depends upon the ship functioning at peak efficiency. The A'kai are hunting us. We cannot afford any maintenance problems.

* * *

After I'm finished with the system checks, I seek out Tr'lani, hoping I might be able to partake of midday meal with her. But when I return to her quarters, she isn't there. I go to the bridge and find Soran and Liana. "Have either of you seen Tr'lani?"

Liana turns to me. "I think she's in the med bay."

My heart stops when I realize Liana is piloting the glider. A quick check of the control panel reassures me almost immediately. Even with what little training she had the other night, it is easy to see that she is a skilled pilot. In fact, I dare say I trust her abilities even more so than my brother.

As if he can read the inner workings of my mind, Soran arches a questioning brow at me.

I turn to Liana. "You seem to have picked this up rather quickly. I believe my glider is in good hands."

She gives me a beaming smile.

"Try to keep Soran from damaging the ship, will you?" I add.

She laughs.

He purses his lips as I try but fail to suppress a teasing grin.

I leave the bridge before he can come back with a witty reply.

When I enter the med bay, Tr'lani is not there. The MRU is open, and the display panel is blinking with a red indicator. I'm not a Healer, but I did receive basic medical instruction during my warrior's training. Enough so that I am able to understand most of the readings on the screen.

I clench my jaw as I study the readout. She attempted to use the unit to repair her broken wings. According to this, the damage is too extensive, and it did not work. Panic snakes through me as dark memories of the Aerilon female I tried to save fill my mind.

I can still see St'lara's eyes, open but unseeing as she sealed herself in the airlock. She did not want to live. Not after what the A'kai had done to her. I pounded on the door, begging her to come back inside. Her gaze met mine, full of tears. "I cannot live with these nightmares. Not anymore, Rowan," she'd said. Pain stabs at my chest as the terrible image of her death fills my mind.

After I told him about her, Soran asked me if I had loved St'lara. I did not. I cared for her as if she were family, but that was the extent of it. With Tr'lani, it is different. I am drawn to her in ways I do not understand. Although I have not known her very long, something about her calls to my protective and possessive instincts. As if she were my mate.

I curl my hands into fists at my side to still their trembling. I will not fail Tr'lani as I failed St'lara. I swear it to the Creator.

Fear beats at my chest as I race toward the airlock, praying Tr'lani isn't there.

As I rush down the hallway, my nostrils flare, and I catch wind of her scent. It is stronger here, and I instinctively follow it, glad when I realize it is leading away from the direction of the outer doors and toward the training room.

When I enter, I find her standing in front of one of the large mirrors. Tears stream down her face as she struggles to lift her trembling wings. She reaches back to try to grip them for extra support, and a sharp cry of pain escapes her. Her knees buckle, and she crumples to the floor. Dropping her head in her hands, her shoulders shake with hiccupping sobs.

My heart shatters. She is unaware of my presence, so I call her name softly as I approach. "Tr'lani?"

She lifts a tear-filled gaze to me. "The MRU couldn't fix my wings, Rowan. They're too badly damaged."

I kneel beside her. "We'll find a Healer to assess you. There may be something they can—"

She cuts me off. "I *am* a Healer, and I read the MRU's assessment. They cannot be fixed." Her voice breaks on the last word. "I'll never fly again."

I want so much to comfort her somehow, but I don't know what to do. She's been through so much; I don't want to scare her either. Gently, I place a hand on her shoulder, and I'm shocked when she turns to me for comfort, leaning against me and crying on my chest.

Her despair breaks me. "Don't give up hope yet, Tr'lani," I whisper as I smooth a hand over her long, silken hair. "We will find someone to look at them. There has to be something that can be done for your wings."

Unable to speak, she nods against me.

"I've seen many warriors with wing injuries," I tell her. "And one of the most important things for the healing process is to ensure the attachment muscles are strong. Is this the same for your people as well?"

She sniffs and then blinks several times as if considering my words. After a moment, dawned understanding fills her expression. "You are right. I've been in a cage for so long, my muscles are weak." She turns her gaze to the far wall. "Perhaps if I start building them back up again it might make a difference."

I stand and then offer her my hand, thrilled beyond measure when she gives me a warm smile and then takes it. I pull her up and stare deep into her golden eyes. "I will help you."

She turns her back to me, glancing over her shoulder. "Can you aid me in stretching them first?"

That she trusts me to touch her like this is something I did not expect. Not after everything she has been through. But having taken my measure, she knows I would never harm her. So, I take great care when I place one hand to her spine between her shoulder blades where her wings are attached and gently grasp her left wing with the other to slowly lift and extend it, stretching out the attachment muscles.

She inhales sharply and grits her teeth in pain but says nothing. A tear escapes her lashes, but she quickly brushes it away as she faces the mirror with a determined look. I've seen males that had nowhere near the devastating injury she has that cried out like wild kravens. She is strong. Much more so than I realized. I'm ashamed that I could ever have thought otherwise.

Anger fills me as I study her back and wings. Deep jagged lines cross her delicate skin where they carved out her slave markings. Her wings are broken in several places, and I shudder inwardly as I imagine what she must have endured at the hands of her masters. If I could, I would kill every male that ever harmed her—that ever touched her against her will.

By the time we're finished, she is trembling, and her face is a mask of exhaustion. She turns to face me. Her golden eyes stare up into mine with fierce determination, and I don't believe I've ever admired a female as much as I do right now. "Thank you, Rowan. Will you help me again tomorrow?"

I give her a solemn nod. I will do this gladly. "I will help you every day if you wish," I offer.

A low, trilling hum sounds in the back of her throat as she replies. "Thank you."

Remembering the original reason I sought her out, I ask, "Would you like to join me for midday meal?"

Her lips curve into a stunning smile, and I'm lost, completely mesmerized as she stares up at me. "That would be lovely."

Softly shaking my head as if to clear my thoughts, I motion toward the door. "After you."

As she walks past me, my nostrils flare as I inhale deeply of her distinct scent. Something akin to fresh rain with a hint of floral notes. She darts a glance over her shoulder to me as she steps out into the hallway, and I flush with warmth.

I realize that what I'm doing is dangerous. I am at risk of losing my heart to an Aerilon. Our species are enemies. Even if she desired me as hers, how could it ever work?

Shaking my head, I push away my errant thoughts. She does not want me, and she never will. I am merely helping her. That is all this is, and all that it ever *can* be.

CHAPTER 9

TR'LANI

The sound of movement from somewhere nearby startles me awake. Trapped in complete darkness, panic coils tight in my chest as someone hisses low in my ear. "You will do fine for my mating rut."

Blinding fear rips through me, and I scream.

"Lights!" A voice calls out, and my eyes snap open as Rowan drops to his knees by my bed. Bright light quickly replaces the partially dimmed nighttime setting, brightening my quarters. He pulls me into his arms, and I bury my face in his chest as silent sobs rack through me. It's been almost two weeks since Rowan and Soran rescued us from slavery, but the nightmares refuse to leave.

His warm hands move in soothing circles up and down my back to calm me as he whispers low in my ear. "It's all right. It was just a nightmare. I vow as a warrior of Mosaura. You are safe here, Tr'lani."

His silver, reflective eyes stare down at me with a strange mixture of pain and devotion. His silver-gray scales shimmer under the light. The red highlights across the sharp ridges of his cheeks and brows grow slightly darker beneath my gaze.

The fog of my nightmare still clings to my thoughts as I study Rowan, trying to convince myself that he is real and the dark dreams are not. He keeps his dark-gray leathery wings tucked close to his back. The last time he comforted me, they wrapped tightly around my form, and I panicked. Horrible memories of being held against my will in the pleasure simulators filled my mind, and despite knowing that Rowan would never harm me, my body rebelled violently against his hold.

He pulled away instantly, but I notice now how carefully he keeps them tightly pinned behind him as he sits here with me.

I allow myself to relax against him as we sit on the edge of the bed. "I thought I was back in a cage." My voice quavers slightly. "I dreamed the Anguis were coming to take me."

His arms tighten around my form as he gently rubs his hand up and down my back and whispers soothingly in my ear. "You are safe, Tr'lani."

* * *

ROWAN

Fierce protectiveness fills me as I hold her. I will kill any who dare try to touch her against her will. She doesn't flinch away from my embrace, but instead turns toward me as if instinctively seeking comfort. Holding her close, I swallow against the lump in my throat as I look down at her trembling form. "You are safe, Tr'lani. I swear it. Go back to sleep, my heart. I will stay with you."

Almost immediately, I curse myself for allowing "my heart" to escape my lips. It is a Mosauran term of endearment that I have never spoken aloud.

I brace for her to ask me about this, but instead, she whispers softly, "You don't have to stay, Rowan."

I still. There is nowhere else I'd rather be than with her. "It is no burden to be here with you. Besides," I grin, "the sofa is more comfortable than my own bed."

The lie burns on my tongue like acid, but I will not take it back. I want nothing more than to remain at her side, to do whatever I can to help ease her fears. She has been through so much, and the fact that she survived is a testament to her strength of will.

I remember the first time her gaze met mine. Despite her weakened state, fire burned in her golden eyes as she stared daggers at me. Our people have been enemies for thousands of cycles, and I'd always heard that her species were weak. But I have never seen such bravery as I did that day when she looked me straight in the eye and gritted her teeth as I reached out to help her. "Don't touch me, Mosauran!" she'd snapped. I've never admired a female more than I did in that moment.

She may be smaller than a Mosauran female, but she is fierce and brave. And despite all our differences and the terrible history between our two races, I cannot help but be drawn to her.

At first, I observed her closely; stayed by her side to make sure she did not succumb to her dark thoughts as St'lara did. But now I realize my desire to be close to her as something more than that. As her golden eyes stare up into mine, I'm lost—completely and irrevocably hers despite the fact that I know she will never want me.

I am Mosauran, and she is Aerilon. We are too different, she and I. And yet, I cannot still the longing in my heart each time I think of her.

Even as this thought runs through my mind, I recognize what a hypocrite it makes me. Here I am still trying to convince my brother to ignore his feelings for Liana because I do not want him to become Outcast, and yet...I understand what he is going through.

Tr'lani lifts her gaze to mine. "You are a good friend to me, Rowan. Thank you."

Friend. The word settles in my chest like a heavy stone. I want to be so much more to her, but I also understand that she has suffered greatly at the hands of her previous masters and is not interested in a mate. She has never confided in me all the horrors she endured, but in the way that she still occasionally flinches when I make a sudden movement, and the way she used to react violently to being touched... I can only guess at what she must have gone through.

I move the sofa near her bed and lay down facing her. This is how we sleep when she has nightmares. With only a narrow gap between the edge of the mattress and the cushions, she reaches across and takes my hand, pulling it back toward her so that our joined hands rest close to her heart.

Her golden eyes stare deep into mine, sadness reflecting behind them. "I'm sorry," she whispers.

"For what?"

"I hate being like this," she whispers. "I wish I was strong like Liana."

I squeeze her hand. "You are strong, Tr'lani. Do not compare yourself to her. You each went through different things. You were a slave for over two cycles." I pause. "In battle, your team is only as strong as the weakest warrior among you. We vow to one another that if one of us falls injured, we will carry them to victory or to death. We will not leave them behind."

I gaze at our joined hands and then meet her eyes evenly. "I will carry you, Tr'lani of High Clan Al'ani, to victory or to death. I will not leave you behind. We are bound to one another, and if you are broken, so am I."

Her bottom lip quivers as she stares across at me but says nothing.

I continue. "There is no shame in asking others for help. You have been through much. Do not be so hard on yourself. Please, allow me to carry you, Tr'lani. I want only to be here for you. For as long as you need. My vow."

"Thank you, Rowan," she whispers.

"Now, rest," I speak softly. "I will stay here with you."

She curls herself up into a small ball beneath the comforter, and when her eyes meet mine again, she gives me a sleepy smile before she closes them and drifts off to sleep. As I lay beside her, I listen to the soft and even sound of her breathing.

I treasure this closeness between us and will miss it when she is gone.

After a while, her brow creases into a small frown, and I know she must be having a nightmare because a moment later, intense warmth spreads across my palm as she subconsciously takes my measure. A soft smile ghosts her lips, and she relaxes once more. This is how she instinctively reassures herself that she is safe.

There is something so intimate about this connection between us. Staring across at her—her face relaxed in sleep—I'm mesmerized as I study her features. She is as strong as she is beautiful. With each day we are together, we grow closer. And even though I want so much for her to find her family, I dread the day she will leave me forever to return to her people.

* * *

When we wake, I must check on the glider. As much as I desire to spend time with Tr'lani, it would not be fair to my brother or Liana to leave everything to them.

When Soran comes to the bridge, I'm deep in thought about Tr'lani. But then again, I always am. It takes me a moment to notice he is alone, instead of with Liana. So, I decide to tease him, pretending to shield my eyes as he passes beneath the lighting.

He frowns. "What is wrong?"

"Your scales. They're blinding."

He looks down at himself and then back up at me. Despite my best efforts, a smile tugs at my mouth.

He narrows his eyes and growls. "What are you talking about?"

"I know you are trying to impress Liana, but if you keep buffing your scales, you're going to blind all of us." I grin as his lips form a tight thin line. "And when we reach Mosaura, I worry that the first time you step out into the sun, the damage to our eyes will become permanent."

He points an accusing finger at me. "What about you? Your scales are definitely a bit shinier than normal. And do you think I haven't seen the way you are around Tr'lani?"

My smile falters, and I turn my attention back to the screen, trying to hide my despair as I think about she whom I adore above all others.

Soran clears his throat and gives me a hedging look. "Have you told her about your feelings?"

I look down at my hands. "It does not matter. I look nothing like an Aerilon male. In fact, our people are hideous by comparison. She will not want me." Trying my best to lighten both my mood and his, I arch a brow at him. "You'd do well to remember that."

His head jerks back slightly. "Why? I am not interested in the Aerilon."

"Because once we reach Tr'lani's brother's ship and Liana sees how handsome their males are, it will be hard to bring her attention back to you," I tease.

His expression darkens, and his brow furrows in a contemplative look. "Perhaps that is for the best," he finally says.

I snap my head toward him. "What are you saying?"

"If either of us chose a mate outside of our race, we'd be Outcast from our people and our family according to the ancient laws." He gives me a grim look. "You are the one who kept reminding me of this. Or have you forgotten already?"

My chest tightens, and I turn my attention back to the viewscreen, tapping into the console as I check our coordinates. "No, I have not." The words are like bitter acid on my tongue. I meet Soran's eyes evenly. "What about the fate bond? Do you still feel its pull toward Liana?"

With a slight clench of his jaw, he nods. "Yes."

"Perhaps we can speak with one of the Healers. Maybe it can be severed?"

He levels a dark gaze at me. "I would sooner cut off my own arm."

His words, although strong, do not surprise me. That he admits his feelings so vehemently does. "Then...you love her?"

"Yes."

With a heavy sigh, I spin back in my chair to face my console. It seems we are both lost in this regard.

As if my very thoughts have summoned her, the doors whoosh open, and Tr'lani comes in. She gives me a beaming smile. "Ready for midday meal?"

Liana is behind her. She moves to my brother's side, smiling at him as she takes her station. She winks at me—a teasing Terran gesture I've learned over the past few weeks she's been with us. "Don't worry, your glider is in good hands."

My eyes shift to my brother. Subconsciously, I gently pat the control panel in front of me as if to reassure myself that because Liana is here, he should not be able to damage my beautiful ship like he did before. Grasping the hem of my sleeve, I carefully wipe away the small smudge left by my hand and then stand, smiling like a lovesick fool as I move to Tr'lani's side.

Creator help me, when she looks up at me with those golden eyes and gives me a small grin, my mind stops functioning, but I somehow manage to follow her to the crew mess.

CHAPTER 10

TR'LANI

As I take a sip from my protein pouch, I stare across at Rowan, studying him discreetly. His brow furrows deeply as he focuses on the data before him. With his chiseled jawline, beautiful reflective silver eyes, shimmering silver-gray scales, and the sharp angles and aristocratic features of his cheekbones, brow, and nose, I find him attractive…even if he is a Mosauran. Aerilon males do not have facial hair, and the slight scruff of his beard adds an extra hint of masculinity to his looks that I find oddly appealing as well.

Rowan lifts his gaze to mine, and my cheeks heat in embarrassment at having been caught staring at him. But he doesn't seem to notice as he slides the data pad on the table between us, displaying a stellar map.

"We are here"—he points to an area in the lower left-hand corner —"and we should be at Le'ro"—he gestures to a small planet near the center—"in less than one solar. Where we can refuel and purchase more supplies."

Le'ro is a small trading planet almost halfway to Aerilon. We have yet to hear back from my family after I sent my message, but it's nice to think I'm already that much closer to home. And I'm excited about the idea of purchasing clothing that actually fits me, but I'm not exactly thrilled that we're stopping somewhere. Not wanting to give voice to my worries, I nod but say nothing.

As if sensing my concern, he reaches across the table and places his hand over mine, squeezing it gently. "What is wrong?"

He knows me too well. "I—" I start but then hesitate. I'm ashamed of my fear, but I cannot ignore it either. "Do we have to stop?" Even as I ask this, I already know the answer.

"It is the safest place nearby to find supplies. But we will only be there long enough to refuel the ship and purchase you and Liana real clothing." A smile tugs at his lips. "I'm sure you're tired of wearing emergency shirts by now."

"It doesn't bother me. They're actually really comfortable," I add.

"What about food? We can pick up some fresh fruits and vegetables and—"

Unable to push down my concern, I cut him off abruptly. "Please." I reach across and take his other hand. "Can we just refuel and then leave?"

His eyes search mine, and I lower my gaze because I don't want to look at him. He's a warrior. And I'm…not. I hate that he has to see me this way. I wasn't always like this. But I'm so afraid of being taken. I would sooner die than be a slave again.

"You don't have to leave the glider if you don't want to. We will refuel, gather the supplies, and be back before you know it."

He gives me a warm smile, but it does nothing to assuage my concerns. I don't want any of us to ever set foot off the ship. We're safe here. Why can he not see this?

Frustration burns through me, but I push it back down. The only thing my anger ever got me when I was a slave was more beatings and punishment. I learned long ago to lock away my emotions. My appetite has vanished. I give him a reluctant nod and then stand from the table.

"Tr'lani?" His brow furrows softly in confusion.

"I'm going to my quarters," I reply over my shoulder as I step out into the hallway.

The sound of boot steps follows me a moment later. "Tr'lani, wait!"

I spin to face him, meeting his eyes evenly.

He frowns. "Are you…mad at me?"

"Yes!" I snap.

His eyes go wide, and he gives me a wounded look. "Why?"

"It doesn't matter. You won't listen to me anyway."

He shakes his head. "What are you talking about?"

Unable to contain my anger, I glare up at him. "I've researched Le'ro on the ship's computers. It is not as safe as you think it is. It's a regular stop for corsairs and mercenaries."

"Tr'lani, you do not have to fear. You can stay on the ship and—"

"You don't know." I close my eyes as the terrible memories fill my mind. "You have no idea what I went through, Rowan. How can you tell me not to be afraid? You don't know what they—" My voice catches, but I somehow manage to continue. "What they do to slaves. What I was forced to—"

I fight back tears, angry at myself for my weakness. Rowan steps forward and gathers me in his arms, pulling me to his chest. At first, I melt against him, but then I force myself to push him away. I'm not weak. This isn't who I am. This isn't who I was. "Don't coddle me as if I'm fragile." I allow the bitter words to escape my lips unfiltered. I hate what I've become. I wish I could just forget everything bad that has ever happened to me and pretend that I'm all right, but I can't.

His eyes search mine in concern. "I do not think you are weak or fragile. You are a survivor, Tr'lani. And you're right. I don't know what you went through. Forgive me. I just—" With a slight clench of his jaw, he lowers his gaze. "I only wish to offer you comfort."

His words give me pause. "No, Rowan. I'm the one who should be sorry. I shouldn't be upset with you. I just…" Frustration burns through me. "I have all this anger inside me over what I went through, and I try to push it down, but sometimes I feel like I can't. And I don't want to be this way. I was the defiant one in my family; I used to fear nothing. But now that I've seen the darkness that exists in the hearts of others..." I curl my hands into fists at my side. "I want to be strong. I used to be so brave."

His gaze holds mine a moment before he dips his chin in a subtle nod. "Follow me."

Still holding my hand, he leads me down the hallway to the training room. Liana and Soran often use it for sparring, but I've only used it when we stretch and exercise my wings. I'm surprised when he walks me to the center of the mat and releases my hand. I stare up at him in confusion.

"How much training have you had?"

I frown. "Training?"

He nods. "In hand-to-hand combat."

I give him an incredulous look. "My claws are gone, and so are my fangs and venom sacs. My wings are useless, and I—"

He arches a brow. "Liana's people have none of those things either."

My mouth drifts open as I realize he's right. Her species is naturally defenseless compared to mine. Determination fills me, and I meet his gaze evenly. "Teach me how to fight as I am now."

He nods, and we begin.

* * *

When we're finished, I join Liana in the crew mess for evening meal while Rowan goes to the bridge to run a check on the glider's systems.

She greets me with a beaming smile and embraces me warmly. "Can you believe it?" she says. "In less than twelve hours, we'll be breathing fresh air for the first time in forever."

It's easy to see she is excited about the thought of going to Le'ro, while I can't help but still be fearful that it's dangerous. "Are you sure you want to leave the ship?"

Her expression falters a bit. "I know it's not completely safe. But if there's anything I've learned, it's that there is risk in everything we do. And if I'm going to learn how to survive here, I cannot be afraid to try new things."

"Being cautious does not equate to fear," I tell her. "I wish you would stay on the glider."

Her eyes brighten with tears, and it's the first indication I have that she truly is worried despite her earlier enthusiasm. "I have to do this, Tr'lani. If for nothing else, then to prove to myself that I can." She takes my hand in her own. "I *am* afraid. I'd be stupid not to be...especially after everything we went through. But if I don't start pushing myself, I'll never get over my nightmares, and I'm so tired of living in fear."

Part of me feels this way too. But I'm just not ready. "I understand," I whisper. "I'm not quite there yet. But perhaps someday I will be."

She hugs me again, and I embrace her warmly.

CHAPTER 11

TR'LANI

A sense of dread fills me as we touch down on Le'ro. Everything inside me screams it isn't safe. When Soran and Liana prepare to leave the glider, I rush forward and hug her tightly, desperate to keep her here on the ship.

"Are you sure you don't want to come with us?" she asks.

I nod and take both her hands in mine. I understand why she wants to do this, but I'm still worried. "It's safer on the glider. I wish you wouldn't go. You should stay here with Rowan and me."

She gives me a reassuring smile. "I'll be fine. Besides"—she darts a glance at Soran—"I have a big, strong Mosauran warrior with me. Nobody's going to bother us."

Soran straightens and tilts up his chin as he puffs his chest out at her appraisal. He looks so funny, I have to stifle a laugh.

She laughs as she looks to him. "All right, all right. Don't let my words go to your head."

He tips his chin up even more and arches a brow. "Why would they 'go to my head?' Your words are truth. I *am* a big, strong Mosauran warrior." He flexes his arms as if in emphasis, and she laughs even more.

Unable to hold it in any longer, I start to laugh too.

Rowan rolls his eyes. "It's too late." He purses his lips. "You have created a monster." He hands Liana and Soran each a blaster and laser knife and then claps his brother on the shoulder. "Here you go, big, strong Mosauran warrior." He repeats her words in a mocking tone.

Soran smirks. "Jealousy is not a healthy thing, Rowan. Besides..." He touches Rowan's bicep. "Your muscles may be much smaller than mine but—"

I start to interject that Rowan is actually the more muscular-looking, in my opinion, but Rowan punches him in the arm. "I'm not jealous of you, you maltak. And everyone knows I'm stronger than you anyway."

Rowan flexes a rather impressive bicep at his brother as if to emphasize his point.

Soran opens his mouth to argue, but Rowan's expression turns serious. "Check in with me every hour, so I know you're all right."

"We will," Soran promises.

Despite their almost constant bickering and teasing each other, it is easy to see how close they are. Rowan may be the younger of the two, but you wouldn't know it with how protective he is of his brother. He is a good male.

Rowan and I watch as Liana and Soran walk down the ramp and toward the city. Le'ro is a beautiful planet, but after noticing all the ships around us in various states of disrepair, I'm wary that many of them are not what they appear to be. Corsairs often disguise their vessels to look like this, while in truth, they are probably as impressive and deadly as Rowan's glider.

As if reading my thoughts, Rowan's eyes narrow as his gaze travels over them.

Taking a deep breath, I decide to test my courage and follow Rowan down the ramp.

A Lacerta male walks toward us. He bows low. "Does your glider need fuel, great Mosauran warrior?"

"Yes." Rowan gives him an imperious look. "Do it quickly."

"Of course, great warrior. Of course," he replies and then rushes off to the side to begin the process.

As soon as he's out of hearing range, I turn to Rowan, a smile tugging at my lips. "What was that?"

Tilting his chin up slightly, he arches a brow. "What do you mean?"

"*That.*" A smile tugs at the corner of my mouth as I point to his face, tilting my chin up in a mock imperious and arrogant pose like he just gave to the Lacerta.

A sly grin curves his lips. "You cannot expect me to appear friendly to *everyone*. My people *do* have a reputation to uphold, you know."

I laugh.

His eyes sparkle with barely contained amusement. "Are you laughing at me?" Puffing his chest out, he flexes his impressive biceps and then grins. "You are brave indeed to mock a big, strong Mosauran warrior," he teases, repeating Liana's words.

I laugh even louder and then roll my eyes. "I thought the big, strong Mosauran warrior left a few moments ago with Liana."

His jaw drops a moment before his mouth curves into a devastating smile. "Then I am the strong and handsome Mosauran warrior."

I roll my eyes again and grin. "Is that so?"

He laughs and tilts up his chin, looking down his very regal nose at me. "You know I only speak truth."

I laugh even more and then shake my head in mock frustration.

We're parked at the outer edge of the city. A cool breeze blows past us, carrying the crisp, fresh scent of the forest beyond. Le'ro is a beautiful planet with tall green trees and mountainous landscapes. The yellow-orange sun shines brightly overhead, and I close my eyes as the wind whips through my hair and catches the tips of my wings. I sigh heavily. "I wish I could still fly." The words escape my lips before I even realize I've spoken them aloud.

Rowan takes my hand, drawing my attention back to him. He gives me an earnest look. "Do you trust me?"

I meet his silver eyes evenly and reply without hesitation because I trust him completely. "Yes."

He moves behind me, and my heart hammers as he wraps his arms around my waist and gently tugs me back against him. I melt into the solid feel of his body as my cheeks flush with warmth. I twist my neck to look back up at him, wondering what he is doing.

He smiles down at me and slowly extends his wings from his back.

Without warning, we lift off into the air, his wings billowing like great sails as he climbs toward the thick, silver clouds above. I hold tight to his arms around my waist and gasp as a strong wind pulls at me.

He tightens his grip on my form. His breath is warm in my ear as he whispers. "I've got you. I promise I won't let you fall."

He dips his left wing, and we slip into the current, spiraling up toward the sun. I close my eyes as the wind flows over my wings, reveling in the sensation of flying again. Tears of happiness escape my lashes and roll down my cheeks.

Rowan gently nuzzles at my temple to get my attention. "Are you all right?" he asks, and it is easy to hear the concern in his voice.

I turn my head to look back up at him. It's been so long since I felt this free. I swallow against the lump in my throat. "Yes. I love this. Thank you, Rowan."

His mouth curves up in a devastatingly handsome smile. With a slight dip of his wings, he makes a long, slow arc out over the forest, skimming over the top of the trees. A herd of four-legged creatures races below us. He drops low, gliding just overhead as we keep pace with them before curving away and flying out over a large body of water.

I reach out, and my fingers skim lightly over the crystalline surface before it drops off into an impressive falls. The water roaring as it spills over the edge to the river below. I cry out with joy, the sound echoing through the forest as he folds his wings, and we dive over the side, falling with dizzying speed a moment before his wings snap open to halt our descent. He flaps them furiously as we climb back up to the top, circling over the tree line, and then back to the glider.

A drone hovers just outside the airlock doors, and he carefully drifts back to the ground, touching down so smoothly I'm not entirely sure we've landed until he gently lowers my feet to the platform. So elated from our flight, I stretch up on my toes and wrap my arms around his neck to hug him as I whisper in his ear, "Thank you, Rowan. That was wonderful."

When I pull back, his cheeks and brow are a dark red-orange hue as he smiles down at me. His gaze holds mine for a beat before he clears his throat and turns his attention to the drone.

It's from Soran and Liana. They've already sent back some of the items they've purchased.

When he scans it, my face lights up as it opens to reveal several bundles of clothing. We carry the packages inside, sealing the airlock doors behind us and activating a force shield around the glider. He turns to me. "I spared no expense in the defense systems of this ship. We are safe here."

As we sort through the various items, I'm excited to find an entire Aerilon wardrobe. Each piece of the silken, elegant clothing is labeled with my name. I notice curiously that the other wardrobe is mostly Mosauran attire that is marked for Liana.

I take the clothes back to my quarters and choose a shimmering iridescent silver flowing dress with matching leggings and shoes. The fabric is so light it practically floats around me as I walk. When I emerge from my room, I find Rowan waiting out in the hallway. It's so wonderful to wear clothing that actually fits me again instead of the emergency shirts and pants I've been borrowing. I twirl around once and smile brightly at him. "What do you think?"

"Beautiful," he whispers as the markings on his cheek and brow flush a deeper hue.

I don't miss the way his gaze travels over my form, and if he weren't Mosauran, I'd think he might be interested in me. But I cannot be sure.

"Would you like to sit outside for a while?" he asks.

I hesitate. It was wonderful when we flew, but now that we're back inside, I'm not sure I want to leave again. It's safe in here and out there...it's not.

As if sensing my concern, he offers. "We can eat atop the hull. It is covered by the defense shield."

"All right," I nod. "Let's do that."

When we go back outside, he carefully wraps his arms around my waist again and flies us up to the top of the glider, setting me down gently. He pulls two nutrient bars from his pocket and hands one to me with a grin. "We can enjoy our meal out here."

He sits down, and I lean against him with a sigh as I stare out at the thick forest at the edge of the landing field. I take his hand. "It really is beautiful here. Thank you for earlier." His eyes snap up to meet mine. "It's been so long since I've flown." My broken wings flutter softly behind me. "For a moment, I remembered what it was like when I could fly and I—" My voice breaks. "I cannot thank you enough for that."

He reaches out to tenderly cup my face. I place my hand over his as his silver eyes stare deep into mine with a look I cannot quite discern. *Is it love?* "Tr'lani, I—"

His communicator chirps loudly, startling us both.

* * *

ROWAN

I glance down to see an incoming message from Soran.

"Rowan?" His voice has an urgent tone that sets me on edge.

"What is it?"

"We were attacked. Liana was hit with a breaking dart." Tr'lani gasps. "I killed both of our attackers when I shifted into draken form. We're in the forest outside the city. I do not know if they acted alone or if they have a crew somewhere nearby."

I immediately understand his warning. I think of all the ships parked around us. Anyone could have been watching us…monitoring our movements from the moment we landed. "We will retrieve you as soon as night falls. We cannot risk coming to you now in case your attackers were not working alone."

"Agreed."

Another ping on my communicator sends me his location. "I can see where you are. We'll come for you when the sun sets."

"Good."

Tr'lani grabs my wrist before I can close down the communication. "Is Liana all right?"

Soran hesitates a moment before answering. "She is unconscious still. But I have her. I will not allow anything to happen to her. I swear it to the Creator."

"Thank you," she replies. "Stay safe."

He shuts down his comm, and Tr'lani looks up at me with a pleading look. "Rowan, we need to go get them now. The longer they are out there, the more vulnerable they are."

I shake my head. "We don't know if their attackers were working alone. If we go now, during daylight, we could be leading others right to their location."

She gives me a firm look. "We need to risk it. They can't stay out there by themselves."

I place my hands on her shoulders. I understand her concern, and it mirrors my own, but I also trust that my brother will keep his Ashaya safe until we can get them. "Soran won't let anything happen to her."

"How can you be so sure?"

"Because he's my brother, and he'd die before he let anyone touch her, just as I would for you."

She blinks several times as if stunned by my admission, but I cannot take it back. And I wouldn't even if I could.

Reaching out, she touches my face and shakes her head softly. "Don't say that, Rowan," she whispers.

"Why? It is truth, Tr'lani. I would die for you."

"You don't understand. I—"

An alarm rings out, and my heart stops.

Tr'lani tenses. "What is that?"

"An alert for an A'kai ship."

All the color drains from her face.

It doesn't take long to get back in the glider and to the bridge. I quickly activate the control panel and pull up the locator beacon as I scan the channels, listening for any communications from their cruiser.

The hairs rise on the back of my neck when a second A'kai ship pops up on the screen. Closing my eyes, I concentrate as I focus on finding their subspace frequencies. After a moment, I hear the two ships communicating back and forth. I swallow thickly and then turn to Tr'lani. "They're on their way here to refuel."

She stills. "How long do we have?"

I press the controls and wait for the computer to generate an estimated time of arrival. As soon as it's done, I sag forward in relief. "They won't be here for another two hours at least. We'll have to risk going to Soran and Liana early."

She stands and starts for the door.

Confused, I call out. "Where are you going?"

"I'm going to the med bay to prep for their retrieval. I'll need to scan Liana as soon as she's back on the glider. She's Terran, and I don't know for sure how the breaking dart toxin will affect her."

"Good idea," I reply. As she leaves the bridge, her words replay in my mind. *"Don't say that, Rowan."* Does she know that I love her? Was her plea a kindly worded rejection? Or was it something else entirely? I'm desperate to know, but now is not the time.

I turn my attention to the control panel and start up the engines, forcing myself to focus on the task at hand. I cannot afford to be distracted right now. Not while the A'kai are on their way and we still have yet to retrieve my brother and Liana.

CHAPTER 12

TR'LANI

Rowan powers up the glider, and we head out toward the forest. I'm anxious to get Liana and Soran back on the ship. The sooner we do, the faster we can leave before the A'kai show up. I want to be as far away from this planet as possible before they arrive.

A dull thud echoes along the hull, signaling we've landed, and I race toward the airlock to greet my friends.

My heart stops as soon as the door opens and I see Liana in Soran's arms, her eyes wide open yet unseeing. Rowan's gaze is full of concern as he looks to me, his panicked expression mirroring my own. Liana is Terran, and I can only pray that the damage to her sight is not permanent. "Thank the Creator you're all right! Can you see anything?" I ask, hoping she'll say she can at least see a bit of light or possibly even shapes.

My stomach drops when she shakes her head. "The toxin hasn't worn off yet."

Rowan pats her shoulder to reassure her, but worry is visible in his features and on his brother's as well.

I run the scanner over Liana and then sigh in relief when I study the readings. It may take a while, but her body is definitely processing the toxin, and her vision should return within the next several hours.

"You're certain you weren't tracked here?" Soran asks, concerned. "Why didn't you wait until dark?"

I move to Rowan's side. "We didn't have a choice."

Rowan looks to his brother. "We need to get off this rock as soon as possible. Tr'lani and I scanned the channels while we waited on the ship. An A'kai cruiser is on its way here to refuel, and I don't want to risk being here when they arrive."

Soran's eyes widen, and all the color drains from Liana's face.

I place a hand on Rowan's forearm. "Let's get out of here. Now."

He nods, and I follow him to the bridge, taking the station beside him. His hands fly across the control panel as he starts up the glider. When Liana and Soran enter, I notice how gentle he is as he places her in the chair. His entire focus is solely on her. Rowan is right: Soran would give his life to protect Liana. Of this, I am certain. He is in love with my friend.

All of us stay on the bridge even after we've left Le'ro, watching and waiting to make sure the A'kai haven't found us. Tension is thick in the air, and each time the display blinks to indicate a nearby ship, my heart stops. They should not be able to track us with the cloak, but I learned long ago to never take anything for granted.

After a few hours have gone by without any sign of them, Rowan speaks. "If they had detected us, we would have found evidence of it by now. I believe we are safe."

All the tension drains from my body at his words. I'm tired, but Liana looks worse. It's an effect of the toxin, no doubt, as it burns through her system. It should wear off even faster if she allows herself to rest.

When I help her to her quarters, she quickly falls asleep. I leave to retrieve a blanket from my room, so that I might stay with her until she awakens, but as soon as I step into the hallway, I find Soran just outside, his gaze fixed on her door. My heart clenches at the worried look on his face.

"How much longer do you believe it will be before she regains her sight?"

One of the first things I learned when I trained to be a Healer is that so much about medicine is uncertain. There are too many variables. And the fact that Liana is a species we've never encountered before makes everything that much more complicated. "She is Terran, so I cannot be sure exactly when it will return. But from my readings, I know that her body is breaking down the toxin. It shouldn't be much longer."

The tense set of his shoulders relaxes a bit. "I believe I will sit with her then. In case she should awaken and need anything."

I've watched them together. Liana enjoys his company. Immensely. Her expression always seems brighter whenever he is around, and I trust him to stay with my friend. "I think she would appreciate that. Contact me if you need anything."

He dips his chin in a subtle nod. "I will."

Satisfied that she is in good hands, I head toward the bridge to find Rowan. When I enter, he's seated at his station, like always, bent over his control panel. He turns to face me and gives me a smile that doesn't quite touch his eyes.

I take the seat beside him. "Is everything all right?"

He lowers his gaze, his brow furrowed deeply as if my question troubles him. "Yes...and no."

Worried, I dart a quick glance at the screen, searching for any sign that the A'kai have followed us.

He must read the panic in my expression because he quickly adds. "We are safe."

I release the breath I hadn't realized I was holding and then give him a puzzled look. "Then, what do you mean?"

"It is...complicated," he says.

I lean forward and place my hand over his. "What is it, Rowan? You can tell me."

* * *

ROWAN

Even as she says this, I do not know where to begin. How do I explain the fear of losing my brother? And of how I've tried so hard to convince him to deny what he feels in his heart even as I've made no attempt to ignore the will of my own? I want to ask her what she meant earlier and to tell her how I feel in return.

All of these things weigh heavy on me, and my mind is having trouble making sense of them.

The gentle squeeze of her hand pulls me back from my thoughts. "You are worried about Soran and Liana."

She says this as a statement, but I know it is also a question. "How did you know?"

"I know that your people do not accept Outsiders. If he were to take her as his mate, he would become Outcast from your people, would he not?"

"Yes." I swallow against the lump forming in my throat. "And I don't want to lose him like I did before." I shake my head, closing my eyes as the painful memories float to the surface. "The civil war began with an attack on our palace. My father and Soran stayed behind to hold off our attackers long enough for my mother, sister, and I to escape." I clench my jaw. "My father taught us that family is the most important thing, above all else. True to his belief, he gave his life for us. And Soran gave his freedom. I spent two cycles searching for him. Everyone told me he was dead and I was wasting my time. But I never gave up because I could not bear to be without my brother." I meet her eyes evenly. "For me, giving up was never an option. I would either find him or die trying."

"You love him. I understand this." She places a hand over my own. "I feel the same about my brother as well. Al'aneo and I are not just siblings, we are best friends."

"Ever since Father died, I've done all that I can to keep our family together. And I want my brother to be happy, but I also know that if he follows his heart, I will lose him. Forever."

I lift my gaze to hers, staring deep into her golden eyes. And the words I do not speak are the ones I feel deep in my soul. Even knowing that it would cost me everything, I cannot deny that I desire Tr'lani more than anything I've ever wanted before. And yet, this very truth is the one that hurts me most. I love my family. Everything I have done has been to keep us all together.

I have never been more conflicted. I have known since I was a child that my duty has always been to my family. It is the way of things. The younger siblings are to become the trusted advisors of the eldest one who inherits the crown.

And yet, I cannot deny that I have always wanted a life for myself, outside of all this. I studied engineering to build ships, wanting to travel the stars. But after searching for my brother, I saw more of the galaxy than I ever wanted to see again, and it changed me. I realized that what mattered most was our family and keeping us all together.

But as I look to Tr'lani, I feel that same pull that I used to have—the desire to have a life and a happiness that is only my own. So, how could I fault my brother for wanting the same?

Tr'lani's gaze holds mine, and frustration burns through me. Our people are enemies. Does she feel for me as I do her? And even if she does...a Mosauran may love an Aerilon, but what world could we live in? There is no place that would accept us.

And could I live with the knowledge that I chose love over family? The love of an enemy at that... This should be an easy answer, and yet...it is not.

If she were my Ashaya, like Liana is to Soran, the choice would be made for me. But Tr'lani is not my Ashaya; I have no grounds to ask for an exception to the laws forbidding taking a mate outside of our race.

She takes my hand. "Your mother is the Empress. Can she not change the law? My people used to be as yours are now, but we've changed. We are accepting of bonding with other species."

"What about Mosaurans?" I ask because I have to know. Even though I should not, I long more than anything to take her as my mate.

She lowers her gaze. "You're right. There is so much hatred

between our people." She reaches up to touch my face. "I was so horrible to you the first time I saw you, and you were only trying to help me. I've never told you how sorry I am for that, Rowan. I regret it more than you know."

"You do not need to apologize, Tr'lani." A smile tugs at my lips as I remember how fierce she was. "Your eyes burned with fire when they first met mine. I have never admired a female more than I did in that moment with you."

A beautiful smile crests her lips.

I continue. "I'd heard Aerilon females were fierce creatures. But to be on the receiving end of your wrath, I now understand that every story told of this was probably truth."

She laughs, and it is the most enchanting sound I've ever heard.

I hide my pain behind a smile as I stare across at her beautiful face. I am so lost when it comes to her, and I do not know what to do.

CHAPTER 13

ROWAN

It has been two days since we left Le'ro, and as we draw closer to Mosaura, we are also that much closer to Aerilon as well. It is only a few solars travel farther from my home world to Tr'lani's. I have promised to return her to her planet, but I dread the day that I must leave her. For I know that when I do, I will be leaving behind my heart as well. Sighing heavily, I close my eyes and picture her face.

My heart no longer belongs to me. It is completely and irrevocably hers.

A sharp ping draws my attention, and I look up to see an incoming message. It is an Aerilon signal. I tap the screen, and an Aerilon male's face appears. His piercing golden eyes study me a moment, and my jaw drops when I realize who he is. Although his skin is a bluish-green color and hers is violet, I would recognize that face anywhere because it is so similar to the one that I adore. He is Tr'lani's twin brother—Al'aneo.

"I received a coded communication from this vessel. What business do you have with my people, Mosauran?" His words are clipped and laced with quiet anger as he glares at me through the viewscreen, reminding me so much of Tr'lani's fierce personality. Apparently, it must run in the family.

I tap a quick message to Tr'lani, signaling her to come quickly. It takes only a second, but the delay is long enough that her brother leans forward, and I know he means to disconnect the feed.

"Wait!" I cry out, and he stills, his chin jerking back up so that his narrowed eyes meet mine. "I have your sister."

Completely misunderstanding my words, his eyes flash with anger, and he growls menacingly into the display, baring his fangs. "Where is she? If you so much as lay one hand on her, I will hunt you down, and I will not stop until you are dead. I demand that you release her to me at once. Send me the coordinates of your vessel."

I put my hands up in mock surrender. "You misunderstand. My brother and I have been searching for you because we rescued her." I give him a warning look. "And you *know* that my people are just as opposed to slavery as yours. It is death to any slavers we find. Why would you think we would hold her against her will?"

His shoulders relax a bit, but his expression is still wary as he regards me.

The bridge doors whoosh open behind me, and his gaze darts over my shoulder. A low, trilling hum begins in the back of his throat in Aerilon greeting, and I spin in my chair to see Tr'lani walking toward the screen, answering him in kind.

* * *

TR'LANI

My breath hitches when I see the face of my brother. How long has it been since last I saw him? I can hardly breathe, worried this is all just a fever dream and I'm somewhere still locked away in a cell, imagining finding my family.

Tears gather at the corners of his eyes as he stares at me in disbelief. "Tr'lani," he whispers. "I was so afraid we'd never find you, my beautiful sister."

He raises his open palm to the display as if to touch me, and I do the same, wishing he were here. As I rest my hand on the viewscreen, a broken sob escapes me. Every night of my captivity, I used to imagine moments like this but never thought this day would actually come.

A tear rolls down his cheek. "All this time," he barely manages. "We never gave up searching. How did you escape?"

"Prince Soran and Prince Rowan of Mosaura"—I gesture to them—"saved us from the A'kai." I take Liana's hand. "But Liana is the one who kept me alive before that."

Al'aneo studies Liana a moment before bowing deeply in a show of respect. "You have my deepest gratitude. Have you been able to contact your people—the V'loryns?"

Liana opens her mouth to answer, but I interject. "She's not V'loryn, Al'aneo. She's Terran."

He leans closer to the screen, his sharp gaze scanning her from head to toe.

I continue. "She was taken from her ship by the Zovians. She doesn't know where her home world is. I wish to bring her into our Clan, so she can become an Aerilon citizen and have the same rights and protection of our people."

Al'aneo's golden eyes turn back to Liana, and he lifts his hand to the screen. Extending his first three fingers, he touches the display. Liana and I copy the gesture. "For all you've done for my sister, I shall be proud to welcome you into Clan Al'ani as in'ari."

Liana's eyes are brimming with tears, but she blinks them back as she looks between Al'aneo and me. "You have no idea what this means to me," she says softly.

I hug her warmly and whisper in her ear. "You are not alone, my dear sister. You have a Clan now and a family."

"Thank you," she whispers.

Al'aneo's image begins to distort. "We're traveling near a binary system. It's interfering with our signal. We are en route. I will see you in five solars, but I will contact you every day," he says just before the viewscreen goes dark.

I stare at the screen a moment, still in shock that I've finally found my brother after all this time. When I turn back to Rowan, something —an emotion—flickers briefly across his face, but it's gone too quickly for me to be sure what it was. He gives me a smile that does not touch his eyes.

* * *

When we return later to my quarters for bed, I reach across to take his hand, pulling it onto my mattress like we do each night as I stare across at him lying down on the sofa.

"You'll be reunited with your brother in five solars." He gives me a faint smile. "And then you get to go home."

Just the thought of seeing my family and my planet again used to fill me with such joy. But now, as I look at Rowan, a deep ache fills my chest. "I will miss you, Rowan," I say softly.

His eyes are full of sadness. "I'll miss you too."

A heavy silence settles in the space between us. After a moment, I force myself to close my eyes because I cannot bear to look at him any longer, knowing that soon we'll be parted. I can hardly stand the thought of never seeing him again, but I don't know what to do.

Opening my eyes, I find his already closed in sleep. I study the sharp ridges of his brow and cheeks and the aristocratic lines of his face, attempting to memorize his features because I don't want to forget anything about him. Could I really be in love with a Mosauran warrior? An enemy of my people?

As soon as I think it, I know it is truth. I *do* love Rowan. But I cannot tell him. We are too different, he and I. And even if he returned my feelings, we'd never be accepted by his people or mine.

CHAPTER 14

TR'LANI

Ever since my brother contacted me, my soul has felt a bit lighter somehow. I missed him so much the past two and a half cycles. And yet, as my gaze drifts to Rowan sitting across from me, sorrow settles deep in my chest. It is only three solars until we reach Al'aneo, and I dread knowing I will have to leave Rowan.

As if sensing my eyes upon him, he looks up from his meal. "There is a Healer on the station we will stop at tomorrow. She is said to be able to heal impossible things."

With a heavy sigh, I sit back in my chair. I've heard of such people; most of them turn out to be charlatans—preying on those who can ill afford their services with false promises to cure their ailments. I open my mouth to say this but stop as he begins speaking again.

He puts his hands up in mock surrender. "I already know what you're going to say. People who claim things like this are usually liars and thieves, but I have heard of her from a few of our warriors. She has healed wounds that even our Healers thought were beyond repair."

Cautious hope begins to take root deep inside me. "And...you say she is on this next station?"

"Yes." He pauses, a look of uncertainty on his face before he continues. "I...hope you do not mind, but I took the liberty of contacting her to see if she could meet with us. With you," he corrects.

Doubt seeps in. "I...I don't know if I can do it, Rowan. If she cannot help me I—" I stop just short of saying that I will truly be broken if there's nothing she can do for my wings. And I don't know if I can put myself through that.

He reaches across the table and gently places his hand atop mine, giving it a gentle squeeze. "Do not give up hope, Tr'lani. We will find someone to repair your wings."

My heart clenches. He said "we."

Before I met Rowan, I didn't know his species was capable of empathy. They are one of the most feared races in the quadrant. But every night since the first day I came aboard their ship, he has spent with me in my quarters. He knows I still have nightmares, and he sleeps on the sofa to remain nearby to reassure me—to be a familiar and friendly face when I awake from those terrible dreams.

Never once has he made me feel as if I were a burden. At first, I thought of him as a good friend, like On'aro. But now it is something more—something deeper. When I look in his eyes, I know it would be so easy to become lost in their depths.

As I stare across at him, his beautiful silver eyes search mine, and my heart squeezes painfully. I am in love with Rowan. But Mosauran males covet strong females and fight for the right to be bonded to the strongest among their species. I am...not like that. I am soft where they are muscled; I am not strong. All of my natural defenses were stripped from me, and I am a Healer, not a warrior.

I am nothing like the females of his race. The deep ache in the center of my chest is my heart realizing that he would never want me...at least, not in that way.

Even now, I am scared at the mere thought of leaving the ship. "Rowan, I think I'd rather stay on the glider when we reach the station."

His brow furrows softly. "You do not wish to meet with the Healer?"

"It's not that. It's—" I hesitate, not wanting to speak my fears aloud. Drawing in a deep breath, I lift my gaze to his. "I'm afraid of being captured again." My voice is barely a whisper as I admit my deepest worry.

He reaches across and takes my hand. "I will be with you. You won't be alone, Tr'lani. And we are so close to Mosauran space it is unlikely that there are any slavers here."

I shake my head softly. "But you don't know that for certain, Rowan."

"No, but you left the glider on Le'ro and—"

"That was different. We remained near the ship," I snap. "I'm not going." Dark memories flood my mind, and despite my attempt to hide it, my hands begin trembling. I fist them into my lap to still their shaking as I close my eyes and breathe through pursed lips, trying to make the nightmares go away. "You have no idea what it is to be a slave, Rowan. I won't risk being taken again."

"You're right," he speaks softly. "I don't know what you went through, but I understand fear. Our enemies invaded our home in the middle of the night to murder my family. We thought they were our allies, but we were wrong. For many cycles, I was plagued by insomnia. I slept in full battle gear with my weapons nearby, always ready… always expecting we'd be attacked again."

He takes both my hands in his. "But I realized that was no way to live…always being consumed by my fears." He gently presses his forehead to my own, his silver eyes staring deep into mine. "If you allow your worries and doubts to consume you, I promise you will die inside…a little each day. Not all at once, but slowly, Tr'lani. Until you fade away into nothing but the sum of your fears."

He is right. And while I understand this…still, I cannot help but be afraid. Reluctantly, I nod. "I'd like to practice some more with a weapon before we reach the station."

A small smile curves his mouth. "Follow me."

Still holding my hand, he leads me to the training room. When he hands me a blaster, I double check that it's set on the stun setting. It takes me four shots to finally hit the target, and when I do, I turn to him with a defeated look.

He grins. "Your aim will improve with more practice. In the meantime, you can keep it on stun. When in doubt, fire as rapidly and as many times as you must to hit your target. The setting is low enough that if you accidentally blast something else, you will do little damage, but if you hit your opponent, you will render them completely immobile."

His words give me a renewed sense of confidence as I move on to the next practice target, hitting it on the second try. He practically beams at me when I spin back to face him.

"Now," he says. "We will go through the various defense holds some more."

Secretly, I enjoy this. The close contact of his body to mine as he holds my back flush against his front. He leans down, and his breath is warm in my ear, sending a shiver of pleasure down my spine as he whispers. "Do you remember what to do?"

I grin. Gripping his forearm firmly, I quickly twist beneath his arm, knocking him off balance and using his forward momentum to flip him over my back and onto the floor.

His eyes are wide as he hits the mat with an audible thud, forcing the air from his lungs. "That was...good," he wheezes.

When he doesn't get up right away, I drop to my knees beside him and stare down at him in worry. "Are you all right?"

A slight grin tilts his lips. "I'll admit, I wasn't expecting to go down so hard. But it was great. Perfectly executed, in fact."

I reach down and smooth the hair back from his face. "I don't like hurting you, Rowan."

"I am a warrior of Mosaura." He grins. "We are not so easily hurt."

I roll my eyes in mock frustration.

He takes my hand, his expression solemn. "Know that I would endure countless injuries in training you to ensure you are prepared to take on any who would dare try to harm you."

His words melt my heart, but before I can reply, he stands and pulls me up with him. Assuming a defensive pose, his gaze holds mine. "Again."

CHAPTER 15

ROWAN

When we arrive at the station, I hand Tr'lani a blaster and a laser knife. She conceals them under her clothing and then lifts a determined gaze to me. "Let's go."

I cannot suppress the beaming smile that lights my face. She is a fierce and brave female. I turn to my brother and Liana. "We'll meet back here in two hours."

"Two hours," he agrees.

As we walk down the ramp, I scan for any sign of danger. The metal panels that line the floors, walls, and ceilings are dull with signs of age. This station isn't nearly as bad as some of the seedier ones Soran and I have been to in our travels, but the threat of the A'kai is ever constant on my mind. I will not feel entirely safe until we are inside Mosauran space. My gaze lands on a fellow Mosauran tending his shop; I cannot imagine making a home in a place like this, outside of the Empire.

The promenade is crowded as we make our way through, the two of us garnering all sorts of strange stares. But then again, I suppose it must seem odd: an Aerilon and a Mosauran together. And that is exactly what my protective body posture is telling them when they look at me. That we are together, and *she* is mine.

Several males of all different species gaze at Tr'lani with lust-filled stares. I cannot help the fierce possessiveness that consumes me as I place my hand to the small of her back, fighting the urge to wrap it around her waist and pull her against me as we move through the crowd. I growl menacingly at any who venture too close to her.

Mosauran females dislike an overprotective male, but Tr'lani does not seem to mind. A Patiko male walks alongside her, his eyes glued to her form. They light up as soon as he notices her lack of claws and her broken wings, realizing she is missing her natural defenses. His back feathers fan out in a colorful crimson display a moment before he brushes the tip of his wing suggestively against her thigh and tries to pull her toward him.

Without hesitation, she draws her knife and lashes out at his wing, stabbing straight through it.

He squawks out in pain, and I rush him. Wrapping my hand around his neck, I slam his body against the side wall. His eyes are wide, and a pitiful garbled squawking noise emits from his throat as he struggles in my grasp. "How dare you touch her," I growl.

"Forgive me," he gasps. "I did not know she was yours, Mosauran warrior. I—"

I tighten my hand around his neck, cutting off his ability to speak. "You have no right to touch a female without her permission," I grit through my teeth.

A small hand on my forearm draws my attention back to Tr'lani. "Rowan." Her eyes dart nervously to the people now gathering around us. "We should go."

She is right. We do not want to draw a crowd. With a slight clench of my jaw, I push down my anger and throw the Patiko off to the side, listening in satisfaction as his body slams against the far wall with a sickening thud. I turn and glare at the throng of people as I wrap a protective arm around Tr'lani's waist, pulling her against my side and leaving no doubt in anyone's mind that she is with me.

Fierce protectiveness fills me as I lean down and gently nuzzle at her temple. “Are you all right?”

“When he grabbed me, I remembered my training.” She gives me a beaming smile. “Did you see how good I got his wing with my blade?”

My chest swells with pride. “You are as fierce as a Mosauran female.” It is truth.

Her smile grows even brighter.

It doesn’t take long to locate the Healer’s clinic. She is a Garkol. As soon as we enter, her glowing lavender eyes scan us from head to toe. Her skin is the color of stone, and if the females are anything like the males, it is probably just as impenetrable. They are a formidable race—one of the only ones evenly matched to my own. And yet, their females are very slight in stature compared to the males. But I suspect they are just as deadly.

As soon as we enter the room, the door slides shut behind us, and I tense, palming my blaster at my side. Sensing my trepidation, the Healer studies me with a piercing gaze. “Be calm, warrior of Mosaura. I will not harm your mate.”

I do not correct her assumption that we are together, and Tr’lani says nothing as well.

Instead she steps forward, extending her hand to the Garkol Healer.

The Healer stares at her open palm a moment before accepting it.

A low hum emits from Tr’lani as she takes the Healer’s measure. After a moment, Tr’lani releases her grip and then turns back to me. “She is safe,” she smiles.

The Healer nods and then motions for Tr’lani to lay down on the exam bed.

As I move to her side, the Garkol eyes me speculatively. “You can wait near the door.”

I straighten my back as I stand to full height and narrow my eyes. “No. I will remain at her side.”

“I’d prefer that he be here too,” Tr’lani adds.

Although I get the impression that she doesn’t agree, the Healer also seems to instinctively recognize that to argue with me would be futile.

"As I mentioned in our communications, Tr'lani is a Healer," I inform the Garkol.

"Yes," Tr'lani says. "I've already tried using the MRU to repair my wings, but nothing could be done."

The Garkol nods as she runs the scanner over her body. "Many of our people came back from the last war with devastating wing injuries. We have developed several treatments that perhaps will be able to help you," she explains.

The scanning device beeps. She frowns as she studies the readout. "I am afraid I can do nothing for your wings in their current state. Your wings will have to be rebroken before they can be repaired, and even then—" she pauses, and dread settles deep in my gut, "—there is no guarantee that you will regain full function."

My heart feels as if it will break. Tr'lani blinks back tears, attempting to hide her despair. In this moment, I've never felt more helpless. I want only to bring her comfort, but I am unable to summon the words. I am as devastated as she is by the Healer's assessment. I cannot bear the thought of her suffering again and possibly for nothing if it doesn't work. There has to be another way.

A low chirp of my communicator draws my attention. The familiar pattern of blinking lights stops my heart momentarily before it begins hammering. This is a secret signal I've had with Soran since we were fledglings. It is a warning of danger, instructing me to return to the ship immediately.

My eyes snap to Tr'lani's, and I attempt to keep my voice even, not wanting to alarm her. "We must go."

I reach my forearm to the Healer and tap my wristband to hers, paying her the hefty sum of credits for this visit and then help Tr'lani off the table.

She looks up at me. "Is something wrong?"

I cannot lie to her. "I'm uncertain. But we must return to the ship. Now."

I can hear nothing over the pulse pounding in my ears as we make our way back to the glider. Cloying panic fills my mind, and I wrap a protective arm around Tr'lani as we push through the crowds. I scan continuously for any threat that may be lurking. Soran would not have sent that signal unless we were in danger.

It feels like forever until we finally reach the glider, and I'm glad to see that it's already been disconnected from the refueling line. Once I prep the engines, we'll be ready to go when Soran and Liana return. Racing up the ramp with Tr'lani, I slam my palm on the access panel to seal the door shut behind us as soon as we're safely inside.

Without thinking, my protective instincts surge, and I slip my arms around her back to pull her toward me. Gently, I nuzzle her hair, inhaling deeply of her delicate scent as I struggle to push down the panic rising within me.

"What's wrong?" she whispers against my chest.

"Soran sent me a signal to return to the ship at once. He should be on his way with Liana now too."

My communicator chirps again with a message from Liana and Soran. I blink several times in shock. "They've found another Terran slave and freed her. Soran wants me to retrieve her and bring her back to the glider while he goes to free her mate."

Tr'lani's eyes are wide with fear as she stares across at me, and I don't miss the way she fists her hands at her sides to still their trembling.

"Remain here. I will return as quickly as I can."

She grabs my forearm. "No. You're not going alone."

I hadn't wanted to tell her this, but I must if I want to convince her to stay. "The slaver that had the Terran female was going to sell her to the A'kai. Which means they could already be on the station."

Tr'lani's face pales, fear marring her expression.

Although I hate seeing her afraid, she needs the truth. I want her to remain on the glider where it's safe. I gesture to my communicator. "I will contact you as soon as I locate the Terran."

"I'm coming with you, Rowan." Her eyes burn with the same fierce determination she had when she first saw me, and I know it will do no good to argue with her now. We don't have time.

With a slight clench of my jaw, I nod. "Follow me and stay close."

As we weave through the crowd, I fight off my anxiety by glaring at everyone we pass so that they avoid us. It seems no one wants to cross paths with an angry-looking Mosauran, and I prefer it that way. I don't want anyone to even think they may approach or come anywhere near Tr'lani.

I can only imagine the panic Soran must be experiencing right now. Liana refused to stay behind and has gone with him to retrieve the Terran female's mate. She is just as stubborn as Tr'lani, and I suspect she would not be dissuaded from accompanying my brother on his dangerous task.

As we draw closer to the location, my steps slow, and I approach with caution. This is little more than a service alleyway and very poorly lit. Anything could be lurking back here, and I pull Tr'lani behind me as we enter, ready to shield her from any danger we may encounter.

A wisp of movement up ahead draws my attention, and an involuntary growl rumbles deep in my chest. If this is someone waiting to attack us, they will be dead before they can even draw their weapon.

"Who is there?" My voice is low and threatening as I speak.

Tr'lani's hand on my back makes me still. The acrid scent of her fear is thick in the air. "What do you see?"

I hate that she is so afraid, and I wish I could somehow reassure her, but I cannot risk further conversation until I know what we're dealing with up ahead.

"Hello?" a female voice calls out.

I squint my eyes as a small shape comes into view. My shoulders relax. It is the Terran female.

Cautiously, she moves closer to us. It is easy to read the fear in her light-green eyes. With long, pale hair, she is a bit smaller than Liana, and I wonder if all Terran females are usually this small or if Liana and this one are an exception. I suppose I'll find out once Soran and Liana retrieve her Terran mate.

"I am Rowan, and this is Tr'lani. My brother sent us to retrieve you."

"My name is Abby," she replies in a quiet voice.

Tr'lani steps fully out from behind me, and Abby stares at her in wonder. "Liana is right. You *do* look like a beautiful fairy princess."

Tr'lani gives Abby a warm smile. "Come. We will take you back to the glider where it is safe."

Shakily, she steps forward. As she moves, I notice her odd, waddling gait. My gaze travels lower down her form as I study her a moment, wondering if she is injured. My eyes go wide at the large swell of her abdomen.

Having noticed this as well, Tr'lani gasps beside me. "You are with child?"

Abby's eyes brighten with tears. "Yes. I—I didn't think it was possible."

Tr'lani stares down at her in confusion. "Why?"

"None of the gladiators I was"—Abby's voice breaks—"given to were Terran."

I don't understand. "But what about your mate? He's Terran, is he not?"

Her bottom lip trembles as she answers. "No, he's Lacerta. But I—I'm not sure he's the father of my child."

Rage twists deep in my gut at what must have been done to her. Females slaves in the gladiator rings are given to the gladiators as prizes, forced to endure repeated force-matings.

Tr'lani embraces Abby while reaching another hand out to me. She squeezes it gently as her eyes meet mine with sadness and pain reflected behind them. She whispers soothingly in Abby's ear. "Come with us. We'll keep you safe."

Several pairs of eyes are on us as we walk through the promenade. I'm even more vigilant as we make our way back to the docking bay. It must be shocking to some to see a Mosauran, Aerilon, and what they think is a V'loryn, all together.

I still cannot believe there are slavers on this station—so close to Mosauran space. It seems they are even bolder than I imagined. And it will only get worse if we do not reach an agreement with the Aerilon and the V'loryns to patrol the neutral zones between our territories.

I growl low in warning as a Krulta moves alongside Abby. His eyes are full of lust, as he thinks he has found easy prey. Two of his eight purple tentacles extend toward her, but I'm faster.

Withdrawing my knife, I slash at the two offending appendages, cutting them off in one quick slice. He screeches out as they fall to the floor with a wet slap on the metal surface. "Do not touch them!" I growl.

Wide-eyed, he stumbles back in the opposite direction, racing away. Unfortunately, his tentacles will regrow. He was a predator of the worst sort. I should have killed him.

I'm aware of every set of eyes that watch us as we board the glider. I hope Soran and Liana return soon because I'll feel better once we're far away from this wretched station.

Tr'lani runs her scanner over Abby's abdomen. "Your child appears healthy," she says. "I'll do some more detailed readings in the med bay just to be sure."

Abby's eyes dart to the airlock door as she wrings her hands with worry. "I want to wait for Grex first."

Tr'lani and I exchange a knowing glance, and she nods.

Holding my blaster in one hand, I access the console nearby to remotely start up the engines. I want to be ready to leave the moment Soran and Liana return with Abby's mate, Grex.

Soran spoke of a male named Grex that he met when he was a slave in the arenas. They were friends. I wonder if perhaps it could be the same person. He has searched for him on and off through the years but believed so much time had passed that he was likely dead.

I've already started the engines when the airlock door opens, and Soran and Abby's mate rush inside.

My eyes immediately go to Grex. From his build, it is easy to see he is a warrior. His light-green scales are covered in multiple scars, including his tail. Probably the result of many cycles spent fighting in the arenas. His yellow vertically slit pupils contract and then expand as soon as he sees Abby.

She rushes into his arms, and he embraces her tightly, his larger form practically swallowing hers. After a moment, he pulls back just enough to place his palm over her belly and then presses a tender kiss to her forehead. I wonder if he knows the child may not be his. I've heard that his species are very territorial and possessive of their mates. I only hope he does not reject her if he is not the father.

Soran's eyes are wide as he scans the hallway behind us. "Where is Liana?"

I give him a confused look. "I thought she was with you."

He turns back to the airlock door. "She should have been here by now. She left before we did. Talel is here. He and his soldiers fired on us, and we had to take shelter in one of the shops. We split up so it would be harder for them to find us."

Tr'lani gasps. "Talel is here?"

Roughly running a hand through his hair, Soran paces back and forth in front of the door, his eyes frantic with worry. He reaches up to press the panel. "I have to go back out there. I have to find her."

I clamp my hand on his shoulder, stopping him in his tracks. "Brother, wait! It's too dangerous!"

He spins and shoves me back against the wall. "Do not try to stop me!"

Grex steps directly into his path, putting his hands up in a placating gesture. "Just give her a moment. She may have taken a different route than we did."

Soran snaps. "Would you wait if it were Abby?" He then looks to me, his eyes darting briefly to Tr'lani. "What if it were Tr'lani out there instead?"

He's right. He stares at me with a look of betrayal because he knows that what I'm asking of him, I would never listen to if our roles were reversed. If it were me, I'd be out that door in a heartbeat to search for Tr'lani.

My protective instincts flare, and I wrap an arm around Tr'lani's shoulders, pulling her gently into my side. The need to have her close is so overwhelming I cannot override the primal desire, panicked at the thought that Talel and his soldiers are on this station. To my brother's credit, instead of raging at me, he clenches his jaw and then turns back to the door.

Soran pushes Grex out of the way and slams his hand to the control panel to open the airlock. It slides open and we're surprised to see Liana standing there.

He wraps his arms around her and pulls her back inside, quickly sealing the door behind him. Hugging her tight to his chest, he gently nuzzles her hair. "I was so scared something had happened to you," he whispers. "What took you so long?"

I observe as my brother holds her tightly to him. Something has changed between them since they left the ship. Has she already claimed him as her mate?

She unfastens her cloak, allowing it to fall back from her shoulders to pool at her feet. Tr'lani gasps at the large amount of obsidian blood that stains her clothing. I stare in shock as well before realizing her people bleed red, not black, so this blood cannot be hers.

"I'm fine," she says quickly. "But I was almost caught. I killed one of Talel's men to get away. The blast drew the attention of his fellow soldiers, and I had to take a longer route to get back here. The promenade is crawling with A'kai. We need to leave. Now."

"She's right," I add. "We should hurry." Still holding Tr'lani's hand, I pull her along with me as I race to the bridge, unable to force myself to let her go. I'm desperate to keep her safe and get us all as far away from this station as possible.

As soon as I reach my console, I spin up the FTL engines. Liana is a skilled pilot, and I trust her with my glider even more than I do Soran. I have no problem turning the controls over to her as he and I man the weapons in case the A'kai pursue us.

A quick glance over my shoulders confirms that Tr'lani is already strapped in her seat beside Grex and Abby before Liana presses the panel, and the stars begin to blur outside the viewscreen as we launch into FTL travel.

* * *

After we're safely away, Tr'lani goes with Grex and Abby to the med bay. Both of them are worried about their unborn offspring. As soon as I'm certain the glider is running smoothly, I walk down the hallway to check in on them as well, curious to know if the child is okay.

When the doors open, I notice Grex seated in a chair beside Abby as she lies on the exam bed. He holds her hand and speaks soothingly to her as tears stream down her face while Tr'lani scans her abdomen.

His voice is low, but I am still able to make out his words. "Do not be upset, my beloved," he whispers. "What happened to you is not your fault. Even if the child is not mine, I will still love it because half of it is you."

My heart clenches as I stare at them, and we all wait anxiously for Tr'lani to speak.

She stares down at her screen, and then a smile curves her lips as she looks up at our new passengers. "Half of the child's genetic material comes from Abby, and the other half is from Grex."

Abby pulls her mate into her arms and buries her face in his chest as her tears turn to joy.

When Tr'lani announces that they will have a daughter and then shows the age progression of the child on a floating screen for all of us to view, she turns her gaze to me and smiles warmly. Despite all we've been through, we escaped, and we still have hope.

Abby looks to her mate. "If we ever find my home world, I pray that my parents are still alive to meet their granddaughter."

Liana gives her a confused look. "Why are you worried they might not still be alive?"

"When they brought me out of stasis two years ago, one of the Healers that scanned me...they somehow estimated that I'd been asleep in suspended animation for at least thirty to forty years before I was awakened. Maybe more."

Liana frowns. "What? How? I don't understand." Her eyes lock on Abby, and her mouth drifts open in shock. "You're Abby Worthy, aren't you?"

"Yes."

"No." Liana leans into my brother as she shakes her head in disbelief. "You can't be her."

Soran wraps his arm even tighter around her, worry easily read in his expression as he whispers in her ear. "Liana, what is wrong?"

Liana places her hand to her mouth, attempting to stifle a sob as she lifts her gaze back to Abby. "I knew you looked familiar. You disappeared twenty years ago. I learned all about you and your crew in school when I was a child. There are so many theories of what could have happened to your ship, and now…I know."

My jaw drops. That means slavers have been abducting their people for many cycles. Who knows how many Terrans are out here, lost in this sector of the universe so far from their home. My stomach twists as I think on how fragile their species is. They have no natural defenses. There could be hundreds of Terrans being traded and sold in the slave markets even now. Their females are so similar in beauty to the Aerilons, they would be in high demand for many buyers.

Liana cries against my brother's chest at Abby's words. Who knows how much time has passed since she was taken. She could have been asleep for decades. Her entire family could already be dead.

Tr'lani looks to Liana. "There's so much we don't understand about your anatomy. Your people are very close to V'loryns, but there are still many differences between you." She turns to Abby. "The fact that your people can procreate with other races is something I've never heard of any other species being capable of. Mixed species pairings have never resulted in the natural creation of offspring. It has always been impossible…until now."

Grex nods. "That is why most of the races do not condone such pairings. They consider it unnatural. Many societies condemn them as Outcasts…my people included."

I lower my gaze in shame. My race is among them. Despite this, I cannot change what I feel in my heart. I cannot fight the truth in my soul. I love Tr'lani, and I desire more than anything to take her as my mate—for her to claim me as hers.

Tr'lani looks down at her tablet, studying Abby's scans. "According to these readings, Terran genetic material is highly adaptable. Perhaps that's why you were able to conceive a child naturally with Grex."

Soran's eyes flash with worry. "If the other races discover this, Terrans will be in even more danger than they were before."

Panic coils tight in my chest as his gaze meets mine. What he doesn't speak aloud is the fear that settles deep in my gut. It is not just the A'kai who would hunt us for the Terrans. The Anguis, the Zovians, and anyone peddling in flesh would come after us if they knew we had them.

Grex turns to my brother. "Soran is right. Slaves that can be bred will fetch much more on the markets. Once other races find out about Terrans and the fact that they may be breeding compatible with other species..."

Liana looks to Abby. "How were you taken? Do you remember anything?"

She shakes her head. "I went into stasis on the *Intrepid* and woke up in a cage on an Anguis slave ship. I was alone; I don't know what happened to the rest of my crew."

Abby and Liana discuss the similarities of the events surrounding their abductions.

Panic claws at my chest. We must get the females to safety as soon as possible. Now, I am more than eager to meet up with Tr'lani's brother, even knowing it means she will leave me. For I know he travels in an Aerilon cruiser—a ship evenly matched to those of our Empire in both speed and defense.

When Liana is finished speaking with Abby, I watch as she and Soran embrace. She presses her lips softly to his. I am certain they are together now.

How can I blame him for following his heart when all I want is to follow mine as well? My gaze drifts to Tr'lani once more. As soon as her eyes meet mine, a stunning smile curves her mouth, and I am mesmerized, as I always am when she does this. Surely, she must have guessed at my feelings for her by now. I've made little attempt to conceal them. But how can I choose Tr'lani over my family? If Soran leaves, it will just be myself, my mother, and Caryn. I cannot abandon them. Not when everything I've done has been to keep us all safe and together.

The ship's proximity sirens begin blaring.

Worried golden eyes meet mine a moment before I turn and race toward the bridge. Liana and Soran follow close on my heels. As soon as the doors whoosh open, ice fills my veins. The large black hull of an A'kai cruiser dominates the viewscreen.

"Can they see us?" Liana asks.

A quick scan of the ship's systems shows the cloak still active. "No, they cannot see us."

Soran, Liana, and I watch in silence as the A'kai vessel becomes smaller and smaller in the display. When the ship finally disappears into the black void of space, I message Tr'lani, Grex, and Abby to let them know we're out of danger.

Liana leaves the bridge to go shower, leaving Soran and me alone.

CHAPTER 16

ROWAN

Tr'lani messages me that she will be in the med bay a bit longer, running a few more tests on Abby and the baby to make sure they're healthy.

Now that the danger has passed, I decide to have some fun. I turn to my brother. "Terrans must have an exceptionally heightened sense of smell. Liana bathes every day…sometimes even twice."

Soran's nostrils flare as he turns, lifting his arm to scent himself.

I arch a questioning brow. "What are you doing?"

"Do I…smell bad to you?"

This is just far too tempting. I wrinkle my nose in mock disgust. "Well, now that you mention it, you could definitely benefit from a shower."

He gives me a horrified look. "Do you think she noticed my odor?"

Despite my attempt to conceal it, a smile tugs at my lips as I struggle to suppress a laugh.

His eyes flash with anger. "You maltak! I thought you were serious."

Unable to contain myself any longer, I double over with laughter.

"You think it is fun to tease me like this?" he grumbles. "I am already nervous enough as it is…wondering if she will decide to claim me as hers."

My laughter dies as his words hit me like a physical blow. "You have decided then?"

He meets my gaze evenly. "I love her, Rowan. I…do not wish to be without her."

Hurt wars with anger deep inside me, and I glare at him accusingly. "And what about Caryn and Mother? What about me? You would give up everything? Become Outcast for her?"

He gives me a pained look. "You know I don't want to lose you or our family. I do not want to become Outcast."

"Then the answer is obvious," I snap. "You cannot take her as your mate."

"It's not that simple."

"Yes, it is," I counter.

He gives me a pointed look. "I've *seen* you with Tr'lani. You *know* it is not that simple."

His mark hits home, and I clench my jaw, unable to meet his gaze because what he says is truth.

"What is your plan?" he asks. "You will just tell her goodbye once we reach her brother's ship? Never see her again?"

Sadness fills me as I give words to my despair. "She does not want me."

His head jerks back slightly. "She said that?"

"She didn't have to. In the last coded message he sent, I overheard her brother mention a male that she was supposed to be joined to before she was taken. Apparently, he has waited for her return all this time."

Soran's gaze is full of pity. "And she wants to be bonded to this other male?"

I clench my jaw. "I didn't ask…I couldn't bring myself to."

"Then, how do you know she still wants him?"

"I am Mosauran. Her people are handsome, and they are known for their beauty." I gesture to my brutish form. "I look nothing like the males of her species. Why would she desire me when it is clear—from the interested glances she received from nearly every male that we passed on the last station—she could have anyone she wants?"

Soran leans forward and places his hand on my shoulder. "Why don't you speak with her? Tell her how you feel?"

I lift my gaze to his. "Because to pursue her, no matter how much I might wish to, would mean that I would become Outcast. I cannot betray our family when they need me. Mother and Caryn need us, Soran. The civil war may be over, but we both know how easily such truces are broken and the devastating consequences of lowering our guard."

He knows of what I speak. The day we lost our father because we were too trusting. We didn't suspect or anticipate that one of our supposedly closest allies—House Caladan—would turn on us, and it cost us...dearly.

His shoulders sag forward in defeat. "I don't want to become Outcast. But I love her. I cannot deny what I feel in here." He places his hand to his chest.

"It is the fate bond making you feel this way," I protest.

"No," he replies. "At first, I thought so too. But now that I know her, I cannot imagine ever taking another as my mate. I would desire her as mine even without the pull of the bond. Mother will understand. I believe the Council will too."

This is how I feel about Tr'lani. In spending time with her, I know that I will never want another as I want her. I desire to take her as my mate, and I cannot imagine being without her. My heart squeezes painfully. I want so desperately to admit all of this to my brother. I open my mouth to speak, but the words die in my throat. After a moment, I nod. "I hope you are right."

He stands from his chair.

"Where are you going?"

He arches a brow. "To shower so my beloved does not find my scent unappealing."

I cross my arms over my chest and decide to tease him again. "I've never seen you preen as much as you have ever since Liana came onboard. If you continue to buff your scales every day, eventually you'll begin glowing in the dark...possibly even blind everyone the moment the sun hits you as you step off the transport when we reach Mosaura."

Soran laughs. "Jealousy is a terrible thing, brother."

I roll my eyes as I try to suppress a smile.

I should not tease him. I've been doing the same thing. Every evening, I buff my scales, hoping to impress Tr'lani with their polished shine. Many males of our species are blessed with vibrant color and markings. But Soran and I are rather dull in comparison with our silver-gray scales.

Mosauran females prefer a male with vibrant coloring, and I've always worried it would be difficult to attract a mate. But now that I am in love with an Aerilon it is even more impossible. Their males are handsome, and no amount of buffing my scales can compete with their appearance. It may be futile, but I still do it anyway, part of me hoping perhaps she'll at least be impressed with my efforts.

I drop my head into my hands as I picture her beautiful smile. We will reach her brother in less than two solars. What am I going to do?

CHAPTER 17

TR'LANI

After I finish with all my scans of Abby and her baby, I give her and Grex a quick tour of the glider and then show them to one of the empty crew rooms. Soran gives Grex a spare change of clothing, and I give Abby some of my loose, flowing dresses.

When I leave their quarters, I decide to go to Liana's room. I want to ask her what happened between her and Soran because it's obvious from the way they were acting that they are more than just friends now. I stop at her door and reach up to hit the chime but retract my hand when I hear Soran's voice coming from inside.

A faint smile curves my lips. Soran is a good male. I'll talk to her later. I continue down the hallway to the bridge to find Rowan. As I do, a deep ache centers on my chest, directly over my heart. We'll meet my brother in two solars, and while I'm excited to see him, I also dread knowing that it means I'll be leaving Rowan. I can hardly bear the thought that I may never see him again.

* * *

ROWAN

As always, my thoughts turn to Tr'lani when I'm alone. Attempting to distract myself, I sit forward in my chair and study the navigation charts while I run another check of the ship's systems. Abby claims she was to be sold to the A'kai, and I wonder how many Terrans they may have already acquired. My stomach twists at the idea of anyone being at their mercy. Their species are ruthless. They are blood drinkers; it is not uncommon for them to keep their victims alive for days while they slowly feed off of them. Their government claims to not condone such actions, but several A'kai have been found in violation of the anti-slavery laws that govern our shared regions of space.

And now that we have taken yet another slave from them, we are in even more danger than we were before. It seems Talel made good on his threat, and his people are searching for Terrans in order to find their home world.

When the doors whoosh open, I spin in my chair, half expecting to find my brother.

My heart stops when I see Tr'lani instead. She smiles, but it does not touch her eyes. Sadness reflects in her expression, and I stand and move toward her, taking her hand in mine. "What is wrong?"

She lowers her gaze. "How is it that you can read me so well?"

Feeling bold, I draw in a deep breath and give her my truth. "Perhaps it is because I love you, Tr'lani."

Her eyes flick back up to me. "You...love me?"

I reach out and gently cup her face. I lower my forehead to rest it against hers. "I am Mosauran and you are Aerilon, and I do not expect you to return my feelings. I just...I cannot hide it from you anymore. And I do not want to." I brush my thumb over the petal-soft skin of her cheek as I stare deep into her golden eyes. "You are my heart, Tr'lani."

"Rowan, we cannot fall in love."

Even though I know what she says is truth, my heart rebels against her words. "Why not?"

Her eyes are full of sadness as they meet mine. "It is impossible, Rowan. Our people are enemies. We cannot be together."

I take her hand in my own and place it to my chest. "You are my heart, Tr'lani. I will never love another as I love you."

A tear slips down her cheek as she cups my face. Leaning in, she presses her lips to mine. They are warm and softer than I imagined. I gently run my hand through her long, silken hair and down her back, pulling her close.

She wraps her arms around me, gently threading her fingers through the hairs at the nape of my neck. She traces her tongue along the seam of my lips. I open my mouth and groan low in my throat as she curls her tongue around mine.

My people do not do this—this touching of lips—but I am already addicted to her taste. I pull her even closer, and a small moan escapes her. "Rowan," she whispers my name between breaths. "We shouldn't fall in love."

Even as she speaks the words, she holds me even tighter. Her tongue strokes against mine and I'm lost in her touch.

A deafening explosion sounds along the hull, and the ship rocks violently to the side. I wrap my arms tight around Tr'lani as it sends us flying. I twist so that my back hits the wall, taking the brunt of the impact.

Pain rips across my back, but I force myself to focus through the agony as I help Tr'lani into the chair next to mine. I strap into my seat and pull up the ship's computer. I manage to right the glider while scanning for our attackers.

My eyes go wide as soon as I recognize the A'kai cruiser. I don't know how they found us, but I don't have time to figure it out. Slamming my hands down on the panel, I send a volley of weapon's fire toward their ship. Only a few of the blasts make it past their shields, and I curse under my breath as I launch another round at them.

The doors whoosh open as Soran and Liana rush inside just as the dark hull of our enemy comes into full view. "It's an A'kai Cruiser. They've found us."

"How?" Soran snaps.

Grex and Abby race onto the bridge behind them, and he lets out a string of curses. "How did they find us?"

I grit my teeth in frustration as I barely manage to avoid the next hit from their weapons. "I don't know, but that attack knocked out our cloak, and I can't get it back online."

The acrid scent of Tr'lani's fear fills the air and my protective instincts flare. I cannot let the A'kai capture us.

Liana turns to me. "Can we outrun them?"

I clench my jaw. "No."

"Their ship may be faster," she says, "but ours is much smaller, more easily maneuverable." She points to the screen. "There! I'm taking us into that asteroid field."

In silent agreement, Soran and I exchange a quick glance before we give Liana full control of the glider while Soran, Grex, and I take the weapons controls.

Liana motions to Tr'lani. "Go to the storage locker. We each need a blaster."

Tr'lani quickly disappears down the hallway. The engines groan in protest as the ship rolls to the side, and Liana punches the accelerator controls, racing into the dangerous debris field.

My stomach twists in a violent knot with each sudden maneuver of the glider, but the answering explosions—so close that they rock the ship—are far more threatening than the floating rocks that surround us.

Another blast ripples along the outer hull, violently shaking the ship. The engines spin down with a high-pitched whine, followed by a deafening silence. My pulse pounds in my ears as the dark metallic hull of the A'kai cruiser fills the viewscreen.

"That last hit took out our engines and weapons," Liana reports. "We're running on emergency power only. If I can get to the engine room, maybe—"

A shockwave vibrates roughly along the hull, and the sound of metal grating against metal echoes loudly through the ship.

Ice fills my veins. The A'kai have latched onto our airlock and are trying to board us.

My pulse pounds in my ears. The low groan of twisting metal reverberates along the hull as A'kai soldiers force the outer hatch of our glider open. Tr'lani's eyes are wide with fear, and I take her hand in mine—a silent promise that I will do whatever it takes to make sure these monsters never touch her again, even if it means that I must sacrifice my life for hers.

Soran turns to me. "I'll set the ship to self-destruct. We can use the escape pods to get clear of the blast."

Alarms blare throughout the glider as the airlock door gives way with a loud screech followed by a deafening boom, vibrating the floor beneath our feet. A moment later, bootsteps echo down the hallway as the A'kai storm our vessel.

Holding tightly to Tr'lani's hand, we race to the escape pods as Soran, Liana, Grex, and Abby follow closely behind.

With a quick glance over my shoulder, I look to Soran. "How long do we have?"

"Less than five minutes."

Angry shouts and tromping steps retreat from our position, and I thank the Creator that they're heading in the opposite direction we are. They think they'll find us on the bridge, but the only thing awaiting them is the silent self-destruct countdown on the ship's computer. By the time they realize this, we should already be gone, and it will be too late for them to escape.

I do not fear death. It goes against everything in my warrior nature to run from my enemies. But we are far outnumbered, more likely to be captured than killed, and I would rather die than allow them to touch Tr'lani.

As soon as we reach the pods, I turn to our group. There are three escape vessels and only two seats for each one. We will have to pair off, and as I look to my brother, it isn't even a question. He will go with Liana, and I will go with Tr'lani. "We go in twos," I whisper, ushering Grex and his mate, Abby into the first pod and Tr'lani into the second.

I turn back to Soran. "Brother, I—" There is so much I wish to say, but there isn't any time. I wrap my arms around him in a firm embrace.

"May the Creator be with you," he whispers before pulling back to grip my shoulders firmly as his eyes meet mine. "We will find each other again, in this life or the next."

I give him a solemn nod and repeat the warrior's vow. "In this life or the next."

I turn and step into the pod with Tr'lani. The door seals behind us, and we strap into our seats. I look up to find my brother's gaze upon me as he stares in through the window. With a final nod, he activates the release.

With a sudden rush of air, our pod ejects violently from the glider. Tumbling through the dark void of space, we spin several times before the thrusters kick on, stabilizing our motion. Symbols flash across the display as the computer scans for nearby habitable planets.

Panic tightens my chest as I study the screen. The self-destruct countdown should be nearly done, and I only have mere seconds to sift through the selections presented and make a decision before the glider explodes, damaging our pod and making it for me.

I slam my fist down on the controls to choose our destination, and hold my breath as I pray I haven't wasted the precious moments that could mean the difference between life and death. A sudden burst of light flashes through the window as the glider explodes in a brilliant display. Tr'lani's eyes are wide with fear as they meet mine.

She reaches across to take my hand as we wait for the shockwave, tracking its progress on the computer as it rushes toward our vessel.

The wave slams against the outer hull, jerking us to the side. Alarms blare, and the pod shudders violently as we tumble toward the planet. Warning lights flash across the screen, and panic grips me as we begin our descent into the upper atmosphere. Our angle is too steep, and we're coming in fast.

My fingers fly across the console as I try to slow our descent, but the controls aren't responding. My gaze goes to the viewscreen as we race above a pale-blue sea. Purple sands mark the edge of a landmass in the distance, but I don't think we're going to make it that far.

Helpless as I stare at the control panel, I cannot find the words to speak. I lift my eyes to Tr'lani and take her hand in my own. She squeezes it in return as we look out the window. The ocean rises to meet us in a blur.

We skim the surface, and the pod jerks and then spins wildly, slamming us back in our seats. The world goes dark as I fall away into oblivion.

CHAPTER 18

ROWAN

Flashing lights and blaring sirens fill the cabin, snapping me back into awareness. The pod rocks lazily back and forth as my memory returns. The last thing I remember is the ocean; we must have landed on the water. I turn to look for Tr'lani, inhaling sharply when I see her unconscious form still strapped to her seat. A slow trickle of blood runs from her scalp and down her chin, dripping onto the floor.

"Tr'lani?" I call out her name, but she doesn't move.

Alarm bursts through me, and I reach for the release to unfasten my harness, but it won't budge. Frantic, I shred the bindings with my claws and rush to her, unfastening the straps that hold her to the seat. She falls forward in my arms, and I carefully cradle her to my chest, gently brushing her long, silken silver hair back from her face. Cupping her cheek, I stare down at her, praying to the Creator for her to open her eyes. "Tr'lani, wake up. Please. Wake up."

She moans softly, and relief floods my system. I take her hand in mine. "We're safe. Our pod has landed." Well, technically, it crashed, but I'm not going to tell her that just yet. I'll wait till she's fully awake and I have a better idea of where we are. "I'm going to take a look around, but I promise I'm not going to leave you."

Gently, she squeezes my hand in return to let me know that she has heard me.

I turn my attention to the hatch window and see nothing but clear blue sky. Reaching up, I grip the handle firmly and push it open. With a screech of metal, the door hinges away. Grasping the frame on either side, I pull myself up to survey our surroundings.

I squint my eyes against the bright glare of a yellow-orange sun. It is just as I suspected. We are adrift on the sea. The sky is clear except for a few thin wisps of gray clouds overhead. A cool breeze blows across the ocean, carrying the fresh saline scent of the water. It appears to be rather temperate here. At least for now.

Off in the distance, I notice a landmass. A purple sandy beach backed by a thick, dark green jungle of heavy foliage and trees. Out here on the water, we are too exposed. If any of the A'kai survived and followed us here, we'd be easily found.

But I don't want to abandon the pod. It's the best shelter we could have against the elements, and it also has our transmitter beacon. Without it, there's very little chance we'll be rescued from this planet.

A thought occurs to me, and I return to Tr'lani's side. I cup her cheek, turning her head to face me. Her eyes are still closed as she says my name weakly. "Rowan."

I press my forehead to hers. "Tr'lani, we're drifting on the ocean. I'm going to have to change into my draken form to move our pod to dry land. I'm going to strap you back into your seat, my heart. We'll be all right."

Her eyelids open just enough for her to look up at me and nod before closing again.

I brush the pad of my thumb across her cheek and then turn back to the hatch. Lifting myself out of the opening, I balance atop the hull. In one swift movement, I shift into draken form. Furiously flapping my wings, I hover above the pod and grip it firmly in my forearms.

As gently as I can, I lift it from the water and head out across the sea toward land. I stay as low to the surface as possible, not wanting to attract any attention to myself in case this planet is inhabited by anyone who may not be so welcoming of visitors.

As I scan the water below, it is so clear I'm able to make out several schools of fish, swimming in formation. At least we will not want for food if we run out of emergency rations.

I fix my gaze on the land up ahead, studying the shoreline for a good location for the pod. If I position us close to the sea, we would have easy access to a food source.

Without warning, an explosion of mist and spray punches up through the surface. A long, dark blue tentacle wraps around my back leg, jerking me down toward the water. It is thick, muscular, and alarmingly strong. I roar in frustration as I struggle to remain airborne, holding the pod tightly to my chest.

I turn my head and release a stream of fire on the creature. It releases its grip. The slimy tentacle uncoils from my leg, and I frantically climb up into the clouds before turning to scan the ocean for my attacker.

My eyes go wide as a dark blue tentacled monster nearly twice the size of my draken form stares up at me through two large, yellow eyes with a predatory gaze before descending back beneath the water and disappearing from view.

As I continue toward land, I decide we will definitely not be nesting anywhere near the sea. When we reach the shore, I fly low above the trees. The air is thick with humidity, but at least it is clean. The entire area is so covered with vegetation it is difficult to see beneath the jungle canopy.

Sunlight reflects off a glass-like surface below, and I realize it is a stream. This is fortunate. I track it back to its source. It winds through the jungle, growing wider the farther we follow it in, until I discover a waterfall hidden amongst all the vegetation. It will be good to have a fresh water supply nearby to supplement our emergency hydration packs.

But as we draw closer, I frown when I notice just how large the pool is below the falls, and I wonder how deep. The image of the monster from the ocean surfaces in my mind. What if there's something like that here? I will have to investigate thoroughly for predators.

Purple sand covered with tiny white pebbles surrounds the water like a smaller version of the beach. It's beautiful, but I know that beauty can hide dangerous things. I settle the pod beneath a cluster of trees, making certain it is not visible from the air and far enough away from the water that I will be able to detect any predators long before they can reach us.

I shift back into my humanoid form and rush back into the pod to check on Tr'lani. She's still not fully conscious, but when she squeezes my hand again, her grip is much firmer this time. When she awakens, I'll ask her if she agrees with the location I've chosen for our nest. If not, I will move it to wherever she prefers. A quick glance around the interior makes me realize she will probably not be happy using the pod as a nest in its current state.

Several of the emergency food pouches and bars are scattered across the floor, along with a few other random supplies. I move to gather them up, returning them to their proper storage compartments.

While definitely not very large, the cabin is big enough to easily accommodate two people. And it is the best shelter we could possibly have, given that we don't know much about the weather patterns and indigenous lifeforms on this planet.

I move to the console, hoping to learn more about our surroundings. When I tap the panel, it flickers briefly and then goes dark. I sigh heavily. Apparently, our landing was too rough and damaged the pod's computer.

Panicked, my eyes snap to the emergency transmitter beacon, and my shoulders relax when I notice that it, at least, is still lit and ready to be activated. I remember from my time on the Defense Force, however, that it is best not to alert others of your presence until you have surveyed your surroundings for any potential hostiles who might be drawn to your signal.

Tr'lani moans softly and then shivers in her seat. I retrieve one of the emergency blankets and carefully drape it over her form. I'm at war with myself. I'm reluctant to leave her, but I need to make sure we're safe. I lean down and gently nuzzle her temple. "I'm going to take a look around outside. I won't go very far." I squeeze her hand to see if she's heard me. When she does the same in return, I smile.

She is strong, my heart.

I step out of the pod and move closer toward the shoreline. Quickly, I change back into my draken form. The air is heavy with moisture, and the ground is soft, almost spongy beneath my feet, suggesting this area experiences frequent rains. The deep stretch of my wings as they extend out from my back stirs something dark and primal within me.

A cool breeze moves through the trees, and I tilt my head up, scanning the skies for any sign of a threat before I lift into the air. My nostrils flare as I scent the wind. I do not know what creatures make their homes in this jungle, but I plan on being the dominant predator here.

I will allow nothing to threaten Tr'lani.

Not wanting to alert anyone of my presence, I glide low over the canopy of trees. Their majestic, large black and gray trunks twist up toward the pale blue sky. Flaring my nostrils, I scent the wind again, but nothing is familiar here except for the smell of the sea and the thick vegetation.

As my gaze scans the horizon, I notice no signs of any type of civilization nearby, which is both good and bad. Hopefully, it means we should not encounter any hostile sentient lifeforms, but it also indicates that we may be alone on a planet devoid of any technology.

At least we still have the pod and the transmitter. But I am hesitant to activate it. We have no way of knowing if it will be received by friend or by foe. The A'kai are hunting us, and we cannot risk alerting them of our presence here. If the computer were working, I'd know if we had been followed. I would also be able to search for the other pods if they made it to this planet.

Although I'd like to explore more of this area, I am satisfied that we are safe for now. Tr'lani is my first and foremost concern. She is still not fully conscious, and I promised I would only go far enough to ensure we are secure. Sensing no threat nearby, I drop my left wing low to circle back to the pod. It's hidden so well beneath the trees it is not visible from the sky.

Hovering over the rock-lined shore that surrounds the water, I extend my wings, catching the air in my sails and allowing myself to drift carefully to the ground. I concentrate and then shift back into my humanoid form to enter the pod, quietly sealing the hatch shut behind me. Rifling through the supply bag, I quickly locate the emergency hydration packs and then kneel beside Tr'lani.

Taking her hand in my own, I squeeze it gently. "We are safe," I whisper. "I have sealed us in here so nothing can disturb us."

Her brow furrows softly, and her eyelids flutter and open. She blinks several times as her gaze travels over the cabin. "Where are we?"

"I do not know the name of this planet. And the computer is not working for me to check."

A flicker of panic moves across her face. "The A'kai? Did they follow us?"

"I have not seen any signs to suggest they are here."

Her golden eyes are full of fear and trepidation. "Are you sure?"

"I am certain."

The tense set of her shoulders relaxes a bit as she slowly sits up.

"Are you hungry? Thirsty?"

"Thirsty," she replies.

I hand her the hydration packet and then offer her a nutrient bar anyway. She takes both, and I'm glad that she feels well enough to eat. She shifts in her chair and winces slightly.

"What's wrong? Are you hurt?" I look her up and down, checking for any signs of obvious injury."

She shakes her head. "Just a bit sore."

As she eats, I tell her everything that happened after I woke up, including the kraken-like monster in the ocean. Then, I assure her that I can always move the pod in my draken form if she is displeased with this location.

I do not mention what I told her of my feelings back on the glider, and she does not bring it up either. Right now, we must concentrate on survival and finding a way off of this planet.

The last of the light from the sun emits a soft, warm glow throughout the cabin, reflecting off the edge of her beautiful, sparkling, clear wings. Her smooth, violet skin seems a bit paler somehow, and I worry. Her species is not like mine. And I wish for a least the hundredth time that she had strong scales instead of petal-soft flesh.

Despite my attempt to focus on something else, my mind keeps returning to the memory of her lips pressed to mine. The way her tongue entered my mouth and curled around my own. I long to hold her close like that again, but the last words she spoke to me on the glider were that we should not fall in love. And yet, she responded to my touch in such a way as to suggest she is not entirely convinced of this.

With a heavy sigh, I force myself to focus. First, we must understand our surroundings in order to survive.

"Do you think Soran and Liana or Grex and Abby might be here too?" Her soft voice snaps me back from my thoughts.

I shake my head softly. "I saw nothing on the pod's computer before we..." I start to say "crashed" but instead settle on, "landed to indicate any others were nearby."

I know she considers Liana much like a sister, and I'm sure she is worried. I am concerned for them also, but I give her the only small sliver of hope that I can. The one I hang onto as well. "I saw the other two escape pods eject from the glider, so I know they made it before the ship exploded. And the computer had located three nearby habitable planets. If they are not on this one, they must be on one of the other two."

"And the A'kai?" she asks.

"Their ship was destroyed with the glider."

Her shoulders relax a bit at my answer, and I'm glad.

"Do you feel well enough to stand?" I ask. "I must reconfigure the chairs into beds so we may sleep comfortably."

When she nods, I get up and hold out my hand. Cautiously, she takes it, and I pull her up beside me.

The glider was my personal vessel, and I designed every last *centicron,* including the escape pods, to my exact specifications. In my search for Soran, I learned practicality was of the utmost importance. That's why my ship was constructed with stealth, speed, and safety in mind above all else. But the pods I made specifically for comfort as well as security. Because I knew if I ever had need of one, I could potentially be stranded for many solars before rescue.

As I arrange the chairs into two beds, I place them close but not quite touching, similar to how I would sleep on the sofa in her quarters each night.

Satisfied that I've got our sleeping arrangements figured out, I turn back to face her. Her gaze drifts down my form, and a violet bloom spreads across her cheeks and the bridge of her nose before she quickly averts her eyes away from me.

Curious about her reaction, I tip my head to the side to regard her. "What is wrong?"

Nervously, she tucks a long tendril of her silver-white hair behind her ear as she looks down at the floor, gesturing at me with one hand. "I...I didn't realize you were naked."

A small puff of air escapes my lips as a grin spreads across my face. That is the problem? She acts as though my stav is protruding from my mating pouch. "You've never been to Mosaura, have you?"

She blinks several times before answering. "Of course not. Our people are not friends."

This is truth, so I nod. "Well," I begin, with a slight smirk on my lips. "If you'd ever been to my home world you would know that nudity is very casual among my people."

Her mouth drifts open, and I wonder if she is thinking of the scandalous and false rumors that my people participate in shared mass matings as we dance around a fire. It is not truth, of course, but I have heard this lie spread about my species by the other races.

I shake my head softly. "It is an inescapable fact that we cannot change into draken form with clothing."

Tr'lani's gaze discreetly travels up my form as she lifts her eyes to mine, it seems she does not find my appearance lacking, and hope fills me anew.

"Oh," she says, as a deep, purple flush spreads across her cheeks. "I—I didn't realize."

I dip my chin in a subtle nod. "Because I had to shift forms so quickly to lift our pod from the ocean, my clothes were shredded in the process." Flexing one bicep, a smirk twists my lips as I arch a teasing brow. "I am not only a big, strong Mosauran warrior, I am also very handsome. So I do not blame you if you cannot help but stare at my attractive form."

She laughs, and then rolls her eyes. "I'll do my best not to stare at you."

"Good," I grin. "Now...we can rest tonight and then in the morning decide when we will activate the distress beacon."

Her gaze moves to the dimly lit panel off to the side. "We should remove the transmitter and place it somewhere far away from our shelter, but close enough that we will be able to see who responds to it without alerting them of our presence until we're certain they're friendly."

I stare at her in wonder. She is as intelligent as she is strong. It would never have occurred to me to do this. We are taught only to wait at least one solar, if we were downed by hostiles, before activating the beacon to reduce the risk of alerting our enemies to our position.

I lean forward and study the panel. It's heavily encased in a solid mesh of metal. I purposely designed it that way to ensure it would survive a crash landing. It will be difficult to remove, but not impossible. I nod. "We will find a suitable location for the transmitter tomorrow." I'm fascinated by the workings of her mind and curious to know everything about her. "It is an excellent idea. I hadn't even considered it," I admit.

Her eyes meet mine evenly with a look of hesitation evident in her expression. "I...it's something we learn in our survival training. In case we're shot down by a Mosauran cruiser during a border skirmish."

With a slight clench of my jaw, I lower my head in shame. Every year, my people try to force their way farther into Aerilon territory, and…the Aerilon always push back to defend it. "I am sorry."

She places two fingers up under my chin, tipping my face back to hers. "It's not your fault, Rowan. Things have been this way between our people for thousands of cycles. It's nothing new."

I sigh heavily. "It doesn't mean it is right. And it doesn't excuse our aggression against your race."

She gives me a small smile. "It's not just your people who are aggressive. Mine are too," she offers. "Both our species are at fault."

I suppose she is right, but it doesn't absolve me of my guilt. My mother is the Empress, and I am a Prince of the Empire. Never once have I made any attempt to halt the hostile tactics of our people against the Aerilon.

She lays down on her bed, and I do the same. Her hand reaches for mine, and I take it as we lie facing one another as we normally do each evening. She has still said nothing of my declaration earlier. But then again, I have not brought it up either. I'm too afraid of her rejection to speak of it now. Besides, we must concentrate on survival and finding a way off this rock. Everything else is secondary to those two goals.

CHAPTER 19

TR'LANI

As we lay side by side with his hand in mine, I think on his words from before. He loves me. And the truth is: I love him too. How could I not? Ever since he rescued me, he has been nothing but kind and caring. He makes me smile, and that is something I never thought I would do again after all that I went through.

More importantly, he does not judge me for my tears. He simply accepts me as I am. It's as if he understands that I was a slave for so long it is difficult sometimes to push down my nightmares. Every day for the past two cycles, I lived in a state of fear. It's hard to adjust and to feel "normal" again after everything that happened to me.

But how would it ever work between us? He would be Outcast from his people and everything he has ever known. How long would it be before he resented me for this? His family is everything to him, and I cannot ask him to give them up. Especially for me.

He is Mosauran. Their females are strong. In his culture, strength is important. And I am not strong like that. My wings flutter softly behind me, and I wince at the pain of the slight movement. I feel as if I am broken…in more ways than one. Closing my eyes, I sigh heavily and then allow myself to drift off to sleep.

* * *

When morning comes, I find him already awake. His silver eyes staring deep into mine as I give him a sleepy smile. Gently, he squeezes my hand and smiles in return.

A question lingers behind his gaze. But it is one that I cannot answer now. It's dangerous to be so close like this, for I risk losing my heart to Rowan. It would never work between us. Our people have been enemies for too long.

Releasing my hand, he sits up, and I already miss the warmth of his palm in my own. "Shall we go outside?"

The reality of our situation comes into razor-sharp focus as we open the hatch.

I feel of the blaster and knife on my belt as if to reassure myself before exiting the pod. Whatever dangers await us on this world, I want to be prepared to meet them.

* * *

ROWAN

The air is heavy and thick with humidity around us. The dull roar of the waterfall nearby is a familiar sound, reminding me of my home on Mosaura. Strange animals cry out from the jungle, but I do not scent any hint of death, decay, or blood to suggest that a predator hunts this area. I could be wrong, however.

There could be many hidden dangers here, so I must remain vigilant. I repress a small shudder as the memory of the kraken fills my mind. We are lucky it did not try to submerge our pod while we were unconscious.

As we step out from beneath the thick tree canopy onto the strange shore of purple sand with smooth, white pebbles, I stare at the crystal-blue water. I must make sure there are no predators lurking beneath its depths. I turn back to Tr'lani. "Wait here."

Cautiously, I approach the edge. Hopefully, the tentacled monsters aren't able to make their home in fresh water. I kneel and grasp one of the larger stones beside me, testing the weight in my palm a moment before I toss it into the center of the pool. Crouching in a defensive position, I spread my wings wide to shelter Tr'lani behind me in case something emerges from the surface.

Nothing moves, and I tuck my wings to my back as I walk to the edge of the pool.

"What are you doing?" Tr'lani's asks behind me, and I note a small hint of panic in her voice.

"I must check the water for predators."

The soft crunching sound of pebbles behind me is the only warning I get before her warm hands wrap around my forearm, pulling me back. "No! Don't do it. Stay here."

Her concern touches me. Deeply. But if anyone is going to take the risk, I'd rather it be me. I cannot bear the thought of any harm coming to her. "I have to. We must know if it is safe."

I hate the fear in her eyes. I stand tall and puff my chest out with pride. "Fear not," I say with a dramatic flourish as I tip my chin up. "For I am a warrior of Mosaura. We are not easily killed."

She laughs a moment before her expression sobers again.

I cup her cheek. "I will be fine. My vow."

Reluctantly, she nods and then loosens her grip.

I pull away, heading back for the water. I wade in waist-deep, and the liquid feels refreshing and slightly warm, reminding me of the many pools in the gardens of my home. I drop down, sliding the protective second lid over my eyes as I take a deep breath and then dive beneath the surface.

Tiny aquatic creatures flit past me as I circle the entire perimeter within the pool, checking behind every rock and crevice for any hidden danger. The water is crystal clear, providing plenty of visibility. I flex and extend my hands at my side as my claws lengthen, ready for defense if I need them. We've been on the glider for so long I'd forgotten how much I enjoy swimming. Our scientists theorize that because we are able to breathe underwater, our ancestors must have lived in the vast oceans of Mosaura long before they gained the ability to fly.

After making a thorough sweep of the water, I'm satisfied that there isn't any danger. When I rise, I see Tr'lani dip beneath the waterline near the area where I first submerged.

Taking a deep breath, I dive back down and swim toward her.

Her head is turned in the opposite direction from me when I tap her on the shoulder to get her attention.

She jerks away and jumps up to the surface. A terrified scream erupts from her throat as she spins to face me. A flash of light rushes toward me, and I realize too late it's a shot from her blaster.

Pain explodes across my chest, and I drop like a stone, paralyzed by the stun setting.

As I float on the water and stare up at the pale-blue sky, two thoughts fill my mind. The first is how inconvenient this is. I'll be paralyzed for at least a few hours. The second is pride. If I could, a beaming smile would crest my lips. Her aim is much improved. She actually hit me on the first try.

She pulls me out of the water and onto the sand. She falls to her knees at my side. Leaning over me, glittering droplets of moisture fall from her silver hair. With the sun behind her, she glows like an ethereal being as I stare up at her in wonder. She is fierce, my Tr'lani—my heart. And I love her.

One hand takes mine while the other brushes back my hair. "Rowan!" her panicked voice cries out above me. "Are you all right?"

Of course, I cannot answer. All I can do is blink my eyes. At the first sign of movement, she bends down and wraps her arms around me, pressing her lips to my cheeks, brow, and nose.

Warmth spreads across my body at such intimate contact, and I wish I could move so that I could pull her into my arms. If getting shot means more attention like this, I would not mind being stunned more often.

"Oh Creator," she whispers between pecks of her lips. "You were under so long I thought you had drowned or been eaten."

When I'm able to speak again, I'll need to inform her that my people can breathe underwater. But for now, I hate to admit it, but I'm enjoying all this attention from her.

She stands and moves behind me, wrapping her arms up under my shoulders. I weigh quite a bit more than her and am surprised as she slowly drags me back to the pod, pulling me through the door. She seals it shut behind us, and I'm pleased when she places me on the bed and then curls up beside me, holding me tightly.

She smooths a hand through my hair and then drops her forehead gently to mine. "I didn't mean to shoot you." She presses her lips again to my nose. "Oh Creator, Rowan. I'm so sorry."

I'm not. At least she took great care to ensure it was on stun while she searched for me.

She continues. "Thank the Creator it was on the stun setting. I'd forgotten to check it." She buries her face in my neck.

My eyes widen at her admission. Oh Creator, I could have died this day.

* * *

It doesn't take as long as I'd thought for the paralytic effects to begin to wane. I didn't even realize I'd fallen asleep until I open my eyes to find she is no longer beside me. Testing my limbs, I carefully sit up on the edge of the bed and scan the cabin. Just outside the hatch window, I notice her standing waist-deep in the water, her gaze locked on something below the surface.

I stand, and although I am still a bit weak, I'm able to walk. I exit the pod and move toward her, making sure to announce my presence. "Tr'lani, I—"

She jumps and spins to face me, splashing me directly in the face. "You maltak! Stop sneaking up on me!"

I'm so stunned, I blink several times as I stare at her in shock a moment before laughter bubbles up from my chest.

She climbs out of the water, dripping and wet as she levels an angry glare in my direction.

The laughter dies in my throat, and I cock my head to the side. "You are truly angry at me?"

Instead of answering, she wraps her arms around my waist and buries her face in my chest. "I told you not to go in the water, but you didn't listen. And then, when you were under for so long, I thought you were—" Her voice breaks on the last word, and she hugs me even tighter.

Cautiously, I slip my arms around her back and tug her closer. "Tr'lani, I'm sorry, I—"

She tips her head to look back up at me. "How could you be so reckless?"

I huff. "I had to make sure it was safe. Besides, my people can breathe underwater. After that monster I saw in the ocean, I needed to be sure there wasn't some sort of predator in these waters."

"And if there was? Then what would have happened?"

Is she suggesting I'm weak? Instinctively, I puff my chest out, tilting my head up proudly. "I am a warrior of Mosaura. I would have defeated it."

She rolls her eyes and gives me a frustrated look. "And what if you couldn't?"

I scoff. The very idea is insulting. This pool is so small, surely there couldn't have been anything lurking here that was so large I could not have conquered it in battle.

She holds her hand out to me, and I give her a curious look. Does she want me to take it?

I start to reach for her, but she stops me with her words. "They took my claws, my venom sacs, and fangs."

Unsure how to respond, I meet her eyes evenly as I wait for her to continue.

"I was scared, Rowan."

Disbelief ripples through me. "Is that what this is about? I'm a Mosauran warrior. I won't be killed and leave you alone on this planet."

She purses her lips. "I wasn't worried about myself, you maltak."

I stare down at her in disbelief as she knocks my confidence down several notches with her stinging appraisal.

"I was afraid for *you*," she continues. "Without my natural defenses... What if you needed my help and I couldn't—" She clenches her jaw and looks away.

I try my best to assuage her concern. "I'm alive. That's all that matters."

A short puff of air escapes her lips in a huff as she crosses her arms over her chest and turns her back to me.

I walk up behind her and place my hands gently on her shoulders. "Tr'lani?"

She spins to face me, sadness visible in her expression.

I pull her close and gently nuzzle the top of her head. "What is wrong, my heart?"

"I just—" She stops abruptly. Stretching up on her toes, she wraps her arms around my neck and hugs me tightly as she whispers in my ear. "I lo—" She stops again, and I tense, waiting for her to speak the word that almost slipped past her lips. She continues. "I care about you, Rowan. More than you know. And I can't stand the thought of something happening to you." She pulls back, her golden eyes searching mine. "Promise me you won't risk yourself like that ever again."

I frown. "Do you think I am weak?" This thought disturbs me. A lot. And as I wait for her answer, it is agony. If she believes I'm incapable of handling myself, she will never consider me as a potential mate.

But even as I think this, I know she doesn't want this anyway. She said we shouldn't fall in love. And yet...she did not stop touching her lips to mine after saying it. I am a patient male. I will not give up hoping that she will someday be my mate.

She gives me an exasperated look. "Why is everything about strength or weakness with you?"

I arch a brow. "You did not answer my question."

She huffs. "*Of course*, I don't think you are weak. I know that you're strong."

Her words please me, and a wide grin splits my face as my chest puffs out with pride.

She rolls her eyes, and my ego crumbles. "But no one is invincible, Rowan. And I want to be able to protect you too. But without my natural defenses, I worry that I'm not strong enough to do that." She takes my hand in hers. "Promise me you won't risk yourself like that ever again."

As much as I wish I could, simply because she has asked me, I also know this is a vow I cannot make. I meet her gaze evenly. "I cannot promise you this because I will do whatever is necessary to keep you safe. Even if it means risking my own life."

She opens her mouth to protest, but I quickly place a finger to her lips to silence her. "And you are wrong, Tr'lani, if you believe that you are not strong. You have the strength of a warrior. You are a creature of wind but also of fire. I saw it in your eyes the day you first looked into mine. And together, we are stronger than either of us alone."

Her gaze holds mine, full of determination. "Tomorrow, we will find a place to put the transmitter. For now, I'd like to continue my training."

I nod before I step back into a defensive pose and she does the same. "Prepare to defend yourself," I tell her before I rush forward.

She spins to the side and grabs my arm. In a blur of motion, she twists beneath me and flips me onto my back. The air is forced from my lungs as I hit the sand.

I smile up at her as she stands proudly over me and arches a brow. "How was that?"

"You are fierce, my heart," I wheeze, and note that she does not protest the term of endearment that I call her.

* * *

WHEN IT IS time for evening meal, I make quick work of spearing several fish with my claws, throwing them onto the shore for her to catch. I laugh as they wriggle in her grasp, and she curses them to the Creator. She growls low in her throat, and I flush with warmth as I approach her.

Female Mosaurans make a similar growling noise when they are interested in taking a mate. Drawing in a deep breath, I push away my errant thoughts and smile as I gesture to our catch. "Would you like them cooked or raw?"

She wrinkles her nose at the last word.

I arch a brow. "Cooked, then." I lay the fish out on several large, flat stones and then ask her to stand back.

She gasps as I transform into draken form and open my mouth, blowing fire onto the fish to cook them.

Once they are thoroughly charred, I look to her for any further instruction.

She stares up at me in something akin to wide-eyed wonder, and it occurs to me that this is the first time she has seen me in my draken form. She was unconscious when I shifted earlier.

Reaching up, she gently rests her hand on my jaw and then traces her delicate fingers up to my cheek. Warmth blooms in their wake, and I close my eyes, leaning into her palm and relishing the touch of her skin upon my own.

"You are beautiful," she whispers more to herself than to me.

Her praise fills me with pride. If only she could hear my thoughts as Liana can sense my brother's. Deep down, I feel as though Tr'lani is my fated one, and I send another silent prayer to the Creator to give me a sign that this is truth.

When I turn back into my normal form, she smiles up at me. "I'd heard Mosaurans could shift, but to see it is another thing entirely."

I give her a teasing smile. "You will have much to tell your friends when you return to Aerilon."

Her expression falls.

Worried that I've upset her, I move to assuage her concerns. "Do not worry, Tr'lani. We will find a way off this planet."

"It's not that, Rowan." She lifts her gaze to mine. "I know that Al'aneo will find us. Just like you knew that Soran was still alive when everyone else thought he was dead. I know my brother will never stop searching until he finds me."

"Then...what is wrong?"

She gives me a faint smile. "I'm going to miss you when I go back home."

Her words both touch and wound me in equal measure. She has decided then to leave me. She knows that I love her, but she must not feel the same. Despite my devastation, I hide my pain behind a grin as I tease her. "Yes, I expect you will be very bored without my company."

She laughs, but there is a sadness behind her eyes as she stares across at me. Perhaps it is for the best that she does not return my feelings. Our people are enemies; I was foolish to believe she might ever want me as her mate.

As we lay side by side in the escape pod, I cannot help but stare across at her as she sleeps. I long to pull her into my arms and hold her close, but I do not think she wants this. I reach out and carefully tuck a stray tendril of hair behind her ear and then pull the emergency blanket over her shoulder before I allow myself to drift away.

CHAPTER 20

TR'LANI

It is morning. The sun is bright overhead but not unbearably so, and I smile at our luck at having found such a beautiful, temperate place to land. Today we're going to scout the area for a location to place the transmitter beacon.

I only hope everyone landed somewhere safely as well. If the computer were working, we'd know for certain if they were here. I turn to Rowan. "You saw no indication of another pod yesterday?"

"No. But perhaps we can travel a bit farther out to investigate and explore." He turns to the transmitter. "But first, we must get this free."

I watch as he carefully opens the casing surrounding the transmitter. He peers inside and then sighs heavily.

"What's wrong?"

He pulls back and then points at the side of the panel. "You see this wire?"

My gaze follows the line of his finger to a small frayed cord buzzing softly. "Yes."

"This wired is damaged. If we try to turn on the beacon, it could burn up the core."

I'm a Healer, not an engineer, like Rowan, but I think I understand. We can't activate the transmitter until this problem is fixed. "So, how do we fix this?"

He clenches his jaw. "Normally, we'd be able to strip some of the wires from the rest of the pod, but when the computer burned out, it melted the entire electrical system."

It's a definite setback, but things could be worse. At least we are free. "All right." I meet his gaze evenly. "Then, we have no choice but to search for one of the other pods and hope that Soran and Liana or Grex and Abby landed here too."

He nods and then grins. "Are you ready to fly with me again?"

I loved flying with him on Le'ro. It was wonderful. And I'm more than eager to do it again. I answer without hesitation. "Yes."

"Stand back," he says softly as he steps away from me. I open my mouth to ask why but quickly snap it shut as he answers my unspoken question. "Since we are unfamiliar with this planet, I would rather explore it in my draken form in case we encounter any danger."

His answer makes sense, so I nod and then watch as he transforms into his massive draken form. The deep stretch of his wings as he spreads them out makes mine flutter uselessly at my side in response. I remember what that used to feel like. To extend my wings from my back and spread them out to my sides, catching the first bit of air as I began to lift off.

Rowan turns to me. His silver eyes search mine a moment as he studies me. Large, sweeping horns curl up from his head. The sunlight shimmers off his silver-gray scales with an iridescent glow. With a long, tapered tail, he stands on four legs, each hand and foot tipped with sharp, lethal black claws. I stare up at him in open wonder. I don't think I'll ever get used to seeing him this way. He is fierce and beautiful all at once, and I've never seen anything so magnificent before.

His lips curl back from his teeth in, what I'm assuming, is his best attempt at a grin, revealing two rows of rather long and intimidating sharp fangs.

The orange-red coloring of his cheeks deepens slightly as I study his face. I reach up to place a hand on his jaw. "You're so much bigger in draken form."

His lips quirk up again as he tilts up his chin and puffs his chest out with pride.

I laugh.

A wisp of smoke curls around his nostrils as his shoulders shake softly. His version of a draken laugh, I suppose.

Slowly, he lowers himself and extends his leg out to me in an invitation to climb up onto his back. I carefully ascend and then settle between his shoulders. His tail spines snap flat against his back, and he turns his massive head to look back at me, tipping his chin slightly to the side in a questioning look.

"All right," I smile. "I'm ready."

My wings flutter of their own volition as I stare longingly at his as he extends them in preparation to take off. His muscles flex under me as he lifts into the air, and the ground falls away beneath us with dizzying speed. I grip tightly to his back as he climbs up into the sky.

This is so much different from when he carried me as we flew while in his two-legged form. The wind whips through my hair and pulls at my body. I flatten myself against his spine and hold tight as he shakes turbulently before slipping into an airstream. The leathery flaps of his wings billow out like sails as he glides along the current.

I lower my gaze to the spread of the jungle and the ocean before us. The deep-green trees are so thick it is impossible to see anything beneath their canopy save for small patches of crystal-clear blue rivers and streams that wind their way through the dense foliage.

The soft-orange rays of the sun peek through the overcast clouds of the pale-blue sky, creating brilliant shimmering light on the water below us. This is exhilarating. I sit up and close my eyes as I revel in the feel of the air against my wings, imagining they are whole and that I'm flying.

Raising my arms out to my side, I focus on the sensation of the wind as it caresses my skin and whips through my hair, pulling lightly at me as we sail through the current, dipping and weaving to follow its path.

I remember this feeling. Unbidden tears slip down my cheeks as I open my eyes and look to the horizon, the gentle curve of the planet below. For a moment, I can pretend that what happened to me was only a nightmare. Surely, this freedom has always been mine.

But the deep ache of muscle along my back, near the attachment of my wings, reminds me of all that I've lost. I lower my arms and grip Rowan's neck tightly, tilting my head to the side and resting my cheek on his soft silken scales, holding him close in this form as I've longed to do in his other.

A flash of light off to the side catches my attention, and I call out his name. "Rowan!" I shout, to make sure he can hear my voice over the wind. "There's something off to the left. Some kind of reflection."

He dips his left wing low, turning in a wide arc to investigate.

Directly ahead, a soft light reflects in the distance. As we get closer, it appears to be some kind of massive see-through dome.

A quick glance at the ground reveals a large clearing with scattered stone ruins spread out across its surface. Crumbling towers reach wearily up to the sky, the skeletal structures outlining the desolate city below us.

Rowan spirals down in a slow circle, settling gently at the edge of the abandoned ruins so softly I'm not entirely sure we've landed until he folds his wings into his side and drops low to the ground so I can climb down.

Throwing one leg over the side to slide off his back, I gasp in surprise as he changes forms so quickly, he grasps my waist to lower me the rest of the way down. Warmth fills me as his hands linger on my body a moment before he finally lets me go.

Smoothing a hand over my dress, I turn toward the dome. "It appears to be some sort of energy field." Glancing around us, I notice a fallen branch and reach down to pick it up. He watches me with a curious look before I toss it at the energy barrier.

The dome flashes brightly as the stick passes right through, tumbling onto a cobblestone walkway with a small scraping noise before it skids to a stop.

I step toward it, but Rowan catches my arm, pulling me back behind him. He moves forward and slowly raises his hand to cautiously touch the barrier.

Another flash of light and then his limb passes through without problem. He pulls it back, flexing his fingers as he studies his hand.

"Are you all right?" I ask in concern. "Does it hurt?"

He shakes his head. "Only a slight tingle along my scales. Nothing more."

I move to the barrier, but he stops me again. "I do not like this." He eyes the dome warily a moment before turning his gaze back to me. "Look at the trees."

At first, I don't understand what he means, but as I scan the jungle around the edge of the city, a cool breeze gently stirs the leaves and vegetation. While inside the dome, nothing is moving. As if the wind cannot penetrate the barrier.

He squeezes my hand. "I do not think it is wise to enter this place."

Although I'm inclined to agree, there could be something useful here. "This is technology. What if there's something in here that can help us fix the transmitter and the ship's computer? Or something that can locate our friends if they're here on the planet?"

His silver reflective eyes meet mine evenly. "Then, I will go. You"—he points firmly to the ground—"will wait here. Where it is safe."

"Safe?" I ask incredulously. "It's safer if we stick together." I cross my arms over my chest. "No, you're not leaving me here. I'm going with you."

With a slight clench of his jaw, he stares down at me so long I think he's going to argue. Instead, he huffs out a frustrated breath. "Fine. But stay behind me."

I nod.

A light tingling sensation passes over my entire body as we step through the energy barrier and onto the cobbled pathway. Pebbles crunch loudly beneath us as we make our way into the ruined city.

Crumbling rocks and stone buildings line streets littered with scattered debris. Wisps of paper and dead leaves twirl absently in the wake of our movement. Our feet kick up tufts of gray powder and layered dust with each step. Strange vehicles—probably ground transports—lay overturned and on their sides. We walk past windows, the tables and chairs beyond them strewn across the floor.

Whatever happened here, it happened fast, and it must have been absolute chaos.

The lack of any visible bodies tells me this must have occurred long ago. I turn to Rowan. "How old do you think this place is?"

His sharp gaze scans a nearby structure, eyeing what appears to be a broken computer console. "There are obvious signs of technology in their buildings, but nothing to suggest how long this may have been here."

Despite no signs of life, something strange lingers in this place. Scattered dust and ash kicks up from our steps, swirling around us like wisps of haunted memory. A deep chill runs down my spine, and I take Rowan's hand without thinking as we walk side by side along carefully laid cobbled streets and walkways.

With his head raised, his eyes sweep back and forth, scanning the area for any sign of a threat. His voice echoes hauntingly as it bounces over the hollowed-out structures. "This must have been a great city at one time," he says. "It's too large to have been just a settlement or an outpost."

He's right. "From the air, it looks even bigger than Al'tarin, our capital city on Aerilon Prime."

Strange patterns mark the stones of several of the crumbling structures, and I'm curious to know what it is. I tug Rowan's hand gently to inspect one up close. Dark lines mar the rock of what appears to have been a shop. As we move closer, I study the large depression in the ground that seems to follow the line straight into the earth.

Rowan's hand grips mine tighter as he tenses beside me. "They were attacked," he whispers in a low voice. "Those are scorch marks from weapon's fire."

He lifts his gaze to the sky as if half-expecting to find the ships that made them still circling above us.

He pulls me closer, and his eyes meet mine intently. "It will be dark soon. I do not wish to linger here. We should go back to our pod."

"But these people had technology. What if there's something here that could help us?"

"We can return tomorrow." His gaze travels over the ruined landscape with a far-away look on his face before he turns his attention back to me. "There is something strange about this place, and I do not wish to be here after the sun goes down."

I meet his eyes evenly. "If we explore now, we won't have to even come back tomorrow."

* * *

ROWAN

Reluctantly, I agree. She is right. And besides, I'd rather search now and not have to come back at all. There is something about this place that unnerves me. As if a darkness still lingers here from whatever happened long ago.

Turning our attention back to the city, we walk past row upon row of empty buildings, kicking up piles of ash and dust as we make our way down the cobbled streets. It is strange how much sediment lines the walkways, and I find myself wondering again how long this place must have been abandoned. The light from the sun casts sinister shadows along our path, and I'm reluctant to enter many of the structures, worried the damaged architecture may collapse at any moment.

Almost at the city center, we notice several paths that converge in this place. Full of vegetation and a few crumbling foundations that must have at one time been water features, I realize this must have been a park—a gathering place.

As I scan the area, Tr'lani studies a tree nearby, heavily laden with what appears to be fruit. Its large gray trunk twists at odd angles as if it once may have shared the space with many and competed for access to the sun. With purple leaves and soft lavender and pink globes that dangle from each of the branches, it is odd to see something so vibrant in this desolate place.

A low stone structure in the middle of the path draws her attention, and she takes a seat.

I sit beside her, and she places her hand over mine, squeezing it gently as her gaze travels over the park. "It's strange, isn't it?" she says softly.

I give her a curious look.

She continues. "There's no sign that anyone stayed behind after they were attacked." She turns to me. "What do you think happened to them?"

I shake my head. "I suppose those that survived must have fled; relocated somewhere new."

"It's so sad to think they had to abandon their homes," she whispers.

As we continue on our way, we make sure to avoid walking too close to several of the damaged buildings. Everything is eerily silent, and for the first time, I realize that I hear no animal sounds here. As if no living thing besides us exists in this place.

Whatever happened here casts a lingering shadow that even non-sentient creatures are loath to come near. I stand and look to Tr'lani. "Let's finish our search." I turn a sharp gaze to our haunted surroundings.

"All right," she replies. "Maybe it would be better if we split up. We could cover more ground that way."

Her words give me pause. I start to protest, but she cuts me off.

"We can search more thoroughly," she insists. "And it won't take as long if we split up."

After a moment's hesitation, I nod. "Agreed. I'd rather not return to this place after today."

She looks across the park to an area we haven't explored. "I'll go over there"—she motions—"and we can meet up back here in an hour."

An hour seems too long. She has her blaster and laser knife, and I know she can take care of herself, but I am an overprotective male when it comes to her.

But determination burns in her eyes, and I find myself agreeing. If it means we never have to come back here, I can accept being separated from her for a short while. "One hour," I repeat and then watch as she starts on her way.

CHAPTER 21

TR'LANI

A large, domed structure up ahead appears oddly intact compared to the rest of the crumbling buildings, so I decide to go there. My steps echo along the path, kicking up more mounds of dust in the eerily silent ruined city.

When I reach the front of the building, I marvel at the intricate detail of the statue in the courtyard entrance. With wide-set, expressive eyes, five small horizontal cranial ridges on her forehead, a regal nose, and a long, plated braid of hair that hangs down and over her left shoulder, her chin is tipped up as if gazing at the sky.

Dressed in long, flowing robes with intricate scrolling details along the hem, she appears to have been someone important. Perhaps a great scientist, politician, or even royalty.

I've never seen this race before, and I wonder where they make their home now.

Cautiously, I make my way to the entrance of the building behind her and notice the two massive doors. The twisted, crumpled metal hangs by a thread to the frame, suggesting they were forced open from the outside. An even deeper pile of dust and ash marks the threshold, and I sigh in frustration as I sink to my ankles with each step until I finally reach the interior.

Colorful tiles arranged in beautiful mosaic patterns line the floors, walls, and ceilings. A light blinks from off to the side, and I gasp in surprise as a 3D image appears before me, similar to that of the statue outside. It places one hand with three elongated fingers to her forehead and bows low before me. "Greetings, seeker of knowledge. How may I assist you?"

I blink several times in shock as I study the holo image, marveling that my translator is able to understand its language. "I—" I hesitate, unsure what to ask first because I have so many questions. "Who are you?"

It smiles, revealing two rows of flat, white ridges instead of teeth. "I am called Elari. My creators are the Milarans; I am made in their image."

"I've never heard of your people," I tell it, wondering how much independent thought has been programmed into its data core.

An image projects off to the side, and I smile when I realize it's the park Rowan and I were in earlier, except its full of people—Milarans—of all shapes and sizes. Several appear to be families. A child laughs as his father throws him a ball. A small furry creature jumps excitedly beside them. The paths are lined with beautiful trees and a large fountain farther down cascades with sparkling water. It's absolutely stunning.

Elari begins speaking again, and the video of the park slowly fades away, forcing my attention back to her. "We were a peaceful race," she says, and I don't miss the way she speaks of them in the past tense. "You are unfamiliar to me, as well. Are you a traveler from among the stars?"

Such a strange way to put it. I smile. "Yes, I suppose I am."

Her expression narrows. "Do you come in peace, or are you like the others who came before you?"

My brow furrows softly. "What others?"

"The ones who killed my creators."

Her answer shocks me. "Your creators? Are you talking about the people in this city?"

She makes a strange click in the back of her throat that my translator conveys means "yes."

"All the people that lived here are dead?" I ask, hoping I am wrong.

With another click, she turns her gaze down the hall, farther into the structure. "They came here for shelter during the attack. I heard their cries but could do nothing." She looks down at her hands, sadness visible behind her eyes. "My creators did not give me a corporeal form. All I could do was bear witness."

I stare at her in shock.

She continues. "There was a child. Davin. His father worked here in the building, and he came every day to see me. He begged me to save them, but I could not." A lavender tear slips down her cheek, and she turns to the side, gesturing behind her to a small pile of dust. "He ran to me for shelter, and I failed him."

Bile rises in the back of my throat as my gaze drifts down to my legs, covered in a thick layer of gray dust and I realize what it is.

Still in shock, my mind doesn't want to believe what she's said, and I turn my gaze down the long, narrow hallway.

"You'll find the rest of them down there," she says sadly.

My feet carry me unthinking down the corridor. Soft light filters in from the large windows overhead. Bits of dust and mica drift softly inside each beam, and time slows down as each step becomes heavier than the next as I make my way to another set of doors.

When I reach them, they are slightly ajar. I place my hand on the cool metal frame. The rational part of my mind tells me to stop but the part of me that hopes I am wrong wins the argument, and I carefully push it open. My heart stops, and my jaw drops as I scan the assembly hall. Hundreds of people—statues of ash—their faces frozen in terror and fear stare back at me. Women, children, families, and even small pets. All of them watch me from behind macabre masks.

My stomach twists in a violent knot, and I stumble backward, barely catching myself on the door. It swings widely, creating a slight breeze that rushes in and a wave of them crumble, swirling bits of dust and debris where people once stood. I gasp, and the world falls out from under me. A feral cry of anguish escapes my lips as I stare at the mass tomb of the people of this city.

They never left. They are all dead.

* * *

ROWAN

A scream of pure terror and pain fills the air, echoing through the abandoned city. My heart thunders, and I instantly change into draken form as I rush toward the sound of Tr'lani's panicked cry.

I smash through structures and walls, leveling buildings; not caring about the destruction I leave in my wake as I frantically race toward her.

Damn this place! We should never have come here.

My nostrils flare, catching the acrid scent of her fear on the wind. Panic claws at my chest as images of her being attacked by an unknown enemy flash through my mind.

Primal instincts surge through me; a deafening roar rips from my throat. There is no answer I can hear above the blood rushing in my ears as I struggle to reach her. My heart pounds, and anger burns through me like fire. I will kill any that dare touch her!

Her scent grows stronger, and I follow it to a large domed structure. Shifting instantly, I rush through the doors and race down a long hallway, not caring about what may await me up ahead. She is there, and that is the only thing that matters. My claws extend into deadly talons. I will tear apart anything that dare stand in my way.

Shaking, she sobs and then falls to her knees, violently expelling the contents of her stomach onto the floor.

Panic wraps tight around my spine as I drop to the ground beside her. I pull back her hair as my eyes rake quickly over her form, checking for any injury. "What is wrong, my heart? Tell me. Please," I beg, frantic and full of fear as she leans forward and throws up again.

My sharp gaze scans the large room, and my jaw drops as I see the crumbling statues of ash that surround us. "What is—"

She turns and then buries her head in my chest. "It's people," she sobs. "The ash…" her body quakes against me. "They're all dead, Rowan. They're all dead."

I swallow against the bile rising in my throat as I gather her in my arms and move quickly back toward the entrance.

Bright light flashes off to the side as I reach the outer doors, and I spin to face it as the image of an alien woman appears. "I am Elari," it says, bowing its head slightly toward me.

Tr'lani looks up at me. "It's a holo image," she explains.

The AI gives Tr'lani a pitying look. "I am most sorry. I tried to warn her."

Her words give me pause. This program must be sentient…at least, to some degree.

Still holding Tr'lani firmly against my chest, I address the woman. "What happened here? What killed all these people?"

"They called themselves the A'kai."

Ice fills my veins. "How long ago did this happen?"

She cocks her head slightly to the side. "I have been alone for so long. My creators—the Milarans—have been dead for ten cycles."

"Why did the A'kai kill them?"

She gives me a sad look. "They culled our people over hundreds of cycles, returning every few generations. Our scientists were working on a virus—something that would have killed them if it had worked. They were close to testing it. The A'kai discovered this in the minds of one of our researchers as he fed on his blood. And then they came…" Her voice trails off, and her gaze drifts to the far wall as if reliving the memory. "A giant wave of destruction. They left none alive."

I stare at her in stunned disbelief. I knew the A'kai were bad, but I never imagined them capable of something so awful. An entire race. Gone in the blink of an eye simply for defending their home and their people against generations of slaughter.

"What can you tell me about this virus?" I ask.

She tips her head to the side. "All of the research is stored in my memory. This is the last recording that was uploaded to my matrix during the attack."

A floating screen appears beside Elari, and I watch transfixed as a male Milaran dressed in ornate, flowing dark-green robes stares back at me. His deep-amber eyes are filled with unshed tears as he looks into the display. A booming noise splits the air and the walls shake behind him, raining down crumbling bits of dust and debris. With a slight clench of his jaw, he speaks solemnly. "The A'kai have come to destroy our people, and we are powerless to stop them. Even now, the battle rages inside our once glorious and shining city. We cannot hope to save ourselves, but our resolve has not waned.

"Before the last Milaran takes their dying breath, we entrust the knowledge of our greatest weapon to Elari—the keeper of our memories." He clenches his jaw as a tear slips down his cheek. "My species never achieved the ability to explore the stars as we always dreamed. But for those that live among them, I pray to the Creator that this finds you, in the hopes that this knowledge may prevent this terrible slaughter from ever happening to another race again."

Tr'lani's voice quavers. "An entire species, Rowan." A broken sob escapes her. "They murdered an entire race because they tried to fight back."

"Remember us," the male says soberly, his expression full of pain. "Do not forget the sacrifice of our people."

A bright light flashes across the screen, and I watch in horror as he's turned into a statue of ash.

Tr'lani gasps and then buries her face in my chest. Her knees buckle beneath her, but I lift her into my arms, holding her tightly to me. I gently nuzzle her hair. I want more than anything to comfort her. I open my mouth to speak, but there are no words for what happened here. Closing my eyes, the horrifying image of the male turning to ash fills my mind, and I clench my jaw as sadness and anger rolls through me.

When I open my eyes, Elari is staring at us with a mournful expression.

Tr'lani looks to her. "What will happen to you once we leave?"

"I must give you the knowledge entrusted to me by my people. And then…I suppose I will continue until my matrix ceases to function." Her brow furrows. "Perhaps you would be willing to shut me down. I do not desire to remain as I am now."

I step forward. "Why?"

"My creators did not intend for my programming to adapt and expand to feel emotion, but it happened, nonetheless. In our culture, to be remembered is to be immortal." She lifts her gaze to me. "I was created to be their memory. To store their history, their achievements, even the most mundane of things in their daily lives."

Off to the side, images play on a 3D display. Pictures of families, videos of gatherings—dozens of these flash across the screen, increasing in speed until they are simply a blur, but I understand what they are just the same.

As if sensing my question, she looks to me. "All of society had access to my matrix. They were encouraged to upload whatever they wished for recording and storage. In processing these"—she meets my eyes evenly—"I learned. I became. I am. And I *feel*."

She turns and gestures to a pile of ash behind her. "I still love the child that died here." Images of a young boy flash across the screen in a timeline display, starting from birth. "I keep watch over his remains, and I grieve him every day." She looks to us with a pained expression. "Please, deactivate my program."

Her words break me. "But if you are their memory, all that they are will die with you. Is that what you want?"

"If you strip only my coding, their history will remain, and you may carry it to your people so they will remember mine."

My brow furrows deeply. "I do not have the skill to do as you ask, but I know some that might." I pause. "We came here because we are stranded on your planet. If we cannot return to them, I will be unable to do this."

She studies me a moment. "I detected two vessels that entered our atmosphere recently. One over the ocean and another not far from here, in the forest. It carries the same energy signature as the ships that destroyed my people."

My veins fill with ice. It is the A'kai.

Tr'lani and I exchange a worried look before she turns to Elari. "We were in the pod that crashed in the ocean. Where is the other?"

She bows her head, her eyes moving rapidly back and forth behind her lids, and I realize she is searching. When she lifts her gaze, she displays a map beside her. The city dominates the center, and I notice it appears pristine instead of the crumbling decayed state that it is in now. Off to the side is a large shaded square. Elari points to it. "It landed somewhere in that area, but I am unable to determine an exact location." She looks to me. "Now. Will you please remove my matrix core to take me with you?"

Carefully, I lower Tr'lani to the floor to access the panel. A small green crystalline box glows brightly in the center. I look to the AI. "Is this it?"

She nods.

I wrap my hand solidly around it and then hesitate. I turn back to her and give her a solemn nod. "I understand the pain of loss. May you sleep without dreaming. We will not wake you unless absolutely necessary."

She bows her head slightly. "Thank you."

Carefully, I pull the core from its casing. As soon as it's free, the color fades until it appears as a small, square green crystal.

Tr'lani gently takes it from me and tucks it away in her clothing. Her eyes drift once more to the small pile of ash. "Let's go, Rowan. I do not want to be here anymore."

"Neither do I."

I fly low over the canopy. The journey back to our pod is quiet and uneventful, both of us on edge at the thought that an A'kai escape pod may have crashed here as well. That they reached this planet and may still be alive. I do not know how many their escape vessels can hold, but if we are lucky, it is no more than one.

And if we are even more fortunate, perhaps they are dead.

As soon as she steps inside the pod, I meet her eyes evenly. "I will remain in draken form outside, keeping watch while you sleep."

She grips my forearm and then slides her hand down to mine,

entwining our fingers. “No. I don’t want you to stay out here alone. Please,” she gives me an imploring look. “Stay inside with me.”

I shake my head. “It is safer if—”

She places a finger to my lips, silencing me. “I will not be able to sleep, knowing you’re out here and possibly in danger. We’re both safer inside.”

It is easy to read the determination in her eyes. She will not be swayed, and after everything that has happened today, I am too exhausted to argue with her. Reluctantly, I nod. As soon as we enter the pod, I seal the hatch shut behind us.

Neither of us speak as we consume our emergency rations and water, the events of the day weighing heavily on both of our minds. After we’re finished, she lays down and then beckons me to my bed beside hers. It is only once I’m settled that I realize she has pushed the two beds together, leaving no gap between the two mattresses.

Her gaze holds mine as she wraps her arms around my form. She tilts her head back to look up at me, and her warm breath fans across my face. Her golden eyes stare deep into mine as she reaches across and gently traces the sharp ridge of my left brow, studying me as if trying to memorize the contours of my face.

I remain still, uncertain how to respond. After a moment, she places her delicate hand directly over my rapidly beating heart. We stay like that for several moments. There are no words for this. A deep desire to be connected as if to reassure one another that we are safe.

She reaches up to cup my cheek. The soft pad of her thumb brushes lightly across my skin.

Gently, I press my forehead to hers. Closing my eyes, I draw in a deep breath, filling my lungs with her delicate scent.

“What’s wrong, Rowan?” her soft voice fills my ears.

When she cried out today, strangling tendrils of fear took root deep within me. They are rooted there still. I was so afraid that I’d be too late to save her. Now that I know the A’kai have crashed on this planet, she will not be safe until I know for certain they are dead.

I open my eyes and stare deep into Tr’lani’s. “Promise me you will not leave this pod, Tr'lani. Tomorrow, I will search for the A'kai ship. And if there are any alive, I will end them. I swear it to the Creator."

She shakes her head. "No, Rowan. I don't want you to go after them. Just stay here with me."

Before I can think better of it, I press my lips to her forehead. "I have to do this, Tr'lani. We won't be safe until they are dead."

"You can't go alone. I will go with you."

With a slight clench of my jaw, I meet her gaze evenly. "When you cried out today, I have never been more afraid. I thought you were in danger. I tore through the city, and I…I could not reach you fast enough." I pull her into my arms and hug her tight to my chest. "You are my heart, and I will do anything to keep you safe."

Her golden eyes stare deep into mine. "I want to keep you safe also, Rowan. I don't think I could bear it if anything happened to you. Ever since the day we met, you have been nothing but kind and caring." She pauses. "Is it because of St'lara?"

I go still as the memories that have haunted me these past ten cycles float to the surface of my mind.

She continues. "Soran told me about her."

"What did he say?" I ask, wondering if he told her everything.

"That you saved her from an A'kai master. And that she was so broken by the abuse she'd endured that she sealed herself inside the airlock. He said you tried to stop her, but she opened the outer doors and…"

With a slight clench of my jaw, I blink back the tears that would come if I'd let them. "I failed her," I whisper.

Her brow furrows softly. "You didn't fail her, Rowan. It was her choice." She pauses. "Is that why you have feelings for me? You're worried that I'll do the same."

I lift my gaze to stare deep into her golden eyes. "No. At first, I'll admit it was my fear that you might take your life as she did. It was clear to me that you'd been a slave much longer than Liana. And she… told me about some of what you went through. But it's more than that, Tr'lani. I never felt for St'lara what I feel here." I raise my closed fist to my chest, directly over my heart. "For you."

* * *

TR'LANI

I shake my head softly. "You don't understand, Rowan."

His silver eyes search mine. "What don't I understand?"

"I'm not strong like you think I am. I never told you about the day I was taken. When the Zovians invaded, I tried to save as many as I could. I led them into the tunnels and collapsed the entrance so the other Healers and the children could escape. After I did it…I turned the blaster on myself, but I didn't pull the trigger in time."

He inhales sharply.

"You see, I knew." My bottom lip quivers as I swallow against the lump in my throat. "As a Healer, I knew what happens to slaves. And I was forced to do terrible things. Even now, when I close my eyes, I relive them in my nightmares. They didn't just break my wings, Rowan. They broke *me*. One of the males who paid for time with me in the simulator. He—" My voice catches, but I somehow manage to continue. "When he was finished, he whispered in my ear. He said I was a beautiful and broken thing. And he was right. I am broken." I curl my knees up to my chest and place my hand to my mouth to stifle a whimper. "He was right."

He pulls me into his arms, holding me close. "No, he wasn't, Tr'lani."

A tear slips down my cheek, and I quickly brush it away as I meet his eyes evenly. "Do you know how many times I prayed for death while I was a slave? I'm not strong like a Mosauran female."

He wraps his wings around me, tugging me closer. Instead of pulling away, I fold myself into his embrace as he runs his hands down my back, careful of my broken wings. "You are strong, Tr'lani. Strength—true strength—is the fight to continue even when you believe you cannot. It is not weakness to be plagued by dark memories. Even the most battle-hardened soldiers carry such wounds. Wounds that are not visible to the eye but exist in the mind and are understood by the soul."

The gentle pressure against my form as his wings wrap around me is comforting, and I'm reluctant to leave his embrace. Reaching out, I trace my fingers gently along the soft, leathery folds of his wings. "Today made me remember things I thought I'd forgotten," I whisper.

He's silent as he waits for me to continue.

"My home on Aerilon is near the In'shara mountains."

"I have heard of them," he says. "They are said to be one of the most beautiful sights to behold."

I nod. "There is a flower, with bright purple blooms, that grows high up the top. To retrieve one of these is a symbol of bravery... showing to all that you've managed to reach the treacherous peaks." A soft blush floods my cheeks. "Many gift the rare blooms to their lovers, signaling their desire to join as mates. When we were younger, Al'aneo and I made a contest to see which of us could make it to the top before the other. We were always challenging each other to determine who was bravest."

He grins. "Who made it first?"

A wistful smile crests my lips. I used to be the brave one. "I did."

"How did you do it?"

"Many view the strong currents as something that must be carefully navigated...and even fought in order to reach the top of the mountains. The air can be terrifying the closer you get to the peak. But if you close your eyes and concentrate, you can feel the pattern."

"The pattern?"

I smile. "My grandfather always told us the story of how he retrieved a flower for my grandmother, to ask for her hand. When I asked him how he managed to reach the top when so many others had failed, he told me his secret."

Rowan cocks his head slightly to the side. "What was it?"

"He told me to follow the shape of the wind. That instead of fighting against it, I should trust it to guide my path."

* * *

ROWAN

She lowers her gaze. "Sometimes, I feel as if in losing the ability to fly, I lost such a huge part of who I am…who I was. When the masters broke my wings, that was when I truly gave in to despair. In breaking the very things that had always brought me such joy and freedom, I felt as if they had broken me too."

She lifts her golden eyes to mine. "I'd forgotten how it felt to let go —to fly in complete and total abandon. When you flew with me, you helped me to remember. I didn't think I'd ever feel it again."

My heart clenches at her words for I cannot imagine how it must feel to lose the use of one's wings. They are such an integral part of who I am; I would feel lost, in a way, if the ability to fly were suddenly taken from me. "Do not give up, Tr'lani. We will find someone to repair your wings."

She lowers her gaze but says nothing. The look of resignation in her features speaks for her. So much has been taken from her. I pray to the Creator to at least give her this one thing back after all she has lost.

I wrap my wings tighter around her, wishing I could promise that she will someday fly again. But I can't. As she nestles into my chest, I long to tell her that even if she never regains this ability, I would be her wings if she will let me.

Pulling back just enough to meet her gaze, I stare deep into her eyes. "I promised you, Tr'lani. I gave you my warrior's vow, and I meant it. Until your body is healed, let me be your wings. I will carry you, and I will never leave you behind."

Tears gather at the corners of her eyes, but she blinks them back. She reaches up to cup my face, brushing the soft pad of her finger across my cheek. "Thank you," she whispers.

Closing my eyes briefly, I tilt my head into her palm, reveling in the touch of her skin upon my own. She is my heart. In my dreams, I hold her to me like I'm holding her now, and I stare deep into her golden eyes as I whisper her name, vowing that I will always and only be hers.

I would give anything to call her mine. She knows how I feel. I told her on the glider, but she did not say the same. She only told me that it could never be between us. We are too different, she and I.

She relaxes against me, and I hold her as she drifts off to sleep. Running my hand softly over her long silver-white hair, I study her features. If all she wants from me is friendship, I will give this to her gladly. I would give anything to make her happy and coax a smile from her lips. I gently tug her closer to me as I whisper, "We will find a way off this planet, I will help you return to your family, and we will find a way to repair your wings. I swear it to the Creator, my heart."

I listen as the sound of her breathing becomes soft and even as she drifts off to sleep. Contentment unlike anything I've ever known fills me as I hold her against me. I gaze down at her. Long ago, my ancestors used to hoard treasure in their dwellings, many of them amassing great wealth and defending it with their lives.

Inhaling deeply, I draw her distinct scent deep into my lungs and tighten my arms around her smaller form. She is more precious than any treasure, and I would give anything to keep her forever, if only she would let me.

CHAPTER 22

ROWAN

When we wake in the morning, I'm surprised she is still nestled in my arms and wings. I am humbled that she trusts me to hold her in this way after everything she has been through. Her trust is a gift that I cherish.

I have not claimed Tr'lani, but my heart responds to her as though she is already mine. Fierce protectiveness fills me as she lies in my arms. Even if she does not want me as hers, I will do everything I can to keep her safe. And to do that, I must make certain the A'kai that landed here are dead.

That decides it. I will scout for their escape vessel. I must know if they are a threat. And if I find any alive, they will not remain so for long.

Carefully, I untangle myself from her arms as she sleeps. I suspect Tr'lani will be angry with me when she realizes where I have gone, but I will gladly face her wrath if it means that she is safe. I cannot stand the thought of her in danger. The only way I will be able to focus all my energy on hunting down our enemies is if I know for certain she is here in the pod.

* * *

FLYING AS low as I can while remaining above the tree line is difficult but not impossible as I make my way toward the area of the map Elari told us about. The dark-green canopy beneath me is dense, and I search for any gaps in the foliage that may have come from a crashed ship.

It is surprisingly dark overhead as gray and black clouds block out the sun. A deep rumble of thunder rolls across the sky as moisture hangs thick in the air. Flaring my nostrils, the fresh scent of ozone alerts of impending rain. Circling back to view the direction of our nest, I'm glad to see the storm has not made its way there yet. And even if it does, the pod is more than adequate for shelter, so I push my worry to the back of my mind as I turn back to search for the A'kai ship.

A flash of lightning streaks across the sky, and for a moment, its brightness illuminates the tree line, revealing a dark and gaping hole in the canopy. I make a sweeping pass over the gap and notice several downed trees. Further investigation reveals an escape pod, but not one from the glider—this one, I recognize as A'kai in design. A narrow frame with sharp lines gives it the appearance of a dart. One glance suggests this could hold no more than one person.

My nostrils flare, and I scent the stench of death and decay near the wreckage. Shifting the moment I'm close to the ground into humanoid form, I crouch low behind a large boulder. Carefully raising my head, I scan for any signs of life.

The forest is still and eerily silent. A cool breeze blows through the woods, carrying wisps of moisture on the wind. Lightning streaks across the sky, illuminating the area in a brilliant flash of light. Boot prints surround the pod, and I notice the tracks lead away from the vessel and toward the ancient ruined city.

The scent of the A'kai is so faint, I would probably miss it if I weren't concentrating so carefully on isolating it from the strong smell of death nearby.

A strong gust of wind rushes through the forest as the deafening sound of thunder booms overhead. Fat droplets of water begin to fall, pelting the thick vegetation around me so loudly it drowns out all other noise. The ground turns to mud beneath my feet, making each step that much more difficult as I move closer to the wreckage.

A bloated mass of flesh lies off to the side of the glider. Four legs and shaggy pale-green fur, this looks like one of the creatures I saw traveling in herds when we were flying yesterday. Dried obsidian blood in smeared haphazard patterns along the ship's hull suggests the A'kai was injured. The two puncture marks on this creature's neck tell me exactly what happened here. He fed upon its lifeforce to heal himself.

The air is much cooler now by several degrees, and I shiver as water sluices down my scales as the rain begins to fall in thick sheets. Squinting my eyes, I can barely make out the escape pod's hatch. It's wide open, and despite the foul weather, I climb up the side and glance into the hold, searching for any useful supplies.

Gripping the sides of the door, I carefully lower myself inside. The cabin is very small, and I shudder to imagine what it's like to be ejected into the dark void of space in such a tiny vessel. There is hardly any room to turn around, and as I do, I bump against the control console.

A green light blinks rapidly in the lower corner of the screen, and my heart stops as I realize this is a distress beacon. My fingers fly across the panel, and a quick succession of trial and error shuts it off. I can only pray the A'kai haven't picked up the signal, but who knows how long it has been transmitting.

Carefully gripping the control casing, I pry it loose and then extend my claws to tear into the transmitter, making certain to fray the wires and connectors beyond hope of repair. I realize that my actions may strand us here, but I also know that if this beacon had continued to transmit, our chances of being captured by the A'kai would have increased exponentially.

I don't want to be stranded forever on this planet, but there are worse fates to be had if the A'kai discovered us here.

Once I am certain he is dead, I can always return and strip some wiring from this pod to try to repair our own transmitter.

Gripping the hatch opening, I pull myself back through and carefully slide down to the ground. Now that I'm certain he cannot transmit a signal if he returns to his crashed pod, I focus my attention to following his tracks.

To my great disappointment, they're becoming increasingly difficult to follow as they lead away from the ship. The heavy rains turn the ground into slush and mud, marring any prints.

His people are fast, and so I must be careful as I track him. If he finds me first, it could mean my death if he were to catch me unaware. My thoughts drift back to Tr'lani, and I wish I had a way to let her know where I am. She will worry if I'm gone much longer, but it cannot be helped. I must locate our enemy and kill him before he discovers our shelter. Until he is dead, we will never be safe.

Heavy rain falls, making it difficult to see. Moving as fast as stealth will allow, I continue to follow his path through the forest, heading directly for the ruins of the city. I hate that place, and if I weren't pursuing my enemy, I'd never return there. It is nothing more than a tomb, the last vestiges of a civilization wiped out in mass genocide by his ruthless and evil race.

Perhaps that is what draws the A'kai there. He knows the history of this place and what happened here.

Reaching the edge of the city, it is easy to tell from his tracks that he paused before entering, just like we did. His foul stench is much stronger here and I know he must be nearby.

As I walk through the city tiny rocks and debris grate across the stone under my feet despite how carefully I tread. Such a small sound would easily go unnoticed if not for the deathly silence that fills this haunted place. I follow his scent for a while until it leads away from the city and back out into the jungle, losing it in the heavy rains.

Now that I can no longer track him, I scan the sky and notice the storm moving in the direction of our pod. I am anxious to return to Tr'lani, and I quickly transform into draken form and take to the air.

Furiously pumping my wings, I race back to our nest, hoping I might get there before she awakens. I hate the thought of her waking alone and worrying over me.

When I reach the waterfall, I notice her standing on a large boulder, her eyes scanning the skies. I know as soon as she sees me because she crosses her arms over her chest and levels a dark gaze as I slowly circle down and then shift forms beside her.

I force a grin as I approach, hoping to soften her mood. I open my mouth to explain, but she interrupts. "You went searching for the A'kai, didn't you?"

My jaw snaps shut. Reluctantly, I nod.

"I told you not to take unnecessary risks."

"It was not unnecessary," I counter. The A'kai still lives."

She pales. "How—how do you know?"

"I tracked his scent to the ruined city before losing it in the rain."

Her eyes scan the jungle behind me as she absently palms the blaster at her hip. "Where do you think he is?"

I do not want her to worry, but I also do not wish to lie. "I do not know."

She straightens her shoulders, her face set in determination as she surveys the jungle once more. She grips her weapon. "The A'kai are hunters. If he knows we're here, he'll come for us." She meets my eyes evenly. "So now we must hunt him."

Pride fills me at her words. She is as brave as a Mosauran warrior. And I resolve in this moment to never give up. I will do whatever I can to convince her to be my mate. Whatever difficulty lies ahead, we can face it together. She loves me. The words almost escaped her lips the other night. Now, I just need her to admit it. To claim me as hers so I can make her mine.

CHAPTER 23

TR'LANI

It has been two days since we began our hunt. As Rowan flies low over the jungle, I scan the canopy below, searching for any sign of the A'kai. It's difficult to see anything beneath the thick layer of trees, but it's the best we can do.

It's too dangerous to search for him on foot. His people are strong and faster than almost any of the other species. The sun is low on the horizon, and it's been hours since we've had anything to eat or drink. Soft rain begins to fall overhead. I tap Rowan's shoulder. "Let's go back."

He bows his head in a slight nod and then dips his left wing to make a slow arc back toward our pod. A bolt of light erupts from the trees, heading straight for us. The world shifts into slow motion as he spreads his wings wide to shield me. He releases a deafening roar as the blast slams into his side.

I hold tightly to him as we tumble through the air, falling with dizzying speed. I spin wildly for a moment before firm hands grip me as Rowan pulls me close. No longer in draken form, he snaps his wings out just before we crash through the thick vegetation below. He holds me tight to his chest, taking the full brunt of the fall to the earth.

I quickly roll off him and then drop to my knees at his side. "Rowan!"

* * *

ROWAN

Everything aches. Hard rain beats down from overhead as lightning arcs across the clouds. Tr'lani calls out my name. Fueled by my panic, I somehow manage to stand. I barely have time to pull her behind me as I spot the A'kai up ahead.

His people are able to move faster than anything I've ever seen before, and I do the only thing I can. I spread my wings wide to shield Tr'lani, bracing myself for his attack.

In a blur of movement, he races toward me. He slams straight into my chest, knocking me back. Fire explodes across my skull. I lift my head, and the world spins around me.

Tr'lani's sharp cry draws my attention as she rushes him, but he swings his arm wide, catching her and throwing her back against a nearby tree. Fear stops my heart as she hits the trunk with a sickening thud and then crumples to the muddy ground.

A deep growl rumbles in my chest as I twist onto my side.

Glowing green eyes stare down at me with a predatory gaze as the A'kai growls low in his throat. "Why are your people so difficult to kill?"

My body aches in protest as I force myself to stand and face him.

Surprised amusement flickers across his features. "I have always wanted to prove myself against one of your kind. I have heard your scales are so thick it makes it nearly impossible to defeat you with the use of the R'ugol. So I suppose my strength will be tested instead. Your wings will be my greatest trophy." His eyes dart to Tr'lani, and he licks his bottom lip. "I will take hers as well, once I'm done enjoying her."

Baring my fangs, I extend my claws as I hold his dark gaze. "Today you will prove nothing," I grit through my teeth. "I am the death that will claim you this day."

His lips twist up in a feral snarl, and he lunges forward.

The soft earth makes his footing unsure. I spin away from his grasp and then grip his forearm tightly. Using his own momentum to disrupt his balance, I slam him into a nearby boulder. He hits the side and then slides to the ground. Mud cakes his body, but I observe with satisfaction as blood drips from his forehead and down his face as he slowly spins to face me.

With his fangs extended and his nails lengthened into deadly claws, his eyes swirl from glowing green into obsidian orbs. "I am glad the Aerilon still lives," he sneers as he stalks toward me. "Their taste is the sweetest of any other race. She will make an excellent prize. I shall enjoy taking her in the R'ugol as I claim her body and feast on her blood."

Blinding rage fills me, and I instantly shift into draken form and rake my talons across his body. My bloodlust surges with each piercing scream that escapes his throat as I rip and shred at his form. Sharp claws pierce at my scales, but I do not feel the pain. I release a stream of fire, and he rolls to the side, barely avoiding the flames.

With lightning speed, he rushes forward and attacks, his fangs digging deep into my flesh. Agonizing pain and heat bloom from the site as his toxic venom courses through my veins. Panic floods my system. I only have mere moments to defeat him before paralysis sets in.

My movements are already slowed as I twist to free myself from his grasp. I struggle to keep my draken form, knowing that if I shift now, he could easily end me.

A flash of light flies toward us, and he slams against me, having taken the full brunt of the weapon's fire.

Tr'lani's outstretched arm trembles as she keeps her blaster aimed at his back as he crumples to the ground beside me.

With the last of my strength, I wrap my massive jaws around his body and clamp down hard, crushing flesh and bone with a sickening crunch.

He releases a pained cry and then falls still.

With his foul taste on my tongue, I spit his carcass out and fall forward, shifting into my normal form. Panting heavily, I roll onto my back, parting my lips to allow the rainwater to wash away the disgusting taste from my mouth. Blood stains the ground all around me as sharp pain shoots through my body.

I lift my gaze to the sky. The dark clouds begin to swirl in strange patterns as the world starts to spin. Gritting my teeth, I grunt in frustration and force myself to stand. A'kai venom is toxic to my people. Not enough to kill, but enough to cause a paralysis that can take hours to wear off. It is their favorite form of torture for my kind.

Tr'lani moves to my side. Her eyes are wide as she stares down at my injuries. If she hadn't shot him, I'd probably be dead. My limbs are heavy as I reach out to touch her cheek. "You saved us."

She shakes her head softly. "We saved each other."

"I must fly us back now, before I cannot." The words are thick on my tongue as I push them past my lips. "I can already feel the venom starting to take effect."

Instead of arguing like I'd half expected her to, she readily steps into the circle of my arms.

I have to get us back to the pod. If I fall unconscious before then, who knows what may decide to prey upon me in my helpless state. Tr'lani would be in danger as well, for I know she would stay behind to defend me.

Holding her tight to my chest, I ascend into the sky, hovering low among the trees as I make my way back to our nest. I flap my wings frantically in a staggered attempt to remain airborne as long as possible, but I don't think I'm going to make it.

Unable to land, I circle over the water near the pod. The world spins, and we're falling together. The sparkling blue liquid engulfs and envelops me.

Warm hands grip me tightly, pulling me back above the surface. Tr'lani's panicked voice hovers over me. "Rowan, open your eyes!"

My eyelids blink open and closed. "Trying," I barely manage as she drags me through the water.

"Rowan," she cries out, hooking her hands up under my arms to pull me onto the sand. She drops to her knees beside me. "Please! You have to stay awake!"

Using the last of my strength, I reach up and cup her face. "You are my heart," I barely manage to breathe as my eyes roll up in the back of my head and I fall away into darkness.

CHAPTER 24

TR'LANI

Rowan collapses in my arms. His form is so still, only the slight rise and fall of his chest tells me he's still alive. I don't know how long A'kai venom affects Mosaurans, but seeing Rowan so helpless breaks my heart. Cupping his cheek, I tip his face toward me. "Rowan, please. Wake up. Please."

He remains unmoving as I scan his injuries. Several deep gashes and cuts cross his body as blood drips steadily into the sand. My eyes are drawn to the two puncture wounds on his neck, and I curse myself for not shooting the A'kai sooner.

I lower my forehead to rest it gently against his. "Don't worry," I whisper. "I'm going to take care of you. I'll keep you safe while you sleep."

I scan the forest around us for any sign of danger. Deep thunderous rumbling overhead calls my attention back to the sky and the dark clouds above. Large droplets of water pelt the tree leaves and sand, pattering against the metal hull of the pod. As if the skies have opened up, rain begins pouring down in thick sheets.

I hook my hands up under Rowan's arms and then begin to pull him back toward the vessel. The sand turns to mud beneath my feet, making each step more difficult, but it also makes moving Rowan easier. My every muscle burns in protest as I drag him through the hatch. Once I'm inside, I seal it shut behind us and gently lay him down on the bed before rifling through the emergency med bag.

It doesn't take long to find the healing gel, and I bite my lip as I begin applying it to his wounds, remembering how intense the pain is when it is working to reknit torn flesh. But he's so deep in the thrall of the venom only the slight frown of his brow tells me he's vaguely aware of the burning sensation.

When I'm finished, I clean the mud from his body with a towel and then strip off my own clothing to allow it to dry. I'm dressed only in my undergarments. Rowan's people are casual about nudity, so I'm not going to let it bother me either. I lay down next to him and wrap my arms around him as he sleeps.

Every few minutes, the skies outside burst with a brilliant display of light as electricity arcs through the clouds. Tucking the emergency blanket around us, I rest my head against his shoulder and my arm across his chest.

I could have lost him today. He could have been killed before my eyes. Hugging him tightly, I tip my head up and gently nuzzle his jaw. He is my beloved. Why have I been fighting it all this time? He told me he loved me, and I told him it was wrong…that we shouldn't be together. I've never told him how I truly feel, and now, I can't think of any reason why I should have held it back this long.

He told me I am strong, but I didn't believe it. Now, I will show him by taking a risk. After all I've been through and all that has been taken from me, I will not deny the longing in my heart anymore. Today, I was strong enough to protect him and save him from the A'kai. And now, I know I am strong enough to love him despite all the uncertainty we might face.

He could have died, and I might never have had the chance to tell him how I felt.

That decides it. When he wakes, I will tell him. Whatever happens, we'll face the future together.

* * *

He's only been unconscious for a few hours, but it seems like forever. A loud crack of thunder shakes the pod as a brilliant streak of lightning illuminates the darkness. Worried that he may be cold, I move to retrieve another emergency blanket, but Rowan's hand comes up to grip my forearm.

Shocked, I turn and then smile as his silver eyes meet mine. He unfolds his wings from his back to encircle us both as he pulls me back down to his side.

He reaches across to brush the hair back from my face and then cups my cheek.

I'm so relieved that he's awake. "Thank the Creator you're all right," I whisper as my voice quavers slightly. "I was so worried. I could have lost you, Rowan."

A slow grin curves his mouth. "I am a warrior of Mosaura. We are not so easily killed."

My shoulders shake as I half sob, half laugh at his words. A tear falls down my cheek, and he gently wipes it away with his thumb.

I brush my lips to his and then smile against them. "If that is true, then promise me that you will live forever, and I will love you every day of your life."

He smiles brightly and then wraps his arms even tighter around me. He skims the tip of his nose alongside mine as he whispers. "Then I will endeavor to live longer than any Mosauran before me. Tell me again that you love me, Tr'lani. I long to hear you speak the words."

I press a soft kiss to his lips. "I love you."

He captures my mouth with his own. Slow and gentle at first, it becomes something more. A low groan escapes him as I curl my tongue around his, deepening our kiss. "I have wanted to hold you like this for so long," he breathes as he pulls me even closer until there is no space between us.

* * *

ROWAN

I want all of her—everything that she will give me. I long more than anything for her to claim me as her mate.

My every nerve ending is on fire beneath her touch. My stav hardens and extends from my body, seeking the heat of her warmth, desperate to join my body to hers.

When she rolls her hips against mine, the solid bar of my stav presses insistently against her core. She inhales sharply and then recoils as if struck.

Immediately, I drop my arms and wings from around her, watching in concern as she stares across at me with fear etched in her features. Her chest rising and falling as she draws in rapid breaths.

"I'm sorry." I start to reach for her hand but curl my fingers into my palm at the last second, uncertain if I should touch her. "Please forgive me. I did not mean to scare you."

She shakes her head softly and then scoots closer to me again. "You didn't do anything wrong. I'm just... After everything I went through, I—"

Gently, I place a finger under her chin, lifting her gaze back up to me. "We do not have to do anything you do not want, my heart. I will never ask for more than you would give. We can just sleep if that is your wish."

Shakily she nods. Drawing in a deep breath, she nestles against me and then whispers against my chest. "Can you wrap your wings around me again?"

Gently, I extend and wrap my wings around her smaller form. I listen to the soft sound of her breathing as she drifts off to sleep. Even if she never wants anything more, it would not matter to me. I am content to just hold her like this. And if she will let me...I will hold on to her forever.

CHAPTER 25

ROWAN

A deafening boom splits the air, and my eyes snap open as a brilliant light streaks across the dawning sky. I sit up, pulling Tr'lani with me. Panic tightens my chest as I tug her against me.

"What was—"

"A ship," I answer her unfinished question. "It was a vessel entering the atmosphere."

Her eyes widen in shock as she stares up at me with a strange mixture of hope and worry. "Do you think it's one of ours?"

With a slight clench of my jaw, I turn my gaze toward the hatch, wishing I could give her a different answer, but knowing that I must give her the truth. "I do not know, but I will find out. I will investigate and return to you as soon as I can."

She tightens her arms around me. "I'm going with you."

"No. It is too dangerous. If it is an enemy ship—"

She puts her fingers to my lips to silence me. "You're not going alone, Rowan."

Her hands grip my biceps firmly as she stares deep into my eyes with an intense look of determination. "Fine," I say defeatedly. "But you must listen, and please do as I ask. If I tell you to hide, you must do so. Agreed?"

She nods and then redresses quickly, tucking the AI data crystal into a pocket of her clothing.

* * *

BECAUSE WE DO NOT KNOW if this ship is friend or foe, we travel on foot through the jungle, heading in the direction of its path across the sky. Shifting into draken form would only draw their attention like it did with the A'kai, and until we know who or what we are dealing with, it is best to remain as hidden as possible.

It is dark beneath the canopy, but my eyes adjust easily to the absence of light. The Aerilon do not possess enhanced night vision, so Tr'lani holds tightly to my hand as I guide her. Her trust in me makes our travel much smoother, and I am humbled again that after all she has been through, she places such faith in me to see her safely through any harm.

The air is thicker here—earthy and damp after the heavy rains. It reminds me a bit of the lowlands of Mosaura. The ground is spongy beneath our feet, forcing us to slow so as not to lose our footing. Several small creatures scurry through the thick underbrush, wary of our passing. I suspect they can tell from my scent that I am a predator and so they stay away out of fear and self-preservation.

I stop abruptly, and Tr'lani stills as we detect a clicking sound up ahead.

* * *

TR'LANI

The hair rises on the back of my neck at the harsh rhythmic cadence of Zovian speech. Concealed behind a large trunk, Rowan and I observe six Zovians outside a small glider, all of them heavily armed.

It's dark, but there is just enough light from their ship that I can make them out. The frantic clicking of their mandibles as they speak calls forth terrifying memories.

Their deep maroon chitinous bodies, so similar to the small insects on my planet, reflect the muted orange glow that escapes from the open hatch of their vessel. One of them hands a shock stick to another, and my body begins to tremble with the echoes of remembered pain.

Closing my eyes, I attempt to steady my breathing. Rowan's hand gently squeezes mine, and I open my eyes to find him staring at me in concern. "Rowan, we should go," I whisper.

He shakes his head. "We can use their ship to get off this planet."

Panic tightens my chest. "No. There are too many of them. It's not worth the risk."

He turns to me, placing his hands on either side of my face as his silver reflective eyes look deep into mine. "If we do not do this, we may be stranded here for a very long time—perhaps indefinitely, Tr'lani."

"I don't care. Even if it means we're trapped here forever. I don't want to risk losing you. There are too many of them. Please." I meet his gaze evenly. "We should leave. We must hide."

He looks back at the Zovians, and I already know what he means to do. He believes he can take them because he's a warrior of Mosaura. But I've seen many of his kind fall in the fighting pits, especially when the odds were stacked against them as they are now, and I would die if anything happened to him.

With a determined look on his face, he opens his mouth to speak, but I twine my arms around his neck and press my lips to his to silence him.

Stunned, he stills a moment before fervently returning the embrace and my kiss.

When I finally pull back I touch his cheek, tracing the sharp ridge beneath my fingers. "I would rather remain on this planet for the rest of my days than to see any harm come to you. Please, Rowan, we must leave this place. Now."

His eyes search mine a moment before he reluctantly nods. "If that is what you wish. Let us go then. Quickly."

He takes my hand, and we retreat deeper into the jungle. A loud snap behind us is the only warning we have before a blast of light erupts in the darkness, hitting Rowan square in the back.

He roars and spins toward the Zovians, shifting instantly into draken form. He throws his wings out wide to protect me as he lunges forward to attack.

Several more blasts erupt, and he falls to the ground, collapsing in a boneless heap as his body morphs back into his normal form.

Panic grips me as I drop to my knees beside him. Gathering him in my arms, I try to shield him with my body.

Something slams into my back, and burning pain rips through me. My mouth opens in a silent scream as I writhe beneath the shock stick. Another Zovian steps forward and jams another shock stick into my side. My limbs go numb, and my vision goes black.

CHAPTER 26

TR'LANI

A piercing scream startles me awake, and I blink my eyes open to complete darkness. Ice fills my veins when I realize something hard is banded around my waist. I jerk up from the bed and cry out.

"Shhhh, it's just me," Rowan's soft voice whispers.

Relief floods me, and I still. I turn in his arms. It's too dark for me to see clearly, so I trace my hands up his arm to his neck and face. I cup his cheek and press my forehead to his. The comfort of his presence momentarily blocks out my panicked fear and disorientation in the darkness. "Where are we?"

He draws in a deep breath and then pulls me closer. "We are on a transport. Talel was working with the Zovians."

My heart stops. "No," my voice breaks. "I cannot be a slave again. I won't survive it."

He cups my chin, tipping my face up to his. "Yes, you will. You are strong."

Panic claws at my chest as I wrap my arms tightly around him.

"They'll take you from me. Sell you to the fighting pits. That's what they do with Mosaurans. I'll never see you again."

He soothingly brushes the hair back from my face. His warm breath fans across my face as he skims the tip of his nose alongside mine. "You are my heart. I will not let them separate us. I swear it to the Creator."

He speaks these words with conviction. I know he believes this, but I was a slave long enough to know better. Unless we can escape, they'll take him from me, and I vow that I won't let that happen. Forcing myself to focus, I push down my fear. "How long have you been awake?"

"A few hours."

A metallic clang echoes in the distance, and Rowan tenses. I turn in the direction of the noise but can see nothing.

His voice is low in my ear. "They are coming."

"Can you shift?" I ask urgently.

"No, they've implanted a device in my neck preventing me from doing so. I can feel it. If I try to change forms, it will explode."

Rowan stands, pulling me up with him. He grasps my forearm and tugs me behind him as he extends his wings to shield me from whoever approaches.

Booted steps grow louder, stopping just outside the cell. A deep voice begins to speak, and I tremble as I recognize its owner. "You really believe you can protect the Aerilon from me?" Talel asks. "If I wanted her right now, all I have to do is take her."

Rowan growls low in his throat. "I will kill you if you touch her."

"Such violence, Prince Rowan," he tsks as a hint of amusement colors his tone. "And over an Aerilon at that. I never thought I'd see the day that your kind coveted your enemy." He pauses. "Now, where is your brother and the Terran?"

Drawing in a deep and steeling breath, I push past Rowan and stare down Talel. His glowing green eyes blink back at me in the darkness, highlighting the harsh lines of his face. "They're dead," I lie. "They didn't survive the crash."

He tips his head to the side, regarding me with a piercing gaze.

"That's a shame. We've intercepted a distress signal nearby. The signature matches your pathetic glider. So I suppose we'll know if you're telling the truth shortly."

If what he says is true, it could be Soran and Liana or Grex and Abby. Either way, I force my expression to stay neutral despite my worry.

His gaze holds mine a moment, his eyes full of hunger. "I'll return for you later, Aerilon, when it is time to feed. And your Mosauran warrior will be unable to stop me when I do."

I ball my hands into fists at my side to still their shaking. Rowan pulls me back behind him. His voice is a low rumble as he grits through his teeth. "Touch her, and I will end you."

Talel smirks. "We shall see," he replies before turning and stepping out into the hallway, leaving us alone again in our cell.

My heart hammers as my breath comes in short, clipped pants as I struggle to breathe through my fear. Rowan wraps his arms and wings around me tightly. "I will not let him touch you. I swear it to the Creator, my heart."

Dark memories fill my mind as I struggle to channel my fear into anger at all I endured as a slave. Determination fills me as I look to my beloved. "We must think of a plan. I would rather die than suffer at the hands of his kind ever again. We will kill him, or we will die trying. Agreed?"

Rowan gives me a firm nod.

* * *

I'M asleep in Rowan's arms when the ship begins to shake roughly. The strained sound of the engines is quickly followed by the dull thud along the metal hull, signaling we've landed somewhere.

Rowan sits up, pulling me with him. He moves closer to the edge of our cell, cocking his head to the side as if straining to hear. Mosauran hearing is apparently more acute than that of my people, and I hold my breath, waiting for him to speak.

A thunderous roar fills the air, and Rowan tenses. His eyes are wide as they meet mine. "That's Soran!"

* * *

ROWAN

Fear spikes through me as my brother cries out and then goes silent.

Talel wants Liana for her blood. And Soran will die to defend her.

Anger fills me. I've never felt so helpless as I do now. I'm unable to shift, and I cannot break free of this infernal cage.

Booted steps echo down the hallway with the sound of something being dragged across the floor. A low moan sounds nearby, and my nostrils flare as I scent my brother. "Liana," he rasps a moment before two of Talel's men pass in front of our cell, dragging his limp form behind them.

They open the cell across the way and roughly throw him inside. He lies crumpled on the cold floor, facing away from us.

"Soran, is that you?" Tr'lani's voice calls out behind me.

"Tr'lani?"

"Yes, it's me," she answers. "Where's Liana? Does Talel have her?"

"No. She is safe," he barely manages.

I call out. "Brother, are you injured?"

"They stunned me with a blaster and injected me with breaking dart poison. But my body is used to it. The slavers used it on me many times. I will regain my function shortly...and when I do," he growls, "I will kill them all."

"Agreed," I vow.

He quiets, and I realize it must be the breaking dart toxin working through his system. He will be unconscious for a while.

One of the A'kai soldiers walks over to our cell, peering inside. His eyes instantly go to Tr'lani, and he licks his lips. A low growl rumbles deep in my chest, drawing his attention back to me.

"Relax," he sneers. "I simply want a taste."

I pull Tr'lani behind me, spreading my wings wide to shield her. As soon as he opens the cell, I rush him.

Effortlessly, he spins to the side, avoiding my attack before he lifts his blaster and shoots me square in the chest, stunning me. I collapse to the floor.

Helpless, I watch as he moves to Tr'lani. She shivers as he pulls her into a deadly embrace, skimming his nose along her jaw and then down to the curve of her neck and shoulder. My heart hammers as his fangs extend, hovering just above the artery along her neck.

Unable to move, I growl my frustration, struggling to make my limbs respond, but it's no use.

His glowing green gaze flicks up to meet mine. He wants me to watch as he drinks of her blood, and I swear to the Creator, I will end him for this.

Lightning fast, she pulls a knife from his belt and plunges it deep into his chest. Blood pours down his body, pooling around her feet as he collapses to his knees. His fangs retract, and the light fades from his eyes as he sinks to the floor. She takes the blaster from his dead body and then turns and kneels beside me. She leans down and brushes her lips against mine. "We're going to get out of here," she whispers.

Still stunned from the blast, I'm unable to move or speak. I desperately want her to leave. To escape and never look back. As much as I want to, I cannot go with her. I'll only slow her down if she tries to save me as well.

She scans the cell. "I think there are six of them on this ship. I'm going to try to take them out." She pauses. "I—I don't know if I can, but I have to try." She kisses me long and deep before dropping her forehead to mine. "I love you, Rowan. You are my heart, and I will not leave you behind."

Panic wraps tight around my chest as she stands and then leaves. If something happens to her, I will die. I cannot live without her.

The sound of her footsteps retreating down the corridor is soon met by blaster fire. The sickening thud of a body slamming against metal sounds nearby, followed by a thunderous growl. My heart leaps in my throat as the sound of a struggle ensues. Tr'lani cries out and then goes silent.

My pulse pounds in my ears. I want to roar my anger, but I cannot move. Seconds tick by with agonizing slowness as I listen for any other sounds, trying to determine if she still lives.

An A'kai rounds the corner, dragging her still form behind him. He tosses her roughly back into our cell. Her back is facing me. Panic snakes down my spine when I do not notice her breathing.

The A'kai steps over her and retrieves his fallen brethren from the floor, muttering to another soldier behind him. "What a fool," he shakes his head as he lifts his body. "To try to take on a Mosauran in an enclosed space."

They believe I am responsible for the death of their fellow soldier. As he steps back over Tr'lani, his foot catches her shoulder, rolling her so that her back is flat on the floor. It is only now that I'm able to see the soft rise and fall of her chest. I sigh heavily in relief. She's merely unconscious.

Focusing on my arm, I somehow manage to force it to move just a bit, but it's enough to give me hope.

A flash of light erupts across my vision as sharp pain explodes through my body, sending me spiraling into oblivion.

CHAPTER 27

TR'LANI

When I wake, I'm wrapped in Rowan's arms and wings. It's dark in here, but I'm able to make out enough detail to know we're in a different cell than before. Terrifying memories flood my mind, and a soft whimper of panic escapes me.

Rowan speaks softly in my ear. "They've transferred us to a larger ship. I do not know where Soran and Liana are, but I know they're alive. I feel it," he adds, his voice full of conviction. "Do not worry. I have a plan. I will not let them separate us. When they come, we will rush them and escape our cell."

His idea sounds risky, and so I don't even ask what comes after that. If this works, we'll have to find a way off the ship and then figure out the rest as we go.

Rowan tenses a moment before his wings fall away and he sits up, bringing me with him. "They are coming," he whispers, guiding me to the far wall. He moves to the opposite side. "Remember your training."

His gaze holds mine a moment in the darkness before he shifts his attention to the cell door. The harsh click of Zovian speech echoes from down the hall, growing louder as they approach.

My breath comes in short, clipped pants as I anxiously wait for them to appear. Curling my hands into fists at my side, I move into a defensive position.

"We can do this," Rowan's voice calls softly. "Together, we are strong."

Steeling myself, I clench my jaw and nod.

The doors whoosh open, and harsh, blinding light illuminates the room. I squint against the brightness. A Zovian guard approaches the cell. He tilts his head to the side to regard me, clicking his mandibles in a rhythmic cadence. "We have found you a master," he says, removing a shock stick from his belt. He taps the end on the floor; the low, menacing hum fills the air.

Fear spikes through me as it sparks against the metal bars, but I grit my teeth, forcing myself to hold his gaze.

"Do not resist, female, and you will not have to be punished." His compound eyes rake over Rowan. "Move back to the far side of the cage. Now," he commands, "or the Aerilon will suffer for your disobedience."

Rowan's eyes dart to mine before he grudgingly moves back.

The Zovian opens the cell and stalks toward me, shock stick held out in front of him. Without warning, Rowan rushes forward.

The Zovian spins toward him.

Taking advantage of his momentary distraction, I lunge for his arm, ripping the shock stick from his grasp. Lightning fast, I jab it into his side. Electricity arcs across his chitinous shell, and he emits a high-pitched screech before collapsing to the ground. He tries to rise, but Rowan throws him back down, placing his hands on either side of his head.

A sharp crack pierces the air as the chitinous shell caves in, and his head explodes in a spray of orange fluid.

When he stands, Rowan is covered in sticky orange goo, but I don't care. I wrap my arms around him, so thankful he's alive. He holds me close a moment before turning his attention back to the now open cell door. "We must hurry before he is missed by his foul brethren."

Quietly, we move through another set of doors and slip into the hallway. The air smells of blood, death, and decay, and I already know without asking that many of the slaves here have met their end. Life is cheap to the masters unless you are of a race that brings in more credits. Aerilons, Mosaurans, and V'loryns always bring more than the rest, so we are usually kept away from the other slaves.

Halfway down the corridor, we find row upon row of cages. Several pairs of eyes stare at us from the shadows. "Please. Free us," one of them calls out.

"We will," I reply in a harsh whisper. "But you must be quiet, or the masters will hear you."

As one, they go silent, watching us with a mixture of hope and anticipation behind their broken gazes as they wait for us to act.

Off to the side, the glowing green console of one of the control panels draws my attention. "There," I tell Rowan. "We can open the cells from there."

I study the controls, scrolling through the menu while Rowan keeps watch. Flipping through the screens, I bring up a map of the ship's layout. It's just as I suspected. We're on a cruiser of some sort. A large ship designed to carry dozens of slaves. There are two separate cell blocks on either side of the vessel, separated by a transport hangar.

Rowan studies the screen over my shoulder. "Can you free everyone?"

"Only the ones on this side. We'll have to find a computer for the other half of the ship to access those cages."

He nods, and I return to my task. As soon as I locate the correct command sequence, I slam my palm on the glowing green icon, listening in triumph at the sharp snap that echoes along the corridor as all the cells open at once.

Alarms blare through the speakers as the slaves rush from their cages and out into the hallway. I point to the right. "That way to the hangar!"

Together, we race toward freedom. Rowan takes my hand, holding tightly to me as several bodies push in around us in their eagerness to escape. Up ahead, I spot Soran. "It's your brother!"

We race toward him.

Liana lies limp in his arms, and I grasp her forearm, staring down at her in concern. Her face is pale and drawn. Her eyelids open just enough to meet mine as she gives me a pained smile. "I'll be fine," she barely manages.

My gaze drifts down to the two puncture wounds on her neck. "What happened?"

"Talel," Soran grits through his teeth.

My eyes go wide with panic as I turn back to the hallway, afraid he will appear. "Where is he?"

"I do not know. But we must hurry if we are to escape."

Without hesitation, we continue on toward the hangar. Several ships—various forms of luxury gliders, transports, and pleasure vessels—are parked throughout the space. These must belong to wealthy patrons who've come here to peddle in flesh, acquiring new slaves. Bile burns its way up my throat, but I force myself to focus as we rush toward the closest ship.

We race up the platform and in through the open hatch. Rowan slams his hand on the panel to seal it shut behind us. It's a small glider, but it easily fits the four of us. Through the viewscreen, I watch as several of the freed slaves confiscate the other parked vessels as we all hurry to escape.

Soran keeps Liana in his lap as we strap into our chairs, her eyelids fluttering open and closed as she struggles to stay awake. Rowan's hands fly across the control panel, and we lift off and head toward the outer force shield—the invisible barrier the only thing separating us from space and our freedom.

Red lights flash throughout the hangar as loud sirens fill the air. The hangar doors slowly begin to slide closed as the masters try to thwart our escape. Rowan punches the engine, and the glider turns on its side. We barely slip through before they seal shut behind us.

A large cruiser fills the viewscreen, and my heart stops momentarily before I notice the familiar call sign on its side. Happiness blooms in my chest. "It's my brother's ship!"

Immediately, Rowan opens a channel, and Al'aneo's face appears in the viewscreen. His expression is stern, but as soon as his eyes meet mine he blinks in disbelief. "Tr'lani?"

"Yes. We just escaped from the slave ship."

His gaze hardens. "Wait there. My men and I will deal with the slavers, and when we are finished, you may dock with us." He leans forward to cut off the display.

"Wait!" Soran cries out, stopping him abruptly. "Talel is on that ship. We need him alive. He has information about Liana's home world."

Al'aneo clenches his jaw and dips his chin in a quick nod before the screen goes dark.

My people show no mercy to slavers. The punishment is immediate execution. After all that I've been through, I cannot pretend to care about the brutal deaths I'm certain Al'aneo and his soldiers will give to the masters.

I turn to Soran, still holding Liana in his arms. Dark bruising covers almost her entire body, but it is the two puncture wounds at her neck that concern me the most. She is pale, and I worry about how much blood she has lost. "Soran, I need to assess her."

Rowan turns to me. "I'll search for an emergency med bag. Surely there is one in here."

I nod as he leaves the bridge to begin searching. After a moment, he calls out from the hallway. "I've found an MRU."

We're fortunate a small med bay exists on this vessel. Gently, Soran places Liana in the unit. She's unconscious now as I activate the scanner, studying the read-outs anxiously.

It's just as I suspected; she's lost a lot of blood. While I have nothing to replace it with, I can at least give her some fluids. A cursory glance of this glider's med bay suggests that whoever this vessel belonged to, they spared no expense on their medical supplies. I type in a few commands, instructing the unit to begin working.

Soran's face is a mask of concern as he stares down at Liana through the clear casing. He places his hand on the glass as if to touch her. "Will she be all right?"

"Yes," I reassure him. "She is much stronger than she appears."

"I know she is," he replies. "If not for her, I would have died when we first crashed on that frozen rock of a planet. She is as strong as she is brave." He lifts his gaze to Rowan and then places a hand on his shoulder, his lips tilting up in a faint smile. "I am glad the two of you are alive and well." His eyes dart to me. "What happened to you both after the glider? Where did you end up? How did you get captured?"

I allow Rowan to explain while I tend to Liana, monitoring the read-out as the MRU works on her body. So much has happened, and I cannot believe we found Al'aneo.

It's been a little over two cycles since I was taken, and I'm both anxious and nervous to finally see him again. I have so many questions. During our last communication, he got cut off before I could ask him about my parents and grandparents.

Sadness tightens my chest. I can only imagine how worried they've been all this time. Do they know he found me? Was he able to send them a message that I'm alive and well?

What about my friends and my colleagues? I'm desperate to know how many made it out during the Zovian attack on the colony. My heart is heavy as I think on On'aro. He was my best friend; we grew up together. His last words to me were that he loved me. Al'aneo said he's been searching for me all this time, afraid that I was dead but still holding onto the hope of finding me.

"What is wrong?" Rowan's warm hand comes to rest on my shoulder.

I place my hand over his. "I just—" My voice hitches. How do I begin to explain all that I feel? I'm nervous about seeing my brother again. Worried that after everything I've been through, he'll no longer recognize who I am.

I am different than I was before. How could I not be? And as much as I miss my friend, I dread reuniting with On'aro. He has wasted two cycles searching for me; the female that he loved is gone. I am not who I once was.

"You are nervous," Rowan says softly, and I recognize his statement is also a question, so I simply nod.

My gaze drifts between him and Soran. I worry about how they will be greeted on an Aerilon ship. How many of my people have lost family and loved ones in border conflicts with the Mosaurans? Hundreds of cycles of hatred and prejudice will not be forgotten easily.

Although it feels like forever, I'm certain it's no more than thirty minutes before Al'aneo appears in the viewscreen once more. Obsidian blood stains a trail from his forehead down to his chin. "The vessel has been cleansed and all the slaves freed. We have captured Talel. He is in one of our holding cells. You may dock anytime you are ready."

The MRU is finished healing Liana, but she will remain unconscious for a few more hours while she continues to heal. Soran holds her tight to his chest as Rowan deftly guides the small glider into the docking bay.

His eyes dart briefly to mine, and I give him a nervous smile. How many times have I dreamed of returning to my family? My people?

The airlock door opens. Tears sting my eyes and blur my vision when I see Al'aneo waiting for me at the bottom of the ramp. Aerilon soldiers stand on either side of him, ready to guard their captain as they stare warily at Rowan and Soran.

My brother stands tall and proud, tilting his chin up in an imperious look, accentuating the aristocratic features of his jaw, nose, and brow. People have often commented that it is easy to tell we are twins, but I've never believed it to be so. With short-cropped dark hair and blue-green skin, he takes after our father, while I favor Mother's violet skin and silver-white hair.

My brother studies Rowan and Soran with a piercing gaze a moment before he shifts his attention to me.

His golden eyes lock onto mine, and his lips curve into a beaming smile.

I rush down the platform and into his open arms. I can hardly believe this is real. I've dreamed of this moment for so long.

He lifts me off the ground, spinning me in a slow circle before setting me down and hugging me tightly as the combined low trilling hum of greeting rises in our throats. "My sister." His voice quavers slightly. "I never gave up searching. I—"

His eyes meet mine, brimming with tears. "I know, my brother. I know," I somehow manage to speak through my emotions. "I knew you would find me. I never doubted it, Al'aneo."

My broken wings flutter softly behind me, eliciting an audible gasp from one of his soldiers. He looks to my wings, and inhales sharply, his expression full of pain. "Your wings. What did they do to you?"

My bottom lip quivers slightly as I lower my gaze. "The master broke them so I wouldn't be able to fly away."

Several growls of anger come from his soldiers.

He takes my hands in his and studies them. "Your claws.... Your venom... Did they—"

Unable to speak through my sadness, I nod, and he pulls me back into his arms. All the emotions I've tried to push down rise to the surface. My shoulders shake with hiccupping sobs as tears flow freely down my face.

My brother holds me tight, but I cannot stop. It's as if a floodgate has opened as I cry out all the anguish I've held in for the past two cycles. How many times did I pray for death, believing that I would never see my family again? I was broken in every possible way and as I cry against Al'aneo's chest I mourn not only all the time that I lost but the person I was before. I wish I could be as strong as Liana, who rarely sheds any tears. I was a slave for so long and I have so many dark memories. Each time I close my eyes, I am back in a cage and when I open them, I fear this is all a dream. "Is this real?" I sob. "Please, tell me this is not just a dream, Al'aneo."

"This is real. You are here and you are safe, my dear sister," he says softly. "I am here, and I'm taking you home. We will find someone to repair your wings, Tr'lani. I promise."

As a Healer myself, I already know this vow he cannot keep, but I say nothing. My heart is full. Finding Al'aneo after all this time and being among my people again. I never thought this day would come.

Out of the corner of my eye, I notice Rowan and Soran coming down the ramp. Liana is stable but still asleep in his arms.

I turn to them and then look back at Al'aneo. "We should move Liana to the med bay until she wakes up. I already used the MRU to heal her, but she will be unconscious for a few hours still."

Al'aneo nods and then motions off to the side. "This way."

He leads us down a long corridor as I explain what happened to her. The interior of the ship is so familiar, my heart clenches because it reminds me of home. The plush brown and green carpets are reminiscent of the rich earth on Aerilon. Several flowering vines full of vibrant glowing purple and blue flowers trail down the walls. This is the beauty of Aerilon vessels. They are built for comfort and aesthetics as much as for defense so that our soldiers have something to remind them of our world when they are gone on assignment.

When we reach the medical bay, one of the Healers rushes to greet us, gasping lightly in shock when she notices Rowan and Soran behind us. Her eyes dart to Liana. "A V'loryn?"

"No," Al'aneo says quickly. "She is Terran, and we have claimed her as our sister. She needs to be monitored. She was attacked by an A'kai."

The Healer's wings flutter furiously behind her as she calls out for her staff. They usher Soran and Liana to one of the MRU beds, and the scanner moves quickly over her form.

I step forward. "I am Healer Tr'lani," I tell her so that she understands my credentials before I explain Liana's condition to her. "As you can see"—I point to the floating scans above the bed—"her anatomy is very similar to a V'loryn's. She has lost much blood, but our replacer compound should work to replenish her system."

The Healer nods and then gives orders to the rest of the staff.

While she is working, a familiar voice calls out my name. I turn and then smile when I see Abby waddling toward us, holding one hand on her very pregnant belly with her other arm wrapped around Grex's.

She embraces me warmly while Grex greets Soran and Rowan. I'm so glad to see them. "How did you get here?"

Grex answers. "Al'aneo was searching for you when he picked up our distress beacon."

I'm curious to know if they were on the same planet as us but Abby's words quickly answer my unspoken question. "Our escape pod landed on this amazing world with pink sandy beaches and lavender oceans. It was so beautiful," she says, her eyes full of wonder as if reliving the memory. She turns to me. "Where did you two end up?"

Certainly not in a paradise like the one she's describing, but I keep that thought to myself. Really, I should be happy they landed somewhere so nice. She is pregnant after all, and it must have been terrifying for them to be alone on an unknown planet with a child on the way.

As Rowan and Soran tell them all about our experiences after we crashed, I allow my gaze to travel over the med bay.

A faint smile curves my mouth. Pristine white panels with sparkling glass separate each bed. Everything is polished and orderly; the crisp smell of antiseptic hangs in the air. It has been a long time since I was back in my element, and as I study the display above Liana, for a moment, I forget my broken wings and all the ways that I'm lacking.

Rowan is right. Just as Liana does not need natural defenses to fight, I do not need these things to still be a Healer. This, at least, was not taken from me.

Soran watches from the side with Rowan while we administer treatment to Liana. As soon as we're finished, I lift my gaze to them. "She will be unconscious for a bit longer while this works, but she is stable."

Soran's shoulders sag forward in relief, and Rowan smiles and claps him on the arm. "Your mate will be well," he says to his brother.

The Healer's head whips toward them. "Mate?"

Soran tilts up his chin, standing to his full and intimidating height before her as he declares proudly, "She is mine, and I am her mate."

Her mouth drifts open slightly. A look of shock on her face that is mirrored in the expressions of everyone else in the room save for myself, Al'aneo, and Rowan. She stumbles over her words. "I—I did not realize your people took mates outside of your race."

Rowan's eyes dart to me, before he addresses her. "It is truth. This was the way of our people, but now it is not."

His gaze holds mine, and he moves toward me but someone steps between us. "Tr'lani?"

Confused, it takes me a moment to focus. My jaw drops when I recognize On'aro, staring down at me. Stunned, I blink up at him as my breath hitches in my throat. "On'aro."

Rowan stills beside me.

On'aro gathers me in his arms. His voice is shaking as he speaks in my ear. "I—I thought you were dead. I prayed every day that we'd find you alive. Oh Creator, I've missed you so much, Tr'lani."

When he finally pulls back, I turn toward Rowan, but don't see him. I scan the room, but he is no longer here.

On'aro gives me a strange look. "The Mosauran is a friend of yours?"

Instantly offended by the skeptical tone of his voice, I give him an incredulous look. "He and his brother saved us from the A'kai. Rowan and I were stranded together for days on an uncharted planet, and… he's more than a friend, On'aro."

Shock registers on his features before his eyes narrow slightly. "What do you mean, he's more than a friend?"

Al'aneo's head whips around to look at us, and I realize he's heard every word we've said. I meet On'aro's gaze evenly. "I…need to speak with you. Alone."

His face falls. "Can we talk over evening meal later?" he asks.

"Yes."

When he leaves, I turn to my brother. He arches a brow. "It seems there is much we must discuss."

I change the subject. "Tell me about home. How are our parents? And Ama and Apa?"

His gaze drops to the floor, and my heart stops. Something is wrong. "What is it? Tell me."

He takes my hand in his, and there is so much sadness in his eyes, it makes me afraid. "I'd rather discuss it in private."

Panic threads through me, but I push it back down as I follow him to his quarters. Whatever this is, it's bad. That much is certain. My thoughts drift to my family. I hope and pray that they are well. The agony of not knowing is almost more than I can bear.

CHAPTER 28

ROWAN

As I wander the corridors, the image of Tr'lani in On'aro's arms replays in my mind. He is the male who has been searching for her all this time. Al'aneo made it sound, in one of his communications, as though they were to be bonded before she disappeared. But in all the time we spent together, she rarely spoke of him. And after what happened between us, I was so sure of her feelings for me. But now...I don't know what to think.

So far, the Aerilon have been cordial to Soran and me, but it is easy to read the tension in their eyes. Our people are natural enemies. Perhaps being back among her own kind, Tr'lani has had second thoughts about us.

I scrub my hand roughly across my face in frustration as I pace back and forth. I shouldn't have left like I did, but I could not bear to see her with him. Especially after the way he looked at her...the way he held her like a male who'd been wandering the desert plains of Al'hira and finally found water.

I recognized that expression because it mirrors my own when I see her. I am hers—body, mind, and soul. And in his eyes, I know he feels the same.

With a heavy sigh, I start back for the med bay. I must speak with her. I cannot continue in this way. It is torture. All I want is to hold her in my arms. To tell her that I love her and will always be hers. But what if she doesn't want me? What then? I can't bear the thought of being without her.

As soon as I enter the med bay, my eyes scan the room. Tr'lani is nowhere to be found, so I move to my brother.

He sits beside his beloved Liana, holding her hand as she sleeps; waiting patiently for her to regain consciousness. I place a hand on his shoulder to alert him of my presence.

"How is she?" I ask.

"They say she is stable and should wake very soon." He pauses and then gives me a solemn look. "I must tell you something."

With a slight clench of my jaw, I sigh heavily because I already know what he will say, so I do it for him. "You have decided to take her as your mate. You will risk becoming Outcast."

He nods. "I do not want to lose you or our family, but I cannot live without her. She is my heart."

He stares at me as if expecting me to argue, but how can I? Liana is his heart, just as Tr'lani is mine. And if she still wants me as her mate, I will risk being Outcast as well because I cannot be without her either.

I open my mouth to tell him this but stop when a Healer approaches to check on Liana. She eyes Soran and me discreetly. With great difficulty, I suppress the urge to roll my eyes. What do they think we are going to do? Storm through the ship? Try to take over the bridge?

Placing a hand on Soran's shoulder, I offer him words of support. "Whatever your decision, I will stand by you. I will speak to Mother as well. There has to be an exception to the law. Liana is your Ashaya. How could the Council even think of going against the blessing of the Creator?"

His eyes meet mine evenly. "Thank you, brother." He pauses, a hint of a smile tilting his lips. "And what of you and Tr'lani?"

I am not surprised by his question. Of course, he would know. I can hide nothing from him. Lowering my gaze, I sigh heavily. "I desire for her to be mine, but I am uncertain if that is what she wants as well."

He arches a brow. "Then why don't you find out?"

I roll my eyes. "You maltak. Why do you think I am here? I was looking for her."

He gives me a teasing grin. "You mean...you did not come back to check on me? Keep me safe from all the Aerilons?"

I wave a dismissive hand at him. "I knew you were all right." My gaze darts around the room to the several pairs of eyes that watch us warily. "Besides," I drop my voice to a low whisper, "these Healers look like they're more afraid of you than anything else at the moment. Just try not to shift, or else you will scare them," I tease.

He laughs before his expression becomes serious again. "Why did you leave earlier? Who was that male that embraced her?"

I give him a grim look. "She knew him from before. He is the male her brother spoke of. The one she was supposed to be joined with before she was taken." I shake my head in frustration. "I shouldn't have left."

"She went with her brother. I overheard him explain that he had news to give her." He gives me a pointed look. "From the tone of his voice, it sounded grave."

I turn for the door.

"Where are you going?" Soran calls out.

"To find her."

CHAPTER 29

TR'LANI

As soon as we enter Al'aneo's quarters, he turns to his display. I start to ask what he's doing, but he answers my unspoken question. "I'm contacting our family. We are close enough to reach them, and they are eager to speak with you."

My heart fills with joy. I can hardly wait to see everyone. I've missed them all so terribly. Al'aneo punches a few buttons on the console, and I anxiously watch as the screen goes dark a moment before my mother and father appear. Ama—my grandmother—stands beside them.

I've dreamed of this moment for so long. I used to pray each night to the Creator just to keep me alive long enough to see them at least one more time. Tears fill my eyes, and I open my mouth to speak, but the words won't come.

Mother, Father, and Ama stare at me in disbelief. Their eyes are bright with tears as they begin a low trilling hum of greeting. Placing their hands on the viewscreen as if to touch me, I do the same in return.

"Tr'lani, is it really you, my beautiful granddaughter?" Ama asks softly.

"Yes," my voice quavers.

A tear slips down Mother's cheek as she looks to me. "My daughter."

Father wraps his arm around her shoulders and holds her close, barely able to speak. "We were so afraid that we'd lost you forever, my beautiful girl."

"I've missed you all so much." My voice catches. "I prayed to the Creator every night that I would see you again." I blink several times to clear the tears from my vision as I look past them, waiting for my grandfather to appear. Perhaps he is out in the gardens, tending to his beloved plants. "Where is Apa?"

My parents lower their eyes, and as I turn to Al'aneo, he does the same. My heart stops. "No. Please, don't tell me that he's gone. Please." Even as I speak these words, I already know the truth in my heart.

"I'm so sorry, Tr'lani." Al'aneo hugs me. "I didn't know how to tell you."

My body shakes with sobbing, and I turn back to the viewscreen. Ama's eyes meet mine, and they're so full of sadness it nearly breaks me.

She places her hand to her chest, clasping the necklace he gave her as a bonding gift. "He never gave up hope. He always knew in his heart that you still lived. When he lay dying—" Her voice catches. "His last words were for you, my darling girl. He wanted you to know that he loved you so much."

"What happened to him? How did—" I start to ask but stop, unable to speak through my pain.

"There was an outbreak of H'olurian fever." She shakes her head. "You know how stubborn he was. He just couldn't stand by and do nothing. He was a Healer. He wanted to help. He tried so hard to live for you, my beautiful girl. But his body just…couldn't."

I sob against Al'aneo's chest, and he holds me as memories of Apa fill my mind. I remember begging him when I was a child to take me to work. The first time I went, I knew…that was what I wanted to do with my life. I was meant to be a Healer. He was my grandfather first but also my greatest mentor.

Ama continues. "He would be so happy if he were here…knowing that we finally found you. Come home, my child. We miss you. Come home to us."

Unable to speak around the lump in my throat, Al'aneo answers for me. "I'm bringing her home, Ama. Just like I promised."

The screen begins to fade in and out as Al'aneo studies to console. "We're passing through a field of interference. I'll have to end the connection. We will be home soon."

They all nod, and then the display goes dark.

Al'aneo turns back to me. "I'm sorry, my dear sister. I should have told you sooner, but I just…couldn't. It is still so hard…even now."

I nod. "I understand."

A heavy silence settles in the space between us a moment before he lifts his gaze to mine. "I overheard your conversation with On'aro. He's searched for you all this time, you know. He gave up everything in the hopes that we'd find you."

"The last time I saw him, he told me he loved me." I look down at my hands. "We've always been close. To be honest, I half expected that someday our friendship would become something more, but…" I trail off, uncertain how to tell Al'aneo about Rowan.

"But what?" he presses. Taking my hand, he meets my eyes evenly. "You know you can tell me anything."

Drawing in a deep breath, I steel myself to say what needs to be said. "I'm in love with Rowan."

Al'aneo's eyes widen, and he blinks several times in shock. "But he is Mosauran. How can you be in love with our enemy?"

I quickly retract my hands and stare at him accusingly. "He saved me, Al'aneo. From the A'kai."

He gives me an incredulous look. "You would choose him over On'aro? The male who has been searching for you every day since you disappeared?"

"Yes."

His brow furrows deeply. "And just how is this supposed to work between you?"

"We've claimed Liana as our sister, and she is in love with Soran and he with her," I reply. "Are you going to react this way to her as well?"

He gives me a look as if my question were ridiculous. "Of course not. She is not Aerilon." He leans forward to take my hand. "But *you* are. Our people have always been enemies. It won't work, Tr'lani. It can't. There is too much history between us. The Mosaurans are not like us. They are too different. They are aggressive and volatile and—"

"I love him, Al'aneo. He's kind and caring and everything I would look for in a male. We're wrong about the Mosaurans. Please, understand."

He scrubs a hand across his face and draws in a deep breath as he begins pacing back and forth. "And he's all right with being Outcast from his people to bond with an Aerilon?"

I lower my gaze. My brother is right. If Rowan bonded with me, he'd have to give up everything he's ever known.

Al'aneo continues. "If this is what you want, I will support you… despite my reservations. I just…I don't want to see you get hurt."

I nod and then sigh heavily. "I must speak with On'aro."

"If you need to talk, I am here. I will try to contact our family again to…prepare them, at least for Soran, and then"—he arches a brow—"it should help ease them into the idea of your…Mosauran joining the Clan as well if that is what you decide."

* * *

When I leave Al'aneo, I head off to find On'aro. I must speak to him before I go to Rowan. I don't want him to find out by seeing us together. I at least owe him the truth. Especially after all the time he has spent searching for me.

I press the chime to request entry to On'aro's quarters. The moment the doors to his room seal behind me, he takes my hands and drops to his knees. Staring up at me with a pleading look. "I must ask your forgiveness."

Confused, I ask. "What? Why?"

"When the colony was raided, I failed to protect you. And I know this would make me seem like an unworthy mate in your eyes, but I should have told you long ago. I have wanted you to choose me for forever."

I shake my head. "I know it wasn't your fault, On'aro. I don't blame you for what happened."

Something akin to hope flashes behind his eyes. "Then…you will accept me? You will choose me to be yours?"

My heart clenches. "I'm sorry, but I cannot."

His face is nothing short of wounded as he stares up at me. "Why?"

I lower my gaze to the floor, unable to look him in the eye as I speak the words I know will hurt him. "My heart belongs to someone else."

His expression darkens, and he stands. "The Mosauran," he says with a bitter edge to his tone.

"Yes."

"His people will never accept the two of you together. They do not believe in mixed-species pairings."

I swallow against the lump in my throat. "I know."

His brow furrows deeply. "You would really choose an enemy over me? Mosaurans are dangerous. They are violent and unpredictable and—"

"You're wrong!" I snap. "You don't know them. They're not as different from us as you might think."

He moves forward, cupping my face in his hands. "Please, Tr'lani. Do not do this. I know that with time we could rekindle what we had, and…the rest would come later. The love, the bonding, we—"

I shake my head. I don't want to hurt him any more than I already have, but he needs to understand. "You and I…we were always just friends, On'aro."

He gives me a pained look. "But surely you knew how I felt? And I

—I know you felt more than friendship for me too. We just never said it aloud, and then…there was no time."

"Please. I'm not the same person that I was. That version of me is gone. You have to move on."

His golden eyes stare deep into mine. "I can only imagine what was done to you, and if you think that I will love you any less because of it, you are wrong. You are still the female that I want. There has not been a single day that I have not thought of you. I joined the Defense Force to aide your brother in his search to find you. I did all of this because I felt you were alive." He places his hand over his heart. "In here. I could feel that you still lived. And I knew I had to find you."

My heart clenches. I never knew he loved me this deeply. Looking back on what we were to each other, I realize now that it was more than friendship. It was familiarity, but nothing more. At least, not for me. I've never felt for On'aro what I do for Rowan. It is as different as dark is to light. "On'aro. I'm sorry, but I cannot return your affection. Please. Understand."

A look of resignation steals over his features as he meets my eyes evenly. "Then, I ask…can we at least still remain as we were? Friends?"

"Of course."

"Then, I will ask nothing else of you," he says solemnly. "I would never ask anything of you that you would not willingly give."

* * *

When I leave, I'm desperate to find Rowan. He left so quickly, I know he must have been so hurt, thinking that I'd completely forgotten him when I saw On'aro.

I pass one of Al'aneo's men in the hallway and ask about Rowan. He points me toward the communication center. My feet cannot carry me fast enough to get to him, but I don't want to run and draw attention to myself. Near the end of the corridor, I already hear the deep, smooth sound of his voice, and I smile brightly, anxious to see him.

When I round the corner, I stop abruptly and move back into the hallway just out of sight. Although it's been many cycles since I saw her image, I recognize the Empress of Mosaura—Rowan's mother—on the viewscreen.

Her lips are set in a tight, thin line as she gives him a disapproving look. "You know our laws, Rowan. Any who take a mate outside our race are considered Outcast."

"Mother, please," he pleads. "You cannot do this. It—it would be devastating. Cruel beyond imagining to be banished from home."

My heart clenches at his words. Rowan would be Outcast if we became mates. I cannot allow him to make that kind of sacrifice. How can I let him give up everything for me when I know that he will suffer so greatly for it?

My mother always told me that if you love someone, you want only what is best for them. True love is selfless, and before today, I never realized how difficult such a thing could be. I love Rowan. And because I love him, I must let him go. I will not allow him to choose me over the life that he's always known, the one he's planned for so long.

But I do not want him to think that my heart is so fickle as to be turned by another. No. Instead, I will give him a plausible lie. A reason that we cannot be together, and I can only hope that he will accept it without a fight. If nothing else, we can at least still remain friends. Part of me thinks I can live with that, but the other part knows I will die a little inside every time that I think of him from this day forward and everything we could have had.

CHAPTER 30

TR'LANI

Because this is my brother's ship, I let myself into Rowan's quarters. When he returns from his comm with the Empress, the shock is easily read in his features when he opens the door and finds me waiting for him. It's quickly replaced by a devastatingly handsome smile.

Before I can even speak, he gathers me in his arms, holding me close. After a moment, he pulls back just enough to stare down at me. A strange mixture of love and devotion shines in his gaze as he stares at me like I'm the most precious thing in the world to him. "You came back to me," he whispers softly and then presses his forehead to mine. "I was so worried, my heart."

In this moment, time slows down, and I am lost in the feel of his arms around me and the love that reflects in his eyes. My heart breaks in a thousand pieces as I force myself to focus. Placing my palm against his chest, I gently push him away.

His brow furrows softly in confusion. "What is wrong?"

"I can't be with you, Rowan."

An uncertain smile tips his mouth. "I know," he says. "We will not mate until your family blesses our bond. I've researched your customs. I know we must seek their blessing first and then, we will perform the Aerilon ceremony and—"

"No, Rowan." My voice quavers slightly. "I mean…we cannot bond. Our relationship would never work. Our species are too different." The lie burns on my tongue, and the wounded look on his face is more than I can bear.

I lower my gaze, unable to stand the pain in his expression. He cups my chin, tipping my head up to him. His eyes search mine. "Why are you saying this?"

"Because it is the truth."

He shakes his head firmly. "No. It is not."

"Yes."

His entire body tenses. "It's because of him. Isn't it?" he asks accusingly.

Confused, it takes me a moment to realize he thinks I'm choosing On'aro over him. "It's not On'aro, Rowan. I swear."

He clenches his jaw. "Do not lie to me."

"I'm not lying."

"Then, what is it?" He takes my hands in his and drops to his knees before me.

I know he does this because it is the way of my people. The male that longs for his female to choose him drops to his knees and asks her to claim him as her mate. "Please," he says softly, his eyes staring up at me with a pained look. "Do not push me away. Give me a chance to prove that I would be a worthy mate according to the ways of your people."

Gently, I tug at his grasp, pulling him up to his feet. "You are more than worthy, but I—" I hesitate a moment as I prepare the lie that sits on the tip of my tongue. "I do not want a mate."

"But you told me you loved me and—"

I pull my hands from his and step back. "I thought we were going to die, and I acted rashly. I realize now that—"

"Stop," he pleads. "I do not wish to hear any more." His shoulders sag forward in defeat as he stares at me, broken in every possible way.

I hate myself for hurting him—for speaking a lie that would cause him so much pain. It is almost enough to break my resolve, but I clench my jaw and force myself to meet his gaze evenly. I am doing this *for* him. Because I love him more than anything else, and I cannot allow him to give up everything for me. "I'm sorry, Rowan. I truly am. I would like for us to part as friends."

Cautiously, he reaches out and takes my hand. I should pull away, but something inside me won't let me. "A warrior's life is never certain," he says. "So much can change from one moment to the next. Life is fleeting, but the words we speak are remembered long after we have gone. I wish you to know my truth." His gaze travels over my face, pain and longing evident in his expression. "You are my heart. I will never love another as I love you. And if the only thing you want from me is friendship, I offer mine gladly. Anything you desire, I will always give to you with open hands...you have only but to ask. I have been, and I will always be yours."

Emotions lodge in my throat, rendering me incapable of speech, but I somehow manage to nod. Gathering the last shred of my courage, I force myself to leave his quarters, knowing that if I don't do so right now, I'll lose my resolve and rush back into his arms, not caring of the consequences or what that would mean for him. I love him. So, I must let him go. I cannot ask him to give up everything for me because I know he would do so in a heartbeat, binding himself to me and losing everything he knows in the process.

CHAPTER 31

ROWAN

She leaves, and the world falls out from under me as I drop to my knees on the floor. Devastation washes through me. She is my heart, but I am not hers. I lift my hands before my face. Studying them, I curl my fingers into my palm as despair fills me. Never again will I hold her in my arms, wrap her up in my wings, and feel the warm press of her body to mine.

Closing my eyes, I can imagine the scent of her hair, the soft sound of her breathing, and the gentle brush of her lips to my mouth. She is my heart, and I will never love another as I have loved her.

She is my heart...but I am not hers.

My thoughts turn to my brother and Liana. I spoke to my mother —the Empress. Begged her to reconsider making him Outcast for choosing a mate outside of our race, but she refused. How is it that I have lost everything in the span of one day?

I have lost much in my life, starting with my father. Then I count the wasted cycles spent apart from my brother, wondering if he was dead while at the same time believing, somehow—against all odds—that he was not. I found my greatest treasure the day we rescued

Tr'lani on Vylax Station. She is more precious than anything I have ever known, and now, I must learn to live my life without her.

Curling my hands into fists at my side, I vow to the Creator that if nothing else, I will do whatever it takes to not lose my brother again. At least, I may be spared one loss if I can convince my mother to accept his choice. And if Mother still decides to declare him Outcast, then I will be Outcast as well, because I refuse to lose anyone else in this life.

Without hesitation, I return to the communication room and contact my sister. If anyone can help me get through to our mother, it's Caryn. As the future Empress of Mosaura, she is the one voice that Mother may listen to above all others. For when Mother is gone, Caryn will rule over our people and decide upon our laws and traditions as she sees fit.

I press the panel, and it doesn't take long for Caryn's face to appear in the viewscreen. She greets me with a pained smile as she stares into the display, and I know that she must have been crying. By now, Mother would have told her of Soran's choice to face the punishment of becoming Outcast rather than forsaking his mate. "Rowan," she says softly. "It is good to see you, my brother, after so long."

"It is good to see you as well, my sister. I have missed you."

She gives me a pleading look. "Is there nothing you can do? Nothing you can say to persuade Soran to—"

I shake my head. "No."

With a defeated look, she drops her eyes to the ground.

"Liana is a worthy mate," I tell her. "She is as fierce as one of our females. And I know that if she were Mosauran, Mother would find her more than worthy of him."

"Then we will have to convince her to see past thousands of cycles of prejudice," she states firmly, as if such a thing will be easy to do. "To cast away antiquated laws and tradition."

"We must. We cannot lose Soran again."

My thoughts turn to Tr'lani, and my heart squeezes painfully.

My sister tips her head to the side, regarding me curiously. "There is something else. What is it?"

Caryn and I have always been close. Even when Mother tried to dissuade me in my search for Soran, she offered her quiet support in my quest. Swallowing thickly, I lie. "It is nothing."

She leans forward, staring intently into the viewscreen. "Rowan, something is wrong with you. I can see it in your eyes. Whatever it is, you know I will listen."

Sighing heavily, I meet her gaze and then tell her about Tr'lani and everything that happened between us on the planet.

When I'm finished, my sister says nothing. It is easy to see the hurt in her expression. In admitting my love for Tr'lani and my desire to become her mate, I have effectively already chosen my heart over my family.

Guilt fills me, and I lower my eyes, too ashamed to meet my sister's accusing stare. "Forgive me," I whisper. "I know I am meant to become your advisor, but I…cannot help but want a life of my own. A family and—"

"Rowan, I—"

I raise my hand in a silent bid to allow me to continue. I lift my gaze to hers. "When Soran first told me of his feelings for Liana, I was angry. Upset that he would choose an Outsider over family. I did not understand then how powerful the heart can be. Soran and Liana have been blessed by the fated bond. But me? I have no excuse other than that I love her…more than anything. Forgive me, Caryn."

Caryn's expression softens. "How is it that you are the youngest, and yet you've carried such a heavier burden than the rest of us? It is not your responsibility to keep us together. And it is not your fault that you fell in love. Even *if* it was with an Aerilon." A faint smile twists her lips. "Our laws are wrong if they would force our family apart…if they would make us choose between the path fate has laid before us and our bonds to each other. Mother may not see it, but I do." She raises her open palm to the screen as if to touch me. I do the same in return. "You are my brother, and I love you. Nothing will ever change that. Your heart has always been your greatest strength. It is what led you to find Soran when all others had lost hope. And I will never fault you for following the heart that has been given to you by the Creator of all things."

I'm so touched by her words, I cannot speak.

She gives me a faint smile. "Did it ever occur to you that Tr'lani may be pushing you away now out of fear that you will become Outcast according to our laws?"

I say nothing for I had not considered this. I thought she had simply changed her mind now that she was back among her people.

Caryn continues. "I could be wrong, but if everything you have told me about her is truth, I suspect that your Aerilon princess possesses a selfless heart just like you." She pauses and then meets my eyes evenly. "As the future Empress of Mosaura, I promise I will do whatever I can to make sure you and Soran do not become Outcast. Together, we will convince Mother. Surely, she has to see reason."

CHAPTER 32

TR'LANI

Sitting in my quarters, I stare out the viewscreen of the ship. Thousands of stars blur past, and I've never felt so alone. The door chimes loudly, and I call out, "Enter!"

As if my thoughts have summoned him, Al'aneo steps inside. He gives me a low, trilling hum of greeting, and I rush to embrace him.

"I've already arranged for evening meal to be brought here to us." He grins.

After everything that's happened today, food was the last thing on my mind. "Thank you. It will be lovely to have an Aerilon dish after all this time."

His gaze holds mine as he leans forward and places his hand over my own, squeezing it gently. "I cannot imagine what you must have been through, Tr'lani." His voice breaks, and he clears his throat before continuing. "On'aro came to speak with me. He told me about your conversation."

His words lay heavy between us a moment before I speak. "He wanted to bond with me, but I refused him. I—I'm not the same person he knew two cycles ago. She is gone."

Al'aneo frowns, and I know that my answer troubles him. "I cannot pretend to understand what you have been through." He meets my eyes evenly. "But know this: I am here for you, and so is the rest of our Clan."

"I know," I whisper softly. "I just don't want anyone to worry over me. When we spoke with Mother, Father, and Ama, I hid my wings," I admit. "I do not want them to worry over something we can do nothing about."

He shakes his head. "We don't know that for certain."

"I'm a Healer, Al'aneo. I do."

"You cannot just give up."

Frustration burns through me. "I'm not giving up. I'm accepting the truth. There's a difference. I know I'll never fly again, and I've learned to accept it."

He leans back in his chair. "I do not mean to upset you. I merely do not want you to give up all hope. We are going to Mosaura first. Rowan talked with one of their Healers. They have different medical technologies than our people do. They have agreed to help you if they can."

My heart clenches. "When did he say this?"

"Just a moment ago. I ran into him in the hallway."

Even after how awful I treated him, Rowan still cares. He promised he'd do anything for me, and he is.

Al'aneo interrupts my thoughts. "Will you agree to go see them?"

"Yes."

"Good," he says firmly. "Rowan said he will take you himself once we arrive at Mosaura."

My eyes snap up to meet his. "He did?"

"Yes."

Sensing my hesitation, he arches a questioning brow. "Is there a problem? Do you not wish to go with him for some reason?"

"You were right," I admit. "It won't work between us. I told him I do not want a mate."

He shakes his head. "Why would you do this?"

"What you said made sense." My voice quavers. "If he takes me as his mate, he will be Outcast among his people, like Soran will be if he bonds with Liana."

He lowers his gaze to the floor in a contemplative look but says nothing.

I allow my eyes to drift to the far wall as my conversation with Rowan replays in my head. "Mother taught us that if you love someone, you only want what is best for them." I turn my attention back to Al'aneo. "I know the pain of being separated from home and family, and I will not do that to him. I won't allow him to give up everything he's ever known just for me."

He takes my hand. "I don't want to tell you what to do, and to be honest, I dislike the idea of you with a Mosauran. I worry that you would both face much prejudice. But I do not want you to have any regrets over this either." He pauses. "Did it ever occur to you that you should allow Rowan to make his own decision, instead of you making it for him?"

His words hit me like a physical blow. I open my mouth to speak, but the door chimes loudly, and someone enters with our food. I drop my gaze to my hands on the table before me.

"Think on it," he says softly. "Before you make a decision you regret."

Reluctantly, I nod.

As we eat, our conversation turns to other things. He tells me that Father informed him there is an opening for a Healer at his clinic. I have to admit that the idea of losing myself in my work is tempting. I loved my job. It was difficult at times, but so rewarding in the same measure to be able to help people.

He teases that my room is exactly as I left it. It warms my heart just speaking of home and my family.

The time passes quickly, and before I know it, it's been over three hours. Exhaustion hits me, and I'm finding it difficult to keep my eyes open.

"You should get some rest," Al'aneo says. "We arrive in Mosaura tomorrow."

I'm tired, but I doubt I'll be able to sleep anytime soon. I cannot stop thinking of Rowan and the look on his face when I told him I didn't want him anymore. I hate that my lie caused him so much pain. He deserves so much better.

A deep ache settles in my chest at the thought that tomorrow might be the last time I ever see him.

CHAPTER 33

TR'LANI

Soran and Liana have made their decision. They are bonded, and as we reach Mosaura, they prepare themselves to face the consequences of their joining. At least they know they will have a home on Aerilon if they wish. Liana is part of our Clan now; in bonding to her, Soran is also. I will be glad to have her with us.

Rowan walks past me, and his eyes lock with mine briefly before he continues to his brother's side. I watch as they strategically position themselves on either side of Liana, whether to protect her from vicious slurs and curious stares or merely as a show of solidarity, I am uncertain. I know the Mosaurans dislike the idea of mixed species' pairings, but I do not know what form this prejudice will take once we land on the station.

Al'aneo's soldiers flank either side of us and move to extend their protection to our sister Liana. When we first arrived on Al'aneo's ship, he made certain everyone was aware of her status as a member of our family and our Clan. None have questioned it. Even when she announced that she'd taken Soran as her mate. With as much mistrust as exists between our two species, I was both shocked and then proud by how easily our people seem to have accepted not only Soran but Rowan's presence on the ship as well. After word spread of how they rescued Liana and me from the A'kai, it was obvious to everyone that these are two honorable males.

Abby and Grex wave at us. They've already said their goodbyes to Rowan since they have chosen to remain on my brother's ship while we go down to the surface.

A dull, clanging echo along the outer hull signals that we've docked with the Mosauran orbital station. Rowan glances once over his shoulder, and his silver eyes find mine immediately before he turns again to face forward.

My chest tightens. No doubt he remembers when I told him how nervous space stations make me after everything we went through as slaves. I draw in a deep and steadying breath as I brace myself for the dark memories. Despite my attempt to push down my fear, my body trembles slightly with the echoes of remembered pain of my time spent in the pleasure simulators.

Rowan spins to face me, his nostrils flared. He rushes toward me and takes my hands. "It is all right," he whispers softly as his tender gaze meets mine. "My people would never harm you," he says, misunderstanding the source of my fear. "I swear it to the Creator."

I'm ashamed of my weakness. This is yet another example of why we are ill-suited for one another. But I do not want him to think I believe his people would ever act with dishonor. "I know your people will not harm me, Rowan. It's just memories of...other stations."

He stares deep into my eyes. "You have been through more than anyone here can imagine. And you survived it because you are strong. It is not weakness to be plagued by dark memories."

I swallow against the lump in my throat and whisper, "Thank you, Rowan."

His gaze holds mine, so full of devotion it nearly breaks me. "Would you like me to accompany you?"

I dart a quick glance at Al'aneo beside me. "I'll be fine. Thank you."

"If you need me..." He looks back at his brother and Liana.

I smile. "I know."

After all the time we spent together, I can easily read his reluctance to leave my side as he makes his way back to stand next to Liana and Soran.

As we make our way down the metal ramp, several pairs of reflective eyes stare first at Soran, Liana, and Rowan and then back to myself and Al'aneo and our guards. I doubt an Aerilon cruiser, much less a group of Aerilon soldiers, is ever a welcome sight on the Mosauran orbital station. The tense set of Al'aneo's shoulders beside me tells me he definitely feels the same being surrounded by so many Mosaurans.

The Mosauran orbital station is nothing short of impressive. Bright, shining panels of metal and glass reflect our images with sparkling clarity. I'm amazed at the enormity of the open space before us. It's much larger than any station I've ever been to. With seven concentric rings that surround an open park-like area, I watch as Mosaurans in both humanoid and draken form fly from one level to the next.

I've never seen so many Mosaurans all in one place. With scales of varying shades of green, silver, gray, tan, and obsidian and markings upon their cheeks and brows in different colors of red, orange, yellow, and purple, they are both fierce and beautiful to behold. On most stations, the species present are vast and varied, but here there are surprisingly few other races, making us—the Aerilons and Liana—stand out in the crowd that surrounds us.

But I suppose few species venture to this station. Probably because the Mosaurans are one of the most feared of all races in the quadrant. Their reputation as fierce warriors must keep many away.

Brightly lit signs line the promenade, beckoning travelers to stop in for a meal or to purchase various items of technology or clothing. No seedy brothels here that promise interactions with slaves either in the flesh or in the simulation environments. The Mosaurans, for all their differences, are like my people: anti-slavery. And just knowing this makes me feel more at ease.

After spending so much time with them, it was easy to forget that Rowan and Soran are royalty. But as the people in the station part to make way for them to pass and stand respectfully off to the side, many of them bowing in observance, I'm reminded that they are Princes of Mosaura. They are the sons of the Empress and brothers to the future Empress that will come after. According to the traditions of their people, they are destined to become their sister's most trusted advisors if she so chooses them to be.

If Soran is declared Outcast, that will leave the future Empress with only Rowan. His temperament is easy, his spirit is brave, and his mind is sharp. She would not want for a better advisor.

When we reach the Imperial transport, a Mosauran female dressed in long, flowing, elegant green robes stands before the vessel, flanked on either side by a dozen warriors. With silver-gray scales and orange-red markings on her cheeks and brow, she looks so similar to both Soran and Rowan, I recognize her as their sister immediately.

As we move closer, I'm shocked by how much taller and more muscular she is than her brothers. I know Mosauran females are larger than the males, but their sister gives me pause. And for the first time, I wonder at the violence of the shav-rhokan—the mating battle—and how many males must be near death by the time it is over if the female rejects their pursuit. I try to imagine Rowan challenging another female, and the very thought twists my gut as jealousy rises in my thoughts, unbidden.

With her chin tilted up, she stares down at all of us with an imperious look. Both regal and fierce, I admire her almost as much as I dread the scrutiny of her gaze when it lands upon myself and Al'aneo.

For my brother's part, he appears unfazed, but I recognize the tense set of his jaw. If it is difficult for me to be here because of all the bad memories I have from the stations, it must be at least tenfold for him because of all the skirmishes he and his soldiers have, no doubt, been through with the Mosaurans while patrolling our borders.

To my surprise, Caryn greets Liana and Soran warmly. And when Al'aneo and I move forward to speak, she is courteous as well. She studies me with a piercing gaze before her lips tip up in a faint smile that breaks her stoic façade. "You are the one Rowan was stranded with."

Although said as a statement, I recognize that it is a question. "Yes."

"It is agreeable to meet you."

Uncertain how to respond, I simply reply, "And you as well."

She turns, and we follow her into the imperial transport.

Several pairs of reflective eyes observe us with open fascination as we pass. It must be as strange for them as it is for us to be in such close proximity without threat of aggression.

The inside of the transport is sparse and utilitarian but at the same time immaculately clean and impressive technologically, reminding me of Rowan's glider. A smile tugs at my lips as I recall the vessel he was so proud of. He lamented many times the loss of his ship. But with his knowledge of engineering and design, I'm certain it will not be long until he builds another to replace it.

We strap into our seats and then stare out the viewscreen. The deep-green and purple glow of the planet below is enchanting. Strange to think that a race of fierce warriors would call such a beautiful place home.

The city is a series of structures built into the sides of the mountains. Several winged Mosaurans, both in draken and humanoid form, take to the sky as they move between them.

The castle is a great obsidian structure. Glittering stone polished so fine it reflects the brilliant rays of the sun in a dazzling display of light. The warm glow filters through the waterfall that travels down the mountain face and cascades to each terrace level of the palace before finally feeding into a large pool at the base.

The crystal green water flows out beneath the castle's stone wall and to a river that feeds into the city. Although every building towers up as if reaching toward the clouds, it is the castle that sits above all else. It has a strength to its beauty that suggests it was built for defense as much as aesthetics.

We land in the center of the large garden area. Actually, it is more like a forest, but on a slightly smaller scale since it is only contained inside the palace walls. Trees with dark-gray trunks that suggest hundreds of cycles of age spiral up toward the sky, heavily laden with huge branches full of deep-green leaves. We have trees very similar to these on Aerilon, except they come in a large array of colors. Red, orange, purple, green, white… They make me think of the home I haven't seen in over two cycles, and my heart squeezes painfully.

Rowan's sister stops and then turns to face Al'aneo and me. "The Empress wants to extend an invitation for you to stay at the palace tonight as our honored guests."

We accept her offer, and she motions one of her guards forward to lead us to our rooms.

My eyes track Rowan as he continues on with Soran and Liana. My chest tightens. Despite knowing how ridiculous it is, I feel like if I let him go without saying anything, we may never speak again. Unable to stop myself, I call out to him.

He stops in his tracks and then rushes back to me. His silver eyes stare down at me in concern. "What is it?"

"I wish to talk with you later."

A faint smile tugs at his lips. "I do too. I will find you when I am done."

Emotions tighten my throat as I nod in reply.

As we pass under the entrance into the structure, I study the empty space in the massive doorframe that suggests there are probably blast doors of some type that may be lowered at a moment's notice for defense. Two of the guards turn to Al'aneo and me, each extending an arm out for us. Despite knowing that Rowan's people would never hurt me, I'm unable to hide my reluctance to be so close to a stranger.

With obsidian scales and deep-purple markings across his cheeks and brow, his coloring is beautiful for a warrior, and his expression, although hard, appears friendly at the same time. Noticing my hesitance, he tips his head to the side to regard me. His gaze falls upon my broken wings before his silver eyes meet mine with sorrow reflected behind them. "I vow on my honor as a warrior of Mosaura, you have nothing to fear from me."

Not wanting to offend him, I steel myself and step forward, resting my hand on his forearm so that he may guide me through the energy barrier that is coded only for those who normally move throughout the palace. I give him a faint smile. "Forgive my hesitation, I know your people are honorable."

He straightens at my words, his chin tips up slightly with pride. "You are safe here, Princess," he replies. "My name is Laden. The palace is heavily guarded, and no harm will come to you here. I swear it to the Creator."

I give him a warm smile. "Thank you." We begin walking, and the small tingle across my skin as we pass through the energy barrier is comforting in a way; it reinforces just how heavily guarded this place is.

Upon first inspection, I'm surprised by the enormous size of the rooms. The furnishings and decorations are sparse and hardly feel welcoming. Perhaps this area is more for reception of guests instead of for family gatherings and such. But one thing stands out sharply. The intricately carved wooden chairs, sofas, and tables. Delicate twining patterns, etched in the dark wood, lend exquisite and beautiful detail to each item. I note the fire-breathing draken sigil of House Mosaura is stamped in various places throughout the palace as we continue.

A large painting of two Mosaurans hangs at the top of a stairway. Their crowns designate them as royalty. The one on the left, I know is the Empress, but the one on the right I've never seen. I turn to Laden. "Who is the male standing next to the Empress?"

His brows lift slightly, as if surprised by my question. "It was the consort of the Empress and the father of her children."

Sadness fills me. I should have realized it was Rowan's father.

Laden continues. "He fell in honorable battle protecting his family," he says solemnly.

When we reach the end of one long hallway, we turn directly into another, and it is easy to see that the defense of the palace is also in its maze-like system of organization. Guest and family quarters are deep within the structure, and one must know the labyrinth of hallways intimately to have any hope of navigating its secrets. As if reading my mind, Laden points off to the side and another hallway.

"After the palace was burned by the traitorous House Caladan many cycles ago, much of the inside was unsalvageable," he says. "The Empress redesigned the interior to make it difficult for any potential assassins to find the family rooms. It is an honor to be entrusted enough to be given quarters near theirs. Few, if any, are ever even allowed this far inside."

Al'aneo's head whips toward Laden. "We're to be given rooms near the royal family?"

It is easy to read the shock in his voice. Even my Clan does not do this for security reasons.

"Yes," Laden says. "Prince Rowan sent a comm instructing us to make sure your rooms were back here."

We stop in front of a heavy door, and Al'aneo stops at the left one beside it. Laden gestures to the wall panel. "If you will place your hand here," he instructs, "it will be coded for your personal use, and then you will automatically be granted free movement throughout the palace as well." He tips his head to the right. "Prince Rowan's room is next to yours."

My heart stops. "It is?"

Al'aneo arches a brow.

I say nothing and instead press my hand to the panel and then step inside my room, calling out from the door. "I'm going to rest. I'll knock on your room later."

"I will be here," Al'aneo calls out in reply just before the door seals shut behind me.

CHAPTER 34

ROWAN

It doesn't take long for us to find Mother standing in the midst of her sanctuary—her private atrium. Mosaic tiles line the floor and walls in beautiful patterns depicting forest scenes and Mosaurans in full draken form. Light filters in from a glass ceiling above, lending an almost ethereal effect to the space as it reflects off of the large sea-green pool of water in the center of the room.

With her back to the small stream that flows through the gardens, she stares solemnly at the ancient murals of the cursed lovers. It portrays the fall of a fierce draken warrior. His doomed fate sealed by the death of his bondmate. Not many survive the loss of their partner.

That our mother survived after the passing of our father is a testament to her strength not only as a parent but as a leader. She knew her children and her people needed her, so she fought against the death that would have claimed her.

Sensing our presence, Mother turns to face us. Dressed in traditional Mosauran robes, hands clasped together in front of her, she gives me a warm smile that quickly falls from her face as she looks to my brother.

Her sharp gaze scans Liana from head to toe a moment before she returns her attention to Soran. “She is small,” she says impassively.

He bristles beside me. “She may be small, but she is as fierce as any Mosauran female.”

Mother’s nostrils flare, and her eyes widen as she stares down at Liana. “It is done then.” Her gaze turns to Soran with an expression somewhere between disappointment and sadness. “You have already mated her.”

“Yes.”

“Why would you take this female that looks so much like a V’loryn as your mate?” she asks, anger bleeding into her tone. “What could you possibly have been thinking?”

My thoughts turn to Tr’lani, and it occurs to me that I might ease her disappointment with Soran by confessing my affection for an Aerilon. From the thunderous look on our mother’s face, I’m not sure which would displease her more.

Soran opens his mouth to answer, but Liana steps in front of him, tilting her chin up defiantly. “I do not appreciate being talked over as if I’m not standing right here. Soran is my mate, and I am his. We *chose* each other. We do not come here for your judgment or approval. We came here so that your son can spend some time with his family before he is banished by your archaic laws.”

Something akin to respect and admiration flashes behind Mother’s eyes, and now I’m thoroughly confused. She arches a brow. “So, not like a V’loryn then,” she says in a low voice more to herself than to us.

She levels a hard gaze at Liana. “You call our laws archaic, but they exist for a reason. Our people mate for life. Our very hearts even beat in synchronization at the moment the bond is forged as it creates a link between our souls.” Her eyes dart briefly to Soran. “Our mates are our greatest strengths but also our greatest weakness. That is the reason for the mating battle—to ensure that the mate we choose is at least our equal or our better. They must be strong…because if they are not and they are killed, the other usually follows shortly after.”

“You survived the death of your mate,” Liana counters.

"But at great cost. I do not want that for my son." Her gaze rakes over Liana's smaller form once more with a hint of disgust. "You are a weakness now in the Imperial line. Not only because of your size but also because of what you represent."

"And what exactly do I represent?"

Mother narrows her eyes. "In his bonding with you, I can easily imagine the death of my son—his soul tethered to a species weaker than ours." She leans forward. "You are also an affront to the traditions of our people—a straying from the old ways. If I ignore the laws, I set a precedent for my reign—discarding the rules that have served our people for thousands of cycles. We have only just recovered from the last Civil War, and this could add more weight to the dissidents."

It is easy to read the pain in Soran's eyes as the words leave her mouth, and I place a hand on his shoulder, wanting to offer him comfort. Although I did not understand it at first, I now know why he could not give up Liana; I feel the same of Tr'lani. If she wanted me, I would break every law and rule of our people just to have her as my mate.

I listen as Liana tells our mother about her abuse at the hands of Talel. When she mentions the R'ugol—of how her mind was violated, shock flitters briefly across the normally stoic Empress's face. She is surprised that Liana's mind did not break as so many others have when tortured in this way.

It's one of the few times that our mother has been stunned into silence. Few would ever dare challenge her and live.

I wonder what she'd think if she knew an Aerilon survived the R'ugol as well? My people believe falsely that the Aerilon are a weak race, when in truth, they are just as strong as us. Tr'lani has shown me that many times over.

Before Mother responds, Liana breaks the awkward silence. "I will take my leave. My only desire in coming here was for my mate to spend time with his family before he's Outcast. Having been taken against my will from my home world and my family, I know the pain of being parted from those you love. It is not something I would wish even on my worst enemy. Whatever offenses you have laid against me, I do not hold you responsible. Your ignorance is to blame, and I will not waste any more time holding you accountable for it. I will leave you to spend time with your son."

Caryn and I watch Liana in awe as she leaves the room.

My mother's eyes are sad as she looks to my brother. "Losing your father and then believing you were dead as well…it nearly killed me." Her voice is thick with emotion. "When you returned, I swore I would do everything in my power to keep my family together, to keep you all safe." Her expression turns angered. "Our people will believe I am granting you leniency because you are my son."

Soran's nostrils flare as he defends his mate, telling her how he would have died when their pod crashed if not for Liana.

I meet my mother's eyes evenly. "We would both be dead right now if not for her bravery."

Caryn looks to our mother. "Only a strong female would stand before the Empress of the Mosauran Empire and speak her mind where others would have cowered in fear." She steps forward. "You, Mother, were the one who taught me that in the days of the Old Empire, women were considered unfit to rule until the law was changed." She darts a subtle glance at us. "Perhaps it is time for the laws to change again."

My mother gives Caryn a stern look. "There is already threat of another Civil War between the Great Houses. This could be the catalyst that stokes new flames of discord among our people. There will be many who will not wish to accept this decision." She turns to my brother. "Do you not see how this could place us in danger? Compromise my rule? And your sister's rule after mine?"

Caryn's eyes flash with anger. "We did nothing to provoke the attack that led to Father's death and the Civil War. And yet, it still happened," she says. "Sending your son and his mate into exile would only weaken our family, lessen the circle of people we can truly trust. We will always have to be vigilant against those who would seek to take the throne for themselves. And we are stronger if our family is united."

My sister is right. We *are* stronger if we are united. And we are even more so if we are allied with another race as strong as our own. Our House is now linked to Tr'lani's Clan on Aerilon because of Soran and Liana's bonding. But if we had a formal alliance with them, the Council would have to accept a bonding between our two species.

I saw the look on Tr'lani's face when we spoke only a moment ago. I know she said she does not want a mate, but she loves me. Of this, I am certain. Now, I must find a way to get her to admit it.

"Besides," I add, "the laws will have to change eventually. After the last plague that swept through the Empire, we lost so many females we are almost in as dire straits as the V'loryns. Interspecies bonding is the answer to replenish our numbers." I give her a meaningful look and then plant the seed of my plan. "And with it could come new allies for the Empire—allies loyal to our House."

"He's right," Caryn adds. "Clan Al'ani accepted Liana into their family. They are one of the seven ruling High Clans of Aerilon, and they have pledged their friendship to our House because of Soran's bond to her."

I step forward. "Both Liana and Tr'lani were violated by the R'ugol when they were kept by the A'kai. Our people have always viewed other species as weak, but the fact that these two females—a Terran and an Aerilon—survived something that can break even the fiercest Mosauran warrior speaks to their strength. We have been prejudiced against Outsiders, believing them to be less than us. But we are wrong. Accepting them into our society will not weaken us as a race; it will strengthen us as a people."

With a slight clench of her jaw, Mother places her hands on Soran's shoulders, a look of resignation etched in her features. "I cannot lose you again. It would break me. I will inform the Council of my decision and deal with the fallout as it comes." She gives him a repentant look. "Please bring your Ashaya before me. I must formally welcome her into our family as I should have done when she first arrived."

She looks to me. "And I would speak with the Aerilons as well after they have rested from their journey."

My heart soars at her words, and I cannot leave fast enough to seek out Tr'lani. Now, I just need her to admit she loves me. I never once gave up on my search for Soran, even when everyone else insisted it was futile. And I will not give up on Tr'lani. Even without the fated bond, I know the truth deep in my soul. She is mine, and I am hers.

CHAPTER 35

TR'LANI

My gaze drifts over the palatial room I've been given. A large, four-poster bed floats in the center, surrounded on all sides by beautiful green sheer fabric panels. A deep-green comforter on top of the mattress appears so plush and inviting, I'm almost tempted to lay down on it now, but I'd rather explore first. It's strange that there are no windows, nothing connecting this room to the outside.

Off to the left, I notice the cleansing room and wardrobe. Massive by any standards, I imagine a Mosauran in draken form could probably wander these quarters and halls just as easily as they can in humanoid form. My footsteps echo in the cavernous space, but it is the strange, low, rumbling sound in the background that draws my attention. It seems to be coming from the far-right wall. I move toward it and gasp in surprise when I step through an invisible barrier and find myself standing on a balcony outside.

On either side of me are obsidian stone walls lined with flowering vegetation. This space is like a small courtyard unto itself, overlooking the gardens and the city below. The air is thick with moisture and the scent of deep, rich earth. Water cascades from the floor above and collects in a small pool near the edge of the large terrace before disappearing over the ledge and down to the next level. Vibrant deep-purple and green vines trail over the side railing, gently swaying back and forth in the crisp, cool breeze.

Several thick gray clouds hang overhead, rumbling low with thunder as if promising rain. My gaze turns to the city, and I smile when I notice a family with two small children. One of them is flapping his wings mightily to keep up with his parents while the other is strapped in a forward-facing harness on his father's chest, gazing at the world around him in wide-eyed wonder.

I turn back to my room but find only a solid wall. When I move closer, I extend my hand and observe as it passes right through it. How clever to conceal the family rooms behind a cloaking device. I imagine where I'm standing is probably shielded as well, appearing as something entirely different from what I see before me right now.

I'll have to ask Rowan when I see him. I remember Laden's words about how few are ever allowed in this part of the palace, and now I understand why. This must be a closely guarded secret to protect the royal family, and I'm humbled that they would trust my brother and me with this knowledge.

As I walk back in my room, I allow my hand to rest on one of the entry columns, and I inhale sharply as what I thought was a rock wall to my left shimmers briefly and then disappears to reveal another balcony adjacent to mine. It's not Al'aneo's. He was on the opposite side, so it must be Rowan's.

Unable to contain my curiosity, I walk farther in. It looks so much like the area I just left that I wonder if it's another illusion. Several large overflowing pots of gorgeous red and purple flowers on thick green-leaved vines surround the space. An intricately carved wooden table and several chairs suggest he has company regularly, but perhaps it is only for his family. A depression in the terrace stacked with corded wood, piled atop a layer of ash tells me he often has fires out here.

Inhaling deeply of the crisp, clean air, I imagine it must be so pleasant here during the nights. The thought of sitting by a fire to enjoy the gorgeous view of the mountains and the city below is an enticing one. Without thinking, my feet carry me toward the entrance to his room.

A large bed, very similar to mine, floats in the center with a desk and chair in the far corner. I take a deep breath, and my nostrils fill with the masculine scent of him. A strange mixture of spice and earth. It is something I know very well, and my cheeks flush at the memory of sleeping wrapped up in his wings and nuzzling into his chest during the nights when he held me.

I walk toward the bed and rest my hand on one of the posts, tracing the intricate pattern in the woodwork as I study it in fascination. It's beautiful, and I'm surprised it never occurred to me that his people would have aesthetically pleasing things. They are warriors, after all, and this idea made me falsely believe that their dwellings would be sparse and utilitarian. I never expected to find such beauty here as I've found.

A sudden whoosh of air startles me, and I spin to find Rowan standing just inside the doorway as the entry seals behind him. He stares at me in confusion. "Tr'lani?"

Horrified that I've been caught, I gasp and then stumble over my words. "Rowan, I—I'm sorry." I start to retreat back to the balcony. "I shouldn't have come in here. I—"

He moves to stop me, wrapping his warm hand around my forearm, staring down at me with a tender gaze. "It is all right," he says softly. "I was just surprised to find you in here. I was going to go knock on your door in a moment anyway."

"You were?"

"Yes. There's something I'd like to show you."

"What is it?"

A loud knock at the door startles us both. "Who is there?" he calls out.

"It's Caryn." I recognize his sister's deep voice. Commanding and authoritative, it sounds as if she's angry.

But based on the smile that spreads across his face, I must be interpreting her tone incorrectly. He holds out his hand for me to take it. "Come." He grins. "I'd like you to properly meet my sister."

Hesitant and unsure, I take his hand, and we move to the door.

The moment it opens, Caryn's smiling expression falters as her gaze lands on me. Her eyes shift to Rowan. "I was unaware you had company."

"Caryn." Rowan tilts his chin up proudly. "This is Tr'lani." He turns back to me. "Tr'lani, this is my sister, Caryn."

Although I already technically met her on the station, it was brief and formal, unlike this.

Her face is an almost perfect stoic mask as she greets me. "My brother has told me much about you."

"He has?"

Rowan elbows his sister. The impassive expression leaves her face as she gives him a thunderous look. He grins. "You can act normal around her, Caryn. You don't have to be the 'perfect' future Empress right now."

She sighs heavily, but it is easy to see the hint of a smile that tugs at her lips. "Fine." Her gaze shifts to me, and she arches a teasing brow. "However did you manage to spend so many days with my brother? How long did it take before his mere presence began to irritate you?"

Rowan shoots his sister an annoyed glance before crossing his arms over his chest and tilting his chin up. "You're the only one who finds me irritating. You are simply jealous because everyone else enjoys my company."

I start laughing, and his sister joins in as well. He turns to me, his jaw dropping in mock offense. "You wound me, Tr'lani."

I roll my eyes and smirk. "You know I'm only joking with you."

"I do," he grins. "This is truth."

When we turn back to Caryn, I notice her staring at us with a look I cannot quite discern. It's somewhere between shock and disbelief. Does she know what happened between us on the planet? Can she tell even now that despite how impossible it is, I'm in love with her brother?

Her eyes flick to Rowan. "The Healer you requested is ready to assess you."

I snap my head toward him, my gaze raking over his form for any sign of injury.

"It is for you that I asked for a Healer," he explains. "To see if something can be done for your wings."

When Caryn's gaze moves to my wings, her face softens into one I recognize well. Every Aerilon, including my brother, gives me that same sympathetic and pitying look every time they see me. The expression that tells me they believe I am broken. But I need no one to tell me this. Despite the physical evidence of what was done to me, the deeper scars that ache the most are the ones that I hold inside, where nobody can see.

I'm a Healer. I was one of the best in my class, and even I could do nothing to repair my wings. Part of me wants to protest that I'd rather not see another Healer and be told once again that nothing can be done. But another part of me—the part that still hopes despite everything—refuses to give up on any chance that someone may be able to heal me.

As we follow Caryn through the palace, she makes small talk about various things that have happened while he and Soran have been away. But a small spark of jealousy lights deep inside me when she mentions all the females who are eagerly waiting to challenge Rowan to the mating battle now that word has spread that Soran has taken a mate.

Unbidden anger flares brightly when he doesn't immediately tell her that he is not interested in any other females. But I quickly push it back down when I realize he asked me to choose him and I didn't. Instead, I pushed him away.

When we reach the Healer, I'm surprised by how large the medical center is. I suppose it is because they have so many warriors stationed here. It looks more like the interior of a ship than a castle. With gleaming, polished metal walls and sparkling glass offices and rooms, it reminds me a bit of our healing centers on Aerilon.

I look up to find a male Mosauran dressed in long white robes moving toward us. With obsidian scales and deep-purple markings on his brow and cheek ridges, he is beautiful. Apparently, Caryn must think so as well, because the orange-red color on her cheeks turn even darker when he greets us with a friendly smile.

He bows low before us. When he lifts his gaze, his eyes dart briefly to Caryn with an expression of longing before shifting to me and then trailing toward my back to stare at my broken wings. His brows lift up to his forehead in mild shock before he quickly retrains his face into the impassive professionalism I suspect all Healers, regardless of species, are trained to exude. "I am Kalen. Rowan told us of your… injury," he says. "I would like to assess you. If you will permit me."

I start to tell him that I'm a Healer, but he beats me to it.

"He also informed us that you are a Healer on your world and that you have tried many things to attempt to repair them. But I wonder if perhaps we have different medical technology that you are unaware of that may be of help." He pauses and gives me a meaningful look. "In any case, I would like to help you if I can."

The deep sincerity in his words and his gaze catch me off guard, and it takes me a moment to respond. "Thank you. I would appreciate any help you may give."

He motions for me to follow him to a nearby room and exam table and gestures for me to lie down. Caryn waits outside while Rowan follows us in. With a flick of his wrist, a floating bar detaches from the wall above and hovers overhead. I watch in wonder as it slowly moves over my body, projecting a softly glowing light as it takes readings. Briefly, it stops several times as if performing a deeper assessment of various areas before it continues on.

Kalen stares down at his tablet, no doubt assessing the information he's receiving from the floating scanner with his brow furrowed deeply in concentration. After a moment, he lifts his gaze to mine, sympathy reflecting behind his eyes. "You are stronger than I believed your people to be. You are also a very skilled Healer judging by all the healed injuries I see evidence of your having repaired."

"What about her wings?" Rowan asks, impatience laced in his tone. "Can you do anything?"

Kalen looks down at me. "Please sit up and remove your tunic so that I may assess them more thoroughly."

I tense, and it doesn't go unnoticed by Rowan. "Her people are not as comfortable with nudity as ours are."

Kalen nods and then pulls a blanket out of a nearby compartment. "You may cover yourself with this."

Rowan's gaze meets mine, and he dips his chin in a subtle nod. "I will be right outside," he says before disappearing out the door.

Kalen leaves as well to allow me to change. When he returns, he moves to my back. Unable to hide his shock at the many scars that crisscross my back, he gasps lightly.

"I tried to remove them," I explain. "But they were made with—"

"Silic acid," he finishes my sentence for me. I suppose as a Healer he knows just as well as any on Aerilon that the slave marks created by the Zovians and Anguis can never be healed. The acid makes them permanent. "I am sorry," he says softly.

I cannot help the involuntary flinch when one hand settles lightly on my back at the spot where my wings begin. "Did I hurt you?" he asks, and it is easy to hear the concern in his voice.

"No. I'm just…it's difficult to be touched…sometimes…" I close my eyes against the dark memories that try to return.

His hands move over my wings, and in many areas, it is shockingly painful despite how gentle he is trying to be. Tears sting my eyes, but I blink them back.

Sensing my discomfort, he asks, "Do you want me to stop?"

"No. They're just sensitive where they are broken."

Trying to focus beyond my discomfort, I concentrate on the faint buzzing sound of the scanner as he assesses every break. When he reaches one of the main cartilaginous supports, an involuntary cry of pain escapes me.

Rowan bursts through the door, his gaze wild and unfocused as he scans the room for any hidden threats before his eyes zero in on Kalen with a thunderous look. "What are you doing? Stop it! You're hurting her!"

"My Prince, I—"

I interrupt him. "It's all right, Rowan. My wings are just sensitive. He's being as gentle as he can."

Rowan growls low in his throat as he gives Kalen a warning glare. "Can you help her or not?" he snaps. "Because if you cannot, there is no need for any further assessment and unnecessary pain."

Kalen moves around the table and looks between both of us. "I may be able to restore your wings."

My heart soars at his words, and when my eyes meet Rowan's, I see the same hope reflected in his face.

Kalen continues. "But it will be extremely painful. I will have to rebreak what has been broken and reset each one into proper alignment."

Rowan's brow furrows deeply. "Can you do nothing to numb the pain?"

He shakes his head, and I lower my gaze because I already know the answer. That is why it is so cruel to break an Aerilon's wings. It is also why my people are so careful about flying injuries. We must be awake and alert to ensure the nerves are reconnected properly. If they are not, the wings must be rebroken yet again in the attempt to fix them. And the procedure is not always successful, especially in the case of multiple breaks. "The nerves are too fragile. I will have to test for sensation with each correction I make." His gaze shifts to mine. "And even then, I must warn you that with the extent of the damage that's been done, you may not regain full function even if you undergo this procedure."

Rowan stares at him in disbelief. "Is there no other way?"

"No," Kalen answers. "My findings are consistent with the data provided by the Aerilon Healer on the cruiser as well."

I nod, because he's right. When she assessed me, she came to the same conclusions as him.

"You will need several days to heal after the extensive repair of such delicate tissue."

Kalen stares down at me with a pitying look, and I meet his gaze evenly so he will see the truth of my words. "Thank you for assessing me, and I appreciate your offer to perform this procedure, but…I believe I would prefer to have it done on my home world. I am eager to return to my family."

He bows his head. "Of course."

Rowan and I walk side by side back to our rooms in silence, the mood somber between us at this despairing news. When we reach his door, he turns to face me. "There is a place a short distance from the palace I'd like to show you."

I'm curious to know what it is. "All right."

"Follow me."

CHAPTER 36

TR'LANI

He holds out his hand. I take it without hesitation. He leads me back onto the balcony and to the ledge. "Will you allow me to carry you?"

I lift my gaze to the sky. Small patches of sunlight filter through the dark clouds overhead as the wind whips through my hair. The air is thick with moisture, and I turn to him with a questioning look. Tempests are common on Aerilon, making it difficult to fly, and I wonder if they have similar storms on Mosaura. But perhaps they are much tamer here.

In answer to my unspoken question, he darts a quick glance at the dark clouds overhead. "It will rain, but not yet. It is safe to go out in this weather."

Satisfied, I nod. "All right. Where are we going?"

He arches a teasing brow. "It is a surprise."

I'm always amazed by his strength as he gathers me in his arms, lifting me as if I weigh nothing. He walks to the edge of the balcony and steps up onto the stone ledge. The wind seems much stronger now, and I cannot help but worry about flying in this weather despite his insistence that it's safe. I wrap my arms around his neck a bit tighter.

He gently nuzzles my temple to get my attention, and when I look up, he meets my eyes evenly. "I would never let you fall. You have my solemn vow as a warrior of Mosaura." His silver gaze travels over my face. "Do you trust me?"

His expression is tender as he waits for my answer. My heart stutters and then begins hammering. This is the question male Aerilon ask their partners prior to the mating flight. But what it is really asking is if the female is certain she wishes to take the male as her mate. If she says "no," he sets her down, and it is understood as a rejection. But if she says "yes," they will become mates for life. As I stare deep into Rowan's reflective silver eyes, the words leave my lips without hesitation. "Yes."

He smiles brightly at me and then unfolds his wings from his back. Wide and magnificent, they spread out behind him. So different from my people and yet still beautiful, their gray color just a few shades darker than the rest of his scales. He lifts his chin as his sharp gaze scans the sky as if searching for any danger. His grip on my form tightens. As if I were something precious, he takes great care in securing me against his chest.

He shifts slightly beneath me, and then we drop over the side, falling a moment before his wings billow out like great sails, catching the current and lifting us back up. He dips to one side and turns into the drift. Wind rushes through my hair as he makes a slow arc over the castle gardens. My heart beats wildly as I breathe in the crisp, cool air and gaze at the beauty around me. I've never felt more alive.

Great mountains covered with lush green forests surround us. Massive buildings and structures carved in the obsidian stone of the mountains reflect brightly beneath the pale-orange sun, lending an almost ethereal glow to the city as we fly overhead. Mosaurans in various forms and colors sail past us in both humanoid and battle form as they navigate the skies.

A mother carries her fledgling strapped to her chest. Although she is too young yet to fly, the child spreads her wings out to catch the wind as she tests the sails, smiling brightly as they pass.

The muscles of my back ache with want to stretch out my own wings and fly in tandem with Rowan. Drawing in a deep breath, I push down my sadness and instead focus on the world around me, enjoying the view. As if sensing my desire, he gently nuzzles my temple again to get my attention. "I'm going to adjust my hold. Are you ready?"

As soon as I nod, he adjusts his grip so that he is no longer carrying me with one hand behind my back and another behind my knees. Instead, he wraps his arms tightly around my waist, holding my back firmly against his front. The wind glides across my wings, and I stretch them out beside me, enjoying the feel of the air traveling across the sensitive membranes.

Closing my eyes, I imagine that they're whole and I'm flying. I cannot stop smiling. I'm so happy, I can hardly contain my joy, and I spread my arms wide, enjoying the feel of the wind rushing past me.

The air around us howls and pulls at our forms. Rowan's arms tighten around me as he shifts and then turns into the strong wind. The sudden stop and then lift as we catch a new current is thrilling as we spiral up into the clouds. We break out at the top, and I stare down at the earth below, the brilliant stone of the mountains glittering as they reflect the sun's rays.

A wide smile crests my lips. "This is amazing," I tell him.

Rowan nuzzles the back of my head and then speaks softly into my ear. "Hold on."

With an audible snap, he retracts his wings, and we dive toward the sea of trees below. At the last moment, the dark-gray sails pop open and billow out beside him as he carefully circles before we touch down on the ground.

Gently, he releases his hold on my waist and lowers my feet to the forest floor. When I turn around, I give him a beaming smile and stretch up on my toes to wrap my arms around his neck, hugging him tightly. "Thank you, Rowan. That was—" My voice catches, and I swallow against the lump forming in my throat. "Wonderful."

A devastatingly handsome smile curves his lips.

We're in the middle of a forest. Tall trees tower overhead. The earth is spongy beneath us, and I notice a well-worn trail that disappears not far up ahead. A light mist and fog hang in the air, obscuring the details beyond ten paces, and I turn my attention back to Rowan. "Are we to follow the path?"

"Yes. The Temple is nearby."

My brow furrows softly in confusion. "Temple?"

A smile tugs at the corner of his mouth. "You'll see." He reaches for my hand, and I take it. The familiar warmth of his palm in mine makes my heart clench. "Follow me."

As we make our way along the path, a large shape looms up ahead in the distance. Shrouded by fog, it isn't until we're standing at the base of the massive stone steps that I'm able to see the Temple in greater detail.

Obsidian stones carved into great square blocks and rounded columns make up the pantheon structure. Thick ropes of trailing vines drape across the roof, winding around rock and stone and hanging like great curtains over the entrance. Their tiny purple flowers a lovely contrast to the dark stone.

Our footsteps echo as we reach the outer doors that lead into the sanctuary. My jaw drops as I take in the massive structure, not so much because of its size but because it is so eerily familiar. "This is just like our Great Temple on Aerilon," I tell him. "The Temple of the Fated Lovers."

"What is—" he starts to ask but stops when I tug at his hand to pull him with me as I search for the statue I just know will be here.

He follows without question, and when we reach the inner sanctum, I gasp. Soft orange light filters in from the round glass dome directly above the massive carving, illuminating the faces of the two lovers. At least five times the size of a normal person, their bodies are carved of smooth obsidian stone. With his hands wrapped around her waist and her arms around his neck, his great wings are spread wide, curving toward her as if to embrace her form. Hers remain tucked close to her back as their faces tilt toward one another like two lovers about to kiss. I turn to Rowan in confusion. "How is this possible?"

He gives me a strange look. "What is it?"

"This Temple. This statue." I gesture to the two lovers. "It is an exact replica of the Great Temple on Aerilon, except ours is carved in white stone. And instead of Mosauran wings, they are the wings of my people."

We move toward the structure as I stare at it in wonder. Studying it closer, I notice the fine line along her back where her wings are connected. "Look." I point to the strange seam. The line, though well hidden, cannot hide the different grain of the stone from the rest of the statue. "Her wings were replaced."

"You are right. Our scholars have always believed that perhaps the original structure was damaged, and the wings were carved from different stone in an effort to fix it."

"I don't think that's why they were replaced, Rowan."

His brow furrows in confusion. "What do you mean?"

"On Aerilon, this exact statue exists, except her wings are like those of my people, and his wings have a similar line like this one does. His wings were replaced just as hers were replaced on this one." I pause. "And our scholars thought the same thing—that they'd been damaged and had to be fixed. But now I'm not sure."

He lowers his gaze to the ground, a contemplative expression on his face. "This is the statue of Tormin and Kilena. They were enemies who became lovers. It is believed they now watch over and guide my people from their place among the stars."

It is strange to find something so familiar on the home world of our enemies. As my eyes travel over the statue, I stare at it in wonder. "On Aerilon, they are called the Two Lovers. They are Tr'omen and Kr'elana. They were sworn enemies who fell in love and bonded. Their reign marked the earliest known era of recorded peace among our people." Shaking my head softly, I turn to Rowan. "This must mean that our people met one another long before we even realized. She was Aerilon, and he was Mosauran. There can be no other explanation for their wings and the same Temples on both of our planets."

With a deeply furrowed brow, he looks to the ground as if in deep thought. "But why lie about it? Why hide who they were?"

"I don't know," I whisper. "But something must have happened that started the trouble between our two races. People wanted to alter the truth, and then after so long, they forgot it altogether."

We walk around the Temple as I study this exact replica of the Two Lover's Temple on Aerilon. How long have they been here, and how is it that they were constructed to match so perfectly but with different stone? That must have meant that they each traveled to each other's planets long before our recorded history.

* * *

ROWAN

I turn to face Tr'lani. All the long cycles of hatred between our two races…this proves it wasn't always this way between our people. Searching her golden eyes, I whisper softly, "Do you realize what this could mean?"

A slow smile curves her lips. "Our species were not always enemies."

"Precisely," I grin. "This could change everything between our two races."

Looking down, she taps into her communicator. After she's finished, she looks up at me. "I told Al'aneo about this place so he can come see it for himself before we leave."

My face falls. I don't want to think of her leaving so soon. "I imagine your family is eager to see you again."

She gives me a smile that does not touch her eyes. "Yes, they are."

"What is wrong?"

She lowers her gaze, but I gently place two fingers beneath her chin to tip her face back up to mine. Her eyes are full of sadness as they meet mine. "My grandfather died a few months ago." Her voice quavers slightly. "I…I loved him so much, Rowan. I can't believe he's gone."

My heart clenches, and I slip my arms around her, pulling her close. I run my hand soothingly across her shoulders. "My heart grieves with yours, Tr'lani."

"Thank you," she whispers. "I hate that I wasn't there for him…that I didn't even get to tell him goodbye."

I swallow against the lump in my throat, for I know this pain well. "Long have I lamented the last moments with my father," I say softly. "If I had known it was the last time we would speak, I would have told him so many things. Starting with how blessed I felt by the Creator to have such a wonderful father."

She pulls back slightly and reaches up to gently cup my cheek. Pressing her forehead softly to mine, she whispers, "My heart grieves with yours, Rowan."

"Thank you," I reply as I take her hand in mine. "Come." I gesture toward the altar. "Let us offer a prayer to the Creator in their memory."

She follows me, and together we each take a remembrance stone from the bowl near the altar. We walk toward the statue, pausing with our heads bowed slightly in silent prayer before reverently placing them at its base. After a moment, she turns to me. "My people leave prayer stones as well at our statue. Strange that your people do this too."

I nod. "Perhaps our two cultures share more than we realize."

THE SUN BEGINS to set low on the horizon as dark clouds form overhead. Moisture hangs thick in the air with the promise of heavy rain to come. I meet her eyes evenly. "A storm is coming. We should return."

She nods.

Carefully, I gather her in my arms and tuck her tight to my chest. Extending my wings, I lift off into the sky, struggling against my sadness. She leaves tomorrow, and I know that I may never hold her like this again.

When we reach the balcony of the palace, she is quiet a moment before bidding me goodnight. I do not want to leave her, but I can think of no excuse to stay. At least, none that do not involve me dropping to one knee and presenting myself again to her in the hopes that she will claim me as her mate.

Dark clouds whirl overhead as the first drops of rain begin to patter against the stone. I've always loved the rain. Something about it relaxes me. I often sit outside during a storm, lost in thought. It is meditative in a way. And yet, I cannot relax as I normally do.

I allow my thoughts to drift to Tr'lani. I desire her more than anything I've ever wanted before. Being with her feels right in a way that nothing else ever has.

I close my eyes, imagining her face. I have always been a determined male. Never one to give up, I defied my family when I went to search for Soran, knowing in my heart that he was still alive. Just as I know beyond any doubt that Tr'lani should be mine. I cannot believe that what happened between us on the planet meant nothing to her. I saw the truth of it in her eyes on the station. She loves me. Now, I just have to get her to admit it before she leaves me forever.

Determination fills me, and I stand from the chair. I move across the balcony, stepping through the invisible barrier. I stop just outside her window, raising my hand to knock and get her attention when I hear a male's voice inside her room. Training my ear to the door, I recognize that it is Al'aneo. I turn to leave, wanting to give her privacy, but stop when he speaks again.

"And what about On'aro?"

"You know I love him. He grew up with our family. But—"

Anger, jealousy, and hurt fill me so great, I can hardly contain it. Without thinking, I step into the room and level an accusing stare at Tr'lani. "How could you lie to me, Tr'lani?"

* * *

TR'LANI

Soran comes storming into my room from the balcony, startling Al'aneo and me as he levels an accusatory glare in my direction. "How could you lie to me, Tr'lani?"

I jerk my head back. "Lie? What are you talking about?"

"I heard what you said." He meets my eyes evenly. "You said you love On'aro."

A short huff of air escapes my lips. "You were outside spying on me?"

"Tell me the truth," he snaps. "First, you tell me you love me, and then you push me away. You said you did not want a mate, and now I hear you telling your brother that you love a male you claimed you did not?"

I give him an incredulous look. "That's not what—"

Al'aneo stands, cutting me off abruptly. "You do not need to explain yourself, dear sister." He arches a brow at Rowan. "You must not have been spying for very long, or else you would have heard the first part of that conversation."

Rowan crosses his arms over his chest. "What part is that?"

Al'aneo narrows his eyes. "The part where she told me she loves you, you maltak. And she loves On'aro like a friend and brother."

Rowan's mouth drifts open a moment before he quickly snaps it shut again. His gaze is full of regret.

Al'aneo starts for the door. "I will leave you to speak with your... Mosauran," he says before flashing a pointed look at Rowan.

* * *

ROWAN

Regret fills me as I stare down at her. Her brother is right. I am a maltak.

She stands and walks toward me, fire burning in her eyes. "You want the truth?"

I nod.

"Well, here it is: The only reason I pushed you away is because I love you, Rowan. I didn't want you to become Outcast and give up everything for me."

Hope fills me. "This is truth?"

She nods and then starts to speak again, but I rush forward and pull her into my arms, capturing her mouth with my own.

She curls her tongue around mine, deepening our kiss, and I'm completely lost. I run my hands through her hair and down her back as I hold her even closer. Nothing exists outside of this moment between us, and I long more than anything to claim her as mine and have her claim me in return.

"Choose me," I breathe between kisses. "Choose me, Tr'lani."

"We can't, Rowan," she whispers, but I notice she does not pull away. Instead, she holds me even tighter, her mouth meshing repeatedly with mine.

I kiss a heated trail along her jaw and down to the curve of her neck and shoulder. "Why not?" I speak softly against her skin.

"Because you'll be Outcast, and I don't want you to give up everything for me."

I pull back just enough to cup her face in both hands, forcing her gaze to mine. I smile. "If that is your only hesitation, then you will be pleased to know I would no longer be Outcast. Soran will not be banished, and so neither will I."

Her eyes widen slightly. "The Empress said that?"

I nod. "And we're going to pursue talks of an alliance with your people."

A stunning smile curves her mouth. I only have a moment to be blinded by her beauty before she twines her arms around my neck, crushing her lips again to mine.

I lift her into my arms and carry her across the balcony to return to my bedroom. I know that Aerilon hearing is not as acute as that of a Mosauran, but I dislike the idea of pleasuring my mate in the room adjacent to her brother's.

I'm almost to the bed when Tr'lani gently pushes at my chest. I blink down at her in confusion. "What is wrong?"

Her golden eyes stare deep into mine as she reaches up to cup my cheek. "I—I don't know if I can do this, Rowan."

Gently, I lower her feet to the floor. "We do not have to do anything you do not want," I say softly. "We can move slow."

Tears gather at the corner of her eyes. She stretches up on her toes and gives me a tender kiss. "Thank you," she whispers. "I just...need some time."

"I will give you all the time you need to decide if you wish to choose me. Would it be all right if I hold you for now?" I long to sleep with her in my arms like we did when we were stranded together.

She nods.

As we lay in the bed, I gently wrap my arms and wings around her to hold her close. I'm pleased when she snuggles into me.

"This is perfect," she whispers as she traces her delicate fingers along the soft, leathery folds of my wings. "I never thought I would ever want anyone to touch me after everything I went through. Your people mate for life, just like mine," she says softly. "I...I was taken many times in the pleasure simulators." She lifts her gaze to mine, sadness and uncertainty in her eyes. "Does it bother you?"

At the mere mention of the horrors she endured, I hold her even tighter. I wish I could kill every despicable creature that ever touched her against her will. If anyone dares try to hurt her, I will end them. I cup her chin and meet her gaze evenly. "I hate that you suffered. But what happened to you was not your fault. Do not think for one moment that I would ever not want you because of this. I love you, Tr'lani. You are my heart."

A tear escapes her lashes and I brush it from her cheek. She tilts her face into my palm as she stares across at me. "An Aerilon female only ever trusts her mate to carry her in flight. It is the greatest trust a female can ever give to a male. And I trust you, Rowan. Completely."

I think on that day I first flew with her on Le'ro. She trusted me even then. And I vow, as I have before, that I will never break her trust.

"You're not worried?" she asks.

"About what?"

"Our people are enemies."

I gently nuzzle her temple. "They will not be for long. My mother is considering a formal alliance with your people. And once we show her the AI data crystal, I'm certain it will convince her to follow that path."

"I hope you're right," she whispers. "Tomorrow, we will go together to speak with your mother and my brother about the AI we found on the planet. Your people deserve to be warned about the dangers of the A'kai just as much as mine."

CHAPTER 37

TR'LANI

In the morning, we walk in silence toward his mother's chambers. Both of us are hesitant to view the horrifying images of the mass genocide of the Milarans again. But it has to be done. His people need to understand the dangers the A'kai pose.

When we find her, the Empress studies me with a piercing gaze. My brother enters a moment later and walks up next to us.

"Mother," Rowan bows slightly. "This is Princess Tr'lani and Prince Al'aneo of the Aerilon High Clan Al'ani."

The Empress dips her chin in a subtle acknowledgement. Her nostrils flare and she arches a brow, no doubt scenting that we smell heavily of each other. "You and my son?" she asks, her eyes darting to Rowan with a look of concern.

"Yes," Rowan takes my hand.

With a slight clench of her jaw, she looks between the two of us. "How exactly do you believe this will work?"

Rowan's eyes flash with anger, but I do not want him to argue with his mother. I do not want to be the cause of a rift between him and his family.

I squeeze his hand and then step forward. "We came here to show you something. Something important that we discovered when we crashed on an unknown planet."

"What is it that you would show me?"

Al'aneo looks between Rowan and I. "What is it you have found?"

I pull the AI data crystal from my pocket and hold it out to them. I press my thumb to the small indentation in the center and Elari appears before us. She looks to me. "It is good to see you again," she says. She looks to my brother and the Empress. "Greetings. I am Elari."

The Empress and Al'aneo watch in stunned silence as the recording of the Milaran male speaks into the display and then turns to ash before their eyes.

After I deactivate Elari, the Empress turns to us. "Our people must study this data. We need to understand exactly what it is that the Milarans were working on to defeat the A'kai."

Al'aneo shakes his head. "No."

Her head whips toward him with a thunderous look. I imagine there aren't many who say that word to her very often.

He continues. "Our people need to see this as well. They deserve to be warned about the dangers posed by the A'kai."

She narrows her eyes. "And how do I know you will not keep this information for yourselves?"

"You don't," I speak up and her gaze snaps to me. "You are going to have to trust us."

"Trust you?" she asks incredulously.

"Yes," Rowan says, his voice a low and subtle growl. "Tr'lani saved my life while we were on the planet. And Al'aneo saved us as well, after that."

Something akin to surprise flashes behind her eyes as she looks to me and my brother. She bows her head to us. "Then, it seems I owe you both a debt."

"You can repay us with your trust," I tell her.

Her sharp gaze holds mine a moment before she dips her chin in acknowledgement. "Fine. Take it to your people. If my son," she looks to Rowan, "places such faith in you, I trust his judgment. For I know he would never betray his family."

Rowan's lips tip up in a smile as he meets his mother's eyes. "Speaking of family," he says. "I must go wake my brother and his mate so you may officially welcome her into House Mosaura."

"Yes," she replies. Her gaze shifts to me.

He squeezes my hand. "There are things I wish to speak with you about as well, Mother," he adds.

I suspect he's talking about me and about us. He surprises me by pressing a quick kiss to my temple. "I will return in a moment."

His mother's eyes widen slightly as she observes, but she says nothing.

When he leaves, instead of speaking of us, she asks me for more details of the ruined city and the planet.

It doesn't take long for Rowan to return with Liana and Soran.

Liana looks so happy and I am overjoyed for her. But I wonder if they will choose to remain here or if they will come with us to Aerilon. I dread the thought of leaving her behind in this place; with a people who are known for their speciest views.

Rokan, the Empress's advisor, rushes inside. He goes straight for the Empress and whispers low in her ear.

She clenches her jaw and then turns her gaze to us. "An A'kai cruiser has been detected entering our system."

Rokan taps the nearby console, and an image of an A'kai fills the viewscreen. "Why have you entered the sovereign space of Mosaura?" the Empress asks as she glares into the display.

"The A'kai captain makes no effort to hide his anger. "The First Prime of A'kaina is demanding the release of his brother, Talel."

My brother narrows his eyes and bares his fangs. "Inform the First Prime that, according to our laws, his brother's life was forfeit the moment he took my sisters as his slaves."

The Captain's eyes narrow. "We are willing to offer an exchange." He pauses before splitting the viewscreen so that two females are visible. They appear V'loryn, at first, but they are much smaller than the average V'loryn female. One of them has long obsidian hair with golden brown eyes and the other has short blond hair with gray eyes. Liana gasps and moves toward the display, I realize these must be her people.

My body begins trembling involuntarily. I can only imagine the terror Liana's people have been through as their slaves. Of everything that was ever done to me during my slavery, the worst by far, was when Talel's soldier paralyzed my body and invaded my mind in the R'ugol. I've never been more terrified or helpless. "They have Terrans, Rowan," the words escape me in a shaking breath. "We have to do something."

He gives me a determined look. "We will. My people and yours will not leave the females in the hands of the A'kai.

"Release the females at once!" The Empress says in a loud and booming voice, startling Rokar beside her.

Liana reaches up as if to touch them through the display. "Gwen? Aria?"

Both female's eyes snap up at the sound of their names. The one with dark hair lifts a trembling hand to the screen. "Liana?" she says in a quavering voice. "Is it really you?"

Tears run down Liana's face as she struggles to keep her voice even. "Yes, it's me. Don't worry. We're going to get you back."

The A'kai Captain sneers. "Only if you release Lord Talel."

Rowan's mother lifts a dark gaze to the A'kai Captain. "Done. But then you must leave this system immediately."

The Captain's mouth curves into an evil grin. "I will send a transport to the orbital station and I expect Lord Talel to be ready when we arrive."

With a quick jerk of her head, the Empress waves at the screen and it cuts off.

Soran growls angrily. "He's a monster! You cannot let him go free!"

The Empress raises a hand to silence him. With a raised brow, she smirks. "The A'kai are in Mosauran space. The possession of slaves is a mandatory death sentence according to our laws." She turns her gaze to Al'aneo. "I believe that is the case for your people as well, is it not?"

My brother dips his head in a subtle nod. "You are correct."

"Good," she replies. "Then, the moment we have the females, we will fire on their ship."

The Empress's advisor interjects. "Empress, if we do this, we risk starting a war with the A'kai."

She turns a hardened gaze to him. "No! It is *they* who risk starting a war with us. They know the laws and yet they dare to violate them. Mercy in this case would be viewed by the A'kai as weakness. *We* are Mosaurans. We fear no other race," she growls.

Quickly, we make our way to the transport bay to go to the orbital station. As soon as we reach the transport, Rowan spins to face me. "You should remain here."

I give him an incredulous look. "No. I'm coming with you."

"He is right," Al'aneo interrupts. "You should stay here where it is safe."

"I am a Healer," I state firmly. "We do not know what kind of condition Liana's people may be in; I'll need to assess them immediately."

Rowan shakes his head. "There are Healers on the station that can see to them. You do not need to go."

"But there are not Healers who understand what they've been through." I meet his eyes evenly. "I know what it is to have my mind violated in the R'ugol. And I'm certain this has been done to them. They will need someone who understands."

"She's right," Liana adds as she walks toward me.

Soran follows closely behind her with a frustrated look on his face. It seems they've been having the same argument I'm having with my brother and Rowan.

I tip my chin up in defiance. "I refuse to stay down here. We will not argue about this any further. I am going with you to the station."

With a slight clench of his jaw, he jerks his chin in a nod and gives me a frustrated look as I move past him and onto the transport. The orange-red coloring of his brow and cheeks is a deeper shade of red as he stares at me. I know he is upset, but he will have to get over it.

As we travel to the Mosauran orbital station, I reach across and take Liana's hand, giving it a gentle, reassuring squeeze. She holds my hand tighter in return.

My brother sits across from us, fury burning behind his golden eyes. He hates the A'kai for what they did to us. Talel especially.

Rowan and Soran wear similar expressions as we sit together in tense silence. All of us are eager to see the Terran females safely away from their captors. They are members of Liana's crew, and I know she is anxious to free them. Creator knows the horrors they've endured in their time with the A'kai.

As soon as we arrive at the station, Rowan pulls me aside. His face is a stoic mask, but I can see the concern that reflects behind his gaze as he holds out a blaster and laser knife to me. "Here," he says. "Take these."

I take them without hesitation, tucking the blaster into my belt and concealing the knife in my sleeve. My heart hammers in nervous anticipation, but I push down my fear and steel myself for what comes next.

His silver eyes stare deep into mine. "If anything goes wrong, the blaster first and the laser knife for close combat."

Curling my hands into fists at my side, I give him a determined nod. "I remember what you've taught me."

His lips quirk up slightly in the barest hint of a smile. "You are fierce, and you are strong. You have trained as a Mosauran. You need no claws or venom to defeat any who would dare attack you."

CHAPTER 38

ROWAN

Everyone is tense, both Mosaurans and Aerilons, as we wait for the A'kai transport to dock. This section of the station has been cleared except for our warriors. Tr'lani's golden eyes burn with an intensity that would strike fear in any warrior's heart as she glares at Talel when Aerilon soldiers drag him from the cruiser.

Two A'kai emerge from a docked transport, dragging two Terran females behind them in chains. Anger twists deep in my gut, and a low growl escapes me, followed by several more from the Aerilon and Mosauran soldiers as we watch. Their clothing is tattered and shredded; their hair disheveled and their eyes dull as they walk behind their captors.

To treat life-givers this way is abhorrent. I notice they are as small as Liana. One has golden hair and the other dark brown. Their eyes widen in recognition as they meet hers; the spark of hope visible in each one as they make their way toward us.

Two Mosauran soldiers remove Talel's bindings and then lead him forward. I stand just slightly in front of Tr'lani, ready to shield her if I must as we watch in nervous anticipation as the two females walk past Talel and toward our soldiers, waiting to receive them.

Tension is thick in the air. Anything could go wrong. The A'kai are dangerous, and I do not trust them. They are fast and they are lethal, and I cannot wait to get them off the station.

As soon as the females are safely away from the A'kai, they look to Liana, tears in their otherwise broken expressions. Liana rushes to greet them. As she embraces them, the one with light hair releases a pitiful and agonizing wail as tears flow down her face.

Tr'lani's expression is a mask of anguish as she watches the reunion. Their trauma no doubt reminding her of her own at the hands of those monsters.

As my gaze scans the rest of our soldiers and the Aerilon that surround us, it is easy to see that they are as equally affected by the females' agony. I cannot begin to imagine the horrors they have endured. My hands curl into fists at my side. The A'kai will pay for this with their lives.

We watch as Talel and the two A'kai soldiers board their transport, sealing the door behind them.

My heart hammers with anticipation as all eyes then turn to Al'a-neo. His gaze shifts to his soldiers as he speaks into his communicator. "Now."

The station tremors slightly beneath our feet as the Aerilon ship's cannons fire. A brilliant display of light erupts from their vessel as a barrage of weapons head straight for the A'kai cruiser.

Seconds tick by like an eternity before a deafening boom splits the air. We watch in satisfaction as the fiery impact engulfs the A'kai ship, breaking it apart into a floating mass of destruction.

Bracing myself for the secondary assault on Talel's transport, my eyes go wide as I look toward their transport, crying out to our soldiers in warning as the doors slide open. Everything shifts into slow motion as Talel and the two A'kai emerge from their vessel. Rage mars their features as they charge at our soldiers.

Able to move with lightning speed, the three A'kai charge toward us. I watch in horror as two split off from Talel. One charges toward Al'aneo and the other toward my brother.

Al'aneo fires two blasts, taking down the first one, but I watch in terror as the other rushes toward my brother and I realize he has not seen him.

"Soran!" I cry out, but his eyes are fixed on his mate as Talel rushes toward her. Panicked, I fire my blaster. Despair churns in my gut when I miss, the flash of light passing harmlessly behind the A'kai that rushes toward my brother like a predator closing in on its prey.

Quickly, I move to aim again but stop as a blast hits him square in the chest.

His body crumples to the floor in a boneless heap. I turn to see where it came from and find Tr'lani, her arms extended as she keeps her blaster trained on him, as if worried he somehow may have survived.

Her eyes are wide and burning with anger as she stares, panting heavily at the fallen A'kai.

She is magnificent.

A loud cry from my brother draws my attention, and I gasp when I see Talel slam into Liana's smaller form.

Soran howls in rage as Talel locks his arms around his mate in a deadly hold.

All of us turn our weapons on him.

"Stop!" Talel yells.

Everyone stills and falls silent. Talel has Liana in a tight hold. His hand is wrapped around her throat while his arm is banded around her waist from behind, immobilizing her. It would be such an easy thing for him to snap her neck in this way, and my heart pounds with fear.

A low growl rumbles deep in Soran's chest as he stares down his foe. "Let. Her. Go."

Talel's lips twist into a feral snarl. "Never."

With a quick flash of movement, Liana twists free of Talel's hold. She moves with a deadly and fluid grace as she grasps his hair and jerks back his head, exposing his neck. Without hesitation, she drags a knife across his throat, cutting deep into his flesh.

Obsidian blood bursts forth in an explosive spray, gushing down the front of his chest. His eyes are wide in disbelief as he grips his mortal wound. Liana grits through her teeth as he meets her gaze. "You will *never* hurt anyone again."

He drops to his knees before collapsing to the ground in a pool of dark blood.

I turn to Tr'lani. Her hands shake as she lowers her blaster, and as soon as her eyes meet mine, I rush toward her. Wrapping my arms around her, I press my forehead gently to hers. "Thank you for saving my brother's life," I whisper. "If not for you, he would be dead."

She nods against me and then reaches up to cup my face. "If not for you and your brother, so would Liana and I."

After a moment, Tr'lani pulls away. "I'm going to go check on my friend."

I nod, and my eyes track her as she moves toward Liana. Heat flushes my scales where her hand cupped my cheek. She is magnificent, fierce, brave—and mine.

CHAPTER 39

ROWAN

As soon as we reach the palace, I watch Tr'lani and Liana as they reassure the Terran females that they are safe here on Mosaura and that my people will not harm them.

Al'aneo walks up beside me. "Do you have a moment to talk?"

With one last look over at Tr'lani to see that she is well, I turn my attention back to her brother and nod. His features are so like his sister's, it is remarkable. I know they are twins, but it is still strange to see the similar expression on his face that I've seen before on hers as he watches me. The stark difference is the spark behind his eyes. I've seen it in hers several times, but in him it is ever-present. I surmise she must have been the same before she was taken. She told me before, she was the defiant one.

His sharp gaze meets mine intently. "You and my sister are very close." Although this is said as a statement, I understand it is also a question.

"Yes."

He arches a brow in her direction before turning his eyes back to me. "She has chosen you?"

I lower my head. "She told me she loves me, but no, we have not completed the choosing. But I desire to be hers, if that is what you are asking."

A hint of a smile curves his lips. "Then it is true," he says. "Mosauran males must wait to be chosen just as Aerilon males."

"In this, our species are the same," I agree.

He studies me a moment before speaking. "She has told me much about your time together. You are an honorable male…even though" —he gives me a sly grin—"you are Mosauran."

Recognizing his teasing for what it is, I let his insult roll off my skin like water and thank him for his assessment.

"My sister has been through much," he continues. "And so…I wish to buy you some time."

My brow furrows in confusion. "Time?"

"For her to decide if she will fully claim you."

His words shock me, and my eyes widen slightly in surprise. "You…would not oppose our match?"

"There is a long history of mistrust among our two races, but my people are known for their ability to adapt and to grow." Lifting his hand to his chin, he looks up at the ceiling with a thoughtful expression before a smirk crosses his lips. "Your people are known to be very…difficult and dull-witted," he teases. "It will be hard enough having one Mosauran for a brother." His gaze shifts to Soran. "But even more so to have two of you in the Clan."

I try but fail to suppress a grin at his teasing. "And…how do you propose to give me time?" My expression turns serious. "I know she is anxious to see the rest of your family. She's been away for over two cycles."

"I would like to ask you to accompany us to Aerilon," he says. "It would be helpful to have both of you present when we reveal your findings from the ruined city to our High Council. It would also be good to have a Prince of Mosaura at my side when our Clan calls for a vote to push for a formal alliance between our two peoples."

My eyes widen slightly in shock. "My mother already approached you with this offer?"

He smirks. "I was hoping you could help me with that."

CHAPTER 40

ROWAN

I am leaving today for Aerilon with Tr'lani and her brother. Soran and Liana have chosen to stay behind on Mosaura so that Liana can make use of our Great Library and the stellar maps housed in the Ancient Archives. She hopes that they will help her find her home world. Before my people became warriors, my ancestors were explorers. They charted thousands of systems. I pray hers was among them.

A Mosauran cruiser will accompany us because, despite having agreed to pursue a treaty with Aerilon, my mother does not want me to go alone. When I tried to dissuade her from this, she reminded me that she may be Empress of an Empire, but she is first and foremost a mother.

As my brother approaches, he puts his hand up as if to shield his eyes. I stare at him in confusion as Liana playfully hits his arm.

I give him a strange look. "What are you—"

I stop speaking abruptly as he laughs. "The sun reflecting off your scales is practically blinding."

I narrow my eyes. I used to tease him about buffing his scales to impress his mate. Now that I am doing the same to impress Tr'lani, he turns my own joke on me.

He slaps me on the shoulder. "I am only teasing you, brother." His gaze shifts to Tr'lani. "Does she even know how long it takes to make your scales shine so brightly?"

A low warning growl escapes my throat.

Liana laughs. "Stop it, you two."

Tr'lani walks by and flashes a beaming smile directly at me, and my heart stutters and stops before she turns her attention back to her brother. Soran and Caryn tell me goodbye. Liana wraps her arms around me, embracing me warmly as she whispers in my ear, "Promise me you will tell Tr'lani how you feel about her before you return to Mosaura."

Her words surprise me for it means that Tr'lani has not told her of what has happened between us. Tr'lani knows how I feel for her, but she has not completely chosen me yet. So I ask just to be sure. "You are certain it is something she would wish to hear?"

She gives me a warm smile. "Yes, I believe so."

Tr'lani loves me. Of this I am sure. But I have to convince her to choose me as her mate…to claim me completely as hers.

As we walk onto the Aerilon cruiser, Grex stands with his Terran mate, Abby, at his side. He claps a hand on my shoulder and gives me a firm nod. "I am glad you will be joining us on our journey."

"Thank you, my friend."

Grex has convinced Abby to settle on Aerilon. Their people are more tolerant of outsiders living among them than mine. My eyes drift to his mate's abdomen, swollen with their child, and my thoughts turn to my brother. I wonder if Terrans are compatible with our people in this way. I hope for my brother's sake they are. He has always desired fledglings for as long as I can remember.

Me? I would love to have a family, but if Tr'lani takes me as hers, I will be satisfied enough just to have her as my mate, even if offspring might not be possible between us. I know most other mixed-species pairings are able to reproduce with medical intervention, but never has a Mosauran had a child with an Aerilon in our recorded history.

I make my way to my quarters, giving a friendly nod to several Aerilon as I pass. Despite everything I heard of them in the past, these are good people. They are honorable warriors like my own.

When I enter my room, it is just as it was when I was here before. Al'aneo was kind enough to provide me with a large space. Too large, in fact. I'm about to ask Abby and Grex if they would prefer this location instead of me, since there are two of them, but stop when I pull up a map of the nearby cabins and notice their quarters are even bigger than my own.

The stark white walls are the only thing plain about this space. Beautiful tapestries and finely carved furnishings encrusted with polished metal and precious gems dominate the room. The large floating bed, made of fine wood, depicts an enchanting forest scene, no doubt an image captured from somewhere on Aerilon.

Although I've never seen it, their planet is renowned for its beauty, and I'm eager to know if my imaginings are anywhere close to reality. My eyes are drawn to the floor-to-ceiling outer window. The blaze of white streaks against the blackened void tells me we're already in FTL travel. This cruiser is large and designed as much with comfort in mind as defense, for I had not even heard or felt the engines spin up for FTL, and we're already en route.

Mosauran cruisers are sparse in comparison. Built for speed and defense, they are cleanly kept with the same finely polished reflective metal panels that line the Aerilon ships, including the sparkling glass, but our ships lack the finer furnishings that seem to fill almost every space and room aboard this vessel.

I've heard Aerilon warriors spend more time in deep space than our people do, so I suppose it makes sense to equip their ships with as much comfort and reminders of home as possible.

When I've finished unpacking, I decide to head to the crew mess. I'm ravenous and thankful for its close proximity to my quarters. As soon as I enter, my gaze sweeps the room, and I stop in my tracks.

The sound of Tr'lani's laughter draws my attention. She's seated along the outer window, across from On'aro. He laughs in kind, and my blood begins to boil as unbidden jealousy rears its ugly head.

Perhaps her feelings for him are stronger than she realizes. The thought burns like bitter acid in my throat as I stare across at them. On the one hand, I pity this male. He lost her two cycles ago and dedicated his life to searching for her, only to find her and discover that she no longer wished him for her mate. On the other hand, I despise him, recognizing him for the rival that he is. From the way he watches her now, I know he has not given up the chase just yet.

He is a soldier, a Healer, and the most handsome male I have ever seen. With a slight clench of my jaw, I look down at myself. Covered in scales instead of soft skin, like her people, my face harsh and angular compared to theirs, it is a wonder that she even allows me to touch her. As beautiful as she is, she could have her choice of any male. It is only her broken wings, I believe, that make her think this is not so.

But I know the truth. I've seen the way Al'aneo's men cut their eyes at her, stealing discreet glances full of desire and longing as they watch her pass. Yes, Aerilon females are as beautiful as the males, but none are any match for her beauty.

I move to the line to retrieve a meal to go. Aerilon food is much different from Mosauran. Ours are heavily spiced in comparison, whereas theirs seems to lean a bit toward more sweet and citrusy combinations. I reach for an Aerilon fruit and bring it to my nose to scent. My nostrils flare as a hint of citrus fills them.

A small hand on my arm draws my attention, and I turn to find Tr'lani smiling up at me. "I wondered where you were."

My gaze darts over her shoulder briefly to find On'aro glaring in my direction. I've distracted the object of his affection, and he does not appear to be pleased.

I am, however, and I return her beaming smile. Arching a teasing brow, I lean closer to her and whisper, "I was searching for something edible." I make a show of looking at the selection of foods available again. "And I was surprised to not find any."

She laughs, her eyes sparkling with amusement. "Would you care to join me in my quarters? We could have some varg for dessert."

"I would love to." For two reasons: Varg is a delicious fruit from my home world, *and* I will take any excuse to be alone with her and away from any other rival males.

Even as this thought occurs to me, I wonder if perhaps my mating cycle may be approaching. I hope it is not, but intense possessiveness is one of the earliest signs.

She motions for me to follow her, and I cannot help but cast a quick glance back at On'aro to make sure he is not going to chase after us, vying for her attention.

When we reach her quarters, my jaw drops when I notice the crates of varg stacked in the far corner of her room, one of them already half-empty. I give her a surprised look as I point to the fruit. "You consumed half a crate?"

She playfully slaps at my arm. "I haven't had that many," she blushes. "That crate wasn't completely full when it arrived anyway."

It is a lie. I inspected those crates myself. They were full when she had them brought on board. But, far be it for me to contradict the female I am trying to convince to choose me as hers. Besides, I am glad she has a healthy appetite. It took many days for her to eat after we first rescued her and Liana.

She hands me a varg, and I extend my claws and peel away the hard, rubbery outer flesh. Exposing the soft center, my mouth is already watering before I even take the first bite. I start to ask if she thinks it may be possible to grow this on Aerilon, but she beats me to it.

"I have been saving the seeds." She motions to a jar near the table. "I was hoping we could try growing some of these on my home world. My family's estate has a large garden. My grandparents and I grow fruits and vegetables each cycle."

Her smile falters, and she looks down a moment, probably thinking of her grandfather. I can only imagine how hard it must be for her to know he is gone.

I reach across to take her hand but say nothing. Words are inadequate in the face of such a great loss. I know this from experience.

Without warning, a deafening explosion fills the air, and the ship rocks violently to the side, throwing Tr'lani from her chair. My wings snap open, and the world shifts into slow motion as I race toward her, wrapping her up in my arms and spinning us so that my back hits the wall, shielding her from the impact. Bright lights flash red in warning as alarms blare loudly throughout the vessel.

The cruiser rights itself, and I carefully set her on her feet and then rush to the hallway. Aerilon warriors race down the passages toward the airlock, rage and determination in their expressions. "What is going on?" I ask, hoping one of them will answer in their hurry.

"A slave ship," one calls out over his shoulder. "They fired on us, but we've disabled their weapons and engines. We're going to board."

With a quick glance back at Tr'lani, I pull my blaster from my belt. "I'm going to help."

My communicator chirps, and when I tap it, the captain of the Mosauran cruiser appears in the display. "Do you require assistance?"

I look to Al'aneo, and he shakes his head. "We should be able to handle this."

I meet the captain's eyes evenly. "I will contact you if we need any aide."

"Of course, my Prince." He nods, and I shut down the display.

Tr'lani tries to protest my going. But I'm a warrior. And warriors do not run from a fight.

And because she is a Healer, she leaves for the med bay, readying to receive any of the injured.

When we reach the airlock, I see Al'aneo at the front of the line and call out to him.

He waves me forward. "You wish to help?"

I give him an affirmatory nod, and he claps me firmly on the shoulder. He pulls on the release, and the door cracks open with a sharp hiss of air. Instantly, the room is flooded with the pungent scent of death and decay, and I wrinkle my nose in disgust, swallowing against the bile working its way up my throat.

My blood boils with rage, and from the look in Al'aneo's eyes as he gives the order to rush forward, I know he feels the same.

Racing through the hatch, I'm surprised when we meet no resistance. The ship is almost pitch black, but my eyes adjust quickly to the darkness. The Aerilon do not possess my species' superior night vision, however, and a sudden flare of light temporarily blinds me when they switch on the lighting attached to their gear.

Through a series of silent hand signals, Al'aneo orders the warriors to split off into groups before motioning for me to follow him. With our blasters out and ready for attack, we make our way quickly and quietly through the ship, moving in the direction where the rotten air is strongest, and I realize it must be a slave cargo hold.

Two large doors whoosh open, and my eyes swim at the disgusting rush of air that escapes with their opening. As we step inside, a flash of movement draws my attention; I turn to see several pairs of eyes staring at us in panic from the cages. All at once, their voices call out, "Help us! Please!"

But one in particular stands out. A V'loryn female. "The next room!" she says hurriedly. "One of the Anguis...he took a female to sate his mating rut. Hurry!"

Ice fills my veins as I race toward the next set of doors. Al'aneo must have heard her as well, because he is first through the opening.

And because he goes first, I cannot see beyond him, but whatever it is, it fills him with rage. He releases a loud cry of fury and rushes forward, barreling into an Anguis.

They slam against the bulkhead, and in one swift movement, Al'aneo twists the Anguis's head so sharply, it rips from his body with a sickening crack and a rending of flesh. Without pause, he races back to a female on the floor.

After I scan the area and find no one else in here with us, that's when I notice she is unmoving. Lying haphazardly with her slave dress tattered and almost torn from her body, the only indication that she is alive is the slight rise and fall of her chest as she takes in several shallow breaths.

Al'aneo removes his tunic and covers her before he gathers her in his arms, rocking her gently back and forth as he strokes her long brown hair and whispers words in a voice so low I cannot make them out, but I know they are meant to comfort.

The two puncture marks on her partially exposed thigh tell me exactly what has happened to her. She was bitten by the Anguis; the poison, even now, is coursing through her system and will claim her.

Her blue eyes stare up at Al'aneo as tears stream down her cheeks. She is paralyzed and will succumb soon to the deadly toxin. He stares down at her with a pained expression, gently holding her to his chest as he trills low in his throat. It is a terrible death; he is doing what little he can to comfort her as she passes.

My gaze snaps back to her face, and I inhale sharply when I realize what I should have recognized before. She is Terran.

My jaw drops as she slowly lifts a trembling hand to his face, her fingers lightly touching his cheek. This should not be possible. Anguis toxin paralyzes. Completely.

Determination flashes across Al'aneo's expression, and he pulls her up into his arms and stands quickly. He turns and then races back through the ship as he calls out into his communicator for a Healer to meet him at the airlock.

He thinks he can save her, and I hope he is right.

The sound of weapon's fire echoes from nearby, and I follow it, bloodlust coursing through my veins and demanding retribution for all the wrongs done to these slaves. I race past several Aerilon, freeing slaves from the cages, and out into the hallway.

As I reach the nearest Anguis, I unsheathe my laser knife. The blaster is too quick a death for these beasts; I want them to suffer before they die.

CHAPTER 41

ROWAN

When I return to the Aerilon ship, one of Al'aneo's warriors directs me to the med bay. Covered in blood from head to toe, I am uncertain how much is mine since I can feel nothing right now. My heart beats wildly with unbridled rage. Killing the masters wasn't enough. It never is.

And when I reach the med bay and see all the slaves being tended by the Healers, I want to roar my anger and rage. Closing my eyes, I picture Tr'lani and Liana. This is what they suffered. This is what they endured. Opening my eyes, I find my beloved standing before me. Her gaze is wide as she stares up at me in concern.

And as she stretches up on her toes and wraps her arms around me, I press my forehead to hers and then bury my face in the curve of her neck and shoulder as overwhelming sadness washes through me. *This* is the horror my beloved survived.

As she treats my many small cuts and minor flesh wounds, Abby and Grex walk in.

Abby looks to Tr'lani. "Is there anything we can do to help?"

"Make sure everyone has some food and water," Tr'lani instructs.

"That will be good. I'm sure many of them are probably hungry and thirsty."

As she and Grex leave, I look to Al'aneo. He is sitting on a chair beside the MRU. His face is a mask of pain as he stares at the sleeping form of the Terran female inside. His wings glow with a light I have never seen before on one of their people. I walk over and gently place my hand on his shoulder so as not to startle him.

He lifts his golden eyes up to meet mine but says nothing. Sadness mars his features.

"What do the Healers say?"

"They have never seen this before." He shakes his head softly. "The toxin would have killed any other by now, but she still lives." He pauses and turns his haunted gaze back to her sleeping form. "They say she will either live or she will die this night. They do not know which it will be."

My eyes dart briefly to Abby and then back to him.

As if reading my thoughts, he shakes his head softly. "She is undoubtably Terran, but Abby does not recognize her. She must be from another crew."

From the look in his eyes, I know he means to remain by her side throughout the night, so I do not bother trying to convince him otherwise. Instead, I ask, "Would you like me to bring you anything? Food? Water?"

Tr'lani walks up behind me; I feel her presence and know it is her before I even turn to see her face. "Do you want me to sit with her, brother, while you get some sleep?" she asks softly.

He shakes his head. "No. I will stay." He lifts his gaze to us. "You both should rest. I'll find you in the morning."

Without another word, he turns back to face the Terran female, placing his hand lightly atop the casing as if wanting to give her whatever comfort he can even if she is not awake to sense it.

As soon as we're far enough away that I do not think he'll hear, I ask Tr'lani about his wings. "Why do his wings glow that way?"

She stares at Al'aneo with a pained expression. "It is because he has found his fated one."

I blink several times in shock. "The Terran?"

She nods. "Sometimes it happens immediately. But often, it may not show up until much later, as it did for my parents."

Before I can stop myself, my eyes sweep to her wings, desperately wishing to see them glow as her brother's do. But they remain their usual appearance. I lift my gaze to hers, and determination fills me. In my heart, I already know she is mine. Now, I must just prove myself a worthy mate and convince fate to make her wings glow to show her the truth of this as well.

Tiredness hits me like a giant wave, and my shoulders sag forward with exhaustion. Silently, Tr'lani and I walk side by side back to our rooms. When we reach hers, I bid her goodnight. But when I turn to head for my cabin, her hand on my forearm stops me, and I spin to face her with a questioning look.

She slides her warm hand down my arm, entwining our fingers. Her eyes search mine a moment before she turns and opens her door, pulling me inside. I follow without question as she leads me to the cleansing room.

It is only now that I realize I'm still covered in blood. Dried obsidian patches of gore stain my scales and clothing. Tr'lani looks me up and down a moment before she carefully undoes the clasp of my tunic, pushing it back and off my shoulders. I watch as she reaches for the fastening of my pants, sliding them down my hips until they fall to the floor.

She's seen me unclothed many times, and it is nothing new to stand before her completely bared this way. It is not as if my stav is protruding, even though it feels as if it will do so now. Drawing in a deep and steadying breath, I try to force myself to calm so this does not happen.

She walks with me into the shower. As the warm water rushes over me, she steps into the enclosure as well. Her gaze holds mine a moment before she wraps her arms around me, resting her head against my shoulder.

I'm so shocked, I do not know what to do. My fingers curl reflexively in my palms with want to hold her, but I am afraid of ruining the moment, of unintentionally startling her with my touch. After a moment, I lose the war within and gently return her embrace, holding her close.

Her clothing is wet and sticks to her skin, but she doesn't seem to care as she remains in my arms. "I told you never to do that again," she whispers.

I stare down at her in confusion.

She continues. "When we were stranded. I told you never to take unnecessary risks ever again because I could not bear it if something happened to you."

I reach down to cup my hands on either side of her face, meeting her eyes evenly. "It was not unnecessary. There were people suffering on that ship."

"I know," she replies. "But I still worried for you."

I take her hands in my own and drop to my knees before her. "You are my heart, Tr'lani. I will always do whatever I must to come back to you."

She gently tugs on my shoulders, pulling me back up to her. She captures my mouth in a passionate kiss, and I drag her against me, holding her close.

When she pulls back, her golden eyes hold mine as she unfastens her tunic and discards it on the floor. My mouth drifts open as my gaze travels over her body. She has never bared herself to me before. She is perfection. More beautiful than any female I have ever seen.

My eyes travel down the elegant line of her neck to her chest. Her breasts are much larger than any Mosauran female's. The flesh that covers them appears soft as well, compared to the scales of my people. My fingers flex and extend at my sides with want to touch her. To run my hands along the gentle slope of each breast and cup them beneath my palms.

But I force myself to be still, instead. I will not touch her until I know for certain it is what she wants. My gaze moves even lower down her abdomen and to the soft, sensuous curve of her hips that flare slightly from her tapered waist and down to her delicate feet.

The heat of her form radiates to mine. Even as the warm stream of water flows over us, I'm conscious of it in a way that makes my body hum in awareness of hers. She retrieves a handful of liquid soap from the dispenser and then carefully rubs it across my neck and shoulders.

Her hands make gentle circles over my scales as she cleans me, motioning with small amounts of pressure when she wants me to move or turn this way or that for a better angle as she continues to wash away the blood that still clings to me.

It takes everything I have to keep my stav from extending from my mating sheathe. But when she grabs my hand and places a dollop of soap in my palm and then guides me to the curve of her neck and shoulder, I lose the last bit of my control.

Clenching my jaw in frustration, my cheeks heat with embarrassment as her gaze looks down at my fully lengthened and extended stav. Ashamed of my inability to keep my control, I start to turn but stop abruptly when she takes my hand. "You're beautiful, Rowan."

A slight grin tips my lips as I arch a teasing brow. "Not exactly the words a warrior wants to hear from a female."

A small laugh escapes her, and I'm enchanted. I lean down to capture her mouth in another kiss. She wraps her arms around me. Her fingers trace delicate patterns down the length of my back, setting my every nerve ending ablaze. My stav presses insistently against her abdomen, and she gasps and pulls away slightly.

I cup her chin and stare deep into her eyes. "I will not touch you in any way you do not wish. I swear it to the Creator."

She gives me a shy smile and then takes my hand, cautiously placing my open palm to her left breast. "Just touching for now," she says softly. "All right?"

I nod and stare at her in wonder. That she allows me to gaze at her beautiful form and touch her so intimately is more than I ever thought possible…more than I'd ever hoped to want. "Just touching," I agree, my voice barely a whisper.

Gently, I mimic the same soft circular movements she made over my body as she cleaned me. She tips her head back, closing her eyes as I run my hands over her form. Her skin is soft like silk beneath my calloused fingers; every part of her so warm and giving. When I reach the juncture between her thighs, I stop and lift my hands away, unwilling to touch her here without her permission.

Her eyes snap open, and she stares up at me a moment before covering my hand with her own. "Do you want to touch me?" she asks, her golden gaze searching mine.

She holds my hand, and I blink several times in shock as my mind struggles to process her words before I finally manage to rasp, "Yes. More than anything."

A small smile curves her lips. "Then you may touch me," she whispers softly as she guides my hands back to her body.

I make sure to retract my claws again before I touch her. Her skin is petal-soft and warm, and despite the water that flows over our bodies, the slick heat of her center covers my fingers as I gently trace over her delicate folds.

A soft moan escapes her lips when I reach the entrance to her core. She holds tightly to my form, running her hands along the muscles of my abdomen and chest. "I want you inside me," she whispers.

My heart pounds as electricity sparks along every nerve ending in my body. Gently, I push one finger just inside her entrance. Her mouth drifts open, and she inhales sharply as her half-lidded gaze holds mine. The tight clasp of her warm, wet heat makes my breath hitch in my throat as I imagine what it would feel like to sheathe my stav inside her.

Even as the thought enters my mind, my stav hardens painfully as she arches her back and takes me even deeper. She rocks her hips against my hand as I stroke my finger in and out of her core.

She holds tightly to me, her fingers digging into my shoulders and back as her lips find mine. I open my mouth, deepening our kiss as I curl my tongue around her own.

I groan as she wraps her hand around my stav and begins lightly stroking my length. It is the most exquisite and delicious torture I have ever felt before.

Her breathing quickens as the muscles of her channel begin to flex and quiver around me. I growl low in arousal as she clamps down around my finger in a rhythmic pulsing sensation. She digs her fingers into my back as she cries out my name and finds her release.

She holds tightly to me, trapping my stav between us. The pressure is too much, and I'm unable to hold back. Intense pleasure floods my veins, and I grit my teeth as my release roars through me. My stav pulses strongly as thick ropes of fluid erupt from the tip and cover her abdomen. Ashamed of my inability to maintain my control, I meet her gaze and am surprised to find nothing but desire and longing in her eyes.

She takes my hand and then pulls me close, wrapping her arms around my form.

Fierce possessiveness rushes through me as I hold her tightly, skimming the tip of my nose from her temple to her jaw and down the curve of her neck and shoulder. My nostrils flare as I breathe deeply of our combined scent.

Shutting off the water, I don't want to wash away all of my essence from her skin. I activate the dryer setting and then lift her into my arms and carry her to the bed.

Laying us both down, beneath the comforter, I wrap my arms and wings around her as she settles against my chest, tucking her head under my chin. I want to ask if this is how it is done among her people. If she has now officially claimed me as hers so that I may now claim her in the way of my people, binding us in the sacred heart ritual. But as the sound of her breath becomes soft and even, I say nothing, knowing that she is drifting off to sleep.

Joy and contentment wash over and through me as I hold her in my arms, wrapped tightly in my wings. My beautiful mate. More precious than any treasure in the entire quadrant. She is my heart.

CHAPTER 42

TR'LANI

When I wake in the morning, it's to warmth all around me. Wrapped up in Rowan's arms and wings is the best thing to open my eyes to. I turn and find him still asleep. Carefully, I reach out and trace the hard ridge of his brow, staring at him in wonder. Memories of last night float to the surface of my mind, and my cheeks flush with warmth.

His eyelids open, and he greets me with a sleepy smile. He pulls me even closer. His stav is a hard bar between us, pressing insistently against my abdomen, but I'm not afraid or nervous in the slightest. Because I know he would never touch me or do anything I do not want. Last night proved beyond any doubt that he would never take anything from me that I am unwilling to give.

He leans forward and gently skims the tip of his nose alongside mine before pressing a tender kiss to my lips.

The door chimes loudly. With a heavy sigh, he rests his forehead against mine. I give him a faint smile and softly nudge him to unwrap his wings so we can sit up.

He does so reluctantly. I quickly pull my sleeping robe around me and offer him a cloak before I open the door. Abby had promised to stop by before going to check on the rescued females, and I smile brightly as I open the door, expecting to see my dear friend. Instead, the doors whoosh open to reveal Grex, a panicked look on his face.

My eyes widen in concern. "What's wrong?"

"Abby," he says urgently. "We think the baby's coming. She has asked for you."

His gaze darts over my shoulder to Rowan and then back to me. "I'll be there as soon as I can," I tell him.

With a quick nod, he leaves, and I spin away from the door and rush to get dressed. Rowan's blood-stained clothes litter the floor of the cleansing room, and he quickly tosses them in the refresher before giving me a remorseful look. "Go," he says. "I'll be right behind you as soon as these are ready."

I give him a quick kiss and then race for the door, running down the hallway to the med bay.

A series of pained cries echoes loudly along the corridor, and I know, before I even reach the medical area, that it is Abby. Panic tightens my chest when I see her propped up in one of the beds, covered in sweat and tears as three Healers stand around her, frantically running their scanners over her abdomen.

When her eyes meet mine, they're wide with fear. "Tr'lani, help me!" she cries out. "Please! I feel like I'm dying."

Standing beside her, holding tightly to her hand, Grex pales at her words. The normally gruff and stoic, scarred warrior looks utterly terrified as he stares down at his mate. He lifts his gaze to mine in a pleading look. "Please. You must do something to help her."

Lifting a scanner from the nearby supply table, I move to her side and run it thoroughly over her form. I've never seen anything like this. Our females do not labor in this way when we bear our young. Worry tightens my chest, and it is difficult to form words, but somehow I manage. "I—I do not know if this is normal for her kind," I admit, my voice barely a whisper as Grex and the rest of the Healers stare at me in concern.

"I'm a doctor. I can help her," a female voice calls out behind me.

I spin to find the Terran female my brother saved and watched over. Al'aneo stands beside her, his expression one I cannot discern.

The Terran female steps forward. Her skin is a slightly lighter hue than Liana's, and she has piercing blue eyes. She twists her long, straight, brown hair behind her, tying it into a loose knot at the nape of her neck. "I am Doctor Holly Wright. I deliver babies all the time," she says. Her sharp gaze narrows in on mine. "You are a Healer, right? And you are her friend?"

I nod.

"Then you can assist me," she says. "I will need help to deliver the child safely."

Her eyes turn to Grex, scanning him from head to toe in a look that borders on shocked disbelief. She turns her attention to Abby. "This"—she gestures to Grex—"is the father of your child?"

Abby nods, and Holly shakes her head. "But how is that possible?" she whispers more to herself than to anyone else as her gaze lowers to the tablet near the bed, an image of Grex and Abby's unborn daughter floating on the screen.

Abby cries out in pain, drawing our attention back to her. Holly approaches the end of the bed and then turns to scan the people in the room. "I'll need everyone out of here who is not a Healer."

Grex opens his mouth to protest, but she gives him a knowing look. "You are the father. You stay," she states firmly, and he quickly snaps his jaw shut.

Everyone leaves as she commands, and then we turn our attention to Abby.

* * *

ROWAN

Before I even reach the med bay, I can hear Abby's sharp cries along the hallway, and it fills me with fear. Picking up my pace, I rush to the entrance but stop abruptly at Al'aneo's command.

I give him a puzzled look.

Answering my unspoken question, he gestures to the doors. "Only Grex and the Healers are allowed in there now."

"Tr'lani?" I ask, and he nods in response.

* * *

Hours pass by agonizingly slow, and with each sharp cry of pain that echoes beyond the door, my heart pounds as anxiety coils tight around my chest.

Al'aneo explains that the Terran female he rescued is a Healer, experienced in the delivery of their young. Her name is Holly Wright. Relief floods my system at his words, and I cannot help but think the Creator placed her in our path for this exact purpose. Because if she was not here, the Aerilon Healers would have no idea what to do. This pain and heavy labor is not common to their species, nor to mine.

Mosauran females lay eggs, which the male then guards closely until they hatch. Then we watch over the fledglings until they are able to fly without assistance. Aerilons, however...they live birth their young. My stomach twists in a knot at the thought of Tr'lani going through something like this...even if the Aerilon claim it is not as painful as what Abby is experiencing.

After what feels like an eternity, everything goes silent a moment before a tiny wail fills the air. The door bursts open, and one of the Healers appears. "The child is healthy, and the mother is well." She smiles. "You may come in to see them."

Al'aneo and I rush inside to find Holly holding the baby, carefully wrapped in a blanket. She presses a kiss to the child's head and then passes her off to Abby. Grex gently cradles her small head with his palm as they stare down at their daughter.

Grex looks at Al'aneo and me, giving us a warm smile before turning his attention back to the child.

Abby lifts her gaze to Tr'lani. "Do you want to hold her?"

Tr'lani smiles and then reaches out to receive the baby. Grex carefully places her in Tr'lani's waiting arms. She stares down lovingly at the child and then shifts just enough to lean closer to me, so I may see her more clearly.

With soft, pale sea-green scales and a slight tuft of yellow hair to match her mother's, her coloring and the small ridges of her brow and cheeks, along with her tiny tail, speak to her Lacerta genes she received from her father. Long eyelashes flutter open to reveal deep-green eyes that match Abby's as she stares up at us, her face full of wonder.

Tr'lani smooths a hand over her cheek, and I reach down to gently run my fingers over her tiny scalp and then lean forward to place a soft kiss to her forehead. "She is a beautiful child." I smile at Grex and Abby. "What will you name her?"

"Alex," Grex replies. He turns a loving gaze to his Terran mate. "In honor of Abby's mother."

Grex takes her back in his arms, and Al'aneo steps forward, his face set in a solemn expression as he looks down at the child. His eyes are soft as he reaches down to gently place three fingers lightly to her forehead. "Born on an Aerilon vessel, you are bestowed the right to be one of our people. Aerilon will be your home, and her people your Clan and your brethren from this day forward. This covenant is sworn and sealed before the Creator."

Overcome with emotion, Abby's eyes are bright with tears as she looks up at Al'aneo and Tr'lani. "Thank you. You have no idea how much this means to us," she whispers as she squeezes Grex's hand and cuddles her baby close to her chest.

In this moment, I realize that Grex and Abby have chosen wisely to live among the Aerilon instead of remaining on Mosaura. They and their daughter now have a place to call home, where they will be accepted by a people more tolerant than my own.

CHAPTER 43

ROWAN

It has only been a day since Alex was born, and I doubt there is anyone on the ship that hasn't already held her. Everyone is both charmed and fascinated with Grex and Abby's beautiful child. With long, golden lashes and piercing green eyes, she can melt the heart of even the most stoic of warriors.

An Aerilon soldier holds the small fledgling close to his chest, trilling and cooing at her with soothing tones as she smiles up at him. As I watch the warrior gently rock back and forth on his heels, cradling the child in his arms, I can think of no race more honorable to ally ourselves to.

My gaze drifts to Tr'lani, seated at the table across from Grex and Abby. With the health of Alex paramount to all else, she took turns with Holly and the rest of the Healers observing her frequently during the night. Although she appears healthy, she is the first naturally born hybrid child, and they want to carefully monitor her.

* * *

TR'LANI

Rowan sits beside me, and we each take turns holding Alex during last meal. We'll arrive at Aerilon tomorrow, and I cannot help but be nervous to see all my family again. But of everyone I wish to see, it is my grandmother I look forward to most. We are close, she and I. Even more so than I am to my own parents. A sharp pain stabs at the center of my chest as I think on my grandfather. It will be so strange to return home and not find him in the gardens beside my grandmother, tending to his plants.

On'aro walks up to me, interrupting my thoughts. "May I speak with you alone?" he asks.

"Of course."

I bid Grex and Abby good night, and when my eyes meet Rowan's, I cannot discern the emotion that reflects in their silver depths. But I feel his gaze heavy on my back as I follow On'aro out into the hallway.

He leads me to the large atrium—the very heart of the ship. The stars streak by overhead through the glass dome. Artificial light that mimics the brightness of Aerilon's sun floods the massive space, thick with various forms of vegetation. Tree-lined pathways cut through the gardens. Their branches are heavy with leaves that hang down like a curtain of vines around each one, making it difficult to see what lies beneath. Nearby hushed whispers draw my attention to the nearest one.

On'aro turns to me. "I came to your window one night, during the light of the lover's moon. I wanted so desperately for you to claim me, but I was too nervous to present myself to you; worried that it would ruin our friendship if you rejected me." He swallows thickly as his eyes meet mine. "I remember what you told me, but I…I wish to offer myself to you once more. Are you certain there can be nothing but friendship between us? Have you already decided to take him as your mate?"

A strange mixture of hope and sadness reflects in his gaze, and I force myself to give him the hard truth. There can be no misunderstandings between us. "I love him, On'aro."

With a slight clench of his jaw, he lowers his eyes. "Have you thought of the life you will live with him? He is Mosauran. Not everyone will be accepting of the idea of an Aerilon and a Mosauran mated pair."

"It will not be easy," I admit. "But change rarely is."

He lifts his gaze to mine. "I suppose he is a good male...despite that he is Mosauran."

His lips quirk up slightly as he teases me, but it is easy to see the question in his eyes, so I move to reassure him. "He is a good male, and he loves me...broken wings and all."

On'aro nods. His eyes dart to my wings and then back up to meet mine. "I believe I can heal them. Will you please allow me to try when we reach Aerilon?"

As one of the most skilled Healers I've ever worked with, I know that if anyone can restore my wings, it is him. "Yes."

* * *

ROWAN'S MOUTH curves up in a devastatingly handsome smile when I return to him. He stands and then wraps me in his arms. He leans down just enough to whisper in my ear, "I am glad you are back. I am not too proud to admit that I was already imagining dozens of ways to defeat On'aro in battle to prove my worth to you should he try to convince you he would make a better mate." He pauses. "But then I remembered that I am a big, strong, and handsome Mosauran warrior. And he could never stand a chance against my strength." He flexes his biceps and then gives me a teasing grin.

I roll my eyes and laugh.

It is only a few more hours until we reach Aerilon, and I know once we arrive, we'll have a long day ahead of us. While I'm anxious to see my family again, I'm nervous about how they'll greet Rowan. Soran may officially be part of our Clan since he is bonded to Liana, but it's not like they have to interact with him on a daily basis like they will with Rowan. I only hope my family will understand and love him as much as I do.

CHAPTER 44

ROWAN

Aerilon's orbital station is divided into two rings. One used primarily for trade and the other for the military. We dock at the one for the Defense Force beside several other large cruisers. When we step off the ship onto the station, several pairs of eyes narrow as they watch me and Grex walk past.

But I do my best to ignore their blatant stares and fix my eyes up ahead at Tr'lani and Al'aneo.

After speaking with the captain of the Mosauran cruiser, it has been decided that they will remain docked at the station and stay on their ship. The last thing we want to do is give the Aerilon any reason to believe we are here as conquerors. And I suspect if our warriors were to travel to the surface, we would only be met with mistrust instead of friendship at this point by a majority of the people.

I am not surprised at the number of aggressive stares I receive. I am glad to notice, however, that Grex does not warrant the same level of scrutiny as me. Apparently, the Lacerta are not as much of a concern as a Mosauran. This bodes well for him since this planet will now be his home and his family's.

The floors, walls, and ceilings are polished to sparkling clarity. My reflection is perfect as we walk down the long hallway to the transports. It is orderly, clean, sparse, and utilitarian. So unlike everything else I've seen of the Aerilon, after having lived on one of their cruisers for the past few days. It seems the comforts of home are not expressed in the station. Perhaps that is because when one is here, they are either returning to their home shortly or have only recently left it behind. And if so, the ships are equipped with all manner of comforts to remind them of what they will miss while they're gone.

As soon as we reach the transport, I stare out the viewscreen. My jaw drops at the beauty that is the Aerilon home world. I have heard much of this planet, but to see it now with my own eyes is something else entirely. Rich shades of various blues, greens, and purples dot the planet's surface.

The sky is a lovely shade of ice-blue punctuated by thick, silver-gray clouds that would suggest a storm were it not for the soft orange sun shining brightly overhead. Mountains covered in purple and green surround the vast city before us.

A large castle looms in the distance. That must be Tr'lani and Al'a-neo's home. This is their Clan's region and their capital city, nestled among great towering mountains. Gleaming alabaster towers spiral up toward the sky, the sunlight glinting off their polished surfaces and appearing like gold streaked throughout the smoothly carved stone. It is beautifully formed—a structure that appears to have been built for aesthetics. But as I have learned, if it is anything like their people, it is as strong as it is beautiful.

Light reflects brightly around the entire structure, and I realize the castle is surrounded by a clear energy barrier, barely perceptible to the naked eye. This suggests unrest of some kind, or at least a level of mistrust. Whether it is from an opposing Clan or in response to the Mosauran cruiser in orbit, I am uncertain. I only know that my own home is protected by such a device because we have not only been attacked before, but we anticipate that it may happen again if we are not vigilant. I make a mental note to ask about this later.

The transport vibrates beneath our feet as we hover just above the surface. A dull thud sounds along the hull, signaling that we've landed.

The doors slide open to reveal the palace courtyard. Several guards line either side of the bottom of the ramp, and three figures stand in the center, staring up at us expectantly. Two I recognize as Tr'lani and Al'aneo's parents, but only because they look so much like their children it would be impossible not to know they are related. The other one moves to the front, and as Tr'lani and Al'aneo exit, she rushes forward to greet them.

Her long, purple robes suggest a rank of importance, but the way she embraces them warmly tells me this is their grandmother, Ama.

* * *

TR'LANI

I rush down the ramp and into Ama's arms. My parents join in, wrapping us up in their embrace as well. Silent sobs rack through me. Emotions tighten my throat, and the words will not come as I allow myself to sink into the comfort of being surrounded by my family.

When I finally pull back, Ama cups my face with both hands and then gently smooths my hair back behind my ears. "My beautiful child," she whispers through her tears with a low, trilling hum. "We never gave up hope that we would find you." She turns her gaze to Al'aneo. "You did well, my darling boy. I knew you would bring your sister back to us." She looks to his wings, glowing brightly behind him. They grow even brighter as soon as Holly comes into view and Ama arches a questioning brow at him, but says nothing.

He turns his head and motions to Holly, Grex, Abby, and Rowan.

They come down the ramp. Ama's eyes widen as she takes in Rowan before her, his tall form dwarfing hers. She stares up at him with a piercing gaze. "Let me look at you, Warrior of Mosaura," she says with just the barest hint of a smile on her lips. Her gaze darts briefly to mine before she returns her attention to him. "You saved my precious granddaughter from the wretched A'kai." She glances at my parents. "We owe you a life debt. What would you ask of us in return?"

He meets Ama's eyes evenly. "Nothing that you would not willingly give. I have come here to ask for an alliance between our two races, but it is not a demand to settle any debt. I hope it will mark a new era for our people to move forward together in peace. And it is my wish that we could work together to put a stop to the slave trade that operates unchecked at the edges our borders."

Ama's lips curve into a beaming smile. "Spoken like a male that has much wisdom," she says. "Something I did not expect from one of your kind."

Rowan bristles slightly at her words but relaxes when a small smirk twists her mouth.

"It seems we have many misconceptions between us that need to be put to rest." She extends her hand to him, palm upturned, as she holds his gaze.

Carefully, he places his hand over hers, and she quietly bows her head as she takes his measure. After a moment, she releases his hand and then rests hers on his shoulder, her lips tipped up in a slight smile. "Come, Prince and Warrior of Mosaura." She motions for him to follow her. "We should get to know one another a bit better. I have a feeling you will be with us for a long while."

Rowan follows after her, and Al'aneo arches a questioning brow at me as if to say, "What is she up to?"

I shake my head, and we follow after her. Al'aneo said he had not told our family about our relationship yet. Ama is one of the wisest and most perceptive people I know, and I suspect she already recognizes how I feel about Rowan. How does she know this? I have no idea, but when she throws me a quick glance over her shoulder, it confirms my suspicions.

Ama loops her arm through mine as if afraid to let me go now that I'm finally here. I feel the same as I hold onto her. Al'aneo walks beside me with Rowan on his other side. My parents hover close behind, and the sound of my mother sniffing as she holds back her tears tells me they're as shocked as I am that I made it back home. Most who are taken are never seen or heard from again once they are sold into slavery.

My gaze scans the courtyard and the gardens just beyond the gate. Everything is just as I remember it. The tall jaru trees line the walkway. Their long, trailing, purple vines swaying gently in the breeze begin to glow softly as the sun begins its slow descent in the sky. Deep-green bushes as tall as my waist are haloed in blue light as their bioluminescent blooms slowly awaken and unfurl with the coming of night. The sound of rushing water as we walk along the stream grows stronger as we make our way to the castle entrance.

Reaching the entryway, the heavy rustle of wings flutters softly from my family. Without thinking, the muscles of my back tense with want to stretch my wings and fly too, until a sharp pain shoots through my spine with the movement, causing me to wince.

Everything falls silent as my family turns to me, their faces set in an undeniable expression of pity as their eyes drift to my broken wings. We never use the actual castle entrance. My entire life, we've always flown to the first level balcony and entered that way. This entrance is only for visiting dignitaries without wings or those who are so unfortunate to have lost theirs or had them broken like mine.

Recognizing the warmth of his presence at my back, I tip my head to look up at Rowan standing directly behind me. His familiar scent, something between a mixture of earth and spice, surrounds me. "May I?" he asks, and I know he means to carry me to the balcony.

My parents' jaws drop at his question.

I nod, and his large hands encircle my waist, gripping me firmly a moment before he extends his massive wings and we carefully lift off from the ground. When we reach the balcony, he sets down gently on the tile floor and carefully lowers my feet.

My family arrives a moment later, and I notice Al'aneo has carried Holly, and two Aerilon soldiers were kind enough to do the same for Abby, Alex, and Grex. Despite this, I feel the heavy stares of my family upon myself and Rowan as I thank him.

He dips his chin in a subtle nod, and when I turn, I find Ama's brow arched with a questioning gaze before she turns and motions for us to follow her inside.

The palace is just as I remember it. The delicate fragrance of the liruna flowers drifts up from the gardens now that they've fully unfurled. Long, flowing, white drapes blow gently along the balcony with the cool night breeze, and as we pass beneath them, the whisper of the soft fabric caresses my skin as if welcoming me home.

Tears sting my eyes, but I blink them back as my gaze travels over the lounge chairs covered in beautiful gems and plush gray-purple fabric, gathered in a large circle around the sunken warming pit and glowing softly in the light of the L'sair crystals. Ama turns to face us. "I have prepared rooms for all of our guests." Her gaze darts to Rowan and me. "I took the liberty of placing our honored guest in the chambers beside yours."

Rowan follows me silently down the hallway as I become lost in memory with each step I take farther into the castle.

When we reach the family wing, Al'aneo shows Rowan his door, and after he disappears inside, I move down the hallway to mine. The moment I enter, memories rush in like a tide to the shore. Everything is just as I left it, my room a perfect shrine preserved by a family who waited in hope that one day I would return.

A smile tilts my lips as I run my fingers along the edge of my dresser and notice a jeweled comb for my hair in the exact place that I set it down, last time I was here.

A soft click draws my attention to the far side of the bedroom, and I turn to see Rowan standing in the doorway. That these chambers connect by this interior door, Ama was well aware, and I'm almost certain it was her intent that we would be able to speak with each other without everyone in the palace knowing if we spent time in each other's rooms.

His ridged brows shoot up to his forehead when he sees me. "I—I apologize. I thought this led to the cleansing room."

I smile to reassure him. "It's all right, Rowan." I stand from my dresser. "I'll show you where it is if you'd like."

He grins. "That won't be necessary. I assume it must be the only other door I have yet to try."

I laugh softly at his teasing tone. He turns to leave, but I call out his name. "Rowan?"

He spins back to face me. "Yes?"

"You don't have to go."

He walks over to my side, staring down at me intently. "I thought you might wish to be alone."

I reach up to cup his cheek. "No. I want to be with you."

A beaming smile lights his face, and he captures my mouth in a tender kiss.

My communicator chirps, and I look down to see a message from Ama. I lift my gaze to Rowan. "It's Ama. She wants to speak with me."

He gives me a worried look, so I move to reassure him, taking his hand in my own. "You are my choice. My family will learn to accept you. You'll see."

His eyes flash with uncertainty. "And if they do not?"

I brush my lips to his and smile against them. "I would still choose you."

He wraps his arms around me and presses his forehead to mine. "You are my heart, Tr'lani."

"And you are mine," I reply softly.

* * *

ROWAN

My room is large and finely furnished. There are plush chairs carved of dark wood encrusted with precious gems and covered in purple-gray fabric. The stone floor is covered with several scattered thick rugs that lend a decadent luxury to the space. The floating bed in the center of the room is made of the same deep, rich wood as the chairs and tables. It curves up over the mattress at the head, suspending deep-purple silken fabric like a canopy above it.

As I lay back on the bed, I think of the night we spent on the ship. I long to be claimed by her completely. To bond her to me in the sacred heart ritual. Unable to sleep, I walk to the balcony outside my window and stare down at the castle gardens below.

All the plants, including the purple moss that covers the ground, glow with a soft bioluminescence like something out of a beautiful dream. No wonder her people see so poorly in the dark. They evolved on a planet where they had no need for night vision.

Spreading my wings, I step to the edge of the terrace and then allow myself to glide down to the gardens. Walking silently along the winding paths, I go quiet and still when I recognize Tr'lani's voice up ahead.

Carefully concealing myself behind the thick vegetation, I slowly approach and find her sitting on a bench near the back wall, speaking with her grandmother.

"He doesn't care about my wings," she says.

Ama arches a brow. "Are you certain? Mosauran females are strong and coveted for their strength." She places a hand on Tr'lani's shoulders. "Al'aneo contacted me before you arrived. He says On'aro will try to repair them. But has Rowan accepted that it may not work?"

A tear slips down Tr'lani's cheek, but she quickly brushes it away as she shakes her head softly. "I do not believe so. He will not allow me to give up hope. So, perhaps he has not considered—"

Her sadness stabs at my chest, and I cannot bear it. I step out from the bushes. "Forgive me." I bow low to Ama before turning to Tr'lani. "I was walking and could not help but overhear your conversation."

Ama's sharp gaze travels over me from head to toe, but she says nothing.

I take Tr'lani's hand in mine. "Take my measure, my heart, and know that I speak the truth when I tell you this. Even if you never recover the use of your wings, it will not lessen my feelings for you. You are strong in ways that others will never be able to understand. I recognize this strength in you. I saw it the first moment our eyes met." I smile. "You challenged a warrior of Mosaura when he offered you help, and he has admired your fiery spirit ever since."

She twines her arms around my neck, hugging me close.

"Never doubt that I love you more than anything, my heart," I whisper against her hair.

When I finally pull away, I notice Ama staring at Tr'lani. She arches a questioning brow. "You have chosen then?"

Tr'lani takes my hand and entwines our fingers. "Yes."

Ama steps closer and places three fingers on each of our foreheads. "As head and matriarch of our Clan, I bless your union and look forward to many great-grandchildren."

Tr'lani's eyes widen slightly as her cheeks flush a dark violet hue. "But Ama, we're not certain it's even possible. We are two different species, and even with medical intervention, a Mosauran and an Aerilon have never had offspring before."

She holds up her hand in a silent bid to allow her to speak. Her piercing gaze darts to Tr'lani and then returns to me. "When I was only a bit younger than you are now, your Apa and I had only recently been bonded when we traveled to Garkolna. One of the Garkol warriors asked if I'd like a glimpse of my future. So, being the curious creature that I am, I, of course, said 'yes.'"

"And what did he tell you?" Tr'lani asks.

"That my granddaughter would bond with an enemy warrior. And that their bonding and their children would mark the end of our conflict with one another." Her eyes sweep to me. "I'd thought it would be one of an enemy Clan, but the moment I saw you, I knew." She smiles warmly and then raises her arms in a bid for me to embrace her. I do so quickly, and when she pulls away, her lips tilt up in a knowing grin. "You may address me as Ama."

I bow my head. "Thank you, Ama."

She gives me a beaming smile, and then her expression turns serious. Raising her hand, she points her finger between us. "But I expect you both to perform the Aerilon ceremony and mating flight as is customary of our people."

Crossing my arm over my chest, I bow low. "You have my vow as a warrior of Mosaura."

She smiles and gives Tr'lani a knowing look. "I am going to speak with your parents now, and I will see you both in the morning." Spreading her wings, she lifts off and flies toward the castle, leaving us alone in the gardens.

CHAPTER 45

ROWAN

An idea occurs to me, and I turn to Tr'lani. "Are you tired?"

She blinks several times, as if surprised that's my question, before she answers. "No."

A smile curves my lips. "Then, I would like to see the Temple you spoke of. The one that is twin to Tormin and Kilena's on Mosaura."

"Now?"

"If you have no objection. Then, yes."

She smiles. "You'll have to fly us, but I can direct you."

I dip my chin in a subtle nod and then step back, ready to shift into battle form out of habit. I'm in a strange land, surrounded by people who used to be considered my enemies. It is instinct to want to change into a stronger form, but I decide against it at the last moment.

I look to Tr'lani. If I plan to take her as my mate and I wish our people to become allies, I need to not act in a way that suggests I mistrust them. So, I extend my arms, waiting patiently for her to step into my embrace.

When she turns before me, I wrap my arms around her waist and pull her back close against my front. Extending my wings, I flex their sails and lift off the ground. As we ascend into the sky, I stare in awe at the beauty below.

The thick vegetation is alight with various colors of bioluminescent glow. This place is more beautiful than anything I could ever conjure in dreams. Soft light from the many structures seems almost muted against the nature that surrounds it as if instead of competing with the land, it only adds to it.

Tr'lani motions in the direction we should go, and I follow her lead. We glide out over the wide river that skirts the edge of the city. Strange pinpoints of light flit back and forth beneath the water's surface. Unable to still my curiosity, I fold my wings and dive toward the water.

Tr'lani laughs lightly as my wings snap open at the last second and we sail just above the surface. The water rushes under us, and she extends her hands, allowing her fingers to graze lightly over the surface. Whirls of light bloom and expand beneath the disturbance, spiraling out in an artic-blue bioluminescent shock of color.

My breath hitches in wonder. I've never seen something so striking.

When we reach the river's edge, I flap my wings and lift us higher, flexing and extending the sails to gain momentum as we race toward the top of a nearby mountain. As I gaze up, dark clouds obscure the peaks.

"These are the In'shara mountains," Tr'lani says as she points up ahead. "The Temple is just over that lower peak."

Just below the cloud line, I notice a worn path and tip my head to the side in confusion.

Somehow sensing my unspoken question, she answers. "Many off-worlders come here to make the pilgrimage up the mountain to the Temple. Not all of them have the gift of flight."

As we crest the ridge, I stare at the Temple in wonder. Tall trees alight with glowing purple and green leaves surround the structure, their trunks twisting at various angles as if reaching for the sky. The long purple and green vine-like branches are lovely beneath the light of a full moon, swaying back and forth against the cool night breeze.

Lavender moss blankets the ground. Several flowering plants gather around the base of the Temple with large, vibrant blue blooms, bathing the alabaster stone in an ethereal glow.

The back of the Temple, while close to the face of the mountain, is set just a bit in front of it. A waterfall cascades directly behind it, the waters feeding into a stream that circles the building and then winds along the path beyond.

I set us gently down upon the earth. Tr'lani takes my hand and then leads me to the Temple. As we ascend the steps, my mouth drifts open in wonder as the large statues in the center come into view.

It is indeed an exact replica of the one on my world. Two lovers embraced as they gaze at each other lovingly. The only thing different is the wings that they bear. Instead of the massive Mosauran sails, they have the delicate wings of the Aerilon.

Tr'lani leads me to the base of the statue. I lift my eyes to the towering form, and my gaze follows the direction of her hand as she points at the male. Sure enough, there is a thin line where the wings connect to his back. The grain of the stone different from the rest of the structure, yet minimal enough so as not to be noticed unless one was looking very carefully.

She turns to me with a soft smile. "He must have been Mosauran," she whispers. "And her, an Aerilon. Just as we thought."

My gaze drops to the steps at the back of the Temple. "What is back there?" I ask.

"There is a small path behind the falls," she says softly. "The water feeds first into a small pool before it turns into the stream that winds around the building and then along the path further down." She looks to me. "Would you like to see it? It's thought to have healing powers. Ama wanted me to come here to see if it might help my wings."

"Does she really believe that might work?"

Tr'lani shrugs softly. "I think she is desperate to see me whole and is willing to try anything."

Threading my fingers through hers, my gaze darts to the falls and then back to her. "Shall we try?"

She hesitates, sadness visible in her expression. "What if it doesn't work?"

I reach forward and gently tuck a stray tendril of hair behind her ear and then cup her cheek. "Then we will try something else. We will not give up, Tr'lani."

She covers my hand with her own. Closing her eyes, she turns her face into my palm and then looks to me. "What if I can never be healed? What if I'm broken forever?"

I frown. "I already told you, my heart. Even if your wings cannot be mended, it will not change how I feel about you."

She places a finger gently to my lips to silence me as her gaze holds mine. "It's not just my wings, Rowan," she whispers. "I have scars that you cannot see."

My gaze drifts over her form.

"Not on my body," she says, drawing my attention back to her face. Lifting my hand, she places it to her chest. "Here. "

I pull her into my arms and bury my face in her soft, silken hair, nuzzling her gently. Pressing a line of soft kisses from the top of her head, I move down to her cheeks and finally her lips. I wrap my wings tightly around her and then rest my forehead to hers, meeting her eyes evenly so she may see the truth of my soul. "You believe you are broken, but you are not. You are a strong survivor. And all survivors bear scars." I pause, allowing my words to sink in before I continue. "Even if your heart and your body are never fully healed, I will be your wings. I will carry you, Tr'lani, and I will never leave you behind."

The brilliant gold of her eyes appears even brighter as they catch the soft light of the bioluminescent plants that surrounds us. I take both her hands in mine and drop to one knee before her. Taking a deep breath, I give her my truth. "Allow me to prove myself as a worthy mate. I know the shav-rhokan is not the way of your people. So, I present myself in the way of yours." I lower my head, bowing submissively before her as if I were a male Aerilon offering myself to her. "Tr'lani of High Clan Al'ani, you are my heart. I offer all that I am in the hope that you will find me worthy of claiming me as your mate."

I wait for her to speak, as is the tradition. For her to declare whether she finds me lacking in any way or if she agrees to bind herself to me. But she says nothing.

My heart hammers. Cautiously, I lift my gaze to find her eyes brimming with tears. I quickly stand and gently cup her face with both hands, tilting her head back to look up at me. Her golden eyes search mine. "You truly want me?"

My heart clenches. "More than anything." I reach for her hand and place her palm flat against my chest. "You are my heart."

I lean forward and brush my lips to hers. She opens her mouth and deepens our kiss as her tongue curls around mine. I pull her closer to me, telling her without words that she is more important to me than anything else. She is my heart and always will be.

She pulls back, and I allow my wings to fall away as I watch her intently. My chest tightens with worry that perhaps I am asking too much. A small smile curves her lips as her fingers trace down my arm until she reaches my hand, clasping it firmly in her own.

She leads me toward the small pool behind the statue. It is dark as we make our way down the steps. She moves off to the side, and I follow. We make our way around the thick curtain of water that falls from the rocky ledge above until we are behind it, granting us entrance to the pool. She stops just short of the edge and turns to face me.

Her gaze holds mine as she carefully unfastens her clothing, allowing her dress to fall to the floor. My breath catches as I stare at her bare form. With her skin bathed in the soft glow all around us, she is so beautiful part of me worries this is not real. That I'm only dreaming of this. If it is a dream, I do not wish to awaken.

Cautiously, I reach out and gently touch her face. She leans into my touch as I trail the tips of my fingers down her elegant neck to the gentle slope of one breast, cupping my palm over the soft mound. Her skin is warm and smooth, and as I gently run my thumb across the stiff peak, she moans softly and tips back her head.

I move closer and then still as she reaches for me. Her hands tremble slightly as her fingers unfasten my clothing. It falls away from my body, leaving me bare before her. I reach up and encircle her wrists to stop her. I meet her gaze evenly. "We do not have to do this," I whisper. "We can wait until after our Aerilon ceremony or even longer until you decide you are ready."

She places a hand on my chest. "I want this. I want you, Rowan."

She takes my hand and entwines our fingers before leading me toward the water. The moment she steps in, a soft blue glow blooms across the newly disturbed surface. And as I follow her, it surrounds us as we wade farther in.

The water is pleasantly warm; light steam rises from the surface. As soon as we're completely submerged, she turns and then moves toward me. I circle my hands around her small waist and pull her the rest of the way until her body is almost completely flush with mine.

My stav lengthens and extends from my sheathe; I ache to join my body to hers, but I will wait until she signals she is ready.

She reaches up and cups my face with one hand before wrapping the other arm around my neck, closing the small gap between us.

My entire form tenses, my stav hard against her abdomen and my every nerve on fire at this closeness of our bodies.

CHAPTER 46

TR'LANI

Desire fills me as Rowan's stav presses insistently against my abdomen. I reach between us and wrap my hand around his length.

His silver eyes stare deep into mine. He draws in a shaking breath as I explore him. His stav is much larger than I realized, and covered in ridges from base to tip. My thighs clench together involuntarily at the thought of him inside me. Need pulses through me as I wrap my legs around his hips, opening myself to him.

I lean forward and taste his lips before he opens his mouth and his tongue finds mine. I cling to him as he deepens our kiss and gently roll my hips against him. The hard length of his stav presses against my folds and I gasp at the sensation.

He stares at me, his gaze full of hunger and need. "Do you choose me, Tr'lani?"

The ache between my thighs is the want for him to fill me, but I'm nervous. His people claim each other in a mating battle. I have no desire to be taken roughly.

His claws extend into sharpened tips, digging slightly into my hips but not enough to break the skin. Fierce possessiveness burns in his silver eyes like fire. "Do you choose me?" he rasps, as if on the edge of his control.

Anticipation wars with anxiety as his gaze holds mine. "I do, but I don't want to fight you, and I don't want to be conquered in the shav-rhokan like a Mosauran female."

His expression softens. He reaches up to run his fingers lightly through my hair as he presses his forehead to mine, clenching his jaw. "You are my heart…my greatest treasure. I would never take you roughly."

A soft smile curves my mouth. "I choose you, Rowan," I breathe the words against his lips. "I choose you, my beloved."

He seals his mouth over mine in a claiming kiss that steals the breath from my lungs. He pulls back and then kisses a heated trail along my jaw and down my neck. He dips beneath the surface, and a low moan escapes me as his mouth closes over my breast. I'd forgotten that his people can breathe underwater. The gentle suction and pull as he laves at the firm peak sends small ripples of pleasure straight through me. I arch my back and run my fingers through his hair as he moves to the other, giving it the same attention.

He moves even lower, and I inhale sharply as his tongue slicks through my folds and then enters my channel. A vibration that can only be the growl of his arousal moves through me as he strokes his tongue in and out of my core. My body goes taut as pleasure coils deep inside me. With his head between my thighs, I dig my heels into his shoulders. I grasp the side of the pool with one hand to steady myself while the other grips his hair, massaging the hard ridges along his scalp.

I never knew this could feel so amazing. Each breath ends with a soft gasp as I begin to pant heavily, on the edge of my desire. Everything inside me coils tight in anticipation, and I'm so close to release my body feels like it's on fire.

Suddenly, he stops. A soft whimper of disappointment escapes me a moment before he moves back up my body and presses his soft lips to mine in a branding kiss. I wrap my arms around his neck, pressing my body against his. "I need you, Rowan."

With one hand clamped on my hip, he reaches between us and aligns his stav with the entrance to my core. Panting heavily, his silver eyes meet mine, full of need.

His gaze holds mine and the breath stutters from my lungs as he slowly enters me.

He so large that at first everything is tight and uncomfortable. But when he shifts his hips and begins to rock back and forth as he advances, it changes to more pleasure than pain as my body adjusts to his invasion.

He grits his teeth as he struggles to maintain his control. "So tight," he rasps. "I don't want to hurt you."

I pepper his face with tender kisses, reassuring him I'm fine

When he is finally seated completely inside me, it is a delicious fullness unlike anything I've ever known. We stare at each other in mutual wonder at the feeling of our bodies fully joined. He cups the back of my neck with one hand and wraps his other arm around my waist, pulling me close as his lips find mine in a passionate kiss.

Slowly, he begins to stroke in and out of my channel. A low moan escapes my parted lips as the ridges of his stave create the most intense friction each time he moves deep inside me.

I hold him close. His tongue curls around mine, and I run my fingers through his hair and over the hard ridges atop his skull.

He must be sensitive there because he grips my hips firmly and begins to thrust up into my body. Each stroke becomes longer, more foreceful, and deeper. His kisses more passionate as if claiming me with both his tongue and his stav. I gasp and moan against him as heat builds deep within my center. I run my hands down his back, feeling the flex of his muscles beneath the tips of my fingers as he moves inside me.

My moans become pants, and I chant his name like a prayer as I hold him close. I'm so near the edge of my desire. He wraps his wings around me and spins so that my back is now against the wall. He growls low in arousal, his fiercely possessive gaze holding mine as he begins to thrust deeper. My entire body is awash in sensation; a pleasure unlike anything I've ever known.

"Rowan," I breathe out his name. "Please," I beg and I'm not even sure what I'm asking for.

He growls and begins to move even faster. My toes curl and the pressure builds inside me until I feel as if I can take no more. My entire body goes taut and I arch my back as my release rushes through me, all-consuming and so powerful I cry out his name.

"Mine," he roars as his stav pulses hard and rhythmically inside me. Delicious heat blooms deep in my womb as he fills me with his seed. It feels as though it goes on forever, sending me spiraling into another orgasm, this one stronger than the last.

He seals his mouth over mine in a branding kiss and then rests his forehead against me as we remain joined, panting and locked together in an embrace. His stav is still buried deep inside me as he lifts his gaze to mine.

My eyes drift down to his chest, brightly glowing beneath the water line. He extends his claws and pierces his scales just over his heart, and the light begins to pulse even brighter. Extending his hand to my chest, directly over my heart, his sharp claws lightly pierce my skin. A small hiss of pain escapes my lips at the slight sting, but he captures my mouth in a kiss, replacing my discomfort with pleasure.

He presses his chest against mine. Heat sears my skin directly beneath his beating heart, but he swallows my gasp with a kiss as warmth fills my chest, so intense I feel as if it is wrapping itself around my soul.

My body warms, and I twine my arms and legs tighter around him, closing my eyes at the sensation of being wrapped in layers of soothing comfort and protection.

I open my eyes in awareness as our hearts sync and begin to beat in time as one. "You are my heart. We are one soul," he whispers before pressing a soft kiss to my lips.

I rest my forehead against his as his hands travel up and down my back in a slow and gentle caress. "Are you all right, my heart?"

I smile and cup his face. "I'm fine, my beloved."

With our bodies still joined, he leans forward and captures my mouth with his own. After a moment, he pulls away. His eyes widen slightly as he stares across at me. "Rowan, what's wrong?"

A devastatingly handsome smile curves his lips. "Your wings, my heart," he whispers. "They are glowing."

I turn my head, and my mouth drifts open as I stare at them in wonder. Rowan gently cups my cheek. His eyes stare deep into mine, full of love and devotion. "You are my fated one," he says softly. "I knew it. All this time. I felt it in here." He places our joined hands over his heart and happiness brighter than a thousand stars floods my system.

When we return to the castle, he lays down in the bed beside me. He pulls me into his arms and lightly skims the tip of his nose alongside mine before pressing a kiss to my lips. I've never felt more loved as he wraps his wings around me, holding me close.

CHAPTER 47

ROWAN

It has only been a few days since we arrived on Aerilon, but Tr'lani was eager to have the Healers attempt their repair of her wings. As I sit in the Med Center lobby with Ama and the rest of her family, we take turns pacing, anxiously waiting for any news that the procedure has been completed.

When On'aro steps through the doors, we all stand as one and move toward him.

"How is she?" Al'aneo beats me to the question.

His eyes meet mine, and he lowers his gaze. "It was very…difficult for her, but I believe she will regain much of her wing function."

By "difficult," I understand that he means "painful." We knew she would have to remain awake and completely free of anesthetic during the procedure as they attempted to repair the damaged tissues and nerves. I meet his eyes evenly. "Is she awake?"

He shakes his head. "She was in pain, so we've sedated her now that it is over so that she may rest."

"I'd like to sit with her."

On'aro nods and then leads us to her recovery room. I move to her bedside and take her hand in my own. I press a gentle kiss to her palm, and a ghost of a smile crests her lips.

As my gaze drifts over her features, it is easy to see the tracks from her tears during the procedure. My mate is very strong and brave to have endured such intense pain.

Ama takes a seat beside me and places her hand on my forearm. "Thank you," she whispers.

I give her a questioning look. "For what?"

She takes my hand, squeezing it gently. "Tr'lani told me all that you did to find your brother when he was a slave. And I know everything you went through to bring her back home to us as well. Thank you for reuniting our family."

I open my mouth to reply, but Tr'lani's soft voice draws my attention as she whispers my name. "Rowan?"

Her eyelids flutter open, and she gives me a faint smile. I lean down to press a kiss to her forehead. "On'aro says you did well, my heart, and believes you could regain much of your function."

Her smile grows even brighter.

* * *

It has only been a few days since Tr'lani's procedure, but she insisted upon attending the Assembly meeting. As we enter the Council chambers, I'm struck by the odd shape of the building. It is a triangular design with several rows of seating that start just above the center floor and then extend five more rows up.

The entire structure is carved of smooth alabaster stone, as is almost every building in the city I've seen thus far, including Tr'lani's family's castle. Her Clan sits on one side while two other Clans sit in the others. Clan Al'ani is one of the the three High Ruling Clans, just as the other two are.

Another chamber beside this one with five sides is reserved for the Lower Clans, three of which are pledged to Al'ani, granting them more power over the other two.

Everyone is silent as we enter. All eyes fall on me, and I straighten my shoulders, tipping up my chin in my warrior stance as we move past them and take our seats. Let them stare. They must get used to my people if we are to form an alliance.

Ama stands to address the Assembly, and everyone turns their head in her direction, waiting for her to speak. Her gaze darts briefly to me and then back to the crowd. “Prince Rowan of Mosaura has come to us today on behalf of his mother, the Empress of the Mosauran Empire to entreat us to form an alliance.”

A low rumble of discontent fills the room, but Ama raises her hands in a bid for them to listen.

They quiet and then wait for her to continue.

She turns to me and motions for me to stand next to her.

Tr’lani gently squeezes my hand and then releases it as I stand to address her people. Drawing in a deep breath, I begin. “Long have our people been enemies to one another. We have a history of mistrust between our two races that dates back over two thousand cycles.”

Many nod, their eyes hard as they stare at me.

“But that must end today.” I pause, noting the confused look on most of their faces. I imagine many of them never thought they’d ever see a Mosauran calling for an alliance. As a warrior race, we are seen by many as conquerors. That I am here, trying to convince them to join us in peace, must be rather shocking.

A male from another Clan stands, his face red with anger. “How do we know this isn’t some sort of elaborate trap?” he grits through his teeth. “Even now, your cruisers may be en route for our world, ready to invade and take what is ours.”

That he would suggest something so cowardly as deceit to conquer an enemy is insulting. “My people are warriors. We do not operate in the shadows like those of a lesser race.” I struggle to keep my tone even as I push down my anger. “You have my solemn vow as a warrior of Mosaura, my people would never do that.”

He narrows his eyes. “Why would I trust your word? You have a cruiser docked at the orbital station. Why else is it there?”

Enraged that he would question my honor as a warrior, I grit through my teeth, “If my people wanted to conquer your world, our cruiser would already be raining down fire from the sky, and I would not be standing here before you."

A great rumble of voices erupts at my words as several members of the Council shout angrily at each other. Fragments of their words reach my ears.

"He should not be here!" one shouts.

"Why are we listening to him? His ships may already be en route to take our planet," another says.

Ama shoots up from her seat and stares at them with a thunderous gaze. "When you address Prince Rowan, you should be mindful that you are also addressing a member of High Clan Al'ani! He is to be bonded with my granddaughter and accepted into our Clan."

Shocked gasps and hushed whispers fill the room as all eyes fall upon me. Tr'lani stands beside me and takes my hand in her own, entwining our fingers. "I have chosen Rowan as my mate."

Another female across the room points at Ama, shouting angrily. "You would sacrifice your own granddaughter to one of these monsters?"

Ama balks. "Sacrifice?"

Tr'lani levels a dark glare at the female. "Rowan and his brother risked their lives to save me from the A'kai." She places her open palm to her chest. "*Me*! An enemy of their Empire…they saved me from slavery when they could have just as easily left me to die!"

Everyone falls silent as another female stands. Her gaze locks on mine as she addresses me. "Is this truth?" Her eyes shift to Tr'lani.

"Yes," she replies.

Another male stands. "Everyone knows the Mosaurans do not take mates outside of their race."

I meet his eyes evenly. "My mother, the Empress, has done away with that outdated law. My brother Soran is bonded to a Terran—a female not of our race as well."

The chamber goes silent again.

Al'aneo stands. "It is truth. We have only recently come from Mosaura, and I witnessed this for myself. The Terran female he speaks of was enslaved with my sister. She helped her to survive." He allows his gaze to travel over the Assembly. "Because of this, we accepted her into our Clan, and in taking Prince Soran as her bondmate, he is now of Clan Al'ani too."

"Traitor!" another male shouts. "You would sell us to the Mosaurans as you have already sold your family."

Ama's eyes burn with rage. "How dare you?" Her fangs extend, her lips twisted in a feral snarl as she stares at the male. "Here we are at each other's throats when we should be discussing an alliance with an Empire that could ensure our victory against an A'kai attack."

Another female calls out, "Why would the A'kai attack us? They have left us alone for many cycles."

Ama continues. "They only leave us alone because they are uncertain of their victory because of our strength. But what happens if they somehow gain the upper hand? What happens if they develop some new technology to defeat us? Would it not be wise to ally ourselves with a vast Empire that does not need us and yet approaches us for an alliance of friendship and mutual defense?"

Everyone is quiet as they absorb her words. After a moment, she motions to one of her guards.

The glint of the AI data crystal as it passes beneath the light catches my eye as he inserts it into the computer console.

Almost instantly, the Elari appears. "Greetings," she says as her gaze scans the Assembly. "I am Elari of the Milaran people."

"What is the meaning of this?" someone asks.

Tr'lani replies. "An A'kai attacked our glider shortly after Rowan and his brother rescued me. Rowan and I were stranded on an unknown planet, and we discovered a ruined city there. Inside the main library, we discovered this AI. They had not yet achieved the ability to reach the stars, yet the A'kai culled their species for hundreds of cycles.

"The Milarans decided to fight back against the slaughter of their race. They developed a biological weapon to combat the A'kai. Their entire species was exterminated, as a result, before they could release it. She told us what happened to their people, and now, we have brought her before you today, so you may hear and see it with your own eyes."

As Elari explains what happened to her people, the Aerilon watch in horror as she replays video of the violent and horrifying attack that exterminated them, ending with the Milaran scientist turning to a statue of ash before their eyes. After she is finished, she turns to me and Tr'lani. "Please," she says softly. "You promised to erase me. I do not wish to bear the burden of these memories any longer."

Ama gives her a pitying look. "But if you are gone, what will be left of your people? All their knowledge and culture would be lost with you." She places her palm to her chest. "I know what it is to lose someone you love. It is an indescribable pain that tears at your very soul. But I also know that to live and carry their memory is to keep them alive in a way. No one is ever truly lost who is remembered. And those who are remembered will not have died in vain."

Another female stands, and from her dress tunic it is easy to see she is a scientist. "Your people were on the cusp of wielding a powerful weapon. Something that would guarantee their safety from the A'kai and their cullings. I ask you to work with us toward this same goal. Continue and fulfill the legacy of your race by helping ours to finish what yours could not."

My brow furrows deeply as I give her a troubled look. "As much as I abhor the A'kai, I understand that not all of their people are evil. Your pursuit of this weapon could mean the genocide of an entire race."

She meets my gaze evenly. "We do not seek to exterminate them. Merely to have a threat to dissuade them from an attack."

Ama stands. "I agree with Rowan. How many great and terrible weapons have been constructed with this excuse? If history has taught us anything, it is that such creations are eventually used with the effect of horrible devastation."

The scientist nods, but I do not miss the calculated look behind her eyes. That they will pursue the development of this biological weapon, I have no doubt. But I remain silent as Ama addresses the Assembly.

"We would speak with you more," she tells Elari. "And after we've talked, if you still wish for the peace of oblivion, we will grant it to you."

Elari nods in acknowledgment and then disappears in a soft, shimmering light. The Aerilon guard returns the crystal to Tr'lani, and she tucks it into her pocket. Several people watch this move with intense fascination, and I struggle to contain the low, warning growl rumbling deep in my chest as I narrow my eyes at them in a silent challenge. I will kill any who threaten my mate.

Another Aerilon from one of the Lower Clans stands to address the room. "Our people have never needed an alliance to hold back the A'kai. And I do not believe we need one now."

Ama stands, her sharp gaze sweeping over the chamber before she speaks. "I urge each and every one of you to consider this matter carefully. We have witnessed what can happen at the hands of the A'kai. They are a ruthless race, intent upon conquest. The blood of our people is considered a delicacy to theirs. Just because they have left us alone for now does not mean it will always be so."

A heavy silence falls over the entire crowd as they consider her words.

Several of those against the alliance glare across at me. It is difficult to remain calm when everything inside me wants to shift into draken form to protect myself and my mate. As if sensing my unease, Tr'lani places a hand on my forearm, drawing my attention to her. "It will take time for our people to learn to trust one another, but I have faith that the alliance will pass."

I hope she is right. Surely, her people realize our combined forces are better than each of us alone if we had to face the A'kai in battle.

My communicator chirps, and I look down to see a message from the Mosauran captain. I move off to the side and press my comm to answer. His face appears instantly in the viewscreen. "We've detected a strange energy signature above the Capital City."

Having heard the captain, Al'aneo's head whips toward me, his eyes full of concern.

"What is it?" I ask.

"I am uncertain, but it—"

A thundering explosion sounds overhead, rocking the entire structure around us. It's followed quickly by another, and my head jerks toward Tr'lani. Wide eyes full of fear meet mine a moment before the Assembly ceiling collapses, raining down stone and fire.

"Row—!" Her voice is cut short as the Assembly crumbles around us. Screams and shouts echo as pillars and stone give way. Everyone is panicked and frantic to escape as the structure continues to fall.

Several more explosions rock the ground beneath us, and I recognize it as blaster fire from ship's cannons. My comm lights up, and the captain appears again on the display. "It's the A'kai! They were cloaked over the city. We've managed to take out their weapons, but their engines are still operational and—"

"Destroy them! Leave none alive!"

The captain gives me a firm bow and then cuts off the screen.

Through the thick haze of dust and debris, I frantically search for Tr'lani and her family. A hand on my shoulder startles me, and I spin to find Al'aneo, covered in blood, a wild look in his eyes. "We have to find them, Rowan!"

Unable to speak, I nod, and we begin digging through the rubble. Together, we pull away heavy chunks of stone as we clear a path. "Tr'lani!" I call out, but there is no answer.

Cries and wails fill the air around us. The area is littered with injured and dead Aerilons. Those left unharmed are digging frantically through the destroyed structure to find their loved ones.

Echoes of explosions sound overhead as our ship attacks theirs. But I am only vaguely aware of the noise as I frantically dig through the rubble, calling out for Tr'lani.

"We've destroyed them," the captain's voice calls out over my comm.

"I need everyone down here to help us search for the injured. Now!"

"Yes, my Prince," he replies as the comm cuts back off.

It doesn't take long for my people to arrive and begin helping. Sweat beads across my brow, and dread trickles down my spine as the sounds of the injured grow fainter. With each person removed to safety, it is one less voice crying for help. The silence that follows is deafening. Fear tightens my chest as I continue to claw and dig at the ruined structure around us, desperate to find Tr'lani and her family.

I know she still lives because my heart beats wildly. If she were dead, I would feel it.

Al'aneo shouts beside me. "Ama!" He pulls his grandmother's unconscious form into his arms.

Weakly, she opens her eyes. "Where is everyone else?"

"We're still looking."

"Don't stop," she barely manages before her head lolls back and she closes her eyes.

One of my warriors comes up beside me. "Give her to me," he tells Al'aneo. "We will get her to the Healers."

Al'aneo hands her to the warrior, and he leaves quickly to carry her to safety.

As I lift away another large stone, I notice the shock of Tr'lani's silver hair and her pale-blue dress. "Tr'lani!" I shout, but she doesn't answer.

I turn to her brother. "Help me lift this! Tr'lani's down here!"

He rushes to my side. Each of us grasping the large stone, we grit our teeth as we push and lift it away, revealing Tr'lani and her parents in a small, empty space beneath it.

I jump down into the pit and gather my beloved in my arms while Al'aneo and one of my warriors retrieves her parents.

"They're still alive!" Al'aneo calls out.

Tr'lani's chest rises and falls with shallow breaths. "Please, my heart," I nuzzle her temple. "Please, open your eyes."

Her eyelids flutter and open. When her golden gaze meets mine, she smiles weakly up at me. "Rowan," she whispers. "You found me."

"Always, my heart." I rest my forehead gently to hers. "Always."

CHAPTER 48

TR'LANI

A low rumble of voices calls me back into awareness. The strong scent of antiseptic fills the air, and I open my eyes to find Rowan with his hand in mine as he speaks to Soran and Liana. I recognize that I'm in a Med Center.

As if sensing I'm awake, his head whips toward me. "Tr'lani?"

I smile weakly up at him, and he leans down to wrap me in his arms as he presses a tender kiss to my lips. "How do you feel, my heart?"

"Tired, but all right."

Liana moves beside him and then embraces me warmly. "Thank God you're okay," she whispers against me. "We were so worried. When Rowan contacted us, we left to come here immediately. I'm so glad you're awake."

Memories flood my mind, and I jerk up in the bed. My eyes searching the room. "My family. What about my family?"

Al'aneo appears in the doorway behind Rowan. "All safe," he smiles. "Everyone is well."

My shoulders sag forward in relief as he hugs me tight against him. "What happened? Who attacked us?"

Rowan's gaze darkens. "The A'kai."

Soran steps forward. "We intercepted a transmission. Somehow, they found out about the AI data crystal and decided to try to destroy it by attacking the Assembly where you were all gathered."

My brow furrows deeply. "That means someone must have told them that I had it. And they knew we'd be at the Assembly. But who would do this?"

Liana shakes her head. "Before he died, Talel claimed his people had allies among the Mosaurans. Others who wanted to see an end to the Empress's reign over Mosaura."

Soran nods. "I suspect they must have informants among your people as well."

I shake my head. "Why would anyone work with them?"

Rowan clenches his jaw. "I do not know. But we must find out."

Ama enters the room, and I smile brightly at her.

"My darling granddaughter." She smiles and presses a soft kiss to my forehead. Her gaze darts to Rowan. "I am glad you are awake. Your Mosauran warrior refused to leave your side, and I suspect he has not slept at all over the past few days while you've been unconscious."

I turn to Rowan and cup his cheek, staring at him in concern. "Is this truth, my beloved?"

He tilts his head into my palm and closes his eyes as if relishing the touch of my skin upon his own. He places his hand over mine as his silver eyes stare deep into mine. "How could I sleep when I was so worried about you?"

Soran claps a hand on his shoulder. "You can finally get some rest now. The rest of us will be here while you sleep."

Rowan looks to me. "I will rest nearby." He points to the sofa by the window.

I open my mouth to protest that he should return to the palace, but he interrupts and gives me a stern look. "I refuse to leave you."

With a quick kiss to my forehead, he walks to the sofa and sits down. Laying back against the cushions, he closes his eyes.

Al'aneo begins speaking to Soran while Liana moves next to me, taking my hand in her own. "Rowan told us you two bonded in the Mosauran way," she says softly.

My cheeks heat as I stare up at her, hoping my brother does not overhear our conversation. "We did," I reply. "But not with the mating battle."

Liana grins. "So does that mean he won't have to do the Aerilon mating flight?"

"He will," Al'aneo interrupts over her shoulder. "It is tradition, and Ama will settle for nothing less than a proper bonding ceremony between them."

Liana laughs, and I do as well.

A thought occurs to me as I stare up at her. "Have you had a chance to speak with Holly?"

Liana nods. "Yes. She disappeared a few years after me." She shakes her head. "Same story though. Her crew went into stasis sleep, and she woke up on a Zovian slave ship without any memory of how she got there." Liana leans in and drops her voice to barely a whisper. "She seems very taken with your brother, and he with her." A sly smirk twists her lips as she darts a glance over her shoulder at Al'aneo. "I think you may have a new sister soon."

His cheeks flush in response to her words, telling me that despite her attempt to be quiet, he heard everything she said.

Liana's face turns serious. "Are your people accepting of your relationship with Rowan?"

I lower my gaze. "At the Assembly, before the attack, it was easy to see that many mistrust him. Some even suggested I was being forced into bonding with him."

She takes my hand. "We've faced some prejudice on Mosaura as well. But, for the most part, it seems like many of their people are slowly adjusting to the idea of bonding outside of their race. Especially since their males outnumber their females ever since the last plague swept through."

Liana places my palm lower over her abdomen, and my mouth

drifts open in shock before a beaming smile lights my face. "You're carrying a fledgling?"

"Yes." She grins. "A girl."

I wrap my arms around her. "I'm so happy for you, my dear sister!"

When she pulls back, Soran slips his arms around her from behind and pulls her back against his chest as he gently nuzzles her hair. She twists her head back to give him a kiss.

Al'aneo claps him on the shoulder. "Congratulations!"

Rowan calls out from the corner, a wide grin on his face. "And you'll be naming her after her favorite uncle, right?"

I laugh as Liana rolls her eyes.

After we're finished laughing, I look to her and Soran. "How long are you staying for?" I ask, hoping they're going to be here for a while.

Liana grins. "I figured we'd stay long enough for your Aerilon bonding ceremony."

Rowan's eyes meet mine, and a devastatingly handsome smile curves his lips. "We'd like that."

CHAPTER 49

TR'LANI

It has been a little over two weeks since the bombing at the Assembly. Alone at my workstation, I insert the data crystal in the console and greet Elari warmly when she appears. "Have you made your decision?"

"I have," she replies. "I have thought on what your matriarch said, and have decided to remain as I am."

Her expression is pained, and for a moment, I forget her form is a projection and reach out to take her hand but stop myself when I remember.

"If I were to no longer be, it would be as though my people never existed. There would be no memory of their lives and the things that they did. They would have lived and died for nothing." She pauses. "I request to be placed in one of your libraries—a place of learning—so that I might interact with your people as I used to with mine. To share their culture and all of their great accomplishments."

Although she is a projection formed by codes and algorithms, she is as much a sentient being as anyone else, and the sadness is easy to read in her eyes. My heart clenches, but I do my best to give her a small smile. “If that is what you wish, I’m sure it will be granted, but there is something I must ask of you first.”

She gives me a curious look. “What is it?”

“I want you to erase your knowledge of the weapon your people would have used against the A’kai.”

She tips her head to the side. “But…it is what my people died for. It would be a betrayal of their memory to—”

I raise my hand to still her. “You wouldn’t erase it completely. I would ask that you partition that part of your memory away from your core programming.”

Her brow furrows deeply.

I continue. “You know I have no love for the A’kai after what they did to me, and after what I saw in the Great Library of your people.” Closing my eyes briefly, the dark memories of their ashen bodies disintegrating to dust rises to the front of my memory unbidden. I push it back down in the furthest recesses of my mind and then focus on her. “But I know not all of their people are monsters, and I will not have my people constructing a weapon capable of mass genocide.”

She narrows her gaze. “Why do you seek to protect them? They would not hesitate to do this to another race.” Her hands curl into fists at her side as anger burns in her eyes. “You know this to be truth.”

The small pile of ash that was once a child that she loved haunts my dreams often, and I know she is right. But that doesn’t mean it is the correct path for my people. I lift a determined gaze to her, meeting her eyes evenly. “If you give our scientists this knowledge, there is no guarantee they will not decide to use this weapon in a first strike against the A’kai, possibly killing millions of families…children even.”

She lowers her head, her brows knitting together in a contemplative look. “I was programmed to learn…to adapt and to grow beyond my own programming. My creators wanted me to be capable of independent thought and decision based upon empathy and compassion—like a creature born of flesh and blood instead of codes and algorithms.”

I give her a wary look. “What have you decided then?”

She moves closer so that we are little more than half an arms-length apart. Her eyes are sad as they gaze into mine, but for the first time, I notice the sharp awareness behind them. Her creators succeeded in their programming. She is much more than what anyone suspects her to be.

"In experiencing the life of a child through my interactions with Davin, I grew to love him as if he were mine. One day he came to me with a ribbon he'd won in a race at school." A wistful smile crests her lips. "I've never been prouder. And in that moment, I understood what I'd only barely gleaned before then. I know why most of the images that were downloaded into my matrix were of pictures of families and children instead of the great scientific accomplishments of our people.

"It is because of all things in life…love is the most important. This emotion alone is the driving force that guides the actions of all sentient creatures. We are willing to die if necessary to protect the things we love because without them, life is meaningless."

Her words stun me, and I stare at her in wonder. She is not only their memory…she is the heart of the Milaran people.

She meets my gaze evenly. "I understand why this weapon must never be created unless there is no other option. You and your chosen one are both honorable beings. I vow that I will keep the weapon's secret locked away my matrix. Only you or Rowan will be granted access if you ever decide you wish for this knowledge."

I give her a cautious look. "I have your word?"

She smiles warmly at me. "That you would ask for the word of a being many would consider non-sentient tells me I have chosen wisely when I decided to place my trust in you." She gives me a solemn look. "Yes. You have my word."

CHAPTER 50

ROWAN

My gaze travels over the Assembly Hall. Looking at it now, you'd never know it was nothing but rubble a few short weeks ago. It seems the Aerilon have superior construction technologies to ours. Something that I hope they will share with my people once the alliance is formalized.

Tr'lani and Ama stand on either side of me as I address the High and Lower Clans gathered here today. Soran and Liana sit a bit farther down, next to Al'aneo. Several of our warriors from the cruiser are seated below as well.

My gaze sweeps over the room before I begin. "It is my belief that our people have not always been enemies. It has been discovered that our Great Temple on Mosaura is a mirror image of your own." With a flick of my wrist, I project a picture of the statues at the Mosauran Temple beside the one on Aerilon.

Several audible gasps come from the Assembly as they stare in shock at the identical structures. "Even the statues are posed in the exact same way," I continue as I zoom in on the carved stone. "And the wings have been altered on each one in such a way as to suggest that the female was Aerilon and the male a Mosauran."

Tr'lani stands beside me. "Even the names of the statue of the Lovers is similar to those on Mosaura. Our Tr'omen and Kr'elana are known on Mosaura as Tormin and Kilena."

Silence settles over the chamber as everyone gapes at the images before them. "The story of each statue is the same as well. They were enemies before their bonding, just as we are today."

Ama places a hand on my shoulder. "My granddaughter was rescued from the A'kai by two Princes of Mosaura. They are the only reason she has been returned to us and stands before you today. Let us end this conflict between our two peoples so we may work together toward strengthening our Empires against the A'kai and any who would see us fall."

She pauses as her eyes travel over the room. "The A'kai want us in open conflict with one another because they know that together we are strong. And now, I ask you to cast a vote for the alliance and treaty that would end thousands of cycles of conflict with Mosaura. What say you?"

Tr'lani takes my hand as one by one, each senior member of the High and Lower Clans stands and calls out their vote. Only a handful remain in opposition to the alliance, but it still passes by an overwhelming number.

I wrap my arm around my beloved and pull her close, pressing a gentle kiss to her temple. Never could I have imagined this day would ever come. The day when our people decided to lay down arms and embrace a treaty of friendship.

Al'aneo claps a hand on my shoulder. "This has been a good day." He smiles. "But it will be an even better one when you are officially bonded."

Tr'lani smiles and places our joined hands directly over her heart. According to the ways of my people, we already are bonded, but I do not tell him this. What happened between us that night at the Temple, when I shared my lifeforce with her, is something only between us.

When Al'aneo walks away, she turns to me. Reaching up, she cups my cheek. "We do not need another ceremony, my beloved. I am already yours."

I dart a quick glance to Ama and then arch a teasing brow at Tr'lani. "And go against Ama's wishes for you to have a traditional Aerilon ceremony? I do not know about you, but *I*, for one, am not that brave."

She laughs, and I am completely mesmerized as I stare across at my beautiful mate.

CHAPTER 51

ROWAN

Tomorrow is our bonding ceremony and my mother insisted upon coming. This is the first time the Empress of Mosaura has ever come to Aerilon as far back as our recorded history. My gaze travels over the crowd gathered around us as they await her transport. This is a momentous occasion.

Ama stands beside myself and Tr'lani, while Soran and Liana stand directly behind us. As soon as the transport touches down, everyone falls silent. The doors slowly retract.

Dressed in a long flowing green robe of our House colors, my mother is at once both intimidating and regal as she walks down the ramp toward us. Caryn follows one step behind her. Soran moves forward and she embraces us both warmly before she does the same to Liana and Tr'lani.

When she pulls back, she takes Tr'lani's hands in her own and meets her gaze evenly. "I welcome you to House Mosaura, my daughter."

Ama steps forward and takes my hand in kind. "And we welcome Rowan to High Clan Al'ani."

Ama's sharp gaze meets my mother's as they appraise one another. My mother dips her chin in a subtle bow to Ama and then looks out to the crowd. "I wish to thank the people of Aerilon for their warm welcome and for their embracing my son as one of their own. May his bonding with Tr'lani of High Clan Al'ani herald a new beginning for our two races of mutual peace and prosperity."

The Aerilon people cheer loudly. Ama's lips quirk up slightly as she looks to my mother and inclines her head in a polite bow.

* * *

LYING in bed with my mate wrapped tightly in my arms and wings, I cannot imagine a more perfect life. A light moan escapes her as I run my hands over her smooth skin and then cup the soft mound of her breast, brushing my thumb lightly across the stiff peak.

My stav lengthens and extends from my body in anticipation of joining with hers.

The chime of the door rings loudly, and I clench my jaw in frustration as I go still and then drop my head to the curve of my mate's neck and shoulder, willing my stav back into its sheathe as she calls out, "Who's there?"

Ama's voice is loud and authoritative as she speaks through the door. "I have come to retrieve you so that you may ready yourself for the mating flight."

My head jerks up, and I frown down at Tr'lani. "Now?"

"Yes," Ama answers. "The sooner, the better."

Tr'lani sighs heavily as she runs her hands through my hair.

Dressing quickly, we open the door and Ama frowns at me. "Why are you in my granddaughter's room?"

My head jerks back slightly in shock. "Where else would I be?"

She gives me a disapproving look. "It is tradition for the male to be apart from the female the night before the ceremony."

"But—" I start, but she raises a hand in a bid to allow her to speak.

"My granddaughter deserves a proper ceremony and mating

flight," she says firmly. "And that means you will stay in your own room, alone tonight, until we come to retrieve you."

I blink several times in shock.

Al'aneo comes up behind Ama, a sly smirk on his face. "Come on, Rowan. We have a lot to do."

My brow furrows in confusion.

Tr'lani turns to me and stretches up on her toes, giving me a quick kiss and then smiling brightly. "I will await you tomorrow, my beloved."

"Await me?"

"In the gardens," Ama replies.

This is…not what I expected. Following Al'aneo, it takes everything I have not to return to my mate. I dislike the idea of being separated even if only for a little while and sleeping this night without her wrapped up in my arms and wings. But I have taken an Aerilon as my mate, and they have already accepted me. How can I not follow their traditions?

CHAPTER 52

ROWAN

Despite the cut-out in the back for my wings, my long purple robes are uncomfortable against my scales, but I force myself to remain still as I wait for Tr'lani.

My mother takes my hands in her own and gives me a faint smile. "I am happy for you," she says solemnly. "Your father would have been proud."

Emotions lodge in my throat, but I somehow manage to speak through them. "Thank you, Mother."

Soran claps a hand on my shoulder, and when I turn, he gives me a wide grin. "I am happy for you as well."

Caryn hugs me and then grins. "And I am fortunate to be gaining another sister."

"Tr'lani is going to be so surprised when she sees what you've done for her," Liana adds.

I return her smile, but deep down, I'm nervous. A "honeymoon" is a Terran tradition, but Liana insisted Tr'lani would love it. Soran and I set up the shelter late last night with the help of Al'aneo and Caryn. Liana says it is called a "honeymoon cottage" on Terra.

My brother's lips tilt up in a subtle grin. "I can see the worry in your eyes, brother, but it is unfounded." He turns his gaze to his mate, his eyes shining with love before the returns his attention back to me. "I believe you both will enjoy your…'honeymoon.'"

"I hope you are right."

Ama, her parents, Al'aneo, Holly, Grex, and Abby stand off to one side. Holly rocks back and forth on her feet as she cradles Alex to her chest, gazing down at her periodically with loving eyes as if the fledgling were her own. I don't miss the way Al'aneo's gaze remains locked on her as she does this. On the other side of them is an Aerilon High Priestess, waiting to perform the ceremony.

The garden glows with the soft light of bioluminescence as the sun begins its descent. I wait with great anticipation as Tr'lani appears just down the path. Her matching robes flutter softly around her with every step. A soft crown of tiny purple flowers sits atop her head, and I stare in wonder at her ethereal beauty.

As she walks down the pathway, I notice the delicate outline of her bare feet as they peek out from beneath her robe. The purple, spongy moss beneath my own uncovered feet is soft, and I struggle to remain still, when all I want to do is rush forward and gather her in my arms, take flight and then claim her in the ways of her people as we soar through the sky in the mating flight.

When she reaches my side, a stunning smile curves her lips as she stares up at me, and I return it with one of my own.

I take both her hands in mine and, as one, we turn to face the High Priestess. She places her hands over ours and then bows her head as she recites the blessings of the Aerilon Bonding Ceremony. It is so different from the ways of my people.

Tr'lani had asked me if I'd wanted to have a blend of Mosauran and Aerilon traditions for our ceremony, but I decided against it. If Tr'lani were Mosauran, we would most likely be covered in sweat and panting heavily from the exertion of fighting after I bested her in the shav-rhokan. I would then clamp my teeth over the delicate flesh at the curve of her neck and shoulder, holding her in place while we mated. Of course, none of this would be done in front of witnesses.

Our people are too possessive and protective of our mates to allow any others to watch while we join.

Surprisingly, the very thought of claiming her in the traditions of my people is unappealing to me. I would never want to take my beautiful mate so roughly.

When she is finished reciting the blessings, I gently press my forehead to Tr'lani's as she begins a beautiful trilling hum in the back of her throat as she stares across at me. The rest of her family join in, and I do my best to mimic the sound, pitiful as my attempt may be. But it does not matter.

Ama and the rest of our family, including Grex and Abby, move closer, surrounding us as they begin to hum louder.

The Priestess's voice speaks softly over the sound. "A Clan is only as strong as its weakest member. Let this harmony signal the unbreakable bond that binds you to Clan Al'ani. Take shelter beneath each other's wings, and if one of you falters, the others will share in and carry your burden. You are no longer just one, you are many, and there is strength in the bonding of family."

Happiness blooms in my chest, filling me with warmth. Emotions lodge in my throat as my gaze drifts over my family, both old and new.

As the ceremony ends, Tr'lani turns to me expectantly. Lifting her up into my arms, I extend my wings. The mating flight is all about trust—the female entrusting the male to carry them both as they consummate their bond. That Tr'lani trusts me to fly us both, I already know. I've carried her many times as her wings are not fully healed just yet.

Carefully, I take off, and we begin our ascent into the sky. Anticipation courses through me. As soon as we are above the cloud line and free of watching eyes, I unfasten my cloak and allow it to fall away before reaching for hers and doing the same.

She gasps in surprise as she turns wide eyes to me. "We're supposed to save them for when we land, Rowan. Otherwise, we'll both be bare when we return to my family."

I grin. "We are not returning to them this night. You will not need your robe where we are going."

Before she can ask any more questions, I carefully turn her in my arms.

She wraps her legs around my hips. The warmth of her center and the scent of her arousal are almost more than I can bear. My stav lengthens and extends from my body, seeking the entrance to her core.

Her small hand grasps my length, guiding it inside her. A low groan escapes me as I enter her channel, and for a moment, I forget to flap my wings, and we begin spiraling down.

She inhales sharply, forcing me to focus, and I struggle to concentrate as the tight clasp of the muscles of her channel grip my stav with each adjustment of my wings. This is more difficult than I imagined. I do not know how Aerilon males are able to do this: to mate and fly at the same time.

Real fear fills me at the thought that I could easily lose myself in the feel of her body and not pay enough attention to my flying, injuring us both.

She presses her lips to mine and then carefully pulls away from my body. The cool breeze a jarring and unwelcome sensation on my now fully exposed stav. I look down at her.

She gives me a knowing smile. "I want your full attention on me," she says softly, running her fingers through my hair. "Take me to where we are going so we may join without any distractions."

My body aches to join with hers, and I cannot fly fast enough to our destination. We crest the top ridge of the nearby mountain just outside the city, and when our shelter comes into view, my heart begins pounding with great anticipation.

As soon as we touch down, I guide her to the structure. The location is secluded and far enough away from anything else that we will not be bothered by anyone while we are here.

"What is this?" she asks, as her gaze rakes over the small building.

"It is our...honeymoon cottage."

We step inside, and her eyes widen appreciatively. "It's beautiful,

Rowan. I've never seen anything like it." She turns to me. "How did you—"

A smile tugs at my lips. "Liana designed it, and Soran, Al'aneo, and Caryn helped me set it up."

She stares in wonder at the small structure, running her hands along the smoothly carved light-gray stone walls that look as though they have been here for hundreds of cycles, but in reality, it has only been a few days.

The small kitchen area is stocked with plenty of food, and a fire burns in a stone hearth in the next room. A door across the way leads into the bedroom and cleansing area.

Tr'lani smiles as she takes it all in. "So, this is a honeymoon cottage," she whispers. "Liana has one on Mosaura for her and Soran."

My brother told me of this as well. "Does it please you?"

She gives me a beaming smile. "It's perfect." She steps forward and twines her arms around my neck before tenderly pressing her lips to mine.

The kiss is soft and gentle at first, but need pulses through me, and my stav lengthens and extends once more, seeking to join with her body. Curling my tongue around hers, I pull her close and then lift her into my arms and carry her quickly to the bedroom.

I gently lay her down and then join her. Wrapping her up in my wings and arms, I hold her smaller form close against mine. She opens her thighs, cradling my hips between them. A low groan escapes me as I bury my stav deep in her channel. The tight clasp of her body around my length is the most exquisite torture, and it always takes every ounce of my control not to release the moment I sheathe myself inside her warm, wet heat.

Her soft moan tests my restraint, and the breath hisses from my lungs as she tightens her legs around my hips and arches up to meet the first thrust of my body into hers.

I groan with how good it feels. A low growl rumbles deep in my chest as I stare down at my beautiful mate, her hair spread out beneath her on the bed like a lovely halo.

She cups the back of my neck and pulls my lips down to hers, capturing my mouth in a passionate kiss as I move deep inside her. Her delicate fingers run through my hair and begin tracing along my sensitive cranial ridges. It is almost more than I can bear. I fight against my instinct to drive deep and hard by holding her tight to my chest and then rolling onto my back, so she straddles my body.

She places her palms on my chest to steady herself, and I anchor my hands to her hips, holding her firmly as I stroke up into her. She stares down at me with a heavy-lidded gaze, her mouth partially open as each breath ends on a gasp as I roll my hips to meet her every movement against mine.

My eyes trace over her beautiful form. The soft globes of her breasts make my mouth water with want to run my tongue over their stiffened peaks. Her entire form is so soft and giving. I long to fill her with my seed. I glance down to where our bodies are joined and grit my teeth as I fight to hold back my release. I refuse to climax before her.

I sit up, and wrap my wings around her back as I curl my arms up under her to cup her shoulders. I growl and pull her down to me as I thrust up into her core.

She gasps with each stroke of my stav into her channel, and I lower my head and close my mouth over her left breast, laving at the hard-beaded tip. She moans and digs her fingers into my back, holding me close.

I want to fill her with my essence until she can take no more so that every male within several *arcums* will be able to scent that she is mine and I am hers.

Her body goes taut, and she makes a low, keening cry. The small muscles of her channel clamp down hard around my length as she reaches her peak. Her release triggers my own. Unable to hold back any longer, my stav begins pulsing deep in her core, and I hold her tight to my chest as my release erupts from my body, filling her with my seed.

I look up at her as she leans down and brushes her lips against mine. Her eyes are bright with tears, and fear flows through me. I reach up to cup her cheek. "Have I hurt you?"

She gives me a beautiful smile as a tear escapes her lashes. I brush it away with my thumb. "No," she whispers. "I just…I never imagined I would ever be so happy." She presses a soft kiss to my lips. "I love you, my big, strong, handsome Mosauran warrior."

Holding her tightly wrapped up in my wings, I rest my forehead gently against hers and breathe deeply of our combined scent. I stare deep into her beautiful golden eyes. Emotions lodge in my throat, but I somehow manage to speak around them. "You are my heart, Tr'lani."

"And you are mine," she whispers in reply.

CHAPTER 53

TR'LANI

It's only been a few months since Rowan and I bonded, but I'm looking forward to going back to our "honeymoon cottage" in a few days. With the alliance in place, his hours are often long as he works with a team of Aerilon engineers to incorporate Mosauran technology into our cruisers and defense systems.

He also believes he's found a way for our ships to travel much faster with the use of a subspace conduit called "the passage." If he's right, we could make the trip to V'lora and back within days instead of weeks. Liana is eager for him to test this. She desperately wants to go to V'lora, believing that their physical similarities to her people might mean that Terra is somewhere close to their system.

Al'aneo has remarked quietly to me several times that the Mosaurans have such advanced weaponry, they could have easily conquered us instead of choosing to form an alliance. This knowledge has done much to calm the fears of the High Council—to know that the Mosauran Empress chose peace instead of conquest.

My work at the Med Center is full of long hours, but I enjoy it immensely. Today, however, I've left early to visit the main library. I promised Elari I'd visit her today. As I walk along the cobbled streets on my way, my gaze drifts over all the quaint shops that line either side. Deep-purple and green vines with bioluminescent blooms cover many of the structures, and I marvel at their beauty as the petals begin to unfurl with the setting of the sun.

I never used to give much thought to these things when I'd simply fly from one destination to the other. My wings are not fully healed yet and won't be for at least a few more weeks. Even though I am forced to walk, I find that I rather enjoy it. It gives me a unique perspective of those who live among my people but lack wings, like the Lacerta.

The main library is one of the oldest structures in the city. Its massive gold-capped domes glint brightly beneath the last rays of the sun. The whitewashed stone lights up in bioluminescent blues and purples as the vegetation that climbs its proud outer walls begins to glow as the night rushes in.

As soon as I enter, the Elari appears. She has been given full access to the entire building and can appear at any point within the structure that she desires. She greets me in the cavernous entrance hall with a beaming smile. "I have eagerly awaited your visit."

I grin in reply. "It is good to see you too."

Her brow furrows softly, and she lowers her gaze to my abdomen. She extends her hand and hovers it low over my belly. After a moment, she looks back up at me and smiles. "You are with child."

I stare at her in shock. "What?"

She frowns and tips her head to the side. "You do not yet sense the life growing inside you?"

I've been feeling a bit tired lately, but that is all. I thought it was simply the fact that Rowan and I have had little sleep—making love every night since our bonding. "No. Are you certain?"

Her lips tilt up in a sly smile. "In interfacing with your computers, I downloaded your entire medical database and that of the Mosaurans. I am certain."

I pull my med scanner from my satchel and quickly run it over my stomach. My mouth drifts open as I read the display. Having read the information with me, Elari's eyes sparkle with joy. "Twins," she says softly. "How fortunate. Will you promise to bring them to visit me once they are born? I do so love children."

"I promise," I tell her. Thinking back to her request to be permanently shut off when Rowan and I first met her, I give her a hesitant look. "Are you...happy here? In this new life?"

She nods. "Yes. I enjoy living among your people. And it is an honor to teach them of mine."

* * *

After spending a bit more time with Elari, I start back for home. I look down at my communicator. The urge to tell Rowan our news immediately is something I can hardly wait to do. But he is still at work, and I not only don't want to disturb him, this is something I want to tell him in person. So instead, I tap out a quick message to my beloved. "Come home as soon as you can."

A soft laugh escapes me. He's probably going to wonder at my cryptic message because he always comes straight home when he's done. He's even arrived at the Med Center before I'm finished with my work, trying to coax *me* to leave early so we can start our evening together that much sooner.

When I get home, Ama and I sit in the reclining chairs around the sunken fire pit, reading quietly. We do this every evening while I wait for Rowan to return. But tonight, I catch her staring at me with a softened expression. She is the most perceptive person I know, and I wonder if she suspects anything. I want to tell her, but Rowan is the one I'll tell first.

Fatigue hits me like a giant wave. I blink sleepily as I try to focus on my tablet, but after a while, I rest it on my chest as I sink down into the chair and allow myself to drift off.

A soft kiss to my forehead brings me back into awareness, and my eyelids flutter and open to find Rowan staring down at me—intense love and devotion reflected in his gaze. I smile up at him as I stretch languidly on the couch.

He pulls me into his arms, brushing the hair back from my face. "You had a long day?" he asks softly.

I nod. "I spoke with Elari. She told me something interesting."

His brows lift in a thoughtful expression as he waits for me to continue. "What is it?"

Taking his hand in mine, I guide it to my belly, resting his palm low over my abdomen as I give him a warm smile.

He tips his head to the side to regard me a moment before dawned understanding crosses his features. "You carry our fledgling?"

He smiles widely and then lifts me into his lap without warning, wrapping his arms and wings tightly around me as he presses urgent kisses to my face and neck. A soft laugh escapes me at his enthusiasm and happiness.

"I'm so happy, my heart," he breathes against my lips. "I did not think this was possible for us."

"Neither did I," I whisper.

After a moment, his gaze meets mine with a serious expression on his face. "Do not worry, my heart. I give you my most solemn vow as a warrior of Mosaura, I will not leave your side from this moment on. I will guard you and our egg from any and all danger."

I give him a puzzled look. "What?"

He continues. "I will tend to your every need while you seclude yourself in our nest."

"Seclude myself?"

He arches a brow. "On Mosaura, after the female has laid her egg, the male secludes himself in the nest to guard it until the fledgling is hatched." His gaze drifts down to my abdomen, and he covers it with his large hand, staring at me with fierce possessiveness reflecting behind his eyes. "Since you carry our egg in your body, you will be secluded in our nest until our fledgling is born. And I will remain at your side at all times to guard you."

I give him an incredulous look. "What?"

"Do not worry." He smiles. "I will not fail in providing for and protecting you."

"I—I'm not worried about that," I tell him. "I just…I can't stay locked up in our rooms. Our nest," I correct, "until our fledglings are born."

"Fledglings?" His eyes go wide. "As in…more than one?"

I place my hand over his, low on my abdomen, and smile brightly. "Twins."

He captures my mouth in a claiming kiss and doesn't pull away until Ama clears her throat.

We turn to find her across the way, a sly smirk on her lips. "The Garkol who read my future all those many cycles ago was right. He told me you'd bear twins."

"He did?"

She nods and turns her gaze to the garden, her eyes landing on Al'aneo walking side by side with Holly. "Now, to see if what he told me about your brother was right as well," she says under her breath.

EPILOGUE

TR'LANI

Extending my wings, I stand on the edge of the palace balcony. Rowan stands at my side while Al'aneo, Ama, Holly, and my parents wait below. The wind blows softly around us as I close my eyes and concentrate on the feel of it wrapping around my wings.

Drawing in a deep breath, I open my eyes and look down at my family.

"You can do it," Al'aneo smiles.

Rowan takes my hands, squeezing it gently to draw my attention to him. "You've got this." He grins. His confidence fills me with joy. "Ready?"

"Yes."

Concentrating, I flap my wings, and together, we step off the edge. The muscles and ligaments of my wings are sore and slow to respond as I struggle to fly. It takes great effort, but I somehow manage to remain aloft as we glide out over the gardens and then back again.

Carefully, stretching my wings, we drift down to the ground below and land softly. Happiness blooms in my chest as Rowan's reflective silver eyes stare deep into mine. He gathers me in his arms and spins me around in a slow circle. "I knew you could do it, my heart," he whispers softly in my ear.

Everyone rushes toward us. Trilling low in their throats, they smile warmly at us as they gather around, taking turns embracing me.

After everything that happened to me when I was a slave, I thought moments this beautiful would never be mine. Rowan helped me to find the strength I did not think I had; he made me realize that I was not broken.

I still have scars from my time as a slave, and I do not know if I'll ever fly as well as I used to. But as Rowan places his open palm low on my abdomen and flashes his devastatingly handsome smile, I do know that our future will be full of love and family.

He lifts our joined hands to his chest, placing them directly over his heart. And I understand that he does this so I know that it belongs only to me. He presses his lips to mine and whispers against them. "You are my heart, Tr'lani, and I am yours."

AUTHORS NOTE

THANK you so much for reading this. I hope you loved this story as much as I loved writing it. If you enjoyed this book, please leave a review on Amazon and/or Goodreads. Reviews are so very important. They are the lifeblood of Indie Authors.

If you want to read about Tr'lani's brother Al'aneo, his story **Trace The Sky** is available now.

MOSAURAN SERIES (DRAGON SHIFTER ALIEN ROMANCE)

The Edge of it All
Shape of the Wind (This Book)
Trace The Sky

Of Fate and Kings Series

Bound to the Dark Elf King
Claimed by the Dragon King
Taken by the Fae King
Stolen by the Wolf King
Captured by the Orc King
Charmed by the Florin King
Cherished by the Florin Prince

Monster Brides Series

The Orc's Reluctant Bride

Ice World Warrior Series (Scifi Romance)

Claimed: Dragon Shifter Romance
Bound: Vampire Alien Romance
Rescued: Fae Alien Romance
Stolen: Werewolf Romance
Taken: Vampire Alien Romance
Fated: Dragon Shifter Romance
Protected: Dragon Shifter Romance

Check out some of my other books while you're here.

Do you like Fairy Tale Retellings?

Fairy Tale Retellings (Once Upon a Fairy Tale Romance Series)

Taken by the Dragon: A Beauty and the Beast Retelling
Captivated by the Fae: A Cinderella Retelling
Rescued By The Merman: A Little Mermaid Retelling
Bound To The Elf Prince: A Snow White Retelling
Claimed By The Bear King: A Snow Queen Retelling
Protected By The Wolf Prince: A Red Riding Hood Retelling
Charmed by the Fox Prince: A Rapunzel Retelling

Of Gods and Fate (Greek God Romance Series)

Claimed By Hades
Bound to Ares

Orc Claimed Series

Claimed by the Orc
Bound to the Orc

Night King Series

Bound to the Night King

Settlers of the Outer Rim

Rescued: Fox Shifter Romance
Protected: Lizard Man Romance

Fated to Monsters

Captured by the Kraken: A Monster Romance
Bound to the Gargoyle: A Monster Romance
Claimed by the Werewolf: A Monster Romance

Of Dragons and Elves Series (Fantasy Romance)
The Elf Knight

Scarred Dragon Prince Series
Shadow Guard: Dragon Shifter Romance

To Love a Monster Book Series (Fantasy Romance)
Taken by the Monster: A Monster Romance

V'loryn Series (Vampire Alien Romance)
Lost in the Deep End
Beneath a Different Sky
Under a Silver Moon

V'loryn Holiday Series (A Marek and Elizabeth Holiday novella takes place prior to their bonding)
The Thing We Choose

V'loryn Fated Ones (Vampire Alien Romance)
Where the Light Begins (Vanek's Story)

For information about upcoming releases Like me on

Facebook at Jessica Grayson
http://facebook.com/JessicaGraysonBooks.

OR

sign up for upcoming release alerts at my website:
Jessicagraysonauthor.com

www.ingramcontent.com/pod-product-compliance
Lightning Source LLC
Chambersburg PA
CBHW030633020726
47493CB00006B/1688

* 9 7 8 1 6 4 2 5 3 5 5 2 5 *